# ABSOLUTION

# ABSO

# UTION

## A SOUTHERN REACH NOVEL

# JEFF VANDERMEER

4th ESTATE • London

4th Estate
An imprint of HarperCollins*Publishers*
1 London Bridge Street
London SE1 9GF

www.4thestate.co.uk

HarperCollins*Publishers*
Macken House, 39/40 Mayor Street Upper
Dublin 1, D01 C9W8, Ireland

First published in Great Britain in 2024 by 4th Estate
First published in the United States by MCD Books,
a division of Farrar, Straus and Giroux in 2024

1

A catalogue record for this book is
available from the British Library

ISBN 978-0-00-872597-6 (hardback)
ISBN 978-0-00-872598-3 (trade paperback)

Silhouette of house centipede (Scutigera coleoptrata) on title page and
at back of book by Kazakov Maksim/Shutterstock.com. Photographs used in
display type on title-page spread and following part openers © Andy Marlowe

Text design by Abby Kagan

Set in Electra LT Std
Printed and bound in the UK using 100%
renewable electricity at CPI Group (UK) Ltd

*For Ann*

"There shall be a fire that knows your name."

# CONTENTS

## Initiation

## Integration

## Dissolution

## Immersion

## THE FIRST AND THE LAST

### 1=Fuck That Chicken

# DEAD TOWN

## TWENTY YEARS BEFORE AREA X

## 001: THE BIOLOGISTS

O nce, *the story went*, there had been biologists on the Forgotten Coast, in numbers so great that the ground shook in
the aftermath of their passage. Eager men and women
who without warning bestrode the terrain like conquerors, sent
by the government and funded by money that came in the form
of buried gold bars that could not decay or devalue like the
money kept in banks. Which is why, the conspiracy theorists at
the Village Bar claimed, the biologists had been so stooped and
weighted down when they arrived. Their packs had been full not
of supplies and food but of gold.

That the force or forces that had sent the biologists to the
Forgotten Coast wanted the biologists to be ungoverned by bar-
ter, isolated, free of the sense of neighborly responsibility that
had held the Forgotten Coast together for so long.

That the biologists had been *complicit*, aware of their role,
which was important, Old Jim believed. They had to be complicit
if the folks in the Village Bar were to keep telling the story. Because if they weren't complicit, telling the story meant the story
would at some point peer back and condemn the teller.

In their initial explorations, the biologists, clad in their yellow gloves, carried out a series of ever more arcane rituals. They

plucked clumps of native grasses from the mud flats with a fin-
icky precision, tweezered scraps into vials. They shoved bits of
bark mottled with lichen into tiny metal boxes. Jars small and
large allowed them to sample strange aquatic species like crayfish and mudpuppies.

At night, they slept in space-age sleeping bags that looked at
times like the vanguard of an alien invasion: shimmering silver
cocoons against the dark green of tree islands and the golden
wash of reeds and the drab gray-brown river mud pocked with
the holes of fiddler crabs.

The decision to conduct an initial survey and then, later, biv-
ouac inland had been made by someone higher up. Someone
remote who thought a permanent location on the beach "would
seem to flaunt," according to one biologist in their diary.

(The diary, retrieved, had been gone at by beetles and rot,
and in the searing shades of green, the watermarks that seemed
more like records of tidal patterns, it had the look of an object in
a museum exhibit. Old Jim had run his hand over the roughness
of that faux coastline more than once as he read the faded pencil
marks, before he'd thought, almost quaintly, of contamination
and put the journal back.)

None of the locals ever did get a straight answer about why
the biologists had been sent, this much Old Jim knew from the
files, because it had been ordered that no straight answer ever be
given to "those people." But perhaps that didn't matter, either,
for most of the locals had always seen the government as an invading hydra. The "slid-off" answer, as one local called it, only
reaffirmed the long-held suspicion, the desire forever gestating
in them: to be left alone, left to whatever state of dissolution and
decay or, yes, peace they aspired to in that wild and beautiful
place.

In the transcripts, Man Boy Slim—a rickety thin twenty-year-
old local, with, at a cursory glance, a distinguished career at that
time of stealing hubcaps and hunting deer out of season—made

many claims about the biologists. For example, he claimed to have seen a biologist "leap into the air and catch a dragonfly with his teeth," so delicate this maneuver that the lithe biologist spit the insect unharmed into a jar, where it vibrated a confused blurred emerald, unsure of what had happened.

Already, almost from the start, the biologists were changing from something human in the eyes of the locals into something uncanny. One day, a local would be walking down a weed-strewn trail on the Forgotten Coast, glimpse a biologist from the corner of their eye, and not be sure of what they had seen.

Nothing that happened next changed people's opinions in its particulars, as far as Old Jim could tell.


## 002: THE CAVALRY


In addition to equipment and supplies, the biologists had brought a kind of burden with them to the Forgotten Coast, and it was with a sense of relief that they prepared to release that burden into the marshes before setting up a base camp.

That this burden had been imposed on them could be sensed in how they spoke about the process of transporting their un-wieldy subjects to the release site. That they, in this one particu-lar, shared an affinity with the locals, in not knowing how the burden had been imposed, despite the attached documents, the apparent bona fides of the burden's university sponsors.

"We could not wait to be free to conduct our general explora-tions," Team Leader 1 said, while Team Leader 2 observed that "Megafauna always catch the eye of journals, but I would rather observe the bubble fortresses of the crayfish on the mud flats, because we know so little about their ways."

For, within a week of arriving at the Forgotten Coast, the

biologists would release the alligators they had brought from one hundred miles south into the local ecosystems. This plan would not be common knowledge to the locals for some weeks, for reasons unclear to Old Jim. When it did, the county sheriff spared the expedition a visit, only dissuaded from issuing some kind of ticket, or even warning, by the presentation of so many federal government permits. Or as Man Boy Slim put it, "Quills out, folks. The biologists went quills out over those alligators."

But the locals had a wider, more practical objection to the experiment than just how it had been withheld from them.

"There must be ten thousand alligators up here already," Man Boy Slim's friend Drunk Boat said in disbelief, when word did finally get out. "There must be a hundred million alligators up here. Already."

"Drunk Boat" was Man Boy Slim's nickname for the Village Bar's alcoholic poet in residence—a man of letters who had not been above a bit of night poaching with a flashlight and, of all things, a handgun. (Old Jim had read up on Man Boy Slim's file by then, and his nod to an obscure French poet didn't surprise him. Despite initial impressions, Man Boy Slim had a fine academic record, with a college emphasis on English before he had dropped out from lack of funds.)

As far as the biologists knew, the four large, fifteen-year-old alligators had been captured in the wild. But in the margin of the files, that place where a separate truth often flourished, Old Jim read a shorthand on the alligators that gave them a different origin. Three had been plucked fortuitous from roadside zoos and the fourth—the largest female, "code name Smaug"—came from some prior Central experiment. The university sponsor did not exist.

While under anesthetic at the release location, the alligators were fitted with an adjustable soft harness that the experiment notes promised "had the necessary give and pull to not be slipped nor pose a hazard to the reptile." The harnesses had been attached to a thin but strong rubber-coated wire that led to a radio receiver embedded in a spinner and that attached to a bobber. When the battery ran out, the spinner would power the tracker in the bobber by the reptile's movements through the water and, erratically, by the wind when the beast hauled itself onto land.

One stated goal was to field-test cutting-edge equipment, while the primary purpose consisted solely of seeing if the alligators would, via wetlands and interconnected waterways, return to their prior locations. How, then, did bodies understand the landscape? How did minds flourish or wither, still tuned to a distant frequency?

"In other words, could these reptiles be reintroduced to areas of scarcity and be expected to remain there?" Team Leader 1 posed the question, paraphrasing from the brief imposed upon them, itself a kind of "cover." "What kind of site loyalty has such a beast? What stressors in a new environment might evoke site loyalty? Would what might be called 'cultural mutations' need to occur in addition to what we might call 'normal' adaptations?"

This suggested a life of the mind to Old Jim that he found disturbing, but Central's only scribble in the margin of the transcript noted that Team Leaders 1 and 2 had formed a "close bond" during training.

Surely this information was irrelevant?

Some in the Village would later call the four alligators the Cavalry, despite what happened next. In the fierce and abiding imagination of the Forgotten Coast, the Cavalry remained forever and eternal, still roamed the swamps and marshes. Still lived on in more than memory—cherished yet feared, such that many an unexplained "incident" in later years would be attributed, perhaps comfortingly, to "the Cavalry."

The day of the release, the biologists gathered on a raised berm at the edge of a lake that fed into swamp landward and marsh seaward, a liminal place that held a brackish kind of fresh water, neither one thing nor the other.

It was bright and breezy, with tree swallows darting through the blazing blue sky. The drugged reptiles had been outfitted with their gear and constrained by containers that resembled huge, long coolers with removable wire-mesh tops and collapsible doors in the front. Nothing in the expedition's official journals hinted at errors or false steps in the release, but Team Leader 2 would later write in her journal that "The moment felt fraught, tense, of greater importance than the actual purpose of the release."

Team Leaders 1 and 2 must not have thought the release important enough to record via video footage, in the context of their other work. The team's medic alluded to "some still shots," which did not exist in Central's archives. But, no matter, someone had secretly hidden a grainy surveillance camera on-site, and, even more valuable, the biologists' journals allowed a seemingly accurate reconstruction.

The process only went smoothly for the one once named Smaug but renamed the Tyrant at Team Leader 2's insistence, the harness no impediment. The Tyrant ran-slithered in all her ten-foot glory down to the water's edge and disappeared almost in that same instant, as if the water were as much a portal as blessed release.

Firestorm followed with some complications of timing between final fitting of the harness and releasing the door mechanism via a "deconstructed wire coat hanger"—these "1 followed by 2" operations happening, as far as Old Jim could tell, at the exact same moment, so that there had been a possibility of disaster, despite success—and the disappearance of the reptile into the water so immediate that he did not begrudge the biologists their relief.

Who could blame the biologists for ignoring the alternate

universe in which Firestorm had struggled loose and ravaged bodies until the blood sprayed and sprawled across the mud-banks in waves? Yet, there *had* been blood, "some minor cuts, dealt with on-site." The Medic, quoted in the official report.

Old Jim also noted a margin scrawl in the Medic's record books that "all possible measures were taken but nothing could be done." The ink color differed from the rest of the page, so perhaps the scrawled note had occurred much later, and in his panic during the disaster of that future time . . . the Medic had accidentally written it on the wrong page.

Battlebee and Sergeant Rocker fared less well. The former refused to leave his glorified cooler, appearing disoriented, and the latter became harness-entangled, despite the assurances, and had to be tranq'd and prepped again later that afternoon, by which time most of the expedition had been "drinking."

But what did that mean? Drinking what? Had there been some other impairment also in play?

A glitch in the surveillance tape slowed down their steps, so the biologists appeared to have choreographed a slow retreat, a slow surrender, and then reassembled running, only to part ways again in waves, branching off in opposite directions across the berm. The grainy stick figures appeared tiny against the immensity of wetlands and sky. If not for the glitch, Old Jim would have thought they had been running from something.

Finally, Battlebee made an exit by making an entrance. Sergeant Rocker, though, snapped and skittered sideways toward his well-wishers with such ferocious intent that the biologists fled again, even as one amongst them, Old Jim couldn't tell which, circled the beast while calling out what sounded like an absurd "Here, kitty, kitty!" That couldn't be right, could it? (The video ended there.)

"Hilarious," some prior analyst at Central had written as a note. But it wasn't hilarious. Both this moment and the drinking registered as disquieting, out of place with the discipline one would expect at the start of a scientific expedition. He also distrusted the amount of redaction surrounding the alligator experiment in the archives. It signified a growing level of circumspection, like peering through mist come up over black swamp water, even as he continued to glide forward, unable to see what lay to both sides.

But then, too, there was the assurance, the confidence, in the accounts of the biologists as remedy to allay suspicion. Because Sergeant Rocker, too, had then taken to the waters and disappeared, the biologists using their tracking equipment to make sure they could follow the alligators in their new lives.

The Tyrant kept to herself, while the others remained in close proximity, for a while. None, at least overnight, seemed inclined to leave the area, and by the fourth day, Team Leader 1 put the most junior member of their party on the task of monitoring moments that might include a full day of basking in the same stretch of mud.

On day six they found Firestorm's front leg, bobber wire wrapped around it, the whole prominently displayed on a mudbank with deep boot prints suggesting poachers. There was, one biologist wrote, "a bathetic or pathetic quality to the paleness of the leg, enraptured in the evidence of our experiment, lost so far from her home. I wept for an hour, but do not know if this was an appropriate response."

(No, Old Jim did not believe it was an appropriate response, even as he himself wept at odd hours, for his own reasons, down in Central's archives.)

Battlebee turned up dead and bloated and white, with a chunk ripped out of him postmortem by some creature, possibly Sergeant Rocker, speculation being that stress and the anesthetic had been too hard on him. Postmortem examination revealed stomach contents that included fish, a turtle, mud, and, inexplicably, a broken teacup.

She had also been pregnant, "a fact that surprised us," Team Leader 2 wrote, "given her credentials identified her as a male," amid some general confusion: "To be honest, I cannot now remember when we first took this project on, when we first encountered these subjects. The heat here is abysmal."

Sergeant Rocker opted out of the project by shedding his harness in the water near the tent of Team Leader 1, indicating, as she absurdly put it, "A politeness on the part of Sergeant Rocker in keeping with his personality when I knew him best. I felt this loss much more deeply than expected."

This sentimentality toward an alligator seen as an obligation just days before weighed on Old Jim, although he could not put a finger on why. Nor did he understand why the alligator experiment registered with the biologists in their reports as a great success, and they would even reference it with a kind of beautiful, all-consuming nostalgia when the mission began to sour. The myth of competence, perhaps. The myth of persistence. The myth of objectivity.

Perhaps, both he and the biologists would have been wiser to focus on how Sergeant Rocker had turned into an escape artist, for the harness was intact and still latched, with no tears anywhere. So how had the alligator possibly gotten free? Old Jim kept seeing the biologists by a trick of faulty video running away from the release site, only to re-form in their drinking circle.

He replayed the video so often that it became a disconcerting mess of light and shadow, of pixelated disembodied heads and legs and shapes that leapt out and sharpened, only to become subsumed into the past.

*"All possible measures were taken but nothing could be done."*
Or had the outcome been exactly as intended?

## 003: DEADS TOWN

In the late spring, a week after releasing the Tyrant, the biologists established permanent headquarters in the ruins of a ghost town that had once pretended to be a county seat. Even in those parts, rife with poachers, anarchists, and pot growers, it was remote.

An aerial view would have barely registered the ruins of the buildings under the tree cover, but to the west lay the end of the estuary, to the east an improbable wildflower meadow petering out into mud flats, to the south more marsh, leading to the sea, and to the north an impenetrable bramble of palmettos and blackberry bushes.

The estuary held Dead Town like an open hand that could close into a fist at any time.

The biologists arrived at this remote location via kayaks, a flat-bottomed boat with more robust supplies gliding dutiful behind. A row of old rusting automobiles like huge burly beetles stacked three high would have been their welcoming committee, there by the muddy riverbank, beyond which a double row of unruly swamp oaks led to the town.

Even after the biologists had planted an ironic flag at City Hall and taken their machetes to the worst of the vines choking Main Street, the expedition did not feel comfortable there. "The sounds of birds in these ruins are muffled and we cannot tell the origin except with difficulty, given the odd acoustics."

Old Jim wondered whether the biologists had second thoughts, there on Main Street. About their mission. About their choice of careers. To end up in such a derelict place, in the process of sinking into the ground at a rate of an inch per year. To live amongst the intense nocturnal shrieking of insects and the vagaries of crumbling walls.

Nor was everything as promised in Dead Town. A year earlier, the biologists had been told, a filmmaker had used Main Street to shoot scenes for an indie film, "a fever dream shot in the sticks," and this meant some limited access to electricity. But, in fact, nothing worked, the outlets corroded, and they discovered that the emergency generator was just a shell, with one biologist noting that "the gutted interior contained nothing but half-deflated party balloons."

A replacement generator arrived, a week later, along with fuel—from a Central drop site, Old Jim noted, with a raised eyebrow. By then, the biologists had removed the balloons from the old generator and disposed of them. The sight had caused anxiety, not laughter, and a sense of what one biologist called in her diary "some kind of joke that wasn't funny." Old Jim felt the balloons stank of provocation.

But by who? Fate? A sadistic swamp god?


As soon as the biologists occupied the ghost town, the locals started calling it Dead Town or "the deads town," as in "you're dead to me," after some phantasmagoria adored by Drunk Boat. The biologists never questioned the name Dead Town but almost immediately referred to the place they lived in as Dead Town as well.

Perhaps they thought it an ironic joke of some kind, perhaps they, in their private moments around a campfire too hot for the season, understood how absurd it was to call dead a place so alive with insects and plants and fungi. Perhaps signs and symbols held no power over them.

The biologists established a perimeter, put up white canvas yurts at the tree line that bordered the wildflower meadow, made bonfires at night, found clean drinking water . . . and then they began to roam. Widely. An "invasive species" across a new migratory range, as observed, again, by Man Boy Slim. The yurts, as he described them, were like some vanilla variety of the flourless cakes at a local bakery, which had the novelty of a dusty model-train track running up high, near the ceiling.

Putting up the yurts signaled a kind of initial caving, Old Jim thought. A sign that they knew Dead Town wasn't ideal as base camp, despite their orders. Every last one of them erected where the sea breeze breathed its last before dropping off into a stillness that incubated humidity and palmetto bugs and mosquitoes.

A silent rebellion that stretched the limits of authority, under the guise of processing their finds as quickly as possible--to have these "field stations," as the official report called them, which were actually a form of physical relief from the environment for the biologists.

To process these "finds," to be well and truly named, which were just parts of the Forgotten Coast that the locals had known about for years and that had not needed the formality of the kinds of names that the biologists wanted to give them.

It irked the locals who liked birding to be in pursuit of a rare vermillion flycatcher, only to gaze through binoculars . . . at what turned out to be a biologist wearing a red bandana, staring back through her own binoculars.

"They get in the way," Man Boy Slim claimed, to little disagreement in the bar. Telescopes. Microscopes. More advanced and profane sensors that defied Old Jim's understanding. Metal boxes with blinking lights, into which the biologists funneled swamp water.

By then, "peculiar instruments" had become a stand-in for "peculiar people" in the bar transcripts—Man Boy Slim and his allies at odds with others as to the *intentionality* of it all. A good-natured brawl, forgiven through beer, between the faction who thought the biologists fools and those who labeled them capable of harm, and thus the more formal "Rogues."

By then, the biologists had become embedded in Dead Town, their fate and the fate of Dead Town interwoven, as if they were not an expedition at all, but an outpost, preparing for an assault from some unknown force.

## 004: THE ROGUE

Amid all the debris in the files, the term "Rogue" made Old Jim take notice, because the idea of a Rogue on the Forgotten Coast wasn't "a scoundrel or dishonest person" but the more neutral idea of an outcast or stranger. A Rogue, in the parlance of the Village Bar, required keen attention not because a Rogue always *intended* harm, but because a Rogue might not understand the harm it could cause. This ambiguity bothered Old Jim, even has he understood that the Forgotten Coast had always been a reliquary for Rogues of some kind.

Perhaps worse, though, in Old Jim's estimation, how the Village Bar idea of a "Rogue" had only permutated into a term of art for Central after the biologists' expedition, as if the Forgotten Coast had colonized the corridors of power over time without Central realizing it. Where the danger in that lay, Old Jim didn't know, just that it felt dangerous, like a counter-op or potential double agent.

The stranger who became the Rogue, and would not give the locals a name, appeared in early summer, after the biologists had become established at Dead Town. To those tanned and sun-blessed people, the stranger appeared whiter than the rabbits. As the translucent quality of the skin of some geckos reveals the beauty of a beating heart, so the face and arms of the stranger suggested a kind of vulnerability. He looked to the Village Bar regulars so pale as to have come "posthaste from some extreme northern country," although his accent read local. Otherwise, he was physically nondescript.

The man wore a rumpled blue blazer over a once-crisp light blue dress shirt, the top two buttons missing, with slim tan pants ending unexpectedly in sturdy military-issue boots. As startling, given his overall affect, was the camo-colored pack he had with him, which also read army. The blazer had a rip in one elbow and a tired, defeated quality in how it fell across his shoulders.

At first glance, Drunk Boat dubbed the stranger Sad Sack, but Man Boy Slim amended that to Bad Slack, B.S. for short, before some communal subtext settled on "Rogue" with a capital "R" instead.

He said nothing, framed in silhouette by the door as wiry and thin, surpassed in this regard only by a local arborist who resembled an angry jockey and shimmied up trees like an indignant squirrel. Except the Rogue wasn't angry and he favored his left leg. Everyone recognized his walking stick as the one left at the start of the lighthouse trail loop as a courtesy.

"He made a sound," Drunk Boat observed later. "A sound like . . . like a whimper . . . but a whimper of, well, *relief* . . . and astonishment."

Man Boy Slim demurred that he'd heard no such sound, but Drunk Boat persisted. "Like a man on a long mission who has come home? Except no one knows him here. It was strange."

Yes, Old Jim thought, everyone could see that the stranger was strange. Sometimes, when perplexed, Drunk Boat didn't sound that poetic, like it was a fancy hat he wore most of the time and shared with Man Boy Slim on occasion.

When the pale stranger said nothing but ordered a beer and sat in the back, it took a while for the rest of the bar to regain a certain equilibrium.

"He brought in a smell with him," Sally the bartender noted

before closing that night. "Not like the sea or the marsh. More . . . electric. Like . . . a singe of lightning? I don't know now to describe it. Like, if you touched him you might get a shock."

No one touched him. He seemed untouchable, created an aura of space around him that discouraged conversation. But not gossip.

"He stole a stick," Charlie said. "He stole the lighthouse loop stick." Young Charlie often walked the loop, on his days off from his fishing vessel.

"To him it was just a stick and he needed a stick, and we can find another stick, can't we?" Drunk Boat said, in reluctant defense, and then ever more inebriated and illogical camaraderie.

This line of defense seemed to be met with skepticism, or even the mutterings of open rebellion about how easy it actually was to find the perfect walking stick. With an agitated undertone, however, as if talking about the stick was easier than grappling with other questions about the stranger.

Then Man Boy Slim waded in and described the stranger as "an out-of-work magician, looking to create a new act out of you-all." A wide gesture, repeated at lunch the next day, that encompassed the Village, including Charlie.

"A thief," Drunk Boat said. "A thief of our time, talking about nothing when we could be conversing about *something*."

What something did he mean?

But that was the moment the tension went out of the bar about the stranger—just an out-of-work magician—and, for a couple of days, none of the locals paid the stranger any mind when he came to the bar for a quiet sit-down and a glass of water.

That's what the Forgotten Coast was for, wasn't it, Drunk Boat and Man Boy Slim and Charlie said, a bit sentimental. "To lose yourself. To love to live to be whatever you can be."

So, for a time, the Rogue did nothing but become the kind of semi-regular who sat quietly in the dark part of the bar, said little, had a beer or two, and left. Offering up nothing of himself, so that no one knew where he had come from when he walked in, or where he went home to when he left.

Harmless.

But Old Jim knew. He knew the stranger was a Rogue, and he was inclined to consider this Rogue an agent of sorts—a person who, in Central parlance, would come to mean the familiar unfamiliar, "one who knows us but is not us."

A kind of slant rhyme connecting who he was to what espionage was.

Such a person moved against the pattern of tides, of stars, of seasons and, in that sense, was not bound by the idea of Time as experienced on the Forgotten Coast.

Such a person was dangerous.

## 005: THE VISITATION

For dead people, or "the Deads," as they began to be called in the Village Bar, the biologists stopped often in their labors that summer to curse about the heat and humidity, which, when overheard, surprised the locals, because it was such a human thing to do. That Drunk Boat at night, in the distance (while up to unspecified activities), could sometimes see the bobbing headlamps of the biologists "well out to sea, so to speak," mystified him as much as "if faery lights had swept down low above the marshes."

Perhaps to create a distraction from the conditions, the biologists had accelerated their tagging of so many living things— and the hours across which they spread such endeavors. "A vast human migration across the face of the Earth," Drunk Boat said, downing a shot, for the moment the bar's sole authority,

Man Boy Slim having gone into Bleakersville to fix his car. "Unnatural—and without relief."

No one disagreed, for the scope had expanded almost without a will in place to drive it. The biologists cast nets for tiny fish in shallows. They set net traps for small woodland creatures. They took fine nylon nets and created capture zones for songbirds, often running aghast to the rescue of what they themselves had endangered, for a songbird was a terrible curse: unpredictable and angry and easy to harm.

How fragile those wings, those beaks, heads to the side, small bright eyes staring up at the aliens that held their bodies in half-closed fists. The birds came from far north, guided by a complex knowledge of magnetic fields and the stars. Their brains had a coiled density twice that of humans. They only lived six or seven years, on average.

At the zenith of their powers that July, the biologists' boot prints outnumbered the tracks of deer and raccoons on the mud flats. The blue caps from tranq darts became a common sight alongside empty beer cans and shotgun shells. The sun shone at their backs and the sea wind was in their faces and their bodies glistened with sweat, with the nights full of laughter and good cheer at the end of a hard day's work—or with the work just beginning. Their labor was a rhythm and their labor was a pact and their labor continued, unbroken.

The biologists' sleep was long and deep in their mosquito-proof yurts, and the sounds out of the night did not frighten them, and they did not dream, for they lived within a kind of dream already, doing what they had trained for their entire lives.

It would have been mid-July when the first anomaly occurred, a week after the Rogue appeared, and almost a month before the luck of the biologists could be said to have worsened exponentially. A biologist taking samples on the mud flats in front of the wildflower meadow encountered the rabbit first. She had been chosen for the mud work because her slight frame protected her from being mired up to her knees. But, also, she had a rare knack for navigating that landscape, far greater than anyone else on the expedition.

Watching her spindly form from afar, Team Leader 2 would marvel at "how she manages to seem like an insect using the tensile pressure of the water's surface to glide across, well, in this case, the mud." Old Jim flagged her as "the Mudder" in the files, a shorthand he employed now from habit. When he had an interest in a person. Besides, they should've called her that.

Intent on begging mud into one last vial and placing it in her backpack, the Mudder started at an unexpected crunching sound to her left, just out of her peripheral vision, pivoted on her haunches, and fell on her ass when she saw the source.

A large white rabbit with bloodshot red eyes calmly ate a fiddler crab, crunching on the carapace, gulping it down, and starting on another. The rabbit had a starved look about it, a gauntness under the tangled fur splashed brown.

The matter-of-fact way the rabbit ate the crab unnerved her, the Mudder wrote in her journal, as much as the presence of the rabbit itself. Ragged pink ears edged with matted white fur twitched in multidirectional ways as if receiving data from radio waves.

"The eyes focused on me with what I can only call indifference or even contempt," the Mudder wrote, but then changed her mind: "The rabbit stared through me, as if its eyes could not focus or it was intent on some sight behind me. No, that's not right, either. I just know it was not natural."

This page was water damaged along the left-hand side so another sentence read either "both so still and in constant motion" or "but so still in its consistent motion," the rest of her reaction lost.

Trying to right herself, the Mudder instead wound up on all fours facing the rabbit, while the rabbit continued to eat crabs alive. The rabbit might first crush the crab's carapace with one solid paw before feasting, the soft insides pushing out from the shell, or just crack the carapace with its teeth.

While the crabs let the rabbit devour them as if mesmerized, as if the rabbit registered as an inanimate object. That just happened to be killing them.

The pink workings of the rabbit's mouth as it crunched crabs to death, the inner hint of rows of sharper teeth than she would have expected, sent her into a panic and the Mudder jumped to her feet, to no reaction from the rabbit, and ran for safety. Less a water strider now than a freaked-out teenager in a horror movie.

Halfway to the safety of the meadow, the Mudder hit a hole disguised by mud, foot held long enough for the Mudder to scream as she twisted her ankle, falling heavy into the sucking mud, there to shout for help in between shrieks of pain. By the time Team Leader 2 heard her, she was trapped up to her knee, the other leg flashing white against mud riddled through with crab holes like rough pores.

By the time they pulled the Mudder to solid ground, to the waiting Medic, Team Leader 1 noted, "All of her sample vials had been broken, costing us a day of work."

"The rabbit still just sat there, unfazed," Team Leader 2 noted, its teeth busy with the job of rendering down one carapace after the other to the flesh beneath, while the eyestalks of the crabs, for as long as they were able, watched their own death with only mild interest.

Old Jim read over the transcript of the Mudder's conversation with the Medic more than once. It felt wrong to him—or maybe the word was "estranged." Estranged from what had happened, or perhaps this was how you talked about something in the aftermath. Something peculiar, unsettling.

MUDDER: He has a camera.
MEDIC: Who has a camera?

MUDDER: The rabbit.

MEDIC: Is there something in the corner of your eye that you cannot get out?

MUDDER: Just a fleck of mud. Just a speck.

MEDIC: I have some pills that will calm you down.

MUDDER: I don't need pills. The rabbit had a camera on a strap around his neck.

MEDIC: Did he also have a pocket watch? Was he late for an appointment?

MUDDER: I could smell an odor, damp, or electric, or . . . and it seemed shabby, old, like a cat that's stopped grooming . . . and then the eye, the eye . . . was like a camera . . . but it was wearing a camera.

MEDIC: Your ankle will be fine.

MUDDER: It was eating fiddler crabs. Do rabbits eat meat? No, I know they don't.

MEDIC: There's no reward in the risk.

MUDDER: My ankle will be fine. I'm sure of it.

MEDIC: Your ankle will be fine. *I'm* sure of it.

Team Leader 2 chose to believe the Mudder, that "something, perhaps a camera," had been around the white rabbit's neck. Although, it could have "just been an ornate collar," as if the "lagomorph had been a pet."

No evidence other than the evidence of the Mudder's close observation supported the claim of a camera, for when they had looked out over the marsh in the aftermath of rescue, the rabbit that had been so very visible and so very still . . . was gone as if it had never been there.

"Escaped pet" continued to be the leading explanation in the yurts, as the biologists took a break from their endeavors to wait out the heat until the late-afternoon shadows, along with an urge to dismiss the rabbit as anomaly. One insignificant data point. It was just a rabbit in the wrong place, according to Team

Leader 1, and likely it would die out in the marshes or be eaten by a predator.

The Mudder was heard to complain, drinking only water, but lots of it, that they "didn't know what they were talking about," for they hadn't seen the eyes. The eyes. They hadn't heard the crunch. They hadn't seen how the crabs refused to acknowledge their own peril. That the rabbit *was* a predator. (The Mudder had put the fiddler crabs under the microscope in the absence of the creature that made them interesting, but found nothing unusual.)

To distract from the Mudder's intensity, perhaps, the biologists, at the urgings of both team leaders, returned to a favorite after-work routine, although this too ended in puzzlement. The biologists had found an upright piano in Dead Town, an excellent brand, and the Medic fixed it up enough to play at dusk, by flashlight.

A battered, off-key sound by all accounts, something to wake the ghosts lying in wait in the graveyards now buried under acres of vines or submerged in wetlands. The white rabbit incident turned routine into compulsion, this playing of the piano. They could ignore the mosquitoes, the lingering heat. Some of them could even dance to it.

But about half an hour in, the night began to play their piano music *back at them*, from across the meadow and the mud flats. "A weird echo," Team Leader 1 noted. "A strange effect of water and distance."

The sound had an unsettling clarity. The dancing ended abruptly and the conversation, and then the sound of the piano, and then, mercifully, the doppelgänger of the piano stopped playing as well. Which left the biologists standing there holding their cups of beer, staring out into the darkness at . . . what?

"For that moment," Team Leader 2 recalled, "we felt as if we were the experiment. That whoever had let loose the white rabbit was also responsible for . . . this . . . ghost."

Perhaps they deserved that moment of dislocation for disturbing the silence of Dead Town. But from the Village Bar transcripts, Old Jim knew this was a prank played by Man Boy Slim, who had thought of it because it amused him to make owl sounds so real that owls would hoot back during mating season. Which also served to prank Old Jim's own memories, because his boss at Central knew Old Jim loved a good upright piano. That on their overseas missions, in the long-distant past, Young Jim always checked out the bar or hotel lobby, vain hope, that they might have one he could play.

But how much *time* would someone need, to pull off such a prank? What other motivation might you have? To kayak or canoe halfway upriver, with the rest of the way perilous through thick clouds of biting flies—and then to know a location well enough to hunker down in the dark in the marsh, amongst the sleeping alligators, to play back the biologists' own music at them, thready and altered as an inexplicable haunting rising from the very mud.

"The best part is I waited a couple of nights, so I was playing back at them what they'd played the night before," Man Boy Slim said, as he related this in semi–sotto voce to a select circle in a corner of the bar, "almost the same, but just a little different. That must've messed with their heads, for sure."

Man Boy Slim implicated himself in many another incident with those words, because Old Jim didn't think he had crept up to Dead Town on a lark one night. Old Jim thought Man Boy Slim had bivouacked there for days, and maybe he didn't even have a broken-down car in the shop. At the very least, Old Jim began to think Man Boy Slim must have become obsessed (was this too strong a word?) with the biologists.

Like a child, but also it's true that Old Jim smiled with a grim satisfaction reading that part of the transcript. A kind of home-grown, unknowing revolt against a clandestine Central project they would never know about. Although, perhaps subconsciously, instinctually, they guessed.

That something was *off*, and would only get worse.

## 006: THE GENERATOR

By the middle of August, there came a subtle shift of colors and textures, a drop in humidity, and new strength to the sea breeze, even so far remote inland. The biologists had by then abandoned the piano for fear of the odd echoes.

There had been no further sightings of a white rabbit, nor did they speak of it, but now the Tyrant's tracker came to life. "If it wasn't scientific, I would say the alligator has fixated on us as the source of its discomfort and dislocation," Team Leader 1 wrote. For the Tyrant—who Old Jim came to see as a kind of double agent—roamed ceaseless, even during the day, did not rest or falter, and often seemed to shadow their new encampment. This was unforeseen, the proximity, that rather than a return south, the Tyrant would still "be in our lives," as Team Leader 2 put it.

The meadow became riotous with butterflies, bees, and wasps feasting on a perfumed wildness of goldenrod, milkweed, blazing star. So thick and tall that the biologists reluctantly cut a swath through the meadow to reach the fiddler crabs that had become the Mudder's primary subject of study.

Only the slight chill in the deep bronze light of late afternoon told the greater truth: This bounty would fade soon and deaden into fall. There was a *falseness* to the richness, Old Jim sensed, in the wistful way the biologists wrote about it.

With the change in the weather, the lives of the biologists

changed, too. They shifted from collection and cataloguing to analysis and sporadic forays into experimentation. A kind of gaze turned inward, bringing with it some other quality, hard to define. "The red-tinged eye of the lighthouse shining out distant at dusk seems both comforting and utterly unfamiliar," Team Leader 2 wrote, in a passage expressing homesickness.

Over time, the biologists came to feel that something was not quite right with their expedition. Even Team Leader 1's obsession with "inefficiencies" and "better ways of being productive" felt like a tell. That there was influence or coercion, invisible both to the naked eye and to their instruments. The recording of their experiments in notebooks were driven into the paper with a sharpness that sometimes left holes from the pencil lead.

It was the natural order of things, Old Jim knew, that the biologists may have had suspicions left unvoiced long before this point. Because once voiced they might take the form of accusations or irrational fearfulness. They may have, each of them, throughout the summer, *almost* spoken up, *almost* raised concerns, only to think themselves, as the Mudder put it, "unreasonable, paranoid, or imagining things."

Yet once they halted in their relentless cataloguing, recording, reporting . . . wasn't there so much to give them pause? Hadn't one, in the wet slurp and roll of a glinting dark body glimpsed for just a moment in a natural canal, had to impose a species name on what could not, could never, be intuited from such a glimpse? Wasn't the prickle of unease crawling up the back of their necks tied to some actual shadow in the night? Some distant muttering while they slept?

Drunk Boat called it, roughly in the same month, in a different context, "the null effect—to create a *something* from the nothing in the darkness, the mind betraying you every time." This directed with a nudge at Man Boy Slim, of "the way the human imagination fills in the gaps."

But Man Boy Slim didn't respond to Drunk Boat, appeared

diminished or "somehow finished," as Sally put it to Drunk Boat in a candid moment later.

"Well, that movie we decided to see, it was enough to put anyone off their feed," Drunk Boat said in Man Boy Slim's defense, sounding not at all like a poet.

(Old Jim stared at that line in the transcript for a very long time, trying to parse it. Thinking it meant something. Making a note to check the movie theater schedules for the era, if such still existed.)

Man Boy Slim abruptly changed the subject to speak eloquently of the trials and tribulations of the summer tanagers headed north once more.

The way the vines of poison ivy and cascading native grape turned yellow and there would be days of gray skies with no rain, lending the marshes a dull pallor that made them unfamiliar to the biologists, who had not yet experienced that season, in that place.


In the end, it was the choked, choking sound of their field generator dying that coaxed the biologists' darker thoughts, their self-betrayal, to the surface. The terrible, coughing death of the generator that, in its throes, seemed almost human or perhaps inhuman, but nonetheless something *alive*. It rousted them in the night from their sleep and at first none could identify the source. To most, it sounded like an injured beast that had crept in amongst the tents, come to harm them.

The generator dying: a usual kind of failure that existed in the mundane world of maintenance. Except, the biologist in charge of the generator was unsure of the cause. The mold he found inside the casing had not advanced far enough and the natural sabotage practiced on them daily by their surroundings could not be the cause. That the mechanical failure rested on a part deliberately broken or that had failed to register as factory defect.

This left Team Leaders 1 and 2 with a white rabbit, an echoing piano, and a cognitive bifurcation between sinister and non-sinister explanations, with, as would become typical, one clinging to the mundane and the other opting for the sinister and ordering a perimeter guard around the yurts.

Yet how could they guard against what could enter the mind? For, with the generator broken, the world lived on with "a strange silence," as the Mudder put it . . . and one by one the biologists found also absent a notion or hooked question that had hidden wormlike between skull and brain.

The biologists' journals were riddled through with this worm. The absence felt "more like loss than like freedom."

"I am unmade from what I was meant to be." Scrawled in the margin of a listing of the weights of banded birds, types of parasites, irregularities in blood samples, the mutation in coloration from the norm.

"I'll be more comfortable in the dark." How hard they had fought the researcher, how their heartbeat had felt against the half-closed palm of a trembling hand.

"It is deadly cold and the fire in the fireplace has gone out." Part of an entry on the mapping of wildflowers to pollinators, to accompany a killing board with pinned bee and wasp species.

"Nothing holds us back now." From what?

They craved the generator's hum, but they feared its return. Were they not themselves regardless? One organism might peer out from another organism, but not live there. A piano might be played at one time, but the sound might reach them at another time.

Even as the Medic, contemptuous of the perimeter guard, worked feverishly to fix the generator. There came consistently in his entries the biometrics of the expedition, with little editorializing. All had elevated heartbeats except for the Medic, who took his own vitals, Old Jim noted. All exhibited heightened stress, which caused the Medic to conclude that they should "take steps to lower the levels."

Generator repair appeared high on the Medic's list of "steps," and soon enough the generator once more coughed back into life.

Three biologists, according to Team Leader 1, had protested the return of the generator. Three biologists had in belligerent fashion attempted to stop the Medic from flicking the switch. Three biologists had seemingly then fallen back in line and voiced no further concerns.

"We genuinely understood the concerns, but not the method of expression," Team Leader 1 wrote. "We intend to restore morale by proving that the fears are unfounded, that the uncertainty is behind us now."

That Team Leaders 1 and 2 had had to put down a mini rebellion within their ranks to allow the generator to come back online signaled to Old Jim a situation more volatile than suggested by prior events.

But the night after the generator's repair, the first skeptic donned a contamination suit and waded out into the marsh until something fast and large took him—or this was the consensus. In the morning, the buoy of his red helmet lay bobbing, garish but gentle, against the mud flats. The generator droned on.

When the Mudder was sent to retrieve the helmet, she found no head within, nor any trace of the man who had worn it.

At no point during the rest of the expedition did the biologists find any trace of the man. Nor did they speak much of his disappearance. Nor did they pause in their return to their tasks, not even long enough to hold a memorial in absentia. Nor was there ever any investigation.

It felt to Old Jim like a false beacon, meant to distract. But from what?

"Diaz, Armando, 27, wetlands ecologist, missing, presumed

dead of natural causes," read the line item in Central's files, along with details of the cover story and payments to his family.

They had become twenty-three, the twenty-fourth passing out of history as easily as an alligator sliding into the water.

## 007: THE MYSTERIES

At some point, wandering the half-empty cathedral of Central, lost in the archives, Old Jim began to focus on what he thought of as the "Mystery of the Medic and the Mudder," chaining them together only as fellow anomalies at first, and their brief moment of connection at the twisted-ankle nexus. Because during those months the Medic never left the Dead Town base camp and the Mudder left it the most.

Surveillance footage showed her sneaking off five or six times, three of which coincided with her abrupt appearance at the Village Bar hours later, in the evenings. There to have a beer or two and then to disappear into the night, only to reappear in Dead Town before dawn. Old Jim could sympathize—he too would have snuck off from that dour and dire camp, even if leaving for short periods had disorienting effects on most of the biologists.

There were a number of ways to die in the dark traversing that stretch of wetlands, even taking care. Referring to maps of the area, Old Jim had timed it and the Mudder could not have turned up at the Village Bar as quickly as she did without help. It didn't take a detective to guess the source of that help: Man Boy Slim, who appeared in the Village Bar either before or after the Mudder all three times. And who had been spying on the biologists for weeks.

So at some point, perhaps, the Mudder had surprised Man Boy Slim in the bushes with his piano sounds and blackmailed him or convinced him in gentler ways to pick her up for some R&R in this little green boat he had, then take her back.

At the time, Central either missed it or thought nothing of it, given the two-week lag between taping and the tapes being switched out, brought to Bleakersville, and sent on to Central. And perhaps it did mean nothing but a fling or a friendship or a way to blow off steam.

But Old Jim had also noticed that twice the Mudder's presence coincided with the Rogue in the back of the bar. This fact nagged at Old Jim, even in his hollowed-out state, sitting in Central's bland cafeteria before a group session, contemplating pureed soup with a side of oyster crackers. It even agitated him, a welcome distraction from so much he disliked about the detox process.

Old Jim could discern no contact between Rogue and Mudder the first time, but the second time the Rogue came up to the bar and leaned in next to where the Mudder sat on a stool, to give the bartender his beer order.

Rewinding the tape a dozen times in a basement stinking of cigarette smoke, water dripping from the ceiling, Old Jim couldn't be sure that the Rogue spoke to the Mudder. But if he were a betting man, he would have liked the odds that the Rogue had whispered something to her—and that she responded with no more than a word or two. Before the Rogue retreated to his table in the half shadow of the back of the bar, having successfully turned his body such that the camera did not reveal his face.

Curious, the fifteenth time he watched it, that Old Jim turned his attention to Man Boy Slim sitting at the end of the bar, who snuck glances at the two of them. His left boot tapping on the brass footrail. Tap-tap-tapping. Did he just have to use the bathroom or did something make him nervous?

Did the Mudder and the Rogue make him nervous?

That this possible communication between Rogue and Mudder occurred three days after the generator had been fixed struck Old Jim as possibly significant, although he could not articulate why.

Drunk Boat and Man Boy Slim continued to hold court as ever, apparently unaware or uncaring of the generator issues over at Dead Town. Talk turned to "the Conflagration," as Drunk Boat put it, a bonfire party being held by the lighthouse in November. Man Boy Slim went off on a riff of how they must construct a marshmallow worthy of the roasting. This made Old Jim smile, receiving gladly the warmth of their cheery comfort and reassurance. In how they looked forward to the future of the holiday season and their most cherished rituals . . . even if that season lay in a far-distant land the biologists on the Forgotten Coast might never reach.

As for the Rogue, he had still not registered anywhere in "the system," had been such a perfect, best-behaving self as a RUSO, "ritualized unidentified sitting object," as Drunk Boat put it, that even he had stopped editorializing about the stranger.

Still, Old Jim had continued to scour newspaper and police reports from the era, for the Village and the nearby towns of Hedley and Bleakersville. There was little enough, and because police reports and newspaper clippings hadn't been in the files, Old Jim felt now like he was snooping or prying. Yet still he did it. (He found no applicable movie listing for the time Man Boy Slim had seemed haunted, when he'd seen something with Drunk Boat that disturbed him.)

Traffic stops for DUIs, car accidents, a man shot another man over the "trespasses of a pig." Fishermen fined for catching bass out of season. A death threat against the mayor of Bleakersville. The stealing of chickens. The "misplacing" of horses. All these typical and slightly atypical activities occurred while the biologists grew insular and peculiar in their enclave in Dead Town.

Nagging at him, yet another question: Why had Central bugged the Village Bar? He had no easy answer. But, perhaps, the impulse suggested already an uneasy awareness of some other force besides Central operating on the coast. That something in the myths of the coast, what washed up there, compelled such surveillance.

The heavy suppression and redaction in the files, the sense of not wanting to *name* a nexus of concern, for fear of calling it forth.


Amid all this sea wrack, the excesses and mundanity, the heavy fog of the moment, what none of them—him, the locals at the Village Bar, the biologists—could divine correctly was Time.

Not so much the passage of time, with which the locals were well familiar, as the way in which past, present, and future collapsed into each other. The mind became confused by the intermingled layers and whether the portents were ill or benign. Because so much on that coast, humid and hot and closed off, decayed sprang to life decayed sprang to life. The eye, misled, did not know what was truly and forever dead. The eye did not know where to focus, could not tell what might next be resurrected.

Did a pivotal event or conversation begin in the present or did it begin a decade earlier at the start of a friendship, only to end with an upturned table and a drunken punch while the house band played in the back? Was the faint sound of the cranes headed north—silver and ethereal and cloud-distant—happening now, or was that another season and the sky held merely the memory of their passage?

By then, too, post-generator, the storms had begun to come up the coast, so that, in time, Dead Town would become an island, cut off by flooding even as the generator, given new life, droned on, oblivious. The days would become elongated, compressed, hard to gauge and hard to hold on to.

Soon enough, the Village Bar would be boarded up and empty, but for one "loose shutter that kept banging against the window"—Drunk Boat joking that it was a good description of Man Boy Slim, to a scowl, as they shared a last round before the place went dark. Old Jim, traveler from the future peering down at the past, would become more and more cut off from the Village Bar gossip, the locals too concerned about storms becoming hurricanes—"horrorcanes," as Man Boy Slim called them—to worry about the biologists. To worry about anything other than when to evacuate, when to hunker down.

The surveillance camera on the outside of the bar would become a ceaseless record of the banging shutter—over and over, the transcripts continuing as if unhinged, as if the person listening at Central had nothing better than do than to continue typing "[shutter bangs]." Shutter bangs shutter bangs shutter bangs.

Until it became meaningless, and then, once again, held meaning.

## 008: NIGHT VISITORS

The fifth night after the rebirth of the generator, an all-encompassing susurration came from the sky over the biologists' yurts, and by the light of a bright half-moon and reflections off the clouds, they could see countless ragged, darting shapes, headed north over Dead Town.

At first, no one could identify exactly whether it was birds or bats, until the dislocating truth occurred: both birds and bats, of the same mind, a kind of confusion of tongues and wings. The chittering of the bats as they darted in clusters this way and that, trying to avoid the birds, the alarm cries of the birds of all types, from raptors to swamp sparrows.

"I had never seen such a thing, only read about it," wrote the Mudder. "It was beautiful and obscene and dislocating, but most of all the odd oily sheen of . . . scent from all that effort above us, it wafted down and even seemed to coat the ground. Their panic, their labor. I felt an embarrassment in witnessing, and a shame— as if I were the cause of their flight."

On the ground, a vibration and then a clatter and a pounding of hooves upon the ground as white-tailed deer charged out of the marshes, stampeding around the yurts and forcing the biologists inside for shelter, followed by the sometimes indistinct, sometimes raucous sounds of smaller mammals: raccoons, opossums, skunks, and in amongst their number bobcats, coyotes, foxes, oblivious as to who was predator and who was prey. Revealed by shaky flashlights stuck out the doors of yurts, the two expedition rifles raised in defense, but the animals only cared to scramble north as fast as they were able.

The yips and growls and whines and the other sounds, "the sense," as the Mudder put it, "of a great wall of flesh passing through by land and by sky, the thickness of that, is indescribable." By her estimations, it took more than thirty minutes for the sky to clear, the trembling of the ground to subside.

When the birds, the bats, the animals had passed through but for stragglers, the silence they left behind felt ominous to most. All was so very still except for the faithful rumbling of the generator and "the panicked sound of our own breathing."

"It felt, irrationally," Team Leader 2 wrote, "as if the wildlife had rejected us—had rejected our methodologies, and refused any longer to be sampled or catalogued, or subjected to even the least intrusive experiments. It felt as if the entire reason for the expedition had abandoned us and thus we had no rudder, no anchor, no reason to be. That we did not belong here."

To Old Jim's astonishment, reading the files as he waited on the results of his psych evaluation, the Medic described the night's events as "a lessening of dead weight. A great relief," as if the sheer wealth of wildlife had been oppressive, and joked that "a bird can be a bat, a bat can be a bird, that's just the way of things now."

The Medic noted that "a deteriorating sense of self has fled in the night with the mass panic." But Team Leaders 1 and 2 felt differently and focused on reassuring the rest of the expedition at an emergency meeting held in the aftermath, around 1:15 a.m. Illuminated by flashlights and a small fire outside the yurts, the ground churned and cracked by stampede.

This was a natural occurrence sometimes before a storm, Team Leader 1 reminded the others. It had been well-documented as a phenomenon and thus was no outlier, and if the shock of it still resonated, that was the difference between an account on a page and experiencing it in real life. They should be thankful to witness such a rare event and to "learn from it."

Talk turned to evacuation, despite the ambiguity of the weather reports. "There's no reward in the risk of leaving now," the Medic said, somewhat cryptically, Old Jim thought.

The conversation petered out, mostly from fatigue. Or a kind of peer review pressure bearing down, as if on some level, each member of the expedition knew that, in some form, they were being read, or would one day be read, as Old Jim read them now. That none wanted to say the wrong thing and, as a result, did not know the right thing. (None could know they would never be read again, in the usual way.)

The next day the white rabbits appeared, in great numbers, all over Dead Town.

## 009: HORDE

T he rain or the rabbits? Which came first or did they arrive together? "Drops like dew, a haze, the most delicate mist," the Mudder called the approach of the storms. "Like a kind of veil across our eyesight." Soon it would be hard to see two feet ahead in the torrential downpour, but this outcome would have seemed distant to the biologists that day, and of little consequence compared to the other arrival.

For the rabbits had the opposite effect of appearing all too real, and in such quantity, overnight, *unreal*. Team Leader 1 noted, "In their initially placid aspect, dotting the slope leading to our yurt, dotting the meadow, dotting the cracked concrete of the main street of Dead Town . . . they unnerved because one felt that they had always been here, and that they belonged here. That it was our conception of what belonged that had been wrong. That *we* did not belong, somehow."

Old Jim wanted, across the years, to implore the biologists to pack up and run, ahead of the storm. To cease operations and observations. To join the stampede of animals. To heed the echo of the piano that now came to the biologists in the gloaming of dusk. How casually some noted in their journals that this phenomenon had occurred for several days, even though Old Jim, by means arcane and archival, determined it began the day of the rabbits' arrival, with seemingly no Man Boy Slim hunkered down in the reeds to make it happen.

The rain on the yurts by that first evening, as the biologists adjusted to the presence of the rabbits, had already become a thready message that danced off and on across the rough canvas surface. It would have been a percussive presence above the biologists' heads as Team Leader 1 told them, after dinner, that she suspected "the locals of having a laugh at our expense," although in her journal later, adding the cryptic margin note "beware of falling stars."

Where would the locals find what appeared to be hundreds of white rabbits? How would they afford to buy them? How would they have so stealthily transported them to Dead Town and left them there? Mundane questions to quarantine the strangeness, to not think beyond certain boundaries, beyond which lay . . . what?

Team Leader 2, at cross-purposes with her partner, suggested a counter-experiment, a rival expedition. Or a "foreign entity," as she put it, although what did "foreign entity" mean back then? What *could* it mean?

To Team Leader 2, it meant: "Some other team of biologists conducting invasive species research. Some other team of biologists conducting invasive species research *in our territory.*"

But as the Medic was quick to point out, and with which Team Leader 1 agreed, they had no record of any such governmental survey in the area. They had no other indication of such an effort. Yet still this theory of a rival expedition gained credence amongst the biologists, perhaps because it still accreted some logic to it—like a solid bait on a hook that only over time begins to flake away into the water, to dissolve in the absence of a fish, into nothing.

Team Leader 1 then steered the debate toward communications and a plan of action. She would ask their superiors about what to do, and in the meantime the biologists would continue their experiments while "allocating some time to capturing and caging as many rabbits as possible."

In the Village Bar, just three days before the banging shutter, Man Boy Slim had found out about the rabbits from Charlie, who, from his boat, through binoculars, had discovered the rabbits in the marsh adjacent to Dead Town, if not the extent of the invasion.

"They've set loose lab rabbits that have been altered, look

unnatural, and spook every other living thing," Man Boy Slim said in a tone of voice that contained, if rewound a few times, a hint of reproach, but also a powerful unease. Man Boy Slim's theory covered up some other knowledge that made him fearful. Neither did there come back at him from his friends any of the customary jokes or bravado, just a "least of what they've done" from Drunk Boat.

No one in those discussions (key words in the files: rabbit, bunny, white [incl. plurals]) gave a wink or nudge-nudge to indicate complicity or foreknowledge, although Old Jim had become frustrated with how little footage corroborated the audio, so that he could not glean tone from visual clues.

But one thing was certain by then, on that first day the rabbits took over Dead Town: The Rogue no longer haunted the Village Bar. He had moved on, changed his base of operations, and to the patrons of the bar, it was as if he had never existed at all.

After dark that night, some observed that the invasives shed a slight phosphorescence against the pall of night. "Their quivering bodies as they foraged at dusk appeared like luminous smudges of ghost," Team Leader 2 wrote, uncharacteristically poetic.

This became a contested observation, an opinion shared by only some of the expedition, and not by Team Leader 1. But most agreed that, from the start, they "congregated in tight proximity after sunset," so that the rabbits took on the appearance of "wide swaths" or "rags" of white that in their "persistence of movements similar to shoals of fish" seemed to "glide across" the dark ground, to and fro, back and forth.

What pursued them, or what they pursued, no one could tell.

## 010: ESCALATION

**B**y the second day of their appearance, the white rabbits began to make the biologists' experiments useless or difficult to conduct—distraction, disruption of the landscape, destruction of the (plant) subject matter. They had some of the Old World look of hares, as cottontails did on the Forgotten Coast, along with the elongated stride of a hare. But the whiteness remained a stark reminder of aberration. It manifested in all of them. Too many of them. All of them.

"This continual shock of unnatural color"—for nothing else presented truly white in this soggy backcountry, except the pale underbelly of a dead alligator. This made explicit, as the Mudder put it, "by contrast with the tannins that give the water a dirty, red-tinged finish."

The Mudder pushed back against the assertion that the rabbits had become an obstacle: "The others say that the rabbits throw off our work, make our work impossible. But what is our work, exactly?"

Yes, what was the work? What would the work be now? Old Jim suspected that only the Medic truly knew.

The biologists once more observed, this time en masse, the feasting of the rabbits on fiddler crabs, which in this time of their mass migrations over the mud flats had begun to cross Dead Town in waves.

"The visceral experience of the sound of the rabbits—so many rabbits—crunching down on crab carapace unnerved many of us. The relentlessness of the sound throughout the day seemed to interfere with the essential signal of the mission." This from Team Leader 1, although the Medic noted something similar in his physiological observations.

"The essential signal," like the residue from the piano echo, a mass psychological unhingement. To Old Jim, there lay a wealth of analysis in the issue of sound and the expedition—enough to become its own forensic science project.

But the effect, by the afternoon of the second day, was anger and frustration directed at the rabbits, with any speculation as to how the rabbits had arrived in Dead Town petering out as "pulse" or "impulse" in the journals. Instead, the text and sub-text became: "How can we rid ourselves of this affliction?"

This anger became funneled into "the plan," as far as Old Jim could tell, and Team Leaders 1 and 2 were unable to provide a more productive context or distance from the issue. With this failure, Old Jim felt the expedition had descended into the danger of what he would term "a leaderless state," or a leadership that catered to the anxieties of those being led. Even as the Medic continued to calmly, and with little extraneous comment, chart the declining health of their vitals.

The morning of the third day, the biologists hauled out all available cages, from those that would hold one rabbit, to those that might hold up to a dozen. Large enough buckets with lids that locked, meant for aquatic samples, came into play. Butterfly netting, mist netting for songbirds—some felt that this gauzy material could be thrown over rabbits to capture them. Debate fizzled out over turning the yurt half packed with supplies into a rabbit holding pen.

But when the biologists attempted to capture the rabbits, the creatures moved with an almost uncanny ability for avoidance, anticipating the biologists' moves. Sometimes with hissing sounds or a clacking of their teeth that distracted their attackers as "not like a lagomorph"—or the rabbits stood their ground, snarling, suggesting infection with a pathogen like rabies.

This tactic, too, proved effective in thwarting the biologists. A species acting unlike, or in opposition to, the normal habits of that species put the biologists at a loss. On a very deep level, it confused them. Nor had they any military training or experience with mass extermination to prevent disease.

A rabbit that did not run away was, in some ways, not a rabbit at all. A belligerent rabbit had, in a sense, already broken contain and escaped the range of their intent.

"They seemed both afraid and unafraid, could be docile and aggressive and docile again—the same animal," Team Leader 1 wrote. This, in a section that detailed frustrating attempts to extricate the tiny cameras that graced the necks of perhaps one in ten rabbits.

If the biologists had a worrying lack of concern about the cameras, perhaps the sheer numbers of rabbits so overwhelmed that they had no critical faculties left to devote to the subject.

Even Team Leader 1's observation distorted reality, seemed to be skewed by the inundation. The rabbits did not fear humans in *any* context, Old Jim believed, including his review of the limited video footage. They simply brooked no interference, by a variety of means. The biologists never asked themselves if the rabbits had their own mission to complete, but this thought haunted Old Jim continually in the cafeteria, eating meat loaf or dry chicken breast. Thinking about the crunching of crabs.

When the biologists did manage to capture a rabbit, it lunged to bite with those teeth that had feasted on crab flesh, with a devilish accuracy. Caged, the rabbits thrashed and thrashed, physically in agony at entrapment—terrible to watch, organisms trying to smash themselves to bloody rags to escape. Banging shutters banging and banging, and no way to stop them but to give in to the storm. All while the cameras around the rabbits' necks at times appeared to click, to blink, to record, to process . . .

If not for all that had come before, this situation might have simply engaged the biologists' feelings of "humane and ethical treatment," of "respect for specimens," as fuel to find the energy for release. But, in fact, Old Jim noted, what it did was hollow out that concern, so that afterward it no longer existed in discernible quantities.

Empathy slid toward expediency, but not before the biologists released the most frantic rabbits and attempted to sedate others with the longest needles at their disposal, to limit contact. Protocols continued to be abandoned or ignored in the confusion, as thirty cages in a yurt would vibrate with the scrabbling panic of fifty spasming rabbits, turning white fur red with self-inflicted injury against the wire.

Jabbing, jabbing, jabbing, here and there, everywhere, upending cages as they hurried amongst the creatures, no logic to needle reuse or even dosages. Even as, starting from the center, the cages receded from their terrible juddering as if from some ground zero event, until the outer cages fell silent of the thrum and shaking. While the biologists continued to jitter and ping in their ceaseless banter and chatter, which felt like a disguise to mask a rising sense of horror.

Nor did it reflect poorly on the biologists that so many, even heavily protected, leapt back out of the way of a lunging rabbit, from a terror of infection, contamination, invasion. "I feared they would find me on all fours, eating the crabs raw on the marsh flats, no signal left within me."

The footage the Medic took shook so much, nothing was comprehensible except as blur and vibration, and, sometimes, the wild, rapidly blinking eye of a biologist up close, panning back, a syringe in hand with the dimensions, at that perspective, of a spaceship about to crash-land.

Even the orderly intent in the disorder of this approach became further compromised as, due to either mistakes or expediency, the biologists broke open two boxes of an experimental sedative meant only to be used on seabirds, and instead of putting the rabbits to sleep, it imposed an overwhelming clarity and sharpness—such that they would stop thrashing but then begin to "chatter at high volume" in a "directed and hostile way."

There welled up from the rabbits, then, what Old Jim thought of as a "competing signal," and it appeared to harm the biologists in some physiological way, for the Medic advised them to leave the yurt, discontinue the effort, and regroup. Although even outside they could still faintly hear the group call from the rabbits.

"I did not like how they stared at me," the Mudder wrote, as the reason why she had abandoned her duties in the yurt long before the use of the experimental sedative. And, perhaps, why she then continued to instead catalogue the progress of the rain, "which we have gotten used to, but which has increased in severity."

Team Leaders 1 and 2 reconsidered "methodologies of containment" from the steps of crumbling City Hall, hoping, perhaps, by the change in scenery to provide some relief from the visceral experience of the yurts and cages. While also brainstorming ways to retrieve rabbit cameras, which might hold further insight as to their containment or control. (This again, Old Jim noted, a way of rationalizing the cameras, rather than considering their essential nature.)

As Team Leader 1 noted that they had neither "sufficient quantities" nor the will for "bullet to the brain solutions," Team Leader 2 personally handed out ice-cream sandwiches, a surprise treat, reminiscent of summer camp, that they had been hiding in amongst frozen flounder and ray specimens in the deep coolers, as a reward before their winter break.

"What does it mean that the Tyrant now eats these rabbits? How might this affect the environment?" This from the junior biologist tasked with monitoring the tracking device.

Which had begun to malfunction, a harbinger of a growing problem with the camp's electronics in general. Sometimes the tracker showed the Tyrant nowhere, the dot disappearing. Other times, the dot had bifurcated and the Tyrant existed in two places at once, with no visual confirmation possible to determine the true sighting from the phantom. But on three occasions, the Tyrant had erupted from the water on the meadow side of Dead Town to devour a rabbit that foraged too close to the reeds.

"The Tyrant's behavior now differs from before, as if the rabbits have switched on within its brain some impulse or organizing thought that had lain dormant," the junior biologist had noted in the records. "This 'activation' appears centered on this encampment."

Neither Team Leader 1 nor Team Leader 2 had an answer for the junior biologist, nor the patience. Instead, for a time, the question silenced all discussion and they loitered, standing in a semicircle to eat their ice cream in silence, a scene rendered somewhat macabre by the grainy black-and-white footage and the coldness of Old Jim's table at the viewing area in Central's basement.

"Tomorrow will be better," Team Leader 1 said, after they had finished the ice cream.

But it wasn't.

## 011: THE KILLINGS

By the third afternoon, the rabbits had eaten the wildflower meadow down to nubs, so that the wide expanse looked as if someone "had given it a bad shave," the Mudder wrote, accompanied by a washed-out photo that showed how the marsh and estuary beyond could now be seen from the yurts. To Old Jim, the meadow resembled a field of wheat after the harvest. He could almost smell the straw-hay freshness, soon to fade into a staleness he associated with horse barns.

The white lumps of rabbits dotting that bereft landscape felt fake, false, *added later*. The sand and the marsh flats beyond, the islands of palmettos, the hint of the sea in the distance . . . all of this impossible to coexist with that foreground. And yet it *had* coexisted, for a time, as startling as if skulls had appeared in the wet marsh.

By the fourth afternoon, purple thistles had, with preternatural speed, "even for speedy growers," sprung up throughout the fallow meadow. The landscape appeared almost alien, with the dull brown of flattened dead wildflowers such a stark, neutral backdrop to the bodies of the rabbits and the vivid purple explosions of the thistle blossoms and their multitude of tall green stalks.

The meadow had a wet, boggy texture now. The rabbits, fur ruffled and stained, would not touch the thistles but foraged on the remnants of what they had already destroyed.

The biologists' emergency comms had failed, even though the generator rumbled on. Old Jim knew Central's surveillance cams had begun to fail as well. Privately, Team Leaders 1 and 2 expressed concerns that "something about the rabbit cameras is interfering with our gear, perhaps even the Tyrant's tracker. Some electrical impulse or competing channel."

The rain had intensified to a steady downpour, even if the sun could sometimes still be seen, as was common in those parts. Weather reports gleaned from a battery-operated handheld radio differed on where and how the worst of the storms would hit, whether it would get worse or subside.

That evening, Team Leaders 1 and 2 announced that an order had come down from on high, "By arcane means?" the Mudder muttered in her journal, for no one except possibly the Mudder herself had left the encampment. How could a message be sent out and a reply received?

Team Leaders 1 and 2 claimed that the order was to herd any rabbits *not* in the meadow *to* the meadow and "dispose of them there, with the discretion to then withdraw from Dead Town to a more secure location farther inland," should the storm intensify.

It became clear, as Team Leader 1 outlined the logistics of the plan, how they would encircle and "nudge or otherwise coerce" the rabbits to the meadow . . . that, in the end, they would use flamethrowers to incinerate as many rabbits as possible, with outliers "disposed of by hand," which meant, more than likely, knives, as they had few guns.

The "flamethrowers" were propane-fueled "super weeders" the biologists had been meant to test as a means of controlling invasive plants by disrupting their cellular structure, with the flame "applied a foot or so above the ground and the roots," but also for controlled burns to encourage "renewal of the native seed bank."

The flamethrowers were still in their boxes, as they had been reserved for Phase 3 of the expedition, in the late winter. The propane tanks fit strapped onto the back of the wearer while the weeding apparatus awkwardly curved from the back around to the front. The handheld spigot looking both infernal and as innocuous as a sprinkler head.

The last reliable weather report indicated a lull in the rain the next morning, giving the expedition "a small window of opportunity" to kill hundreds of rabbits with fire.

"What *current* weather reports? Even the radio has stopped working," the Mudder noted, underlined twice, which Old Jim again determined to mean Team Leaders 1 and 2 were flying by the seat of their pants, given the disruption of electrical devices.

Science and logic had given way to mere hope, prayers, and blessings. This applied, as well, to the actions of the evening, when, too wired to sleep, Team Leaders 1 and 2 debated, privately, what to do about the cameras in Team Leader 2's yurt. They had retrieved two ancient cameras from around the necks of rabbits that appeared to be intact and functional. Many were not.

The attendant chatter Old Jim found incomprehensible, a kind of proof that the cameras represented an uncanny bewilderment to the biologists that they wanted to channel into the technological or logistical realm, rather than acknowledge it. A denial reinforced every time they returned to trapping and killing rabbits without knowing what the cameras meant or might one day mean. Because they had reached their limit.

Team Leader 1: "We decided to view the footage together to ensure an objective viewpoint on what we saw. And that we would only view the footage once and then preserve the cameras against the weather and prepare to have them sent on later to our superiors."

Team Leader 2: "I thought something in the video might provide insight into the rabbits, and might in that case affect our mission in the morning."

But from Old Jim's perspective, some other impulse motivated them or coerced them. Standard protocol would have meant bagging the cameras and sending them to a Central proxy immediately. Team Leaders 1 and 2 had no way to make a copy. If viewing the footage destroyed the footage, a distinct possibility given the condition of the cameras, only their eyewitness impressions would remain.

"The cameras were so delicate—the straps we had cut, the tiny micro point of the lens, the screen a little larger than an overseas postage stamp." So small, in fact, that Team Leader 2 had the idea to view the screen through a magnifying glass. Destabilizing: the mysterious quality of the underlying mechanics of the cameras.

The body of the first camera had a slurred quality consistent with having passed successfully through ancient flame and had an acrid scent. It took some time to find the recessed button in the chassis that played the video. Team Leader 2 expressed anxiety about this delay, asking Team Leader 1, who ignored her, if they should abandon the idea.

But the few seconds of video showed grainy footage of other rabbits and then "a flash of light that ended it." Team Leader 2 noted that playing the video made the camera "feel soft and rubbery in her hand," as if the mechanism inside was in danger of malfunctioning. She feared "it might fall apart like old rubber."

With perhaps more confidence but more care handling the camera, they watched the second video. They noted that the video lasted three minutes and twenty-one seconds. They noted that it did not include rabbits. They noted that it did not include scenes of Dead Town. That it did include images of them both, "with close-ups of our faces," but declined to describe what these scenes consisted of or in what context a camera attached to a rabbit at ground level had been able to show "close-ups" of their faces.

"At first, we thought we had hit the recording option and then playback," Team Leader 1 wrote. "But then it seemed more like, for lack of better words, a kinetic viewing that included us. As if the camera observed us and some internal program knew that *we, specifically*, were using it. We did not feel comfortable continuing the experiment."

The experiment? When had it gone from archival to . . . experiment? At what point in the viewing had Team Leaders 1 and 2 realized they had made a mistake?

Old Jim sat back in his chair in the archives to contemplate that statement. Team Leader 1 appeared to be saying that the video was *anticipatory* of being viewed by unauthorized person-nel, like some kind of psychological weapon. That, in a sense, the video was *looking in* at them in a distorted way? Like a crystal ball or a two-way video system? No, not like that at all. But like *what*?

And if the Medic had viewed the video, what would it have shown the Medic?

Nothing about the cameras or their fate made it into the next briefing, which focused on the extermination phase. Nor at any point in the future of the expedition did Team Leader 1 or Team Leader 2 mention to the other biologists that they had viewed the camera footage.

So that next morning—the operation overseen by two people who were romantically involved, who may or may not have viewed unsettling footage the night before—the ten biologists with training on the flamethrowers donned their gear, including protective garments and the tanks, so they looked like sad fumigators fighting some futile war against the landscape.

Under a gray sky and gathering drizzle, the rest took up metal lids and mosquito netting and knives and the two rifles and everyone joined those already on the far edge of Dead Town to drive the rabbits toward the meadow.

"Meat for ages. Meat for miles," the Medic enthused in a boastful fashion, next to his usual physiological readings, which had begun to devolve into observations "from the outside." Many of the expedition members had stopped allowing him to monitor their vitals, poke and prod them, perhaps as a vote of no confidence.

With a kind of relief later that afternoon, Team Leader 1 noted "the cessation of operations," with little other details. What Team Leader 2 admitted "could have been a nightmare" was "pulled off without a hitch." This included "destruction of foreign paraphernalia," which meant the cameras.

The rabbits, by all accounts, had let themselves be herded, with little resistance, to the meadow, to join the rabbits already gathered there, until, surrounded by the flamethrower wearers, the rabbits "were effectively liquidated, as humanely as possible." Although Old Jim doubted a scenario existed in which "humanely" could have played any part as a description.

Soon after, the biologists retreated to their yurts, for the rain came down by dusk in such obliterating rage that the water seemed intent on hiding "any hint of a crime," the Mudder wrote. That there would be no trace of the rabbits in the memory of the world. So that, as the Medic might have put it, "we can get back to our vital work."

No one, even the Mudder, made direct comments in their journals about the day. No footage existed, as all comms save a Central surveillance camera on Main Street had malfunctioned and gone offline permanently. Another layer of information stripped away. He was left with what the journals told him from this point on.

Journals rescued from layers of dirt, green with moss.

Journals with pages torn and ripped and bloody.

"Did not move or register pain as they burnt and died. Did not try to run. Did not care. Did not. Would not. Could not." Found, finally, buried in Team Leader 2's journal, in the margin of an entry from the early spring, when the locals had thought the biologists were burying gold bars.

Old Jim's terrible, unthinkable thought: Had the rabbits kept on eating, crunching down on dead crabs even after their fur had crisped into ash? Even after their hearts had burnt away or exploded from the heat?

That night, the weather changed and the storm became a hurricane and evacuation no longer possible. The biologists would have to wait it out in Dead Town.

That night, too, Team Leader 1 authorized the dumping of "a number of severely damaged, nonfunctioning rabbit cameras into the marsh."

Old Jim did not like the idea of the cameras mingling with the substrata, with the detritus at the bottom of the estuary. To be pulled apart over time, to molecule by molecule become part of the Forgotten Coast.

Even if that was the fate of every living thing.

## 012: DEAD MEADOW

In the morning, the biologists awoke to the sounds of a great rending and tearing of flesh that they did not at first understand. Some anomaly of the winds brought by the storms, lashing against the trees and reeds and bushes. Some vestige of a bad dream welling up again.

But as the sound continued at an unhurried yet amplified pace, flurries of rain welling up, dying away, and welling up against the dull gray horizon . . . as the crackle and tear of it, the crispness to some listeners, the moistness in others, it caused a mass hysteria.

As did the stench of burning from the dead meadow. For there, upon that blackened, blighted field shorn now of any vegetation but for some stalks of thistles, the half-torched corpses of the rabbits lay slumped in a confusion of flesh and bone and parody of sculpture—in blackened clumps still steaming while flashes of white remnants of fur like tattered flags flashed through the gloom as a reminder of what they had once been.

But memory was not needed, for a hundred or more new rabbits, be-muddened and brazen, grazed there now. And what they feasted upon was burnt and crackling flesh. What they ate were their dead kin, and they ate them as methodically and calmly as their predecessors had eaten the fiddler crabs.

At the sight, a handful of biologists vomited into the grass around the yurts, into the mud, the weeds. Others seemed "almost catatonic," according to the Medic. The chewing of gristle, the gentle yet firm way some of the rabbits held the charred heads of their meal and, wrenching with their teeth, pulled strips of skin and meat from the skulls. How, in several accounts, the charnel-house stench released felt like a physical blow.

"You did not want to be there. You didn't want to be anywhere, ever again." "My head will never be right again." "I felt the presence of the Tyrant in their feasting, as if the rabbits had become the Tyrant."

But the Mudder wrote only, "The worm eats its own tail. Will the worm die of it?"

Into the void, Team Leaders 1 and 2 issued forth from their yurt, noticeably shaken, and ordered a new advance. "A final advance." Although rain might hamper their effort, the flame-throwers would still work well enough to "do the job," and other weapons could be assembled and "we can finish this once and for all."

There must have been some resistance, some sense that a war of attrition might end badly, as the biologists had already performed what they had assumed would be the "final advance" the day before. Even the Medic urged caution, that "now we have time to evaluate perhaps a better course of action." Two accounts also noted that the Medic was uncharacteristically emotional that morning. "He was yelling at us, all these half-familiar phrases, like he was whipping a horse in a race"—just, perhaps, not toward a finish line endorsed by Team Leaders 1 and 2.

But what course of action *was* better, Team Leader 1 shouted at the Medic. They had waited too long as it was, and now they simply had to *get on with it*. Only one or two others objected to the plan. Mental reserves at new lows. No better solutions available, depleted by the generator incident, the piano music, the course of events.

*Shutter bang bang shutter shutter bang bang shutter.*

The biologists advanced, shuffling and exhausted and lonely in their duty, to the edge of the meadow, in three cascading 8-8-7 rows, the second two rows meant to expand out to the sides like a human fence to block every last rabbit from escape . . .

. . . and from the other side a glimmering figure arose from the reeds and water and distance. The rain came down forceful enough now that the figure appeared so slight that there occurred a silvering effect "the drops like fish scales, a shield around the figure," Team Leader 2 wrote later, in almost illegible handwriting, like "ethereal armor."

No real identification of the figure could be made, and at first neither Team Leader 1 nor Team Leader 2 assumed the figure posed a threat. Perhaps they thought the missing biologist had come back or a local had decided to check in on them with the hurricane imminent.

Team Leader 1 held up a hand, palm out to indicate "pause," a motion to hail the stranger, to perhaps usher this person out of what would soon be a kill zone. To protect this person against the wide and deep intent of the biologists to exterminate whatever remained alive between them and the figure. As the rabbits continued to eat the dead, amongst the burnt sour smell of bone and charred flesh, and there came, far distant but radiant, the ardor and anchor of the lighthouse lens expressed as a shining out across the expanse to reach even them, so remote.

But the Rogue did not halt. Instead, the Rogue shouted words at them—for Old Jim believed the figure was the Rogue, even if he was alone in this—and by these words the biologists knew the figure to be an enemy, that and the elastic, flailing speed of his approach, sheathed and stained by the raindrops and yet slipping through and between, this unseeable form with the shrieking voice.

The pause of the biologists became a faltering in their advance. They faltered with their flamethrowers and gutting knives, their flare guns and hooks and hammers. They faltered in their hearts. Because they knew not what they looked upon. Just a man. Just a man, surely. *Shudder bang, bang shudder* went the videotape from the Village Bar now, wracked by vicious winds. *Shudder bang* went the biologists, wracked by doubt and dismay.

What word did the Rogue utter? Was it "exhilaration" or "acceleration" or "exhalation"?

The one word they all agreed upon: "Stop!"

At the beginning the Rogue shouted, "Stop!"

The sky had turned a strange and oppressive oval of gray with black around the edges, like a sagging eye, enflamed, "some impossible intensity of red." As the wind forced the rain to lash them, and the white rabbits, soaked, still gnawed with their teeth and scraped with their claws at the flesh of their dead burnt brethren. The smell welling up as of a terrible spell cast upon the world—of decay, of smoldering, the piled meat of fiddler crabs gone bad, and the stench of some other musky animal lancing through.

This they experienced in a way almost ecstatic and otherworldly as the Rogue's screams became overwhelming to the biologists. As if the words, in some heightened register, drew forth the meaning of the smells in a way they had never before understood, and with this came a resentment, beyond measure, of their situation. *The onrushing of the rain, the Rogue, and the word "Stop."*

Perhaps on another day, the biologists might have just . . . stopped. Laid down their weapons. Retreated to the encampment and sank into whatever simple comforts remained available to them. There, in the yurts or in City Hall, to await the Rogue's approach and to parlay with him. To let talk and accommodation be the only part of valor.

But something in the "Stop" after so much had gone wrong, so much in general awry, made "staying the course" more comforting, it appeared from the journal accounts. A feeling that later became meaningless, worthless, as if a heated need to take and hold territory had, too late, fallen away.

And so, with their own roar muffled and choked off by ever greater torrents, in their waders and boots, in their raincoats and waterproof hats, clasping their flamethrowers and improvised killing weapons, the biologists now charged forward across the meadow toward the Rogue. Toward this inexplicable, pitiless, gaunt figure in the gloom. This fugue, this affront, this threat, this *little nothing* who had commanded them, without authority, to stop.

"It felt pure," one biologist would write later. "It felt so very right." That whatsoever the biologists should face there, as they slipped and slid, that they should "hold the line," and achieve, finally, some sort of victory. *Never surrender.*

Perhaps in the face of their aggression, the great shout that arose from them as if an army charging the ramparts of the enemy, the biologists expected the Rogue to come to a halt in surprise. To slip in the mud, to pivot with one hand on the ground for support and disappear back into the marsh. Or even to put his hands up in surrender, outnumbered and outgunned.

But he did not. He did not. The Rogue instead raged across the blackened field toward them, screaming out more words, screaming and roaring phrases, and if he too almost lost his footing, went askew, righted himself, it was from how the power of his intonation careened him off-balance, how those words proved almost too powerful for his body as they cleared his lips. How the words disfigured him, to the few biologists who thought to look up from negotiating the mud to try to view his face.

"He was a signal. His face was a shining light." "There was nothing I could see of him, ever, but slivers."

There filtered through the biologists' recollections a sense, too, that as the Rogue traveled toward them the distortion of the rain formed a silvery wall. That the Rogue lay behind the wall, or that the wall *shivered* and *trembled* forward with him, and that the meadow had widened and lengthened until, despite the charge, they remained miles away from him, and yet so intimate, held by the intensity of his regard.

With this sense of separation of the Rogue from the landscape came also a puzzling yet deep feeling of grief, of shame, that made the biologists weep as they stumbled in their advance yet kept shambling forward, Team Leader 1 urging them on in frenzied mimicry of the Rogue.

The biologists had reached the white rabbits and did not care or notice that they trampled blackened corpses and living creatures both, weapons slack at their sides like a muscle memory that was amnesia, this onrushing surge toward the Rogue behind his veil of silver. Nor did the living rabbits care if they were trampled.

At this point, too, the Rogue's singing or shrieking or shouting changed in pitch and tone and there descended upon the biologists "a slowness" no one understood later. A deep, churning slowness, as if they moved through air as heavy as that around the Rogue appeared light. So that every pump of legs against the mud and yellowed grass, the small bodies of the rabbits, feet disappearing reappearing, ground out into moments of obscenely meticulous detail—the flutter and upkicking of the mud onto each other, the spatter, the jostling of shoulders in close quarters as they fell into each other, the flecks of sweat on the lips that, in their microscopic precision, bore no resemblance to the rain pouring down their faces.

The plastered hair like that of "hyperreal statues set upon the plain," fated to stand motionless in mid-motion, and on some distant day crumble into dust.

Now the Rogue seemed both very near and very far, and through the drumming rage of the rain came, miraculous, the unmistakable song of birds from a place where the sun must still shine and where none of this could possibly be happening. And yet, too, several noticed that the lighthouse had stopped shining out, that the rest of the world had fallen away except for the blackened meadow across which Team Leader 1 led the charge.

Now the Rogue kept opening his mouth wider and wider and the words came out louder and more brutal above the downpour. These words blazed into flame upon leaving the Rogue's mouth. These words could not be extinguished by the rain. These words rose and permeated and cascaded outward and around the Rogue—even as the first wave of biologists surging against that "fey weaponry" crumpled, fell to their knees, slid down on the gurgling mud as if they could evade the fire "that called our names" . . . except it kept calling and each time the desolation within became more final and complete.

"The fire of his words had cloaked him in flame and now rushed out to all sides."

The second wave of biologists came up behind, to break upon the first, down in the mud, crawling, until desperate hands formed fists to grasp at the clothing of those already subsumed—to slow their own headlong rush into the widening bog of dead rabbits, dead flesh, the mud, the rising water, and the third wave after that, so none could stop their "onrushing onrush" . . . and there they lay, grappling with each other, weapons long forgotten, a few struggling to stand, crying out in distress, while those with propane tanks for flamethrowers pawed, frantic, at the straps on their backs, unbalanced by their burden and panicked by it.

And still the Rogue ran through them, like an avenging angel, but avenging what, they grieved, and his voice, that close, rippled out not as a fire but as some kind of visible sonic boom in a circular wave that smashed through whatever it touched, and, caught by surprise in their struggles, the biologists fell again into the mud, to "get low, to escape to the sides" and suffer not "the blades of this new thing."

The wave became "like blood," became "physical" and broke over them, became them, choked and bathed them, "smelling like open wounds and too lost to escape it, but to have it linger in the body, to bind us and even to froth out of our mouths like the sea, to be drowning while on land." Ahhhhhh there came the sounds of a groveling madness and a texture like mangled dead baby birds, neither skin nor feathers, and also "something smooth and shiny that infiltrated the pores, metallic and sour, and left no trace behind but remained nonetheless, unable to get out."

Days passed in that state. Or minutes. Or "nothing nothing nothing."

How the wrongness made them clutch their heads but they could not get the wrongness out. How the sounds built and vibrated and spun and unspooled and in all ways made of them taut twine and elastic stretched to its utmost. To feel attenuated and so thick all at once. To be abomination and unable to cast off the shame of that.

Their heads were filled with wild things and evil things. Their heads were filled with nails and pus. Their heads were filled. They would never remember the words the Rogue used. They said the words sounded "familiar." They had heard the words before, but not in that combination. They had heard the words but not in the same context or intonation or the same kind of light or darkness or they could not recall what was different, why it was different and yet the same, no they could not, please stop asking the question. "Please stop asking. Please stop asking." Please. Stop.

Although after, all were untouched and no sign remained of what had passed through them, and perhaps into them. On the horizon, the lighthouse had become a "pillar of electric green," spilling a fuzzy, rapturous light between fissures of rain.

And still, without relief, the Rogue ran forward and kept running forward, knives emanating from his mouth and blood and light spreading out from him on all sides. Until he disappeared once more, into the wall of rain behind them, and they could no longer see him nor hear him. Nor feel the weight of that presence.

The lack, which they had not recognized as weight, undid the biologists further, so that those handful who had risen toppled once more and there came over all a malaise and sadness that forced them to be still, to be silent, to gather their limbs into themselves and become as small as they could become, to cease their cries and their weeping.

To lie there as if dead in the devastation of the Rogue's passing.

Yet the rain did not stop but intensified until none could see the other but only "feel a hand on a shoulder" or "a foot kick out." The wounded timelessness of these moments so deep and frayed and faded that it left a kind of "smoldering watermark on the soul."

The bones that had come free in what once had been the meadow belonged to the ancient cemeteries and so now the biologists lay freely amongst those bones, amongst the centuries, unable to understand how they had gotten there, to so commingle, and of all the horrors of that, came this perverse comfort: That to be there, almost as floating, in the deep mud, vision blanketed in gray, lying atop and amongst those bones felt natural and right and pure.

Staring at the scarred and occluded sky, mottled with a deeper darkness that matched the darkness that had leaked into their heads, rain runneling the contours of the face and the body left to burrow deeper into the bones and layers beneath, without any terrible, pointless urge to rise, to rise up in the aftermath of the inexplicable.

No one could say how many hours had passed, nor if any of them would feel whole ever again. No one could remove the image of the Rogue from their minds, though one, later, might try with a stab of scissors to the eye, interrupted in this task by three others not so much "for his sake but for ours." No one could get the words to leave them alone, at first like a swarm of biting flies and then as a presence standing always behind them, so that if they turned at the wrong time, it would devour them whole.

So they did not look back much, or go out into the dark, even if they carried the dark within.

Some insisted, too, that as they had lain in the mud, the Tyrant had followed in the Rogue's footsteps, obscuring them with the crawl of its body as it bathed in the spray of blood emanating from the Rogue. That the Tyrant had passed over and under and through them. Crushing them under those smooth and shining scales into the mud and dead rabbits and shells of crabs.

That the roughness of experience and age of the alligator's chiton left bruises on those it had dug beneath and shuddered to the side and with a sense of being peeled away or pushed out of a tube, as if they were glutinous, impermanent, not human. The Tyrant oblivious to their presence and this, somehow, the worst part: that the alligator had no desire for their flesh but instead remained loyal only to the Rogue, joined in purpose by some vision the biologists would never understand.

That the great, the yellow, the armored eye had "discarded us as easily as if tossing a rag doll into the marsh." Receding into a nothing that became just another part of the charred plain. Judging, because how could it not judge? How could they not, now, in this extremity, feel themselves judged.

The aftershocks faded. The rain did not stop, but the sun shone through a hole in the black clouds to illuminate stricken faces, each lit differently by shadow and by light, so that some registered more as silhouettes than people.

Some began to stagger back to the yurts, most on all fours, as if reluctant to stand should the Rogue return. A few croaked out the names, querulous, of friends, of colleagues. A handful spoke the names of dead loved ones, as if they might now be found amongst the more ancient bones, in the aftermath of the expedition.

At City Hall, the biologists found, after a head count, that they had left two dead in the meadow, killed of no visible wound but fear. But also missing: Team Leader 1, Team Leader 2, the Medic, and the Mudder. And because their bodies could not be found, the remaining biologists chose to believe that it had been the *Tyrant* who took them, dragging them one by one or two by two in its great jaws, down into the deep water, to drown them there and open them up and devour them at the beast's leisure.

For that was fitting. For that was what they deserved for the straitjacket of the harness, for releasing the Tyrant out into a foreign land, disoriented and lost.

Also dead: the generator, so thoroughly sabotaged as for it to feel personal, the blunt yet intricate details of that damage—the completeness of how the generator could never again fulfill its function—spoke of rage and brought the image of the Rogue back to them, against their will. Made of them nothing but receptacles for further terror.

For what if the Rogue should return? This possibility assailed them every moment of the aftermath.

## 013: SHUDDER BANG

**N**othing changed the next day, or the day after that, or the day after that. The rain slaughtered the land and the lightning cracked open the sky and sheets of water eroded the estuary banks so that the earth crumbled away from the shore and the rusted heap of automobiles tumbled into those waters, some carried away at the high point of the flood to be found later upended sticking out of the marsh in places where they could not easily be retrieved and so remained for decades, rusting into the reeds. Others found their way into Dead Town, haphazardly and sometimes "parked" upside down on Main Street.

The meadow disappeared under the water, too, and the biologists, in shock, in trauma, gave no account of whether they had time to bring the bodies of their fallen comrades to higher ground and bury them, or if those bodies drifted out into time and distance. The biologists, now seventeen in number, moved like sleepwalkers, clutching what belongings they had thought to take from the yurts and moving into Dead Town to take shelter on the flat roof of City Hall, with the waters still rising.

Some huddled in the stairwell, which, due to a quirk of overtaxed gutters, still poured water down upon them. They had not slept for twenty-four, thirty-six, forty-eight hours. Their supplies had been winnowed by water submerging most of the yurts. None of their comms worked and they had no way to call for help. Nor, looking out across those lands where the Tyrant lurked, a way to send anyone for help.

"We could only wait it out," the young biologist responsible for the Tyrant's tracker wrote in his waterproof journals. "Our provisions dwindled, even risking reprovisioning from the sinking yurts. Our potable water supplies are low, and we fear the swamp water. We fear the return of the figure. We fear the Tyrant. But we are so tired it is difficult at times even to feel fear. We want to be dry and somewhere else. Our dreams come so strange now."

Only three biologists still kept records. Only three to describe these dreams, and yet Old Jim noted a chilling consistency, as if the Rogue held them in thrall still.

In these dreams, the meadow had "become some other place," ill-used by "constant battle." A weird green-gold light came from the horizon, framed by the cleft between two mountains. An army of "scientists and psychics" struggled "across a plain of sand and bones toward the light." Grim-looking men and women, "who looked like veterans of some longer conflict." Oxen pulled war wagons. Soldiers labored to fix the wheel of a catapult. A leader upon a draft horse. Their style of dress was archaic; they wore leather armor and many had crossbows slung across their backs. The army's numbers were so great that "ranks of ten stretched to the horizon" and the light. The army fed itself into the cleft between the ridges, ever advancing, ever disappearing into the distance.

All three claimed to see figures "stitching their way" through the undergrowth outside of Dead Town, and that these figures wore "old-fashioned armor and helmets and some rode upon horses." But these figures had no faces, only the toothed hole of a lamprey's open mouth, endlessly circling a limitless gullet.

"There came the distant sounds of conflict, but always at some vast remove."

But for the Dead Town expedition an end to the dreaming was soon to come. For the remaining remnants of journal entries—what Central recovered of them—recorded a confusion beyond imagination, a descent into a vast internal void, a kind of babbling nothing that Old Jim could not read more than a paragraph of at a time. These dangers to themselves and others. These psychotic breaks. Hints of references to murders, of mutilations, cut off from everyone and everything except what did not bear thinking about. Who could know what on the page had been real and what imagined or outright hallucination. All Old Jim could be sure of is that the biologists' sense of time and reality had been obliterated and put back together differently—and that this had harmed them beyond repair. The flooded yurts were found burnt to the ground by the biologists' own hand. Their tattered flag at City Hall had been ripped from its pole and torn to pieces.

By the time Central's rescue mission reached Dead Town, the rain had stopped, and by that time, too, the rest of the expedition had died of causes both natural and unnatural.

As for the Rogue, little more information could be gleaned from any of the accounts. Just an impossible still shot from a surveillance camera on the northern edge of Dead Town. Water stains from the rain had distorted the photograph and the unnatural light that haloed the figure appeared to have no source, but must have been a quirk of the infrared inversion.

The Rogue existed forever suspended in mid-step, one boot almost blocking the view of the camera, and the forced perspective rendered his gaunt body preternaturally forceful and looming—but looming away from the camera, toward the backdrop. He had a bag over one shoulder and the boot farther from the camera had an insignia or symbol smeared by the rain.

Old Jim probably misread a sense of haggard satisfaction or accomplishment from the set of the Rogue's shoulders, but it was an impression he could not shake.

What had the Rogue's motivation been? In Old Jim's report later, from which he withheld many things—less from a need to hide than a need to think about it first—he identified stealing the cameras and destroying the generator as the objectives. (The generator had been the first of its kind for Central.)

This did not feel like an original observation to him, and being ordered to issue a report felt to Old Jim like a test . . . that Central would compare his "results" with the general consensus before judging him fit to return to field operations. Had all the rest been an extravagant psyops pyrotechnic display? And couldn't the Rogue have destroyed the generator under the cover of darkness and found some less disruptive and ultra-visible way to collect the rabbit cameras? If it were a mission of a sort, why had he been all alone? Shouldn't there have been some evidence of a support team? (And the thought Old Jim buried deep, to protect his own sense of well-being: What if all of it—every last bit of it—had been part of some incomprehensible, gargantuan, obsessive, and obscene Central experiment, including the Rogue? No, this could not be. This must not be.)

And what had the Rogue muttered in the Mudder's ear?

Because the Mudder still puzzled him, even if that puzzlement lived as much in the condition of her journal as in her moment with the Rogue. The journals of all the rest had suffered spectacular fire and water damage, smears of ink, tears, missing pages. But the Mudder's journal, two decades on, maintained a pristine appearance, save for the green moss spread across the lower half of the cover and faded into just a texture but with the illusion of life. Inside, the only disconcerting element remained her use of green ink, which made the words appear organic at first, like the moss.

The handwriting, while it quivered and oscillated at times (betraying a tremor?), held admirable to a steady, centered standard. In fact, the field entries mustered a kind of steel in their calm and precision, as she relentlessly recorded fiddler crab data long after some of the other biologists had been reduced to a gibbering delusion. True, that tidiness and precision did not mean anything. It could be repression of panic, of fear, of anxiety, of turning away from the reality, except . . .

The Medic had been picked up by Central "at an agreed upon exfiltration spot" and Team Leaders 1 and 2 were found hiding in a motel room in Bleakersville, taken to a secure location, and interrogated. Only the Mudder had never been found. At least, such a capture had not made it into the files.

If this fact filled Old Jim with the unfamiliar emotion of hope, it was because in all ways the Mudder's journal suggested someone *with a plan*. Someone so adroit that they could walk across ground that was uncertain for most. Someone who might have used the Rogue as a distraction to disappear, never to be found again. Someone who had already colluded with the locals to sneak out of Dead Town to the Village Bar. Perhaps she had escaped the wreckage of it all in a way that even Old Jim could not.

Yet the Mudder's journal held no mention of the Rogue, and after the blip of a "tell" around the subject of the generator, only her observations of the rabbits were of interest.

Take, for example, her assertion that "the rabbits are not rabbits," which she clinically expanded on to assert that if an organism "acts against its essential nature, it must be a mimic—perhaps to avoid being prey or, as in this case, to disguise that it is a predator. You might then alter your methods of containment or eradication, or slow your efforts long enough to develop a greater understanding of the context."

But the expedition hadn't altered or slowed their efforts long enough. And what did it really mean if a rabbit was not a rabbit? And what had that meant to the Rogue?

The official account from Central put forward an audacious and stomach-churning lie meant to minimize, to absolve: The expedition had been lost at sea during the hurricane, having attempted to leave in their boats and been washed out to sea.

An absence rather than an all-too-corporeal presence was less easily contested, and who would contest it anyway? "Bodies unrecoverable." A story aided by Central tampering with the selection process, so the biologists had been chosen, in part, for their lack of connections to the world. The lack of parents. The lack of siblings. The lack of strong, close friends. The lack of all the normal things that perhaps were less normal than people who had them thought.

"A clear and present threat exists," read the note atop the top-secret summary file. "Open-ended. Existential. Confirmation via uncanny op. Nature of same: Unknown. Initiating entity: Unknown. Priority: High." Yet, it had taken twenty years for the threat to manifest again.

In the Village Bar later, before the inevitable discontinuation of surveillance, Man Boy Slim was heard to say, "They just left. They all just left." Drunk Boat commented on the fickle, ephemeral nature of outsiders. Yet their banter had a subdued quality, and it seemed none of them visited Dead Town thereafter, and Man Boy Slim in particular grew snappish at mentions of the place. Some things were best left alone. Some things did not bear further scrutiny.

This sense after viewing the surveillance, too, of being infected by the very thing Old Jim had been brought in to analyze, even though he could not articulate what that *thing* might be.

A few weeks after the hurricane, the red suit of the disappeared biologist washed up in the estuary by Dead Town. A crumpled, empty figure amongst the eternal reeds, swiftly removed by Central. The Dead Town site had already been cleaned up, wiped of any other trace.

Of the Rogue: no sign, no sightings at all.

As if he had never existed. As if Old Jim had spent his time at Central chasing phantoms and dark faery tales. As if *none* of it had ever happened.

(And, perhaps, it hadn't.)

(At least, not in the way Old Jim thought.)

# THE FALSE DAUGHTER

## EIGHTEEN MONTHS BEFORE AREA X

# IMMOLATION

## 000: GNITSOHG EXT

The Ghosting, Old Jim called it, how he lost his daughter, and only him the one losing her, and he figured he would never know the why and that's why she'd done it that way. So she would never have to talk to him again. When the thought made his heart constrict and Old Jim's breath came rough and uneven, like he might die, he tried to remember he didn't deserve it. Unless he did.

Eleanor Cassandra Kavanaugh, the first name from her mother, French for "shining light," the surname a construct for Old Jim's cover. Little Light when she was younger. The way at age eight she had held the spatula out like a flyswatter to turn over a pancake shaped like a butterfly. The frown into smile as she ignored his advice at twelve playing miniature golf and made a hole in one. That time she tried to run off with a pig at the petting zoo and had been trotted along the fence line, the porker protesting the tight leash, until they'd caught up. Where had she been going?

Eleanor Kavanaugh held weight, but by her teen years she'd gone by "Cass" or "Kavanaugh," as if it made her seem more serious, and Cass had stuck over time. Cass as college undergrad who took poetry classes and published poems, but had graduated with a degree in animal science. But turned aimless, left jobs abruptly, took other ones, started over. It became a tougher life for her over time than he'd wished for her, but he was proud of her.

Most of the time during her childhood, Old Jim was a spook, far from home, reliant on his wife's updates. He'd met Genevieve in the service, which is why they'd never married, just played pretend. Old Jim's boss, Jack, had this intense idea of family to go with allegiances within Central that made it work, for a while.

What it meant to tread foreign soil on some pulse-pounding secret mission, receiving communiqués from home that seemed benign, senseless, benign again. Checking for enemy surveillance along a dusty roadside . . . while reading about 4-H clubs and prizewinning chickens. Central had him hooked by then, or he just liked the adventure of the job and used that as an excuse.

Then, that period of domesticity when, despite bouncing around between home and overseas, he took Cass to soccer matches and for a time he was driving this chatty teenager to regionals and exploring the mysteries of small talk with the parents on the sidelines, commiserating when they lost and celebrating when they won. Then he'd been called overseas for a longer stretch, and for a handful of years Cass had lived with a great-aunt.

By the time Cass left him for good, Gen had been gone eighteen years, the time they'd had together so short. Everyone was so grown up, Cass closing in on thirty and Old Jim used to a haggardness in her eyes as each new opportunity crumbled to dust, and he couldn't parent her into something better at that point. She had her poetry. She wasn't out on the street. She just had a life that hadn't hit its stride, but he thought she knew he had her back.

The day she left Old Jim remembered as being in November, dead leaves on the lawn of his upstate New York house that Central had bought him as a prop. He'd been stateside for some time, Central using him to trap domestic terrorists. A few meetings in public places. Arrests months later, after he'd been forgotten, not a loose end but a thing that hadn't worked out, a person they'd barely known.

A burnt hint of winter in the distant smoke from a premature fireplace. But maybe that was his mood remembering it. Perhaps it had been late summer and the generator had just died, but he couldn't recognize the glimmering hope of that.

No, it was a day you don't forget. In November. The dead leaves on the lawn he left all winter until the snow covered them. She had ghosted him but was still around. Traces over time. Bills that arrived, forwarded—by her. All her mail came to him for a year, then nothing.

In its sparse, impersonal quality, the mail almost broke him, even though he opened each new envelope as if the advertising within would, miraculous, reveal a message. As if he were still receiving her over the transom, if only he could read the signs. Was light. Was matter. Washed up in the sea wrack of some distant shore.

No hospital had held her. No hotel had booked her. No airline had received her. But, then, she was her father's daughter. He'd not let slip the specifics of missions but had entertained her, perhaps too much, with a beer in him, in the art of espionage.

Had she asked him for specifics? He couldn't remember.


At first, he had just a spy's intuition that something was wrong, because her usual letters never arrived, and they'd settled into a good, solid routine with that. But, two weeks after their last lunch, he opened the car's glove compartment . . . and found her note. Not even in an envelope, just scrawled on a lined piece of eight by eleven notebook paper, ripped from a spiral binding.

"Don't follow me. Don't try to find me. Don't contact me. Sincerely, Cass."

*Sincerely* crushed him. Her handwriting, hurriedly scrawled, even if the time delay had broken the chain of evidence, and so he entered his first loop: That someone was running an op on him. Some Central faction, an agent he'd caught with a hand in the till back in the day, or one of the domestic terrorists he'd set up, but, no, they lacked the subtlety. There would've been a ransom note, some other sting in the tail. The note felt real. It felt real because it hurt him so badly.

*Don't follow me. Don't try to find me.* And that was him, too, in a way, cashing in his R&R with Central and slipping their gauntlet, flush with cash and driving a different car. Catch me if you can, but for a long time they didn't bother.

A forwarded letter from a friend of Cass's, early on, he pored over for clues but found nothing. Juxtaposed with unearthing a box of memorabilia that included baby photos and elementary-school essays, crayon and watercolor images she'd made for classes. Green parrots she'd never seen flying across a blue sky, as if predicting an idyllic moment from Old Jim's secret missions. Such a happy child, with such a huge smile. Everything he felt in that moment, looking through the box, was a cliché, even though it cut so deeply.

What did that mean about details of lives, real or made-up? That Central could've made this up, too, if he didn't remember her drawing it? A casualty of his career, these thoughts. Because he'd been so many people, for Central. Out in the field, then as a fixer or enforcer.

Her apartment at the edge of a city forty miles from the house . . . barren, gutted, and after Old Jim's first visit, that December, slipping the landlord a twenty, rented out again, so anything forensic receded into the past. Returning the night of his visit, Old Jim had run a black light across the floor, the walls, the lone futon left in a corner.

What had he expected? Blood spatter?

After he was done and sitting in his pickup truck, in the grips of some dark emotion between grief and rage, he hated himself for turning her disappearance into another special op. Sneaking into buildings after dark with night vision goggles. To trudge the world looking for traces of someone who didn't want to be found—who had decided to become a ghost. What next? Would he construct theories from torn matchbook covers, like a bad noir movie?

The details that became a description for other people as he widened his search. Long brown hair, hazel eyes with dark liner, small upturned nose. Freckles, with a slight flush to her cheeks. The mouth that tightened into determination when she clenched her jaw. Just under five ten and a swimmer's body. Bitten nails with chipped red nail polish.

As weeks became months and the feeling he'd had when she'd missed two regular calls, usually after group therapy, became a constant weight in his heart, his stomach, like a cancer spreading . . . he couldn't take it anymore. No relief from the sadness, the confusion, the sudden disconnection, shocked by the force of these emotions, how they sustained themselves.

He slid past the date on the calendar that he thought of as marking the end of Central's tolerance. He slid into drink, like a natural, like a pro. It was easy enough—it had been the escape that got him through many a mission, in moderation, doled out as a reward or to screw his courage to the sticking place. Just upped the volume on it, to stop hearing her voice. Because her voice came to him at odd times, from different times, so the cooing of Shining Light became the castigation of a teenage rebellion into activism and the arts. And the shame of it: Gen receded even further the longer Cass had ghosted him, as if the two were connected and, both undead in their separate ways, cast loose from memory, reeled back in.

Inadequate, fuzzy, shimmering moments came back to him— his sense of his own daughter. Memories he had to work at, reinforced by old photographs. Here she was right before the petting zoo pony stepped on her foot. There she was staring at the camera in costume for some high school event.

He ate too much, to keep up the drinking, or he ate nothing, to punish himself, until he felt weak, fuzzy. He left the house and spent a month in a crap motel sleeping most of the time and roaming dive bars in strip malls late at night. Got used to the smell of piss from dirty bathrooms, the curling grin of vomit. He wanted to pick fights—with fellow drunks, with rangy men in backward-turned baseball caps playing pool. He couldn't say what held him back.

Instead, Old Jim had conversations with himself at the end of the bar. Except, it wasn't Old Jim he spoke to—he spoke to Cass, reliving the last conversation they'd had, that last Monday. He'd been driving through her area after visiting a hardware store, so it had been by chance, except maybe she'd meant it that way. For the last time.

At a busy diner pretending to be a café, in a booth with cracked plastic covers, with the comforting burnt-grease smell and the line cooks grumbling, tetchy and sharp in the open kitchen. They both drank hot chocolate.

Old Jim had told her about his physical, that he'd "passed it with flying colors," a term that now seemed meaningless. By which he meant he didn't care, but he also didn't know what "flying colors" meant, as he dissected each moment later. UFOs?

Flags? Less or more? Some old way that made sense back in the day.

"That's great, Dad," she said, and she never called him Dad, did she? Or did she? Her face was open to him—and the smile, it seemed genuine in the moment, but what lay behind it? Something else had had to exist behind it.

But he'd been caught in the reverie of relief of getting through another physical, which she couldn't know had meant a trip to Central, along with a full psych eval, too. A process he dreaded. Then, thinking about the things he could not share with Cass for security reasons, and did that mean he'd never been able to share enough, been too on guard, to ever really be her father?

He just hadn't seen it coming—the way they'd laughed and joked with each other for a few years now. How they'd been in such easy contact for most of her middle to late twenties. They'd had one bad argument, yes, a couple of years before the ghosting, but he couldn't even remember most of it. Something emotional, but her shouting at him and him shutting down as a result.

"Don't talk to me that way," he'd said, because of her shouting.

"Something isn't right," she'd said, "and I don't know how to fix it."

But they *had* fixed it. They had fixed it to the point they had been fine later that day. He recalled a nice dinner at a steak house, where she could get a robust salad.

What if he could have focused on what was moving through her, absorbed the hurt, asked a question? Was that it? This strong impulse? If only. If only he could travel back in time and fix it.

But he couldn't.

The familiar sick and hopeless feeling washed over him again, and he kicked his feet against the side of the bar so the men playing pool took note and the bartender's caterpillar eyebrow rose, as Old Jim put up his hand in the universal gesture for "Sorry sorry sorry" for "Peace, peace, peace will never find me, but I'll settle down now." Looking down at himself, at his body, like his own ghost, wondering at the overreaction, get it together, pull yourself together.

Remembered now why he didn't want to fight anyone. Because his training might kick in and he'd be helpless next to the compulsion of that, and he didn't want to kill anyone because he was grief-stricken. Break the pool stick in half, jam it in a biker's eye, take the other half and smash it across the back of the next attacker. Reach across the bar and pull the bartender toward him into a headbutt, or worse. Now he was back there, now he was overseas again and with a mandate to do whatever, whenever, without asking.

He had kept the forwarded letter from Cass's friend, but knew better than to pull it out of his wallet and read it again. Usually, that triggered his need to write to Cass, and he'd done enough of that, with no way to get the letters to her.

Feared all of those letters would turn into the plea he wrote, so short, out-of-his-mind drunk in one of these bars, the one he balled up and threw away, a weird déjà vu in the action he couldn't ever explain. Asking for a sign, an explanation, anything.

He'd passed the physical with flying colors. She'd said she was glad and had touched his hand. No, his wrist. She'd reached across the booth, sitting opposite him, and touched his wrist, glad that he was okay. A daughter who loved her father.

He remembered then that she'd said she appreciated him. "I really do." And that had landed odd at the time, this idea of appreciation, but now it screamed out at him as her receding across the table from him until there was nothing of her left, no way to explain, just this constant absence, re-absenting itself.

What had she thought would happen? That he'd go on with his life, assume she was safe? What was anyone supposed to do with that?

The next time Old Jim came to his senses, he was in a dark bar in the Midwest and didn't know how he'd gotten there. Oh, right, he'd been kicked out of the hotel for being "aggressive" and "disturbing others." That made him cackle but when he tried to stop, he couldn't turn the faucet off. His savings almost gone, and every time he made a withdrawal, the assumption that Central might've closed the account. Or, perversely, did Jack like to think Old Jim was still undercover?

Thoughts that recycled: His daughter had been recruited by Central. She hadn't left him but couldn't tell him, for the usual reasons. She would contact him when she could, if she ever could. She loved her father. She loathed him. Despised him. She'd called him "Dad" in the diner. Had she ever called him that before, with such informality? He didn't think so.

The truth of it was: No way to get out of the raw, bloody scream deep in his throat that he didn't fully understand. The not knowing. The not knowing and no way to tell her . . . anything. He knew it was a circle, a loop, a crashing into the ground from forty thousand feet, but . . .

But he tried. Stupid, maybe, to try the places he knew she'd haunted before but to which she would never return, but that was all he had left. Coffee shops, bohemian bookstores, counterculture performance spaces, laundromats, libraries. He wrote and rewrote a new letter. He left copies of the new letter everywhere. As if his daughter had been lost somehow, to everyone. Kidnapped. In trouble.

If you see this woman, call . . .
If you see this woman, call . . .
If you see this woman, call . . .
If you see this woman, call . . .
If you see this woman, call . . .
If you see this woman, call . . .
If you see this woman, call . . .

Old Jim started doing it seven times and then another seven times, convinced that six was bad luck, five not enough, and eight too many. Seven a day, seven the next day, until he ran out of places. The photo he had to use was grainy, and he didn't know if her hair was still long and brown.

There came strange callers in the night who hung up when he answered, and did he dream them, or did Central test him, or want him back? Or his daughter? Or some third party, like another intelligence service? But he saw signs of Cass in everything, no matter that it wearied him. From the walk of some stranger hunched over in the rain to a singer's voice on the radio to an electronic pulse through a receiver that might mean nothing.

Her poetry came to him during odd moments of sobriety.

*"The upward lilting song / of small birds in the air. / A sweet question in the dark, / mysterious trajectory, / the strafing of a whispered love."*

There came the moment Old Jim vomited in the hot sun on hotter pavement, maybe six or seven months after Cass was gone. He'd tried everything. Found nothing. Burnt up, lit up, sitting down heavy against a fire hydrant, feeling the hardness of it against his back, and letting it dig into him like a punishment.

Ankle hurt, so he'd been limping before he fell. Could've caught fire in that heat—in what city?—didn't care. Didn't care.

Still didn't care, when a woman in a white dress shirt, black blazer, and black dress slacks loomed over him, bounced a quarter off his forehead. He just stared at it where it had landed, on his thigh right above the end of his ragged cutoff jeans.

Except when he picked up the coin and felt it between his thumb and forefinger, the face etched there was not the familiar one. Or, rather, the less familiar one. Central's special quarter, their coin as calling card. The core of their far-flung and invisible land, to have the arrogance to presume their own currency.

He looked up at the face of a model, but hardened despite the youth of her. A jaw from hell, or that promised hell. It was not his daughter.

She didn't identify herself. Why would she? But he knew who she was. She was Jack's daughter. An emissary by which Jack sent a message.

"Shouldn't you be in high school? Not here scraping trash off the street?"

She gave him a cold, appraising look, like a heron about to spear a frog.

"Shouldn't you be somewhere other than puking your guts up, homeless?"

Central didn't care that he was a wreck, he believed. More that he'd made himself a target. By being careless, so he might have made himself visible to foreign agents. Or maybe Central was just, finally, angry he'd abandoned his post.

"Where's my daughter?" he asked.

"'Where's my daughter, where's my daughter?'" Jack's daughter mocked. "She's not there in the gutter with you, is she?"

The way she talked to him was a slap in the face, cold water poured over his head.

"Do you know who I am?"

"I know you're my father's friend," Jack's daughter said, and Old Jim had to wonder how much of Jack peered out at him now. "And I know where you'll be in a year if you don't pull out of this tailspin."

"And where is that?" Old Jim asked, although he knew the answer.

"Dead."

"Are you here to kill me?" He knew the answer was no, but some part of him wouldn't have minded too much.

She smiled, but it was cold, so cold. "No, but I could do that—for you, for them. If need be."

"So young to be so hard."

"So old to be so soft," she replied.

"What do you want?"

"Nothing for now. We just want you to go home."

"Home?"

"No, not the house. Your real home."

The Forgotten Coast.

Except it wasn't.

He'd never been there.

## OOA = Πr²: GNITNUAH EHT

But first, Central. Because they wanted him clean. They wanted him cleansed. They didn't trust him, the way he'd become, even though he caustically joked with the intake team that it was good cover. That he was already undercover and they should drop him, drunk, on a dirt road near the coast and he'd take it from there. Ha ha, not received well.

There was a bird up near the high ceilings in the intake area, a dark fluttering smudge, trying to get out, and he watched it for a while as distraction, until it disappeared from view or became something else. He liked to believe it was free now.

Old Jim didn't like to remember the next months, because he kept wishing he would die and couldn't quarantine the feeling, test it. If a loaded gun had appeared on his bunk in isolation, he wasn't quite sure what would've happened. But there never was one, so he had to just endure until clean, clear, mind as blank as the white walls of Central's echoing corridors devoted to defending the nation against . . . well, whatever it decided was a threat. So white, so brightly white, the whole building, down to most of the underground levels, to be so full of black ops.

He didn't see his handler, his boss, his friend, Jack Severance, for ages, while his body was unspooled into some other form that made his head full of nails and then full of cotton candy and then, roughly, back on his shoulders more or less the right way.

"If you feel this way again, remember that it's natural and that it will pass."

The infirmary offered only one pill, from a blank-faced technician who noted "it will last a year." Old Jim had expected it would be enormous, like a wheel of cheese, but it was just a tiny white tablet, like the discard from a three-hole paper punch, and he felt nothing before or after he took it.

Then, and only then, he saw Jack through the half-tinted glass of the infirmary, staring at him. From afar. Almost suspicious. Turning away and moving out of sight when Old Jim locked in on him. How he'd seen Jack through layers of glass before, on their best their worst mission, in a church, in a different life.

At least the infirmary smelled of something. Not just bandages and iodine but some underlying rot like they brought triage into that space from foreign lands and at the end of the day they couldn't quite mop up all the blood and other bodily fluids. Couldn't quite get it out.

He insisted on his psych eval from the infirmary doctor, a kindly man with a twinkling eye who seemed too good to be true, and as far as he knew they had honored that request.

Because he didn't like the odds of ever getting out of Central if he talked to a Central psychologist, in their separate department. Talk the dark cloud from his mouth, to some young go-getter rah-rah bullshit artist or buoyant "life coach" he could peer inside of in twenty seconds and pull his soul out of his head through his nose, shrieking.

Except, Jack might've gone a step further—given Old Jim over to some even darker soul they kept in one of the flooded basements turned over to the black arts. He imagined these experts at psychic overhaul and rebirth as being like coelacanths: ancient and sequestered in that deep water, and you had to be lowered down into their tanks like enduring some profane baptism, and the psychology of it was you were cured when you spent enough time down in the depths to become like them.

*"How do you feel, Jim? If you were an orchestra, what music would you play? If you were a school of fish, what kind of fish would you be? Think of a point of light deep beneath the sea. Recognize that if you go deeper, you will be released into the burning of that incandescent light. Can you feel the warmth of your burning?"*

Once you could breathe through their gills, you would be released toward the surface, gasping, to deal once more with megalodons like whomever Jack reported to.

But fuck all that, some tiny pilot light flickering inside him kept repeating. No, he couldn't do it. He'd rather die on his feet, in hell, with his grief intact; he had nothing left. Let them try to take it away from him. A flare of rage rising from his indifference, seen by none, that he'd felt before in his love-hate relationship with his job.

He'd be flame hurtling down the corridors of Central, rendering justice to every damn fool who deserved it. Including himself.

But would he? Because, most of the time, he just felt grateful to be at Central and all alone in the world.

Routine at Central meant doing something to replace the routine that he'd lost with Cass and his prior mission. Central gave him structure in how he spent his days, but to replace the letters, the repetition he took up after long absence was the piano. The kindly psych in the infirmary had put the idea in his ear, and he'd really taken to it.

At first, Old Jim just hummed those tunes to himself and drew the keys on a piece of sketch paper from the thrice-weekly Rorschach wellness check disguised as an afternoon art class. To remind himself of the notes of his new favorite piano suite, where his fingers might go on the individual songs.

*"My feet did not ask for rest, / though it was too cold to stand; / my back did not long for caress, / the storm led me through bitter land."*

He had tried to teach Cass piano as a teenager and she'd rebelled, but he could still remember a nice moment before her teens when she'd listened to him playing and enjoyed it, asked questions that meant it intrigued her.

But the piano helped, because he was back in a loop again, and needed the poison out. Worse, because too often there was so little emotion there, or the emotion flared up again raw, and then banked almost into ash, and wasn't that awful? Wasn't that the wrong kind of oblivion? While thinking, If you cut someone out of your life that way, hadn't you become, for a time, a kind of monster? Didn't that deserve the ash?

But perhaps his daughter had felt burning her life to the

ground was magnificent viewed from afar, or somehow admirable in its hardened stance. How close was narcissism to empathy? And was it better confined to an individual or better when the impulse coursed through the veins of an organization like Central, where doing the right thing could become the wrong thing? Oh, he wished her well. He wished for her . . . nothing. And, yet, if she returned, he knew no matter how he tried to cut her from his mind now . . .

As he was let off the leash more and more, Old Jim found comfort in an old dark dim bar with a piano only a ten-minute swift walk away, and with a few others, he'd take a lunch relearning how to play. A quiet group, just four of them, and they didn't talk much. Maybe they were his minders as well as colleagues he'd known forever, but sometimes he imagined they had gathered over a mutual love of an upright piano.

Central would never bring a piano into its hallowed halls. The sound of music there might break the crystal, the test tubes, the eardrums of those in the basement who labored so intensely on the most arcane assignments that their sensitivity to random blips on tapes rewound multiple times was akin to that of mice or rats.

*"When snow flies in my face / I cast off its shroud; / when my heart speaks in its cage, / I sing bright and loud."*

Who knew what other operative in the halls of Central might hear the faint sound and become aware, for a critical instant, of the world beyond what had been hermetically sealed?

After five months, Jack parachuted, unexpected, into Old Jim's routine of breakfast, quiet time, exercise, lunch (sometimes with piano), analysis of the Dead Town Disaster, dinner, some midnight hour down in the deep, deep archives questioning things like alligator experiments and people named only Mudder and Medic . . . all of that and then hey, presto, there Jack was, taking the place of his afternoon group session with a bunch of other burnouts.

Typical. Disruptor of the key element, wanting to be the most important thing in his day. In his head. This old friend. This disastrous remedy. With a big hug and a clap on the back. Just like old times.

Because Jack Severance never could contain himself—broke contain every time. The beatific sheen to Jack's face, the ruddy gleam of a hardworking man that was likely just a skin condition. But it also emanated from the flame that Jack had nurtured within himself for such a long time: That knowledge of the sacred spheres or other incalculable wisdom had been passed down to him from those upper reaches of Central that Old Jim would never see, let alone be able to imagine, well above the tree line, requiring a guide and an oxygen mask. And yet what could possibly exist at the summit?

Maybe just Jack after all.

"Those dipshits would impose themselves without you there," Jack said to him in the conference room, and Old Jim nodded. He felt he'd lost the thread of a conversation Jack thought Old Jim had started.

They sat at a nondescript gray Formica table, leaning back in standard black office chairs, posing a bit for the mirror at the far end that must be two-way glass with a possible audience in the dozens. They had two mugs between them filled, for some reason, with hot chocolate, both mugs displaying the optics of a Christmas cheer long faded from the calendar.

Jack had dressed like a country man, in a plaid lumberjack shirt, scuffed jeans, and work boots, which on him resembled a Halloween costume, at best. He was a smaller man than you might expect, his clothes always too big for him; his hand on the mug handle seemed tiny, despite the iron grip.

"What dipshits?" Old Jim asked, after a skipped beat. His mind had been clear for a couple of months, but often empty, and he had yet to take interest in even the simple things people tended to be interested in. Nothing in the present really made his pulse race, and he'd come from the archives, which felt more real. He'd been reading more of the Mudder's journal and some turn of phrase had reminded him of his daughter's poetry.

"You know, the dipshits you'll be managing from afar," Jack said, on message. "They'd be interested in every third-rate, crackpot haunting. They'd be rapturous over a shipwreck younger than the *Titanic*"—he pronounced it "Tit-tan-ick"—"and there in the back of beyond we'd be fucked if not for our raptor's focus on what's actually important, right?"

So Jackie hadn't lied and the files weren't just distraction, a test of his analytical skills, or sparing some more valuable operative the boredom of cleanup work. It had been prep for a field position. Great. The Rogue fascinated Old Jim, but something about existing in the same space, even twenty years later, froze him in place. He could sense the danger of it, even though, logically, that was the distant past.

"Right. What's important?" Old Jim asked, because Jack expected it and if he cared about anything at all . . . it was not to fail another secret test, like his reaction to being in a bar, and remain at Central another three, four, six, ten tedious months. That, he didn't think he could take. Lurking beneath his calm: blood waves and lost daughters trying to burst out of his skull, smash into his skull.

"We've been running something called Serum Bliss in a place you know pretty well by now from the files—the Forgotten Coast." Flash of the piano keys, Cass's doll flung there after the lesson. A hiccup in his heartbeat.

"And what does Serum Bliss do?"

"Turn rabbits into gold," Jack said, holding Old Jim's gaze in a way that told him to pay attention.

"Sounds dangerous." He'd bit his tongue on "sounds reckless," or "like some alchemist's wet dream."

"It will be."

"You're not going to tell me what Serum Bliss is, are you?"

"Once, Serum Bliss was an expedition that Central hijacked as an op for mind-control experiments. Now it's a hunt. For an 'existential threat,' in the same place."

"What threat?" But Old Jim knew, because he couldn't get the Rogue out of his head.

"Certain intel suggests the capacity for widespread devastation, some new weapon."

"How reliable is the intel."

Jack grinned, like a gambler with a question that lit up his life. "Not very. According to most of Central."

"Why me?"

Jack wagged his finger at Old Jim, drank some hot chocolate, changed the subject: "We're using the cover of a bunch of stupid Ouija Hicks, who've been traveling to 'haunted places' for a couple of decades. They already call the whole coast 'Active Site X,' like they've planted a flag and claimed it or something. But little do they know, we've planted a flag in *them*."

"What're they called? These Ouija Hicks?"

"The Séance and Science Brigade."

Old Jim didn't like brigades, made him think of civil wars and unrest. But also of fools who didn't clean their weapons.

Jack leaned forward to whisper, "You'll use your prior cover name, 'Old Jim,' and most of what comes with that. Your meta cover, for certain factions here, is that you're headed to retirement and the Hicks op just lets us keep an eye on you. From the Central side, officially, S&SB is a 'passive inquiry.' We just observe, extract any useful intel for R&D. Unofficially, I run a much more active operation, with Jackie mostly on-site."

"Who else knows about it?" Besides whoever watched from behind the mirror. If anyone did.

Jack, gleeful, put a finger to his lips. "Shhh. No one. Almost. Let there be some mysteries left."

Sure.

"Where's my daughter?" Old Jim asked. That spike in his heart rate—that was the hope Jack knew, and would tell him.

Jack looked around the empty conference room like it was Shangri-la, said, "Man, those office parties used to get crazy around here, didn't they, Jim. People blowing off steam. Getting up to all kinds of antics. Those were the days. Not like this anti-septic crap the Brutes have imposed so they can see the blood all the better."

The Brutes Jack warred against when he didn't want to an-swer a question were a "new breed" that held most of the power, made policy, and were always trying to impose "an ungodly order" on what was meant to be wild and free—namely Jack's budget. Sometimes Jack also railed about a Central faction Old Jim didn't think existed: "Phantoms, playing their own long game, slipping through the fingers the more you look for them."

All Old Jim said now, though, was: "Sure, sure, the Brutes. Yes, those were the days." Old Jim didn't care to parse Jack's use of the term. You could parse Jack until the cows came home, for miles and centuries, and never get close to the answer.

Jack rambled on, unthwarted by Old Jim's stoicism, and Old Jim made useful noises to nudge Jack forward. It wasn't that he didn't share intense memories with Jack, or a certain brotherly fondness, and Old Jim owed him a lot. So, yes, the good old days with Jack, when ops had less moral complication, because every-thing felt so black and white, and every day had been like holding hands running through a field of daisies.

Those days when no one saw it coming or felt even the slight-est sting of doubt as Jack, as the senior operative, had led Old Jim down rivers, down roads, rutted paths. A river could as easily be a trash-strewn parking lot behind an abandoned strip mall. Not for what it contained, the landscape, but for what you did once there, and had passed a certain point. The way the headlights burnt through the mist or humidity or rain to reveal a silhouette only ever allowed for one outcome anyway.

Jack was still saying. Jack was still talking about. Jack was this. Jack was that. Jack, maybe, was a little bit unhinged, but that was Central for you. That was the old breed.

"With gas—poison gas—you know the birds fall from the sky and plants wither, and the people, Jim"—said with real anguish as he paused to take a sip of hot chocolate—"the people, they cough up their lungs and drown in their own blood. They drown in blood, Jim."

*The silvered figure roaring through the mud, the sonic boom leveling the biologists.* Old Jim wondered if the Rogue had seeped into Jack's thoughts, along with all the blood in people's lungs. He'd always had a thirst for the uncanny, a superstitious streak. No op on the thirteenth, ever. The bad luck of the croak of a raven in a tree that made Jack look up from a scope triangulated on a target. His rule of three, which meant always having a backup plan to the backup plan.

Jack continued before Old Jim could figure out what to say: "But what if it wasn't gas. What if. What if it wasn't gas. What if the birds stayed in the sky and the people went about their business . . . but they were . . . changed, so they were different? And some day, when you wanted them to, when you needed them to, they would, at the snap of my fingers, at the utterance of a single word or phrase, help defeat an enemy. Receive a signal. Sequester and not feel pain on the battlefield. Do even a small, mundane task in the middle of their normal routines without remembering they'd done it. Like, even, introduce something dangerous, even monstrous, but *necessary*, but in between playing hopscotch and not recall. What if in a sense the necessary world of violence in which we live, that violence became so contained it was invisible to the naked eye?"

"You know the Tyrant's still out there," Old Jim said, because he didn't like what Jack had said to him. "Somewhere in the marshes." He wanted to talk about the generator, but figured Jack would deflect, unless this was Jack's way of talking about the generator . . . and he'd rather Jack not know everything he was thinking about. Central's determination: "mass psychosis event caused by errors in hypnosis programming."

"The what?" Jack said, looking at him like he was nuts.

"The alligator. The locals call her the Tyrant. She eats abandoned hunting dogs and can't be caught. Local legend. Part of the Cavalry."

"I'm not following," Jack said.

"The alligator experiment." Even as he uttered the words, Old Jim felt exposed, like Jack hadn't expected he'd go off in that direction.

Jack looked at him with practiced puzzlement.

"The Dead Town Disaster," Old Jim said, because he was sick of playing games.

Some hostile impulse to blurt crossed Jack's face and Old Jim could've sworn he'd wanted to say: *Don't call it that!* But instead Jack laughed. "Always the runts, huh, Jim? You want the sawed-off shotguns instead of the sniper's rifle, the stuff no one else wants. Or needs."

Jack changed the subject to something blithe and cheery that Old Jim didn't remember later because he'd had an image of the Rogue riding the Tyrant enter his head, trying to reconcile the strangeness of that, the ridiculousness.

Because Old Jim was already all-in on the Dead Town Disaster, he couldn't help himself. The Rogue wasn't Central, but the generator was, and maybe so was the alligator experiment, and to Old Jim it felt like Jack had taken a risk in giving him access for a reason. Something there beyond an "existential threat" that Jack didn't want to articulate but still trusted Old Jim to track, like a faithful hound that he might give up to the Tyrant after.

"So, you'll take the job?" Jack asked at some point, as if he'd interviewed Old Jim for assistant manager at a hardware store.

The longer they spoke in that conference room, the more Jack began to feel like a doppelgänger to Old Jim, and lost forever the easy rapport from those first missions in the field, when they'd been brothers who could tell each other anything, everything—any sin, any fault, any obsession, any emptiness.

Maybe the residue of that carried them into the future now, because once it had been pure and true. Jack must believe that hold would be enough. Jack must believe they were still family. Old Jim didn't doubt that.

*"Where is my daughter?"*

Maybe that unspoken pact was also in the look Jack gave him at the door a few minutes later, and the extra squeeze in the handshake. The handshake of a black op.

How black, though? As black as a ruined meadow full of traumatized expedition members? As black as a phantom faction at Central?

Jack thought the Rogue was still alive, still a threat.

The piece of paper Jack had passed him read: "Top Priority: Find the Rogue. Eliminate the Rogue."

Did Old Jim talk in his sleep, because how did Jack know that's what he called the stranger?

Overheard in the hallway his last day before traveling to the Forgotten Coast: "I wish you weren't wonderful in so many ways, because you're so awful."

A wave of blood, spreading out in all directions.

**T**hings you find out right before you leave a haunted cathedral. Things that stay with you. Coordinates you can't unsee. Two sets of coordinates. Surrounded by water. The information Old Jim took with him that made him feel guilty, as if he'd left with dozens of crimson streamers swirling out from his head, each one a different piece of intel, and a wonder that he didn't become entangled, lose a step, trip, become so encumbered there on the curb that he became some version of the same guy Jackie had pulled out of the gutter months ago.

"Oh, and one last thing," a whisper in his ear before he'd left Central, out on the street, about to climb into the black sedan, the crimson streamers obscuring his vision. A blustery day in the shadow of skyscrapers. Dribbled into his ear so the task became obscured by the sound of water. "*A phantom's flaming breath pulled me from my route . . .*"

The one more thing to do, and Old Jim nodded because he'd expected it, even distracted so there was a hazy, heavy sense of someone talking to him while he slept, because whatever Jack wanted him to do seemed irrelevant next to what he'd already done, what had gotten under his skin about the expedition.

*Separate coordinates like a form of death. Maps made into weapons and punishments.*

Team Leader 1's true name was Alexis (Alex) Aguilar and Team Leader 2's true name was Kim Numi. They had been picked up by Central two days after the hurricane abated, in a motel room north of Bleakersville, one of those places unmoored from any town, surviving in the middle of nowhere without an anchor.

Central had "busted in the door" and found Aguilar and Numi "huddled on the floor behind the bed." Two of the rabbit cameras were found on the bed and both expedition members appeared "pre-traumatized," meaning the violent appearance of Central operatives had just been the blood-red cherry on top. Of whatever they had experienced.

"Both were underweight, suffering from some sort of withdrawal, although the drug has not been identified. Minor scrapes and bruises. Aguilar had a slight dislocation of her left shoulder. Numi's blinking left eye appeared to be an existing tic that had intensified to a constant meaningless signal."

Constant meaningless signal. Was there enough contempt in that analysis? What was worse, Old Jim wondered, than being a signal that held no meaning? A receptacle for light where no light need shine. A boat that sank into the depths at the first sign of water.

Numi, from her journal: "We were doing things we never did in life. We saw a terrible thing. We were *doing* impossible things to survive. But most horrible of all was the thought that it would continue on and on for as long as we watched it, so I shut the video off [at 3:21] and tried to sleep until morning."

*We saw a terrible thing.*

*We were doing impossible things to survive.*

All signs pointed to Aguilar's and Numi's intent to flee the country, according to the interrogation. In the file, Central called it a "debrief," perhaps because in the videotape both team leaders appeared resigned to some indecipherable fate and so "coercive techniques had been deemed unnecessary, perhaps counterproductive."

Questioned separately or together their stories remained simple and the same. In the aftermath of the Rogue, the two had fled, despite the conditions, along a route that they had mapped out in advance, to an all-terrain jeep they had hidden in the underbrush along a dirt road. Their sole luck, initially, had been a bridge that had held against the flood, and a vehicle that navigated a dirt road suddenly under two feet of water.

The hiding of the vehicle, the evidence of a scheme for retreat, raised questions for which neither Aguilar nor Numi had
answers.

"When the generator broke, we knew we needed a backup
plan. For the expedition. An alternative way of getting help,"
Aguilar said, separate from Numi.

"It felt like we were on our own," Numi said, separate from
Aguilar. "So alone we needed to take care of ourselves. That's
all."

"But you didn't go for help?" the interrogator asked when
Aguilar and Numi coexisted in the same sad space at Central
again. "Why didn't you *actually* go for help? Why did we find
you hiding in a motel?"

The two looked at each other, the video quality clear enough
to tell that they found the question odd or even nonsensical.

"And the cameras?" the interrogator asked. "Can you tell us
the thought process behind keeping the cameras?"

They had no good answer for that, either. For why they had
taken two rabbit cameras with them and then tried to burn them
behind the motel, but then brought them *back* into the motel
and placed them in the middle of the bed . . . while they huddled on the floor.

> INTERROGATOR: Were the cameras part of the plot? Were
>    you part of the plot?
> AGUILAR: What plot?
> INTERROGATOR: By the foreign entity.
> AGUILAR: What foreign entity?
> INTERROGATOR: The one that overran your camp.
> AGUILAR: We don't know what overran our camp.

Not everything existed on video from those sessions. Old Jim
found the gaps interesting, but put it down to sloppiness.

Central wanted to believe that the gist or grist pried out of

Team Leaders 1 and 2 meant they had believed they could sell the cameras and make enough money to disappear, to flee. That, somehow, they felt they could escape what they had seen on the camera.

"Why didn't you *do* that, then? Why did you try to burn them?"

Old Jim felt the question unfair, intentionally obtuse, understood why Aguilar and Numi ignored it.

A chipper side note declared that "some functionality remains, even burnt," which might "necessitate involvement by R&D," with the subtext, disturbing to Old Jim, that studying the cameras might lead to incorporating the underlying technology of the "foreign entity" into Central's surveillance devices.

Had that happened? Had that actually happened? For a dead second, sitting in the black sedan speeding toward the airport, he hoped that the surveillance they were installing right now in the Village Bar did not rely on knowledge gleaned from the bones of the Dead Town Disaster.

Eventually, in trying to explain their actions, the biologists had descended into a kind of obliterating babble or hysteria that the interrogator acknowledged in his conclusions: "Trauma from Dead Town created a series of glitch decision points, influenced more by general panic than intent to betray."

No evidence of any outreach to foreign governments. Just of two exhausted women in a motel room fighting off sleep and malnourishment, bound only by the need to help each other.

That help never wavered during the interrogations. They remained loyal to each other. They refused offers that to Old Jim's eye resembled "selling out" their partner. The nudge to say more, to assemble words from the abstract into concrete ways that pointed to the other being the ringleader, the one who really would have sold the cameras to a "foreign entity." The one who really knew what was going on.

Nothing in their backgrounds suggested anything abnormal.

Neither had much in the way of family, as was the norm for the expedition. They had both roved widely in their careers, the norm for field biologists, who often were funded (poorly) for a season or two and then moved on. If they had found each other—found each other during the Dead Town expedition, in a way that felt profound to Old Jim, a wanderer as well—it must have been almost as much relief as passion, a falling into an embrace made familiar because they both had been on the same journey.

The quickening pulse of the short half-life of the expedition, the uncertainty of what might or might not occur after.

So much, so vital, that journals could not reveal or articulate, a secret history no one else would ever know.

Shortly after questioning, Central deemed Aguilar and Numi "unfit for further operational duties/security risk," although part of the team leaders' confusion stemmed from believing they had worked for a shell corporation called Soothing Kiss, which used "nature-based solutions for medical problems." They had had no knowledge of Central until capture and interrogation.

Aguilar and Numi were exiled to separate remote islands with one hundred miles of ocean between them. These islands appeared abandoned but had been controlled by Central for decades. An automated radar station on one served as a weather service for the area. A shack on the other had at one time been occupied by a light-station operator and a meteorologist.

The islands existed outside of commercial shipping lanes and did not figure into the military exercises of any nation. Their ecosystems included harsh mountainous regions and lush but malaria-filled jungles. Once every four months, a Central plane dropped supplies into the general area of each biologist's release, but the pilots were under no orders to check on their well-being.

Old Jim wondered with a vague sense of unease how many islands with how many exiles the plane might pass over. How many sets of supplies the crew loaded onto the plane before it flew off from some black ops base a thousand miles away. And if, one day, he might look up at a similar plane from the shores of his own island. Whether Jack would be the one to give the order.

Was the idea of "island exile" a kind of *quarantine* meant to have an end, once they could prove the Rogue, the cameras, had not affected or infected them indefinitely . . . but, then, over time Central just *forgot*? Or they'd been stashed for now, to be decanted in some way, *used* in some way later?

A note in the file, near the very end, read that "these landscapes mimic in many ways those both biologists studied in grad school and thus they should be familiar with them."

An emotion Old Jim couldn't identify washed over him. This suggestion that Central thought it a kind of small mercy, when weighed against the greater cruelty. That at least they might recognize the places they had visited as postdocs and might feel comfortable there.

The two had been fated to live out their lives in a kind of solitude that, Old Jim felt, must still be full of voices and, perhaps, confusion, puzzlement, or worse.

Was it better for them to know or not to know the other's fate?

Did they think about what the camera showed them, every day, or had it faded into the surf, the particular brilliance of light at sunset on the water?

He could not erase the image from the video, together in the interrogation room, holding hands. The last time, and how they held each other before being separated. For the last time.

"Do you have anything to say?" the Central interrogator had asked before they were led away.

But they had already said everything—to the interrogator, to each other.

It just wasn't all in the files. There was something Jack didn't want him to know yet, for whatever reason.

Stepping onto the plane to the Forgotten Coast, taking his seat, looking out the window at a landscape of metropolis falling away into mountains and forests . . . Old Jim tried to forget the Exiles.

Failed.

# INITIATION

## 003: BURNING FILES

**T**hree days later the doorbell rang and Old Jim walked out onto the ramshackle porch of his new place to find an accordion folder of files set ablaze on the steps. An acrid billow of black smoke blew in the opposite direction, released into open sky. Who knew what chemicals they used in the paper.

More improbable, seen through the smoke: An upright piano with bench now stood in the sunlit yard, among the weeds, a mockingbird perched on one corner.

No one in sight.

All right then.

Calmly, Old Jim retrieved a thick kitchen towel and a pitcher of water from the kitchen and walked out onto the porch. He squatted there watching the dossier burn for a few seconds. Such a childish satisfaction watching the red-orange turn black and curl into ash.

He poured the water on the flames and blotted it with the towel, making a smoldering mess that stank of smoke.

No flourish from Central much surprised him anymore.

The piano he'd deal with later.

He could faintly hear one of the telephones ringing harshly in his office. Of course.

Old Jim went back inside and watched the red phone ring ten times, eleven, twelve. He picked up before thirteen. A shift or creak, a hint of shadow falling across him from the window, just the slightest touch as if his anxiety had taken physical form.

He knew it was Jackie before she spoke. Some spy's intuition, the fact she held back a moment to leave a silence, whereas Jack would've plowed right through that.

"Get Jack's message?" She had a rasp to her voice to counter-balance a melodic youth, as if she'd smoked just to sound older.

"I let them burn."

"Suit yourself."

What would the coelacanths in Central's basement think? Had he passed a test or failed one?

"Thanks for the piano," Old Jim said. "I've only seen that piano in my nightmares of Dead Town."

"You're not drunk in an alley pissing yourself anymore. So don't act like you are. This is a new piano."

So young to be so full of knives.

When he didn't reply, she said, "I know how you are, but you report to *me*, not to Jack. I run this operation on the ground. Is that clear?"

"Yes." Was it, though? He had the usual back-channel access to Jack.

"I will now go through mission directives and your cover pro-file. Then I will hang up."

He did indeed know the drill, as Jack might've put it.

"Shoot," Old Jim said, and so she did.

Old Jim in the field felt different than "Old Jim" in the archives. Some perverse impulse attached to that transition from words on the page, the interrogation of dead text, to the sun on his face, receiving real-time detail. Analysis ceding in an almost sensual way to *sensation* and muscle memory, and living, absorbing, trying to see people entire while inhabiting a role.

He might be safer trying to pierce the gloom down in the archives, but being in the field was better for him. Easier to become lost out here, and maybe that was for the best.

Jackie's brief reflected Jackie more than she might realize, Old Jim noticed as she began to supply the basics of his position. He supposed the burning files had included the high-level view and that was why Jackie shied away from that view. Or, maybe, something in the high-level view frightened her, or put her at odds with Jack.

Jack had flagged the whole situation under the vague term "Interference," which usually mean "foreign, hostile intelligence service"—which meant "enemy hindering our cohesion and compliance experiments on the Forgotten Coast," in this case.

It felt odd for Jackie to focus on what was tactical, in a sense, in the present moment, when the situation had become so wide, so deep. Central's official conclusion about the Dead Town Disaster also struck him as relevant to operations currently, and maybe part of his role now was as a kind of secret historian. Mapping the cause and effect, the idea of influence, and even Central itself, in how an organization reacted to failure.

Eighteen years ago an anonymous Central analyst had concluded that "The full extent of foreign interference cannot be grasped from the evidence on hand. For this reason, the Central program should continue, in a different context, and Central should explore more fully why the Forgotten Coast might be of interest."

Could you lose your mind to an unanswerable question, or just your soul? And what would Jackie become in this strange hierarchy, mired in this mystery, if she stayed here long?

Old Jim's instinct was to interrupt Jackie's brief to ask questions about all of this, to make it personal, to draw on the fact that he was part of Jack's family, too, in a way. But now was not the time, as she drove home points in areas where his expertise far outstripped her own—emphasized his cover, for example, which included that he'd been away from the Forgotten Coast, but now he'd come back. Which was the story of so many here. They went into the world to try their luck, and some failed and came back, but others came back because they didn't like it as much out there.

"Avoid a surname whenever possible, just use 'Old Jim.' I aged you in the documents, including the birth certificate on file in Hedley, where you were born."

"Old Jim" retained both a proximity to his real name and also the relicf of continuity with the past few years. But he didn't like his real name anyway, or the atonal way his alias reminded him of it. Some days, in the past, he'd woken up wanting to be stripped of it so utterly that he might never be able to return to it.

"And my parents?" he asked, sure they were dead, which was usual and easy.

"Dead."

"Accident? Or something more interesting this time, like murder?"

"Your parents are both dead, as you might expect," Jackie said, with a hint of exasperation at starting over. "They met in Bleakersville, in the only pool hall back then . . ."

They died in a plane crash when Old Jim was only five years old. He'd grown up in the area, raised by grandparents now also conveniently deceased and unlikely to answer any questions, even via séance. Someone at Central had given him the small mercy of having a reputation as a good piano player, to balance two years at a community college studying business management.

"You manage and part-time bartend at the Village Bar. A silent partner of sorts now come back to the area to help out. So become familiar with the place, act like you've always known it, and soon enough the locals will act like you've always been there. Your name is on the deed for the bar, which leads back to a shell company called Shell Company. You'll need to familiarize yourself with the legal documents."

"Cute." Too cute, the standard Jack swagger.

He'd asked for surveillance on the Village Bar for the usual reasons, figured his cover would be manager, since he'd done it before, but he was still a little surprised they were going to let him actually interact with people, put him in proximity to spirits. Had that been a psych rec? So he wouldn't molder down to nothing, a shut-in? A test of "situational" alcoholism as opposed to the institutional type?

"So you have always been there, on paper. You've always been part of a holding company."

Who didn't want to be part of a holding company? It was why he'd joined up.

"False resident, embedded where I never was, for what I will never be." Something Jack used to say, out in the field.

"Landscape to person, it's a perfect match." As if he were a color swatch, wall paint being matched to the flooring.

"Just how old am I supposed to be?" Placeholder for the question he'd wanted to ask, which lay just beyond his grasp. Something about how much Jackie knew, whether she agreed with Jack.

"Sixty-one."

"I guess the sun and salt spray will age me."

"And the job. You can let your beard grow wild out here, Old Jim. In fact, ops recommends it. The more you look like a castaway, the more you will fit in."

"Just let myself go." Still grappling with having aged almost a decade in a second.

"You have one prohibition."

"From what?"

"The Séance and Science Brigade calls the whole Forgotten Coast 'Active Site X,' but they operate from Failure Island, six miles north of the lighthouse. You are forbidden from visiting the island for security reasons."

"But why?" This he hadn't expected. He felt like a child, asking the question, but . . . why?

Her voice became robotic and he imagined she was reading off a sheet of paper.

"To facilitate a smooth continuation of projects and programs as you right the ship, you will have a liaison who visits the island. This liaison will also report to me."

"Maybe throw in a concierge, too." But his sarcasm masked a growing unease and frustration. He liked to be hands-on. From afar, you missed details, had to rely on the unreliable to be your eyes and ears. He didn't want the extra complication of a go-between.

"I won't waste time with further details. Just a question: Does your unique memory still work?"

The question caught him by surprise.

"Sure, for most things."

For example, Old Jim remembered her as a nine-year-old with water wings in Jack's pool, staring through him into some kid's daydream about probably nothing at all.

For example, Old Jim on the back deck could catalogue each separate waving reed if he wanted, each and every one, lash himself with them to keep the bad thoughts out. Shove the reeds one two three four into his brain until nothing else existed, for a time. So maybe the mission would serve a similar purpose.

She was still talking, although he felt as if more time had passed and they'd existed in a silence longer than most would consider natural.

"I have to caution you. You might be lulled into thinking this backwater isn't worthy of your spy craft and expertise, but we both know the history of this place and the foreign entity that infiltrates it suggests a sophistication beyond the norm."

Still, he felt Jackie brought less urgency to the situation than Jack, and he wondered why.

"What happened to my predecessor?" He'd found the question that had eluded him.

"His head popped at a depth of four hundred meters."

"All on its own?"

"And his bones liquified."

"Jack didn't tell me any of that." He couldn't help a flicker of irritation, which receded because what good was it? The files had referenced "an accident."

"Or, maybe," Jackie continued as if he hadn't said anything, "he died because you wish for something you shouldn't or you look behind you when you shouldn't, and suddenly you're a pillar of salt, and who follows orders from a pillar of salt? Not me."

He frowned, feeling like she'd revealed something personal, but all he could think to say was "I don't think that's how the story goes."

"We're the ones who write the stories, Old Jim."

"And what if I can't be bought by a piano?"

"A gift you never asked for arrives tomorrow. That will be our answer as well as your own."

The receiver clicked and she was gone, rasp no more, wraith no more.


It was a house; he'd lived in many. Old Jim tried not to get too attached to them. Run-down from the outside, on purpose, but clean and solid inside, with a kitchen, a dining-room area, a living room, two baths, two bedrooms, closets, a room for his office, on one level, ranch-style. All the usual things. Central had thoughtfully furnished the place in a kind of low-key coastal "shabby chic," although the ranch-style layout pushed back.

Everything from the large faded green-blue plush throw rug

on the living-room floor to the sagging off-white couch with floppy pillows felt lived in, with a vague beach theme. The white stucco walls of the living room and kitchen helped offset the low ceilings and the dark-paneled wood of a corridor filled with soft seaweed-green shag carpet that led to the bedrooms and office.

In the office, Central had given Old Jim two phones—a red one with a secure line and a black one for "tourists"—as well as a fax machine. He had to enter a code every time he sent a fax. A safe in the corner of the supply closet to the side could be booby-trapped if he liked, but that was the extent of the cloak-and-dagger—unless the ancient alligator tracking device he'd found in the archives and placed at the far edge of the desk counted as "espionage" rather than "shot in the dark."

The huge rosewood desk with its ostentatious leather-bound blotter engulfed the tracker and everything else he'd brought . . . this strenuous desk with its ultra-secure drawers and lion's paws for feet . . . He had become slightly obsessed with thinking about how Central had gotten the desk into such cramped quarters. Lifted off the roof of the house and helicoptered it in? Built the house around it, like the desk had grown up in that spot? Maybe he lingered on the question because it felt refreshingly stupid or unimportant.

A Gothic built-in bookcase facing the desk made everything worse, with its pretentious Doric mini-columns, flashing bone-white against the dark wood of the shelves . . . which held volumes like *The Decline and Fall*, alongside some thick cookbooks he'd never get around to using. The typewriter was a tiny, delicate-looking thing, like a metal beetle on its back with a hundred legs sticking out, tucked into a cubby in the cubicle-like shelves behind the fax machine, under the office window.

The window there peered out suspiciously on the barbed-wire fence around the biohazard facility that was his benighted neighbor—mostly out of view through a forested easement.

Something about how the shadows fell at a certain time of day made the view ominous. Shambling to his desk after fitful sleep, there came the impression of a weight receding from outside the glass.

He had no other neighbors for miles, and the area in general had an unfinished feel to it—unincorporated, mostly public lands or zoned agricultural for timber. The Village not only had no name beyond Village, he'd discovered, but had no mayor or other officials—beholden in theory to a grifty bunch of county commissioners, but in reality left to a kind of semblance of self-rule except for utilities, plumbing, and, most places, garbage pickup. The nearest public airport of note, as he'd discovered, lay seventy miles away, and land was cheap.

In a drawer in the desk, Old Jim had discovered leftover flotsam from his predecessor: multicolored pens, reimbursement forms, a scribbled screed about "secret minders" that didn't seem paranoid if his head had popped like a grape. It would be just like Jack to build in redundancy or fail-safes.

But his predecessor's particular obsession had been reports on what had washed up on the beach. Pages and pages of them in the drawer, with certain items underlined using pens with different-colored ink. (On some level, the fact his predecessor had underlined "bag of dog feces" on one list made the man's idea of a "minder" seem more like a random shadow cast upon the interior wall of the man's skull.)

*Drug kits, baby-doll arm, hair weave, railroad tie, pieces of unidentifiable metal, mousetrap, false eyelashes, mermaid tail for a toy, a green lighter, fuel hose, rubber snake, crime-scene tape, plastic milk carton full of pennies.*

*Dinner plate, bag of cocaine, floor mat, underwear, yard-sale sign, tiki torch, baseball cap, silica packet, plastic dinosaur, dollar bill, dog bowl, seat belt, bike seat, Hula-Hoop, mattress, fire extinguisher, unopened champagne bottle, bones.*

The lists went on forever. They irritated him in the way lists sometimes did, because they represented a kind of raw data, the import of which might only exist in the eye of the beholder. He didn't like to sift through them, suspected a code or a kind of flailing intensity that he recognized in himself sometimes, too. The underlining had no logic to it that he could discern, with "green" emphasized but not "lighter." What had his predecessor been looking for?

Maybe, in the end, Old Jim's skull would burst, too, and out would spill the answer.

Soon enough, unable to resist, Old Jim sat at the upright piano next to the stone path, in the glazed sunlight of the weedy front yard, while cicadas seethed in the trees and among the wildflowers, elderberry, and azalea bushes, grasshoppers and green lizards considered each other with caution, dragonflies skimming along overhead.

It felt like sorcery—that the piano had been brought to him down a dirt road and unloaded without him hearing. Whatever its origins, the piano had recently been refurbished and it shone slick in the sunlight, the gleam of keys white and black. He felt a residual, sentimental gratitude toward Jack for the grand gesture.

Old Jim started to play the melancholy notes of a song, "Rast," part of an eighteenth-century composer's piano suite, *Winter Journey*. Had Jack introduced him to the suite or had he introduced it to Jack, when they were out in the field? He'd had it in his head for some time now.

Most of *Winter Journey* had a kind of universal appeal, and the melancholy satisfaction of existing within someone else's sadness, their expression of that condition removed from his by centuries and situation.

> A *phantom's flaming breath*
> *pulled me from my route:*

*it led me to rocky depths*
*with no hope of getting out.*

*I follow dry riverbeds,*
*in peace, I make my way;*
*every stream will meet the sea,*
*and every sorrow will have its day.*

The first of the cycle that he'd learned to play, and he knew it by heart, sang it silently as he played. Minor key, leaping from low A to high A. *"I am used to going astray, / every path has its end. / Every joy, every dismay."* How would he get to hell, if lost, anyhow? And would the phantoms lead him astray?

A song, a tune, a melody could not save him, but in the pressure of his fingers against the keys, the memory of a voice rising over the notes, there came a kind of comfort. Rising like the mist over the marsh flats out back, on the days when heat became steam.

There was the signal and there was the sound. The signal and the sound, and maybe it was true the piano made him too sentimental and maybe it was also true that he remembered so much he wanted to forget, with a sharpness where it just came to him when he wanted it. One reason they'd recruited him initially—to be the guy who only needed to be told things once, the one who could look at the mission specs and then burn the paper and never once regret the absence of the map. Yet his almost-wife he could not remember except, if he tried hard, vague, out-of-focus moments that he couldn't tell was actual memory or a photograph he'd seen. There was just the sickening crunch and slam of the vehicle smashing into the side of them then . . . nothing. Such a towering silence. It had all been destroyed in his mind, and nothing about the ghosting that had turned into a haunting had brought it back.

What could he do about it? Nothing? Reeducate himself

from old vacation films he'd shot? That wasn't a person, not in the usual way. He resisted that. He kept the photo of her in his wallet. Never looked at it. Sometimes looked at it. Sometimes when he played the piano, though, he got glimpses of her. Little things. Little moments. She'd liked the piano, he remembered. She'd like to hear him play the piano. Maybe it reminded her that he could be things other than a field agent. Maybe it made it seem like they could have a normal life.

What was a person, sometimes, but a wandering fire. But put the flames out, and what was left?

## 004: THE UNWANTED GIFT

The morning after Jackie Severance's call, Old Jim stepped onto his porch with his usual cup of coffee, about to check on the condition of the piano in the dew . . . and *she* stood there, waiting for him. There came a kind of buckling at the knees and he recalled later how strange that his coffee mug had shattered so easily against the wood and neither of them acknowledged it.

Cass had always looked uncannily like her mother, and so it was the mirroring, too, that punched Old Jim in the gut, got into him so deep he felt unmoored. A terrible weight and yet weightless, mired in the mud of a dead meadow.

"Hi, Dad," she said in a chipper tone. "It's good to see you."

But it *wasn't* and yet it was . . . because this wasn't his daughter. Old Jim knew that, didn't know that. A surge of betrayal. Was this a joke? Or Jack's sick idea of operational integrity? How could Central do this to him? He sat down heavily in one of the two wicker chairs, his legs turning to concrete.

"Leave," he managed, but it came out as a rasp, a whisper so faint she didn't hear him. This pain in his heart.

She bent over to collect the largest shards of coffee mug, set them on the rickety oak coffee table, and took the chair next to him.

"Sure, Dad," the false daughter said, after sitting, as if the script had gotten switched, action to reaction, dialogue versus stage business. "Sure, Dad, we can talk out here. And, later, you can let me in."

An emphasis on "let me in," a quiver that felt wrong, and he held her gaze to see what would happen. He knew this was not his daughter, and yet . . . the terrible, ragged feeling welling up out of him along with the shock . . . what did it mean about him that he couldn't tell her to leave a second time?

A flash of worry broke the symmetry of her face, and Old Jim realized he had held her gaze for so long without speaking that she might think he was having a stroke.

"That mug you broke," Old Jim managed to whisper, making her lean close, which he did not want. "That mug was a present for my daughter I never had a chance to give her." She'd been more about Halloween than Christmas, so it had ghosts along the sides. And then he'd forgotten to bring it to the diner, and by then it had been November anyway.

The stain of dark liquid along the slant of the porch. A mockingbird sang a jaunty medley from a fence post in the yard. There was no breeze and Old Jim's neck felt hot.

"Won't you invite me in?" she asked, staring at the remains of the mug on the porch, and this time, no mistake, she was giving away the game to convey that she understood he'd said "leave."

When he still didn't reply, was still trying to compose himself, she said, "There's so much to get started on for the Séance and Science Brigade."

How would she leave, anyway? No car, so she'd been abandoned here to deal with his response, no matter what that might be. Armed with her canned speech, that she had decided to deploy as if it were not words so much as some stilted rehearsal.

He could feel his pulse roaring in his ears like an alarm. The hazel of her eyes matched Cass's, even if achieved by contacts, not real. Matched it to a degree of precision that made him want to weep, imagining someone at Central working on that for hours. A similar sorcery in the line of cheekbone.

This person who had been made to look like Cass in an impervious, trapped-in-time way.

Would he let her in? Would it kill him if he did?

"Let's sit out here a bit," he managed, numb, still trying to process her stiffness. Could she be so green an operative that that was real, not a signal at all? No.

"Okay, we can do that," she said. "Good to catch up."

"Yeah, good to catch up." With this person he had never met before.

*Invite me in.* As if she knew she was something strange, some monster from old folktales that could not pass a threshold without permission.

Terrified, or just anxious, while it was his job to accept or reject her. But he couldn't get there. Not yet. Did Central think someone else, some *foreign entity*, was listening in? Was that it, too?

Even now, clean, he wasn't clean. He wasn't clear.


The leather jacket over a T-shirt for a punk rock band. The gold earrings in a spiral pattern. The faded blue jeans, the black boots. She smelled of the same breath mints Cass had used to cover clove cigarettes. In all the details of the false daughter in front of him, Old Jim realized that Central, on some level, knew his true daughter better than he had. That the fake made the real sharper, more in focus. But wasn't that a lie, too, because weren't his memories the important parts?

"Cass" hadn't changed at all in the year or more since he'd last seen her. She'd been twenty-nine and now was again. It made him picture her in three years, in five. How the endearing crow's-feet would become more pronounced. How the smoking would deepen the rasp in her voice, weather her skin along with her love of the sun. Because no life could escape entropy.

The "Cass" in front of him was as close to his memory of her as she would ever be.

So many things that balanced the bleakness of his profession had been taken from him by removing herself. She had *known* she was taking them, and still she had taken them.

How could she want to take those things from him?

Then a kind of smoldering came over him and Old Jim decided to punish her, this impostor—to unspool her script to the bitter end. Let her think him deranged. Let her think him unrecoverable. He didn't care. He did care.

"I haven't seen you in a while," Old Jim said, choosing his words carefully. He couldn't tell how long they had sat in silence.

No hesitation in the reply, so also from the script: "I just had to go away for a while to work some things out," she said. "You can understand that, can't you?"

"I don't know if I do understand that," Old Jim said, and realized his anger made him tremble. "Or you."

"Listen, Dad, I'm sorry. I am. But now I just want our mission to go well. I want that for both of us." How hard to read worry or deceit from her face.

She leaned forward and took his hand in hers. He could remember when her hand had been tiny in his, and her walk a toddler's lurch. It was too familiar an act, too sudden and too intimate.

He flinched away, and she sat back in her chair. The competing emotion that came with his anger—that he'd *hurt his daughter* by flinching. To discourage the illusion.

"Dad . . . I've spent this time trying to figure things out," she ventured, as if she were extending her hand again and expected him to slap it away. "I've been . . . out of sorts. But I'm better now. I'm here now."

*Dad.* The word sounded odd in her voice—one element Central hadn't been able to coach into the doppelgänger. Cass always had a kind of questioning upturn at the end of most of her sentences, and this Cass never ended with a question, with a voice both too gentle and yet, surprisingly, with more steel behind it.

Enough.

"What's your name?" Old Jim asked. "What's your real name?"

He had to admire that she had recovered herself enough to register no response, no tell of surprise.

"Cass, of course. I haven't changed it."

"Are you sure? Are you absolutely sure?"

"I sure am. Dad." Was that a bit of resistance in her voice? A flare of irritation or exasperation, coming up from down deep.

"What about your true first name?"

"Eleanor, as always."

Such an old-fashioned name, Eleanor, and yet also a favored great-aunt who'd once fended off burglars in her lush garden with a rolling pin, according to family legend.

"A shining light," he said, just to hear it aloud.

For a moment someone else, both older and younger, stared at him. Someone unknowable. Buried there, in her gaze, an emotion or impulse he didn't understand yet. A sadness and yet still that defiance. A memory personal to her that he'd tripped over with *shining light*.

"Stay here," he said. "I've got something to show you."


Jack's perverse idea of a gift, or some new form of torture—his idea of the moment kept changing. A reminder to him, a message? "Cass" would have the bona fides to be his lieutenant, that he didn't doubt—nor that Jack intended that she pose as his daughter. Such a Central-like psyops move. The position had a vacancy, in their opinion, why not use that? So sleekly efficient, but also the emotional maze or riddle meant to hold him in place that almost always meant something else as well. He had come to expect the dysfunctional dopamine rush of that, the exhilaration of the manufactured unexpected moment.

But not this way.

The other, terrible thought, that fed into the same decision, as Old Jim searched for the box he meant to show "Cass," somewhere in the closet of the master bedroom, yet to be unpacked. Why had he buried it so deep? But he knew why.

This terrible thought that couldn't be true: That false Cass was Jack's way of hinting he knew the location of real Cass, and if Old Jim just played along, maybe Jack would give him a clue, or even an address and phone number. But the agony of "then what?" *Then what*, given she didn't want to be found?

And, ah, hell, what did it matter where the hell was the damn box. What else could he do but dust off the old suit and put it on and spiral back into old routines, working for Central?

Because the fact was . . . he couldn't get Dead Town out of his head. And he knew Central. He knew what to expect, which was: anything at all. Central would never abandon him until he was dead, even if it banished him to his own island somewhere. *Jack* couldn't truly abandon him, because Jack so pathologically valued "family" and because Old Jim knew where the bodies were buried. True, or just true enough for now, because he hadn't crossed the fault line yet?

Even if something deeper stared out of him from a dark place, a thought not formed enough to be given voice. A thought so terrifying it might never surface.

Old Jim shambled out onto the porch with the box and upended it at his false daughter's feet. All the letters in their sealed, unaddressed envelopes. They formed a messy pile, sliding out across the wood. So many dozens of letters, since her disappearance.

"Cass" stared at the pile aghast, frozen—then looked up at him. The way she stared undid him and he didn't know if he felt pity or empathy or some secret fellowship.

Did she not understand? How could she not understand? So he made her understand.

"I wrote you so many letters. I wrote you *so many* and there was nowhere to send them." He was standing over her with the empty box still held in one hand.

She had receded into her chair, as if he meant her harm.

Did he mean her harm?

"I just kept writing them. And you just kept not being there." Not even a postcard, unsigned, without a message, that he would know was from her.

All the emotion in that moment lay in the letters and none of it in Old Jim. Seeing them all there like that did not make him want to drink. It did not make him want to wind up on a street corner again with Jackie hovering over him. It did not make him want anything more than for his false daughter to respond, to explain, to try to make it right.

But "Cass" was breathing heavily, staring at the letters like she'd been cornered. Like the letters had triggered something personal to her, not part of the role. The look she gave him was feral, grief-stricken, lost.

"God, this is . . . so fucked up."

The intensity of that, the tone of voice ripping clean through him.

The terrible whisper: Was this actually Cass and he had gone crazy with his grief?

"All this time—I've searched for you. I've sacrificed for you. I . . . I . . ."

"You don't even know me."

Sharp, like an ice pick. All of it crashing down on him, like he didn't know what was happening to him. But he knew what was happening to him. How could he have any defenses left, even to a false Cass. Central hadn't given him that. They'd just gotten him clean and put him back in the field.

"That's not true!"

But he knew she was telling him something genuine, a thing he hadn't known was possible. Because he'd been isolated. Because he'd been so alone in his own thoughts. Because everyone else had been reduced to points of light against a black screen.

She rose and took the empty box from his hand and let it fall to the ground. Something in the gesture extended a sympathy he didn't want.

"Do you want me to read these letters?" she asked. "Because if you do, I will."

Maybe Jack didn't know where his real daughter was. Maybe Jack was telling Old Jim he could have a *version* back, some living memory of her. Because Jack thought family meant everything, because Jack liked to play games.

"No," he said. "No, you don't need to. It's okay."

Strangely, it was okay, at least for that moment. Almost okay enough that he wanted to ask for her real name again.

To break a spell. To live once more in the present, in the real world.

Turning to the front door, he might have fallen, exhausted, except she steadied him with an expertise that spoke to some kind of caregiving in her background, followed by a letting go that left him with his dignity. He could always call it off, he told himself. Shatter the illusion as easily as he'd shattered the coffee mug. Couldn't he?

He still shut the door in her face. He felt he had no choice.

## 005: PILLARS OF SALT

**W**as Old Jim the candle, the flame, or the vessel? The enormous desk, the awkward chair, the way his thoughts accumulated mass, meaning, so he gasped and turned on his side like he'd been drowning, and he couldn't for a moment determine if he was in bed or in his office, with the waters rising fast and an echo of shutter bang, shutter bang he would never escape. Still vibrating with an inner discomfort from the encounter with the unwanted gift, plagued also now by new dreams since coming to the Forgotten Coast.

In the most prominent, Old Jim was a small glass vessel containing a lit candle like a memorial at the bend of a rural road, with a green light leaking in from Central's files. The constraint and prison of that without a body came to him close and suffocating, and the dislocated trickling sound of water somewhere beyond, the sense of a river or creek beyond his view.

This awful sense of not being able to move, not having a body. Of being at the mercy of the world—dead but still having to live. Was that *Winter Journey*, faint, in the distance, just the music, not the words, or some other song?

The question, in the aftermath, when he came fully awake. Was he the candle, the flame, or the glass vessel?

Despite a shiny new sign, the Starlight Lounge outside of Bleakersville had already acquired the world-weary shrug of a dive bar, only two years after opening. Jackie had designated the lounge as the location for debriefs or when he needed to see her in person, and he'd decided to call in that chit already. Maybe to get Jackie's attention. Maybe just because he couldn't read her over the phone.

A few muscle cars dominated the dirt-and-gravel parking lot, along with Old Jim's aging pickup—which made it clear to him that Jack no longer believed him capable of car chases. The low, long building, even with the new bright blue coat of paint, suggested barracks and militias to Old Jim, not the fish market it had once been.

Now it boasted "clean bathrooms," a smattering of pool tables in a sunken back area accessed via purple-carpeted stairs, and, off to the left, a couple of nonregulation sawed-off bowling lanes with bowling balls that looked almost like softballs.

Old Jim took up a position at a less fateful table between the bar and the pool tables. He wanted no part of festivities or the sporting opportunities, a nondrinking chimera, even though he wanted one. But not as much as to be free of his false daughter. He'd become distrustful of any emotion, any sentiment, he'd experienced during their first encounter. Kept seeing the letters spill out and being unable to intuit the look on her face.

Just when Old Jim had begun to wonder if Jackie would show up, she burst in the door, holding a compact duffel bag and dressed in a black pantsuit that looked more military than fashionable.

With deliberate slowness she turned the open sign hanging from the door to closed, walked over, and stood there looming over him.

"Why am I here?"

"You're chipper," he said, noncommittal.

She put down her duffel bag, sat down across from him. "You're not the only project I'm managing. Make it quick. Succinct."

"Send my 'daughter' back to Central," he said.

Grim amusement touched her lips. "Is that all?"

"I don't want her here. She seems . . . unsettled." He meant *unsettling*, but didn't want to admit that. "She seems like—"

"The help you need, but you don't want? Maybe you still think that someday your real daughter will come back."

He forced himself to avoid the bait and abyss of that.

"Why did Jack send her?"

"How do you jump-start a dead battery? You give it a jolt."

Old Jim bit the inside of his cheek to stop from saying something he might regret. So he was a dead battery now and Cass was the jolt. He felt pissed off for both of them.

"Just . . . what's the angle, her deal, this 'Cass'?"

"Angle? She's your daughter."

"That's Jack's profile, Jackie. Not yours. You don't like party tricks, rabbits popping out of hats. Unless you do now?" Dead rabbits. Rabbits eating other rabbits.

"You were harder once," Jackie said. "I remember how you were like bulletproof glass. Jack said once I should be like you."

"He did?"

No answer, and a look he didn't care to decipher any more than he liked what stared back from the mirror these days.

"About 'Cass,' though—I can give you the broad outlines," Jackie said, and it felt like she was relenting, while perversely he didn't want her to. "She grew up poor, joined the ROTC because it felt like a way out, then the military. It took her longer because—"

"Skip ahead. I don't need the whole sob story."

"Not in the mood? Okay. Her first mission for Central, just two years ago, she was on a black op. Middle of nowhere. A shore next to a glittering blue sea under a blazing sky, mountains all around. Such a beautiful place, from a distance. But they were all dead, ambushed. A bullet through her clavicle and two days hiding among the bodies, and then three days, under the hot sun, thinking about her dead friends, before exfiltration. People she'd trained with for almost a year and knew well. Gone. Just like that."

Jackie had leaned closer, as if she were weaving some kind of messed-up spell, so intent on his reaction he reflexively nudged his seat a couple inches from the table.

"Tragic story," Old Jim said. Was it true? He'd felt a pang like it was true, which meant maybe it was the story Jackie had devised just for him, the one to touch the secret heart of him.

"Not as sad as you might think," Jackie said. "People move on."

"Was she? Responsible?" he asked, ignoring the insinuation.

"Are you responsible for the weather around here?" she asked.

"Then, no," Old Jim said.

"Then no," Jackie echoed.

This was getting him nowhere.

"What are you not telling me, Jackie?"

She contemplated him in a way he found unnerving. "Hiding something from you would compromise the mission."

Would it? He tried to be more specific.

"Central *must* know more about the Rogue—the 'stranger' in the files." "Rogue" felt like a word he needed to say to someone here, on the Forgotten Coast. Not just written on a piece of paper back at Central.

"Jack believes in ghosts, but I'm not so sure. Still, maybe this will help, a little." She rummaged through the duffel bag. Tossed a thin file folder onto the table.

But he was thinking about his false daughter again.

"What should I do?" He hated asking her advice.

"About Cass? Nothing. Let her do her job. Which, just so you know, is to push you sometimes."

"She reports to me. I'm her superior."

Jackie laughed caustically like he'd told a bad joke.

"Jim. I still need to make sure you're functional. Jack is less sure it matters—whether you're broken or not. He thinks it's a good sign you let the files burn. I don't."

"Your father is a bastard."

"Takes one," Jackie said. "Definitely takes one." She stood, duffel bag in one hand. It made a dull clank, like she had tools in there.

At the door a thickset mustached man in a cowboy hat, blue denim shirt, jeans, and boots had appeared, waiting for her.

She acknowledged the man, then turned to Old Jim again.

"This wasn't an emergency. Call next time."

"I think you're evil and you're going to kill me," he said.

Her glance made him feel childish.

"Your father's favorite call sign," he explained.

"Thanks for the history lesson. Now go do your job. You used to be good at it. You used to be brutally good at it."

He didn't want to think about that. "And what if I can't work with her?"

She shrugged. "Then you'll be staring at Central's dull walls again. Or maybe you'll be dead."

Typical Jackie. Not so much a threat as a clinical assessment.

Then she was gone as if she'd never been there, like any true rogue.


In that comfortable stillness, that dusk-like darkness, broken only by the soft clack from the pool tables, Old Jim sat for a long time after Jackie left. A low-grade sadness had come over him. For himself, but also for his false daughter. To be lashed to the mast of authenticity after losing everyone you held dear. Something about bonding with your team was hard to describe. The younger you were the first time catastrophe struck, the harder to process what had happened, the more it damaged you.

If he chose to believe Jackie, and for now he did.

Which left him with the file in front of him and while he wasn't going to burn it, Old Jim did feel with a kind of superstitious certainty that he should read the file where he sat, know what it contained before bringing it back to his house. Some information burgeoned, and became even more monstrous the more you considered it. Sometimes people never recovered from that.

Another sip of tap water, a reflexive look around, and then he read the account.

The incident detailed in the file had happened in the late summer of the previous year, in a remote area, estuary-fed, that lay between Dead Town and the coast. The kind of place it took a dirt road to get to and once you were there all you could do besides fish is drink beer, swim a little in brackish water, and maybe shoot off some fireworks.

Two teenagers on their way to the beach reported seeing a naked man on a raised berm in the marsh, with a huge alligator walking beside him. The alligator held a lifeless body in its jaws— that looked exactly like the man walking. Both, from details of the teenagers' account, resembled the Rogue. Except, the one in the alligator's jaws had a "floppy, soft quality, like it wasn't real."

Old Jim was inclined to ignore that last detail, because sometimes the mind filled in for mystery in an erroneous way—and, somehow, he, personally, needed to ignore that detail. Recoiled from it in a visceral way. As if he had come across the body later and found it liquified, peculiar, not right.

The important thing—this had to be the important part?— was Jackie telling him this sighting was one reason Jack thought the Rogue was back. Had been seen. Was doing things that from afar seemed . . . uncanny? Was that the word?

The police hadn't bothered to follow up on the report, as far as Old Jim could tell. Why would they? It sounded insane. They'd probably assumed the teenagers had been drinking and maybe cast a glance at missing person reports, found nothing.

Someone startled Old Jim by using a bowling lane. Such a hard sound, a bowling ball hitting a lane and then knocking over a pin, contrasted with the velvet-crushed clack of a billiard ball. He tried to regain his equilibrium.

A man, a person, who had been here twenty years? As the AC turned on with a startling creak, Old Jim had the thought that the Rogue could be like a soldier who didn't know the war was over. Ordered to hold some remote island outpost, a kind of exile very different from Team Leaders 1 and 2.

But what did that make the Tyrant?

In Old Jim's imagination, the Tyrant breached the surface only long enough to breathe and sometimes snap and tear at the harness of its prison. And then the appearance of the leviathan's head, the body of some swamp god, made manifest.

With one red-eye bobber, embedded in the midst, burning out at him.

## 006: SMASHING THE KEYS

A war of dreams in his head, but he couldn't divine what lay tangled there. Except him as a vessel with a candle inside, teetering on his deck railing in the wind, and the night beyond the deck alive with the flash of some animal and the mutters of the water that almost seemed like words. The flame of him guttering, flaring, but never going out. Sometimes, waking up with coffee, he wondered how long it would take him to get used to the Forgotten Coast, after so long roaming. And how long, too, would it take him to get used to Cass?

The first real attempt at a briefing occurred a few days after he'd met with Jackie and he'd been wading through files and S&SB procedure in ways that made him punch-drunk.

Impressive amounts of paperwork needed to manage psychics, and not enough accountability on budget.

Old Jim just looked at Cass on the stoop, scowled, and said, "Okay, then, come into the damn house."

She hesitated, stood there, shy of the steps onto the porch. Her hair had a wild, disheveled look and she seemed about as awake as he did. She'd ditched the false daughter attire, at least, for a blue T-shirt with a wave pattern, an unbuttoned men's white linen shirt over that, and tan pants tucked into boots.

"Okay, then," she said, reaching some kind of decision. "I will come into the 'damn house.'" She walked up to him like she was calling a bluff, clutching her satchel close.

Already a kind of resistance he could feel seething in the air. But why had he started it? He didn't even know, just that he felt fuzzy, lack of sleep, even though he didn't recall getting up during the night.

Old Jim's mood soured further when she said, "What's with the piano?"

"What about it?" he asked, defensive. "People keep all kinds of things in their yards around here." The truth was, two attempts to get it to the Village Bar had failed. He meant to call a third company after Cass left.

"Not pianos, they don't."

"Forget the piano and come inside. But take off your shoes first."

"Boots."

"Well, take them off. No boots or shoes in the house."

"I don't take my boots off. Operational rule."

"If someone chases us out of the house while you brief me, you'll just have to run away in your socks."

Cass gave him a frustrated look as she struggled to pull her boots off.

"You're wearing shoes. You know that, right?"

Damn it.

"Don't worry about what I do, k—"

*Kid.* He could tell from the look that came over her face that she knew where that had been headed.


Facing Cass over the kitchen table, in chairs opposite each other, had an adversarial edge. He'd placed a pomelo on her side, along with her coffee (black, no cream). The pomelo was an offering that he regretted now. Old Jim felt like eating the pomelo himself. In front of her. As noisily and sloppily as possible.

The slant of the morning sun's rays across the table from the kitchen window happened to be in Cass's eyes, orchestrated that way. Old Jim wanted to see how long she'd last blasted by the light. Most people quickly squirmed their way out of it.

Cass had stopped rooting around in her satchel for something and begun to pull her hair back in a ponytail when she registered the pomelo.

She pushed it toward him. He pushed it back.

"That's for you."

"No, thanks. I don't like citrus."

The citrus smell suddenly seemed bitter and too strong.

"But you always loved pomelos."

Even as he said it, Old Jim became angry at himself. How he'd justified the gift as test of how deep her briefing on him went. But that wasn't really it, was it? Fooling himself about what he wanted out of that. How it undermined everything he'd said about not wanting her to pretend to be his daughter.

"Tastes change, Dad. People change." With her hair pulled away from her face, she looked older, more grown-up, but something about the conciliatory tone flipped another switch on his temper.

"Don't call me Dad," he said, putting force behind it.

"Yes, sir," she said in a calm tone. "Sorry, sir. Won't happen again, sir."

With a slow, deliberate motion, he pushed the pomelo off the table. It landed with a fat, thick sound on the floor, so heavy it didn't even roll. So now it was just sitting there on the floor between them, under the third chair. The exhaustion, still, of constantly having every object, every encounter, put him back in a kind of purgatory—unable to move forward or even fully backward, into the past.

"Don't call me sir, either."

Cass followed the pomelo's progress with a grim set to her jaw.

"Right," she said, "message received."

The light was burning her face for sure and yet she looked comfortable saying that, like she was meant to be there—and he couldn't take it.

"Why are you here?" he asked, trying to match her calm. "What qualifies you to be here? Besides some fucked-up whim of Jack's."

"I'm former military. Central assigned me to this op because I have experience managing people and I am proficient at intelligence analysis."

Her face had gotten more flushed and the freckles under her eyes had become a fiery pink, but her tone remained dispassionate. How could he not admire that? Even as he kept digging a hole.

"What about surveillance? Field ops in general?"

"You're assuming you're still current on the latest methodology in field training."

"Or, standards might've dropped since I joined up."

"Lo those many years ago."

That was kind of funny, but mocking, too, and anger won out.

"I don't like this," Old Jim said. "I don't want to be briefed right now. I don't even know if I can trust you."

He didn't care how he sounded; he didn't know how he sounded. His body was vibrating with tension and lack of sleep. He refused to look at her.

But she was appraising him in a clinical way, said, with no emotion, "I don't know if I can trust you, either. Old Jim." Emphasis on *old*.

"And this arrangement," he said, when she just sat there. "This *pointless*, ridiculous arrangement. I have a hard time with bullshit." Maybe he was being childish, petulant. But he was also ill-served, ill-treated. Manipulated into pretending all of this was normal.

"Your entire life has been 'bullshit,' but suddenly you have a problem with it."

The tone was dispassionate, aloof, and it should have stung. But somehow the rebuke steadied him and he looked at her sharply. Because it felt real. That she'd let slip something about someone who was not his daughter, not just lost her cool behind a clipped delivery.

And what if she was right? That his life had been "bullshit" in the way he lived in a world of deception and often liked it. That the amount of time he'd had to be someone else, or some variation on the real him, had eroded all of his relationships, professional and personal, taken hold in ways that made him, yes, an empty vessel hoping the flame would stay lit.

"I'd like for you to leave now."

"Suit yourself." She pulled a folder out of her satchel, put it on the table. "Read the House Centipede report before we meet again."

"What the hell is a house centipede?"

"And next time try to act like a professional."

"A professional? A *professional*. You know nothing. I have *years* of experience on you." Furious, but on some level he had to marvel at how she was taking him behind the woodshed for a beating. All while her pulse never seemed to rise above seventy.

"Oh, so this is how a seasoned professional behaves? Is this how you learned to conduct yourself over all those years?" she asked, still in a measured tone.

"No," he admitted, then felt like he'd capitulated in some

vague, hard-to-define way. Or that she'd wanted him off-balance. To show she could handle him?

"Jim. We don't have time for this. Look over the files. Something very strange is happening here—and it's intensifying. So we can't afford to do this much longer, whatever *this* is."

He hesitated, unwilling and unable to agree with her, although he did agree with her. This sense of something wrong that he had not yet put his finger on.

"And you need to start acting like I'm your daughter, for the mission. Or you're going to blow my cover."

"I think you know more about blowing a mission than I do," he said, hackles up again.

Even with her prior calm, it shocked him that she didn't register his cruelty. It shocked him that, outwardly, what should've been a direct hit . . . seemed to have no impact. All that registered was that he'd intentionally tried to hurt his daughter, and he felt a deep, burning shame.

"Don't assume that you know me any better than you knew your daughter."

A ringing in his ears and he could feel his face getting red.

"Get out of my house," he managed to say, more like an old man's croak.

She took her time rising from the table, pushing the chair in, retrieving the pomelo. Retrieving it, too, with little effort because he'd begun to notice that not only was she just as tall as him but also twice as strong.

"Okay, *Old Jim*, I'm leaving now," she said, an awful permanence in the word *leaving* that he resented her for, even as she placed the pomelo in front of him. "But I'll be back. We're stuck with each other."

At the door, Cass turned, lit up by the sun coming in from the east.

"If you really care about your daughter, be the kind of person she would want in her life."

"I said get the hell out."

"Also, there's a safe hidden in the floor under your rug—bet you didn't even know that."

"I did know! I did fucking know! I knew that!"

But she'd already slammed the door behind her. And he didn't. He didn't know that. He hadn't checked.

Old Jim picked up the pomelo and heaved it at the door. All he accomplished was to knock a little painting of a fishing boat off the wall.

Fucking hell.

After she had driven off in the stupid little red hatchback his real daughter would never have driven, Old Jim sat at the piano in the front yard and played his heart out. He wanted to smash the keys and get out his frustration. Loud enough to startle the deer and the raccoons and maybe even a stray otter or two. But he didn't care.

*"Now, I find myself weary / as I stop and take in the silence: / my journey kept me hurried, / then held me with a violence."*

This was *Winter Journey* as soul-devouring rage and it didn't need to sound good. His thoughts were a torment, crashing down around the sound of the music and nothing had a melody or a progression or any logic to it at all. He didn't have to sing the words to remember them.

*"I have committed no sin / that should keep me from my kind— / what a wild fool I am then / with endless desert in my mind."*

Because it was how he felt, no matter how Central had cleaned him up. Because "Cass" was right—he could sense that they had little time, that there was a time bomb somewhere in this mission, even if it had started ticking way back in time with Dead Town.

Old Jim had thrown the pomelo against the wall out of a

general frustration, really. He felt wrong, like he was already back to sleepwalking, a recurring problem for him. What point in being rescued just to be put back in a new kind of purgatory? How a dead old file could erupt as a nightmare in the middle of the night or even when he was out buying groceries from the stupidly named Piggly Wiggly.

Maybe he couldn't see the danger clearly now, or what the Rogue had been doing, because she'd destroyed something in him, the real Cass had, and Old Jim couldn't be sure he'd get it back.

If he hadn't been puking his guts out in gutters. If he hadn't been putting her picture up like someone had abducted her . . . and though he felt the loss still, he looked back on the person who had been so distraught with pity, almost with contempt. Although he was that same person.

The fake Cass had just said it straight—and how he resented, hated, the impulse that he should try to be a good person for the fake Cass so that, in some way well beyond logic, the real Cass would love him again.

The ghosting had become entwined, too, with a general sense of being fucked over, and now as he slammed the keys until his fingers pulsed and ached, he wanted to hurt not the fake Cass but the faker Jack, for putting him in this place. For saving him.

Ah, hell, how had he ruined that so thoroughly. Both things, then and today.

When one of his fingers began to throb, Old Jim went back inside and iced his hands at the kitchen sink.

After, with some difficulty, he pulled the edge of the throw rug back . . . and back, and back some more. Stared at the unbroken space beneath in puzzlement for a moment. There was no secret safe hidden in the floorboards. There was nothing at all there.

He laughed, stopped himself when it threatened to become more of a cackle. Except it really was funny.

No safe. Nothing there at all.

Ah, Cass. Good one. Really good. A sense of humor there, mixed in with the pointed reminder to watch his six.

Then he went into his office to read her damned House Centipede report.

## 007: THE HOUSE CENTIPEDE INCIDENT

The file referred to it as the "House Centipede Incident," but Old Jim that night, leaning back in his desk chair as far as he was able, thought of it more as "The Earwig and the House Centipede." Not a real earwig, but something that had infiltrated the mind to incite. A mystery of cause and effect, where he had to keep in mind what came first, what came after, and prioritize the importance of each. The eye could be distracted by the most dramatic part of the story, when the important moment had already occurred, partially out of sight.

Real earwigs he knew already—those pincer fiends that legend had it burrowed deep, but also in the sonic world, an aural sensation that could have mysterious effects. Especially at Central. While a "house centipede," he'd learned, was a six-inch-long, fairly wide, translucent thousand-legged eater of insects in someone's house. It didn't look like any centipede he had ever seen. The feelers alone . . .

In the file, they referred to the House Centipede Psychic as HCP1, a Central operative embedded in S&SB. Old Jim knew her first name was "Helen," but what was better, to think of the person or of her role in the situation? Along with a couple of other notes, he did scribble on his office blotter "kind of fucked up they call her the House Centipede Psychic now."

At first, it appeared Helen HCP1 would have a normal day

on the mainland, after a quick boat ride from Failure Island. She usually rode her bicycle to the Village for lunch, and then came back in the late afternoon.

Old Jim would've called it a "well-established routine that violated current security protocols," but that was the problem with kids today. Or with secret ops accreting around an amateur organization like the Ouija Hicks. The Henry Kage credited with parts of the report had a weakness for dramatic phrasing.

On the way back from the Village, an "uncertain event occurred," in Helen HCP1's words. It felt certain, though, because it had happened. A rut. A rut or a stone, "I'm not sure which." Between the lighthouse and the dock where the boat picked her up. Helen HCP1 went flying over her handlebars, landed in a clump of lacerating grass, knees bruised, "left elbow bloodied from collision with a rock," documented to separate out the injury as occurring earlier.

What did it matter, except as she got up, righted the bicycle, and checked her knees, "a weird sort of panting" came to her across the crashing waves on the one side and the rippling wind on the other. Then a voice she described as "both raspy and sweet, harsh and kind, threaded itself between sea wind and land wind." This was what Old Jim thought of as delivering the Earwig. Some entity that had, through sound, physically altered the life of the mind.

What words did this disembodied harsh-kind voice utter? She didn't know.

"It trickled into my ears like water and it sounded like someone had spoken to me from under the sea or the marsh. But, also, I could have imagined it."

Helen HCP1 had shaken off the sensation, gotten back on her bicycle, and gotten over hearing the Earwig by the time she returned to Failure Island.

The Séance and Science Brigade kept a daily POE (Peculiar Occurrence Event) log, in which HCP1's experience had been added to a list of "nascent auditory hallucinations" that Kage, the designated "Log Leader," felt might be a "natural expression of the 'signal openness' of our extrasensory personnel to an environment that keeps broadcasting an unfocalized 'uncanny presence' as a side effect of the intervention of a 'foreign entity.'"

Log Leader made Old Jim snicker and almost lose his balance on the chair. Well, okay, it was still possible to lean back too far, despite the desk.

The notation gave Old Jim the first inkling that psychics had their own bureaucratic bullshit language, but also that the "extrasensory personnel" might view the "foreign entity" as more akin to a demon or other physical being and not as Jack deemed it an "influence" or "sabotage mission."

That night, Helen HCP1 ate dinner in her quarters within the Failure Island complex that also housed the S&SB's salvage and research operations. Docks and piers led inland to a series of buildings behind a high wooden fence that housed legitimate and more experimental operations. The docks hid the submersibles, in what appeared to be derelict boathouses.

The extent of the submersibles project surprised Old Jim, felt aggressive and almost reckless. This impulse to use sensory deprivation at the bottom of the sea to explore the idea of distant messaging, among other experiments.

After a quiet dinner in her apartment, HCP1 turned in early. But in the middle of the night, reporting no dreams, which would have been put on a "precog descriptive list," Helen HCP1 woke up and "made my way to the bathroom," for the obvious reason. "Halfway there, I felt something soft underfoot and I briefly faltered but was determined to pay it no mind."

Here, HCP1 entered a loop of "no mind no mind no mind" that the interviewer put down to the calming drugs that had been administered to her in the S&SB clinic. But Old Jim read that instead as an activated subliminal command embedded by the Earwig that, by the interviewer ignoring it, intensified the anxiety and suggestibility of Helen HCP1. If he were to accept the premise of the interference of a foreign entity.

In the bathroom, Helen HCP1 "could not deny" a sensation of wetness on the bottom of her right foot but "almost made it back to bed before I gave myself over to the feeling that something terrible and disgusting may have occurred to me. Because of me?"

The surge of guilt Helen HCP1 reported appeared compulsive and debilitating, and this was still the emotion occupying her mind at a later debrief at one of Jack's covert sites. Old Jim noted that Jack (or Jackie?) had chosen not to bring her to Central, almost as if to put her in a partial quarantine.

Next, she walked back into the bathroom, wiped her foot, "although it felt as if I could not get it clean, as if what I felt had become part of the bottom of my foot." She remembered "thinking of soft water and how your palms feel and you cannot get it off, like you've become chalk, and how I must have just stepped in some soft water. Because it's a bathroom—water lives there."

*Water lives there.* Where had he heard that before? The little hairs on the back of his neck rose and he listened intent to the night outside his house, but heard nothing, and then wondered why he heard nothing at all. Except the words "water lives there."

Then, like a hiccup had resolved itself, there came the kinetic thrispy sound of crickets, the croak of a night heron, and some thrashing thing that almost sounded musical. He resumed reading by the calm yellow light of his desk lamp.

Something other than water lived in the apartments, too, because an hour after she returned to bed, Helen HCP1's right foot began to feel "wrong" and she woke to a voice and the voice was coming from her foot and the voice kept saying "Help me help me help me."

A liquid creeping sensation spread across the bottom of her foot, like feathers sticky with oil or molasses.

But she couldn't move, she dared not move. If she moved the

voice would come back and she did not want the voice to know she was still there. She did not want her foot to know she was still there.

And where was she to run to? And how was she to run away from this, at all? From her own body. Old Jim felt a twinge of sympathy.

Yet she shivered. Yet she flinched and the voice came again asking for help and she remembered nothing after the wave of overwhelming fear that roved from her toes to the top of her head, as if she were now covered with quivering oil-drenched sodden birds.

Except they weren't feathers—they were house centipedes.

Her neighbors found her unconscious in the hallway, in shock. She had "done herself damage" with the emergency fire ax, which she had retrieved by smashing her fist through the safety glass. Blood smeared the floor, mixing with pieces of broken glass.

Her severed right foot lay next to her.

She had scrawled "help me" on the floor.

Breath, air, the soul. Debunked, unscientific, that link. But the question became what lived in the body and in the mind, regardless. Could a thing debunked by science still impact a person—if they believed it and had believed it for a long time? Did a *fact*, not, in fact, matter if in a sense *matter* had a different authority depending on one's perception of the truth? Wasn't this, as much as any belief in the uncanny, the reason why Jack found the S&SB research useful? What the generator had wrought for Central. What the coelacanths deep in Central's basement dreamed of delivering up for mission ops.

Would conditioning first mean bringing into focus, or *making live* in the body, that which was not fact, such that it *became* fact for the individual in question? How swiftly could that occur, under the right conditions? Aware that this contradicted Henry Kage's own conclusion, which veered more toward the outright otherworldly.

A rut, a stone, a voice that burrowed into the ear. Old Jim mistrusted the rut, the stone. But if he believed in the Earwig, he could rationalize that a command phrase, not a spell, had caused her to lose control of her bicycle.

Words that had curled into the brain to live there, to murmur and suggest, to begin to eat away at free will, perhaps even at psychic powers. Secret suggestions and directives. The house centipede underfoot and the softness of the body in the alligator's mouth, seen by the teens in the police report, made him queasy. Something about the similarity of texture disturbed him, would not let him rest.

The next night on Failure Island, a disadvantage of the close quarters became evident. The psychic in the apartment directly above that of Helen HCP1 woke screaming in the night, convinced his leg was talking to him. The psychic directly below HCP1 dreamed of being suffocated by house centipedes.

They were found in the same hallway, having "begun to work on each other." The report further noted: "There is a surveillance gap of a similar length. What the two may have communicated to each other is not known."

Both victims received immediate treatment for mutilations, followed by hospitalization. None of the three had come back to work, had hampered the core of the S&SB's work for months.

A quick stab of worry now that it was too late: Should he not have read the report? Because it seemed like farce that the origin of the Earwig could be anyone other than who he sought. *The Rogue with a sonic boom of golden light exploding outward.* He felt no different, but made a note to check how reports like this one were disseminated to Jack and, presumably, to Central. As summary docs, or the primaries.

The remains of a house centipede had been found on the

bottom of Helen's detached foot, "wedged between the third and fourth toes," along with detached centipede legs on a white bath mat next to the shower.

How much did the inciting object matter? Was it like stepping on a mental land mine that had a moment before been innocent of such intent? And what if she hadn't stepped on a house centipede? What if she had woken in the morning and reported to her job in the submersible? Going down into the depths with her team? Would she have gone off like a bomb down there?

To distract himself from a shiver down his spine, he returned to Kage's analysis. Kage, who had risen high in the S&SB ranks, believed that "an uncanny force endemic to the area has either been harnessed to malign effect or simply seeps out like swamp gases from time to time," but this felt decoupled from the idea of "culprit."

He already disliked Kage for that. This idea of some unnatural phenomenon that could not be tracked back to a person. Even if it appeared that someone had conducted a kind of sabotage on a complex op without there seeming to be an end goal or reason. Except, there must be a reason, an end goal.

And did *Jack* believe the Rogue was part of an "incursion" meant to sabotage Central's experiments and in so doing create a disaster or did he think *something* on the Forgotten Coast had strategic or material value for a "foreign presence" infiltrating the area? And that pursuit of this something would lead to disaster?

In matters of nuance, or a pungent scent on the wind despite no sign of the fox, Jack might be vulnerable to using any old excuse to prop up a course of action. If already committed to the idea of a fox. Or if that was the easiest way to secure funding. Old Jim finished reading the report, which included a useless appendix from Kage about "historical precedents," and rewarded himself by turning to the alligator tracker.

The black box had a circular radar screen in the middle. It looked more like a small radio. The device smelled disconcertingly of motor oil. Why should it smell of motor oil? And what would he do if the tracker brought up a latitude and longitude, to indicate a hit? A shot in the dark, after twenty years.

The moment of truth. He flipped the switch, turned the tracker on . . . and watched the steady green blip-blip on the cascading red background of circles for a long time. If the device ever did find a signal, the circles would turn green, the dot red. The dot might even start to move across that primal screen, the return of the Cavalry. Or, at least, the Tyrant.

Disappointing despite the odds, but it felt in sync with how accustomed now he was to the blinking red light through the forest, from the biohazard facility next door. The quiet hum of some mechanism within the facility that kept all in order.

Ah well. He turned the tracker off, forced himself to abandon the office for the bedroom.

Because the main thing to mull as his eyelids grew heavy, more even than a psychic who cut off her own foot, was the fact that in going over the personnel files, he had found a familiar face. One he hadn't in his wildest dreams expected to see, but unmistakable. Older, perhaps, not wiser.

Maybe that was why he couldn't rid himself of a tingling in his right foot.

Because the Medic from Dead Town was part of the S&SB on Failure Island.


## 008: DISTANCE MESSAGING


**T**urn on the lights, sweep and mop the floor; clean bathroom faucets, countertops, and toilets; restock toilet paper, soap, paper towels; unplug the plugs from the taps, wipe clean with a fresh towel.

Destroy the fuzziness in his head by filling the ice well with three buckets of ice. Stanch the dreams spilling out of him by cutting garnish to fill the garnish trays (limes into wedges, lemons into half slices, cucumbers into slices). Escape the weight outside his office window by taking inventory of cups, straws, jiggers.

A waning late-summer morning at the Village Bar, when the coolness of fall had begun to creep into the air and the sun lay not quite so heavy over everything.

Old Jim had decided that the Village Bar had a simple but pleasing flow to it: counter to the left, office on the right. The main space had dark wooden tables in front of a music stage. The left-hand corner held a love seat, with a shelf of old books on the wall. He felt comfortable in that space, once he shook off the night's dreams, with no urge to drink. Hadn't he almost confided his sins to bartenders in many far-flung lands? Hadn't so many bars seemed the same—comfort and curse— as the coordinates that let him forget the intensity of what he had come to do and then the place he assembled himself after a mission, sometimes with Jack sullen or cracking jokes beside him.

After he was done opening, Old Jim sat down at the piano, which he'd placed to the right of the stage, facing the door. He was continuing to work on his rendering of *Winter Journey*. Old Jim didn't know why his affection for it had grown in relation to the Forgotten Coast. Maybe something in the contract of climate and mood, snow for sun, cold for heat.

The words he sang in a foreign language had already been mistaken by the regulars for some sort of rousing drinking song. But the lyrics were stranger than that, the emotion not really jaunty: *"Happily I'll go forth / through wind and rain again! / If no god is here on earth / we will be the gods among men."*

Playing was cathartic. Making the upright piano do what he wanted for these compositions was difficult, it required total concentration. The piano took the edge off a kind of febrile wrongness in his head. Contemplating wryly that there were simple, human things the years took from you. His hands had a bit of a tremor sometimes now, but steadied on the heavy piano keys. These damaged hands, healing well. But what didn't hurt in time?

*Self-proclaimed Gods are the worst of all, but usually they're easier to kill.* Maybe Jack had said that to Old Jim, but more probably Old Jim had said it to Jack, in that space between foolishness and wisdom at a bar after several drinks. So many years ago, when anything seemed possible.

All he knew was: The piss smell in the toilets had been fixed, forever, and everyone but Man Boy Slim seemed grateful.


When Cass walked through the door a few minutes later, Old Jim almost said, "Get out," even though he'd called the meeting. The bar had felt like a neutral site and he had decided to surrender. Which just meant this time had to be different.

He'd almost mistaken the dark gray of her clothing for another fisherman from a boat, come in for a break. But instead it was the severity of her business suit, which had the look of armor and her Joan of Arc on the battlefield or something.

Her cover for the briefings, as his daughter, was as a real estate agent come to the Forgotten Coast to recuperate from an undisclosed illness and to help her good old dad with some holdings on Failure Island. Undisclosed illness was always good, and made the locals do half the work of beginning to like her.

A power suit for a Realtor disguise. But did power and lineage work that way around here? You might look like a derelict and turn out to own a thousand acres. And yet, those boots at the end of the trousers, streamlined yet still anomalous.

"Hi, Dad, I've got that Failure Island property information," she said, patting her satchel.

She gave him a respectful distance by remaining at the bar, so he extricated himself from the piano bench and managed a smile. A little stab of regret: That any closeness shared the first time they'd met, no matter how fraught, had receded— would keep receding. Unless they managed to find a middle ground.

"Oh great, thanks for coming by."

"No problem, sorry it took so long," Cass said, as they continued their stilted conversation.

While Sally looked on with interest, but not too much interest. Old Jim gathered Sally had met Cass before. She'd had a couple of months alone on the coast to set that framework, sell the idea of dear old dad's arrival, too.

"Great. Let's go look it over somewhere quiet." Brushed by her, headed into the office, which unfortunately was still a dump.

The office smelled of sour beer, had some kegs in the corner next to a desk with chairs, and a door leading out to the supply room and then out back. The ceiling always felt low to him, like he should be bending down. He pulled the string that turned on the bare-bulb lighting.

"Take a seat."

Pointless, for there was no seat to be taken until he finished taking the piles of invoices off the chair.

"Is that for me?" she asked, unable to keep the mischief from her voice.

"What?" He looked over at her, standing there in her armor.

"That thing. The grapefruit." Pointing at the huge pomelo.

Ah, crap. He'd forgotten he'd put it there, next to the blotter.

"Pomelo," he said. "And, no, it's for me."

"Sure," she said, sitting down with a grin.

He ignored her, put the beast of a fruit awkwardly on a shelf to the side, because he didn't want to start out this way. Again.

Neither did Cass, apparently, because she got right down to business.

She tossed an evidence bag onto the desk from her satchel.

It had a belt buckle in it, absurdly.

Provocation or important? He held the buckle through the plastic. It had a weight to it, made of brass, or a genuine equivalent, with the words "Champion Angler" on it and "Hedley Regional Finals" underneath, smaller. Nothing odd about that. Nothing inscribed on the other side. Just looked more like a cattle rancher's buckle, that's all.

"Fine craftsmanship," he said, contemplating the buckle.

"An Object of Interest," Cass said. "As opposed to something that is Foreign Entity Related. For S&SB purposes. For what could be related to a 'foreign entity' and what's just the usual weirdness around here. Out in the field, for anything we can't bring to the lab, we use TOT, Trash or Treasure, as a graffiti tag to mark anything interesting for later analysis. So, if you see that, you know. Infantile, but enigmatic to the locals."

Combing through the trash and beaches for evidence of mischief, sorting through it on conveyor belts back at Failure Island. Is this a turd or a piece of gold? Dumpster diving for psychic retrieval. OOI, FER, TOT. It made a rough sort of sense, although he hated acronyms, decided not to use these, either.

"So, how'd you come by the buckle?"

"I found it in the parking lot of the convenience store near my apartment."

"And?"

"First, what do you know about your predecessor?"

She'd said "predecessor" like it was someone undead buried in a coffin in a castle somewhere.

"Jackie told me he died a horrible death. The files back at Central just said 'heart attack.'"

The incident had happened more than a year ago, and so predated the decision to bring them both into the fold. While the rest of the Ouija Hicks likely had been told his predecessor had been recommissioned, along with the body-bagged psychics. Their own deaths that they hadn't seen coming.

"One of the Brigade's submersibles imploded, for no good reason," Cass said. "The House Centipede Incident felt like more of the same."

"The man was obsessed with debris that washes up on the shore. Why?"

"I don't know. The whole submersibles program redirected its attention to searching for sea trenches and other anomalies in the months before he died. So, I guess he was interested in the shallows and the depths."

"Did his last dive have a particular purpose?"

"He was with two Central-trained séance personnel on a distance messaging attempt. He never did field inspections with Brigade members who weren't Central. He'd begun to get paranoid about amateurs."

"By 'séance personnel,' you mean psychics?"

"Yes, psychics. Clairvoyants. Telepaths. I forget all the categories."

"By distance messaging, you mean remote communication between minds?"

"Yes, although it can take various forms or be about two or more psychics connecting to 'solve' some problem, let's say."

"In one of those three-person sunken bathtubs? Those glorified septic tanks."

"Yeah, those," she said. "The Brigade loves them, can't get enough of them. Two more on order."

From the distance messaging reports, he'd gleaned what he thought might be traces of the Rogue, or was that nonsense? This trace of a man with his eyes too wide open: *"There is a crevice in the black sea with a light pouring out. The stranger lives there, peering up at us. Something lives with him close, something beyond understanding. When his eyes open, so too do the eyes of others."*

What he'd been struggling with was . . . if he believed in psychics who might perceive the Rogue, did that mean he also believed in the *Rogue's* ability to trace that link back? To yank on it like it was a physical rope binding psychic to Rogue? It felt like a mystical question, not an analytical one.

"Do you believe in any of this?" he asked, because he sincerely wanted to know.

"Does it matter? What I thought I believed about a lot of things hasn't helped me here. Has it helped you?" She'd fixed him with one of those seemingly impassive looks he'd come to think of as dangerous.

"No," he admitted. "No, it hasn't." Although the truth was, he didn't know what he believed anymore, which might be the problem.

"The Brigade also does more conventional research on sensory deprivation," Cass said. "And the data is sent to other Central projects. The Forgotten Coast also seems unusually rich in reported 'psychic' phenomena."

The S&SB had a fascination with "psychic dead spots and hot spots" on the Forgotten Coast. Which also fascinated the part of Central that seemed to believe warring psychics were the future of combat. Sometimes Old Jim felt they treated the "foreign entity" like unexploded ordnance or a thing currently inert, like a sleeper cell, that ultimately, under controlled conditions, must either be made to blow up or in other ways *react*. If they were to understand it or learn from it, "profit or prophet" from it, as Jack liked to say.

"Tell me more about the buckle." Although he thought he could guess, some of it.

"The buckle belonged to your predecessor. He wore it all the time, but it wasn't on him in the submersible for some reason. Instead, it was propped up on the concrete block at the head of my parking space at the convenience store. Someone put it there while I was inside buying a gallon of milk. Do you want to guess when I found it?"

"When?" He didn't want to guess.

"The week you came to the Forgotten Coast."

"That sounds like a message. Any guesses about who?"

"The locals are much more sophisticated than Central gives them credit for. They definitely aren't as clueless as Jackie seems to think. But I can't figure out how anyone from outside the S&SB could get hold of it."

"What about internal? Anyone disgruntled?"

"Not really, no, but . . ." The hesitation came with a frown, like Cass wanted to handle her own business.

"But what?"

"I've been having some trouble with Henry Kage."

"Kage wrote the House Centipede report."

"Yeah. He and his half sister, Suzanne, came on board a few months before the sub incident. And since then they've, well, I guess you could say they've taken control of part of the operation. The more . . . radical . . . psychics take their cue from Henry, especially. They don't disobey me, but they also do their own thing."

"Is that why you don't live on Failure Island?" He'd noticed she'd ignored Central's place for her on the island and lived in an apartment just six miles from his house.

"One of the reasons I'm glad I don't," Cass said.

That alarmed him. He'd been in situations as the latecomer to a power vacuum, and sometimes an operation would've already become feudal, disguised by mounds of rational-sounding paperwork.

"Who brought them into the operation?"

"Jack. I don't know if Jackie likes them very much."

"Are they Central agents?"

"No, they're civilians, with a history of investigating uncanny phenomena. But Henry has a history of violence."

"What kind of violence?"

"As a teenager, he tried to burn down a gardener's shed, with the gardener in it. Tortured his pet hamster by cutting out its eyes and replacing them with pebbles. Claimed it was the collateral damage from a séance."

From the semi-disgusted look on Cass's face, she felt about the same relaying this information as he felt receiving it. Violence was simple because it could be expressed as "subject-verb-object," but Henry felt more complex than that.

"Do they know about Jack, about Central?"

"Not to my knowledge. They just think I'm a new, unnecessary management level added by someone higher up in the Brigade."

Old Jim considered that a moment. While he also considered that Jack had been expecting him not only to step into a dead man's shoes, but to head up an operation compromised by Jack's obsession with the uncanny, now saddled with his baggage and the relative inexperience of a lieutenant who felt responsible for the deaths of her comrades on her last mission.

For a moment, he felt like he was down there with the dead man, without any wall between him and the water.

*"Why must I stray from the beaten path . . . / looking for the hidden track."*

"What if Henry did put the belt buckle there? What does it mean?" he asked her. Because it still didn't feel like a Rogue-ish thing, and he wondered if half his job would be like Cass's: separating strange wheat from very ordinary chaff.

"Definitely a threat, then, driven by ego," she said. "He was sending the message that he knew you had arrived and telling both of us who's really in charge."

He didn't insult her by pointing out that this would also mean Henry had been following her and knew her routine.

"I hope you use more than the usual security protocols," he said. What if she had a secret minder, too? "Do you feel safe?"

She'd been somewhere else for a moment, but the question brought her back, and she gave him a curious sideways glance.

"I do feel safe, thanks for asking," she said. "I trust no one, and only you and Jackie know where I live."

He looked at his watch, rose from the chair. A contractor would be there in just a few minutes. Certain key obligations to maintain his cover.

"I have to finalize the remodel plans. Get me the file on Henry Kage, if you don't mind. I also want to talk to David Sheers, from S&SB staff, as soon as possible." The Medic. "Can you set that up?"

"Sure. Sheers is one of my main contacts, especially for status reports on morale. He's a loyalist, so a laugh riot. A real patriot."

He could tell she was surprised at the request, but he liked that she didn't ask him why. He also liked that the Medic made her sarcastic.

As he walked with her to the front door, Old Jim felt an urgent need to apologize for last time they'd met. To tell her that he understood she was caught between Jackie and him, between him and Jack. That theirs might be a strange and uneven fellowship, because the mission itself was strange. Because they were both messed up, too, but that was all right.

Instead, he just said, "There was no safe under the floorboards, but there is now."

Let her think about that for a while.

But he could tell from the grin spreading across her face that he'd said the right thing.

## 009: PUNKS IN THE GASLIGHT

The original batch of Ouija Hicks had been UFO conspirators in another life, or counterculture freaks looking for a new fix that wouldn't get them arrested so easily. To this motley crew at the S&SB, many now long in the tooth, Jack had added a stabilizing layer of what Old Jim was tempted to call "the professional psychic class." A series of recruits who didn't come to the organization by chance but by dint of careening careers and the whims of "high command," as he and Jack had joked and toked before Jack had become part of that high command and given up pot.

Old Jim didn't mind the old-timers because they meant well, and most likely the latest direction of the Brigade bewildered them. The overemphasis on submersibles. The sudden hint of danger, the spike in malaise and depression that hinted at the effects of a more subtle application of an Earwig. The way members were there one day, then gone, the change in hierarchy that meant the decision-making was more top-down.

But Henry and Suzanne had a totally different kind of profile. What the Brigade psychics would've called "a bad vibe." Along with an agenda Old Jim didn't think quite synched with Central. Suzanne was five years younger, from another mother, and how did that work? What fucked up lineage meant your half sister joined you, inseparable, in what amounted to a cult? What kind of family? "*A phantom's flaming breath / pulled me from my route: / it led me to rocky depths / with no hope of getting out.*"

Henry and Suzanne sounded like names from a crime-spree news article. That they looked as if they had stepped out of some fascist youth summer camp into their own future gave him one kind of clue. The formal aristocracy of Henry's overbearing mother and father gave him another.

Old money and older appetites, German Hungarian by way of upstate New York, mansion by the river. Henry had been part of the Pickeling Society long before the Brigade, an organization with a nihilistic streak that uplifted and tried to make respectable fringe psychics and other quacks.

Henry had a juvenile record, sealed, that, as Cass had indicated, included torturing a hamster and setting fire to the gardener's shed on his family's property—when he believed the gardener to be inside. Henry's father had "sent him abroad" after that, in the grand tradition of rich people across the centuries. Frankly, Old Jim was surprised Central hadn't tried to recruit him at that point. Disaffected, with a violent streak that could be channeled into a useful aggression.

"Abroad" hadn't helped Henry much, except for picking up an accent that appeared to be affectation, and drinking absinthe out of a half of a human skull, which he boasted about in a privately published pamphlet account of his experiences.

As an adult, Henry had managed to avoid charges on gouging a man's eye out in a bar, sustaining an injury of his own that slanted a shoulder, made his head look not put on quite right. Clearly some kind of payoff from Henry's father, who managed to combine his old money with liquidating material assets from companies he bought out of bankruptcy.

Henry claimed to have had several encounters with "occult influences," usually "in abandoned buildings, alleys," and similarly cheery places. Over time, up north, associated with various fringe groups Central kept tabs on, Henry had gained a reputation for so-called bunking or debunking of a series of "haunted light stations" around the Great Lakes.

He had found "unique if controversial ways to draw specters out of refracted glass" and make them manifest, even speak, while also gaining a reputation as being picky and high-strung. He debunked as much as he bunked. He could also become vicious toward people who scoffed at his "powers." He'd careened from organization to organization in part because he became paranoid and in part because, the subtext indicated, some initial magnetism ceded to dislike, which meant, in the long term, people didn't trust his ideas. Which only made him more paranoid about authority, which also drove him to become ever more knowledgeable about the occult. Not so much a vicious cycle as somewhat pathetic.

At this point in his "career," Jack, inexplicably, had discovered "the once and future magician asshole" (as one of Henry's colleagues described him) languishing in the Midwest and deemed him worthy of the Forgotten Coast op, joining the Brigade "raw," as they put it, which meant Henry and Suzanne had no Central training and, in theory, no knowledge of Central's role in the Brigade. They would need to be managed and controlled from afar, so to speak, through the Brigade hierarchy—which looked like the Medic's tutelage. Even as it was clear Jack wanted Henry to believe he had agency and power in the Brigade.

Old Jim's first, uncharitable thought: Jack was sabotaging the project for some reason. Which gave way to the grudging idea that Jack might honestly believe the Brigade needed an injection of urgency.

Had the rationale been to counter the Rogue with a rogue of Jack's own in the person of Henry?

As for Suzanne, the file contained next to nothing about her. Suzanne had no record of having lived a life at all, except for the basics, and hadn't even gone to high school, let alone college. Suzanne had existed in her father's mansion for many years, like the personification of a Gothic novel, playing pretend scientist with mail-order kits before joining the Brigade as an attachment to Henry.

But she seemed to be the one who made Henry look presentable. Whenever Henry had an analysis, it looked to be Suzanne who made it conform to Brigade format and protocols. Liminal spaces fascinated Henry, especially in the context of the lighthouse, and expressed themselves in stunningly dry and sometimes incomprehensible reports that had been "dictated to Suzanne," which reflected poorly on her editorial skills.

Sometimes, Old Jim thought, she made his batshit theories appear . . . semi-reasonable.

"If you can find the liminal space, neither day nor night, in the threshold, you can receive the dreams or thoughts of others." Henry conveyed this idea in the context of the lighthouse lens, and there being a place, theoretically, "neither here nor there."

Old Jim wondered if he was wrong about the old hands, if they might in fact thrill to hear some of the bullshit issuing forth from Henry's psycho mouth.

"If you could control the effect, if you could inhabit whatever clambered out, that would be spectacular. That would change the world."

Grandiose, but also he didn't much care for the idea of "clambering" and the lighthouse beacon.

Distance messaging. Panic listening. Authoritarian sound. Projection across time and space. Some of Henry's ideas evoked the Rogue to Old Jim. One of them involved "dream bombs" like a "destroyer searching for a submarine below." That this delivery at distance could kill a person remotely, or rewire their personality or beliefs. The psychics seeking strange minds, strange thoughts from the bottom of the sea constrained the Rogue. That he could not leave a zone without being noticed by psychics.

Perhaps the Rogue was trying to take out the submersibles for some reason, not the personnel, and that was just collateral damage. Which led Old Jim back to what might just be another kind of witchcraft. That the Rogue, or someone, was tapping into Central training and protocols. And, again, how was that possible unless they'd interrogated someone from Central or were *from* Central?

A whiff of sorcery, too, in not wanting to evoke Henry too directly, even confined to his office. Only ever "H" in his notes, which he assumed Jack spied on by having a vampire fly in a window at night and hover long enough for the old click-click before leaving again.

Late in the day, he drove to Bleakersville, trying to put the pebbles in a dead hamster's eyes out of his head, but also wanting to *do* something, make some progress he should've achieved by now but hadn't.

He was back in Bleakersville for some of Jack's old-school bullshit, the spy craft of past generations that said loitering half in disguise at a dirty pay phone outside the Starlight Lounge was better than using a dedicated, secure landline in the luxury of his own home. The reason was clear—to discourage Old Jim from contacting him and yet Jack still couldn't quite give up the back channel.

In part, he found it worth the trip for a drive others found boring: thick forest and half-dry swamp, on bridges and perilous curving two-lane roads, most of them dirt. Plus, Bleakersville had the best Piggly Wiggly within reach.

He put in his dime and when the gruff, ultramasculine voice answered, said, "Town and country," with the annoying affirmation of "Living the life, Captain."

Then he waited while the receiver burbled and burped—there, at the far end of the parking lot, as if when putting in the phone, they'd asked the question, "Where can we put it where it's easiest to get mugged at night?" Looking back from the shade into the rusty sunlight of the parking lot, Old Jim already sweating and low on patience.

Then Jack was on the line saying hello and Old Jim, slipping into a well-worn familiarity, said, "You ever going to visit us in the flesh, you think? There's been great weather here. Spectacular. You might like the fishing."

"Sure, Jim, we could go out in a boat. Maybe a rowboat. That'd be nice, two old buddies. But would we both come back?"

"If you give me what I ask for, sure."

Jack laughed. "Well, I don't go out in the field much anymore. Don't need to—I put in my time."

"And I didn't?"

"Yes, you did. But you are the field, Jim. You know that. Plus, a salvage project. Be thankful you're in the field, rather than *in* a field somewhere. So, you settling in? Cass working out? Why the fuck am I getting this phone call?"

He didn't think he could address the question of Cass without anger, so he stuck to what was on his list, first item of which was Henry.

"Settling in fine. Catching up on the files. Getting to know the personnel. You've got some live ones, for sure. Like . . . Henry Kage. He's interesting. How'd you find someone like that?"

A pause. A definable pause, before a reply.

"Oh, you know, here and there. You get a sense for where to look."

"Why use him?"

"Say, Jim, why don't we stop dicking around and get down to brass tacks: Why me, not Jackie, for whatever this is?"

Typical, and Old Jim had expected the question.

"The ask is of Central and not necessarily operational. But I think it pertains."

"So spit it out. Spit it out." Somehow the tone of that made Old Jim *not* want to spit it out.

Item 2: Those who had viewed the camera footage.

"The exiled team leaders of the Dead Town expedition. I need to talk to them. Reinterview them." Maybe it would reassure him to know they were still alive, if he considered himself as a Team Leader 3.

"Out of the question," Jack growled.

"Why not? They're valuable. Central hung on to them for a reason, right?"

"Sure, that I can tell you. Insurance. Monitoring. Someone back in the day thought that if anything about them or their situation . . . changed . . . then it might be like an alarm going off. Because of their contact with the cameras."

"I could submit a list of questions." To wash up on their respective beaches, dot matrix paper shoved into glass bottles.

Jack cursed incomprehensibly, said, "Do you have something serious to ask for? Something I can actually do?"

Old Jim considered that. He had lost the thread for a moment—because he needed better sleep. Needed to stop having a war of dreams in his head, with a thick rustling through the reeds as prologue that he couldn't be sure was in the dream or outside the window.

Item 3: Reexamining the biologist expedition.

"I want to see everything from the Dead Town Disaster."

Jack went quiet, and Old Jim knew he was trying not to blow his top.

"It . . . it wasn't a fucking *disaster*. Fuck no. We learned from the yurts, the meadow, the stranger. You have no idea how much we learned. You ever see the linguistics report on the journals? That alone . . ."

Jack hadn't given him the linguistics report, likely on purpose.

"I'll call the Dead Town experiment whatever you want if

you can get me everything from the expedition. I can come to Central to—"

"No. Stay there. Wait a second. Gotta put you on hold."

The click followed by the hold sounds. Not music. No, it sounded a little like a baby crying, and a snarl on the line he hoped was feedback, or that baby was in trouble. Plus, a hum or mumble of words in the background.

A silence in which Old Jim reflected on Jack. Maybe there wasn't much left of Jack to appeal to. Maybe Jack had started too young and that's the legacy he had left Jackie. Now, aged prematurely, maybe his mind held only the fast-approaching hunger of an aging predator. That kind of hunger could kill you as fast as anything coming downriver faster and more determined than it should've been, trapped in a twenty-year-old harness.

Remembered Jack telling him about some comic strip he liked—two crows with hands, in trench coats, who worked for rival espionage agencies. Immortal, but they kept blowing each other up when, as Jack put it, "they could just explain that explosives are funny and spy agencies do stupid things."

Somewhere in that delayed response, too, he decided to share all of the files on the Dead Town Disaster with Cass. He wasn't quite sure why.

Old Jim wasn't sure how much time had passed until he heard a voice again.

"Okay, Jim," Jack said, with a sound like a foot had picked up the phone, not a hand, "we'll send you everything. Might take a few days. Then someone will get back to you with the details."

"Can that include the linguistics reports and any cameras retrieved from the yurts?"

"There aren't any cameras. The linguistics reports are irrelevant to your mission. I can get you everything else."

"Are you sure that—"

"What about 'everything else' don't you understand?" Jack asked.

"Fair enough."

Jack's intensity, perhaps even a hint of desperation, battered Old Jim over the phone: "And make some damn progress on the Rogue. Apply fucking pressure. Do what you fucking have to. You're running out of time."

Maybe the Brutes had begun to fray Jack's nerves. Maybe Jack was losing it and all he could do was babble about psychics and distance messaging and the rest of Central had had their fill. Hard to adjust your pace to a ticking clock when you didn't know the end date.

The drive back to his house felt long and tedious after that, and lonely as hell. Tossing his keys on the kitchen table, he ignored the impulse to seek a drink somewhere, and went out onto the deck.

The last of the season's fireflies in the dusk, and a lone bird plucking them from the air, snuffing out that tiny light, but what manner of bird, Old Jim could not tell. Also on the deck was a package, delivered by private courier.

Good. The items he'd smuggled out of Central and mailed to himself had finally arrived.

The Mudder's journal.

A little gun.

A bigger gun.

## 010: A PHANTOM'S FLAMING BREATH

The light from the lighthouse that swept out nightly in a thick blade also bore down on Old Jim—exacted a pressure on the far wall of the house as he imagined it, which was also a pressure on the brain from afar, as if Henry were working dark magicks from the top, or it was weighted by an unseen pendulum, achieving a terrible velocity, saying, somehow, direct to him, "I see you, I see all of you, even when you try to hide in the shadows."

His dream of vessel, candle, flame, guttered against that light, for a time, became distant, like it was someone else's dream. The music of *Winter Journey* welled up in him constantly in those moments between rest and wakefulness, but the words were not always the same. The beam of the lighthouse a green weight against the side of his face as he woke and woke and woke . . . even though how could that be true?

Maybe it was just moonlight, transformed, and in shining out quieted the rest, or made the dreams retreat, but Old Jim allied it to Jack's urgency. How he needed a result, even though he couldn't see through the murk yet.

So, a couple of days after going to Bleakersville, Old Jim came to the Village Bar with purpose: a need to interrogate Man Boy Slim about the past. Because who else with secrets could he make feel like they were twisting in the wind? While over on Failure Island Cass concentrated on enforcing "a diminished silhouette" that included canceling shore leave for the psychics, limiting the scope of submersible operations, and making S&SB conform to a two-by-two rule that even on the island turned them into the visual language of missionaries going door to door.

This felt like damage control, not progress, and worse, once he got to the Village Bar he became distracted by an emergency, one calibrated to the more mundane threats on the Forgotten Coast. A local kid, Gloria, had gotten a large fishhook through her foot. He'd seen her on the road on his way home a few times, so he knew she was an adventurer. Hadn't seemed afraid of anything.

To honor that, he poured whiskey, amber and ancient, onto her sunburnt foot after getting the fishhook out and stitching up the jagged part of the wound, right there on the counter. She was a brave kid, wincing but not crying, as he tried to finish as fast as possible.

Sally told him Gloria would poke her head in at least once a week and shout, "Am I old enough yet?" And get a resounding "No—go away" from the patrons. Given she was only nine or ten. A local legend, already.

"She's not a quilt," Man Boy Slim said, critiquing his stitches. "She's not Frankenstein's monster. She's not—"

"Not what?" Old Jim snapped, and Man Boy Slim opened his mouth, thought better of whatever he wanted to say, and took up a position far down the bar. He'd already put up with Man Boy Slim being reluctant to help, even to call Gloria's mom, as if anything Old Jim asked was suspect.

In taking the measure of Man Boy Slim in the flesh it had been as if noting the appearance of some minor celebrity or saint many thought long since turned into reliquary or the dust of a disappointing career arc. The man had a rangy glory, now in his fifties with a long unkempt gray beard and mostly the quality of his cheekbones and tricky green-blue eyes to demonstrate he might be younger than his age. That didn't mean his personality had aged gracefully, as well.

Man Boy Slim had also been by far the most skeptical regular. An edge there, as if Old Jim both fascinated and frightened him. A losing battle anyway: Old Jim had already wooed most of the rest with free drinks, an extended happy hour, and giving the house band, Monkey's Elbow, more gigs.

Old Jim bandaged the wound and got Gloria a soft drink and some ice cream after he finished. Then he talked to her awhile about nothing in particular, because she seemed to need it—and suddenly he was exhausted and he didn't want to think about secret ops or psychics.

He asked her to tell him about Monkey's Elbow, given they had a gig coming up, and he was curious just how obscure they were.

"They call themselves Monkey's Elbow because the monkey's paw is cursed, that's what I hear. So if it's just the elbow, they're cursed enough to make songs, but not so cursed they die over it."

He decided not to say something stupid in reply, but just let her ramble. She mentioned a "Commander Thistle," which sounded like a lot, but was just a thing the locals knew. The name Monkey's Elbow gave to any local who volunteered to sub in for their lead singer around this time of year. Some kind of in-joke about the purple thistles that popped up everywhere. One gig only.

"You did a good stitching job," Gloria said, pivoting abruptly. "Like you have medical training. Like my mom."

"Just good with a needle," Old Jim said.

Gloria considered that while Old Jim thought how ridiculous it would be if a kid blew his cover.

"You should reuse the fishhook," she said. "It's bad luck if you throw it away after it got me."

Old Jim nodded sagely at that, although the fishhook would go in the trash.

Then Gloria's mom, Trudi, burst through the door to collect her, a little concerned until she'd checked his work, and then gave him a quick nod, before whisking her off for some real medical care.

By then he felt confused, found it hard to focus on Man Boy Slim. Which puzzled him, until he figured it out.

For a moment there, he'd wanted to believe that maybe he had been born on the Forgotten Coast. That maybe he really belonged here.


Maybe some of the locals didn't really fit in, either, though. Because digging around a little deeper in some of the ancillary files, Old Jim discovered that Drunk Boat had not just "died"—he had been found torn to pieces on his motorboat, a couple of years after the Dead Town Disaster.

The boat, rocking indolent in an inlet, had been discovered at least a week postmortem, the paraphernalia around him indicative of alligator poaching, but no sign of who or what might've taken offense at him, or that act. More than one Village Bar regular might've remarked how easy it was to make a body disappear, so why hadn't they? Why leave him in full display, like a trophy himself? No one cared to speculate.

If he observed close, too, Old Jim could see what the files spelled out: Under the long pants, somewhere along the way one of Man Boy Slim's legs had become messed up below the knee, apparently due to a bad fall visiting relatives up north. A brace. Although some said it was an alligator attack and Man Boy Slim was too embarrassed at having been surprised by a creature so ubiquitous to the area. Old Jim didn't have a date on that, but he wondered if it coincided with Drunk Boat's demise.

Man Boy Slim had gone outside, so Old Jim went in search of him.

He found the man out front, near the door, smoking a cigarette, where the wind didn't mess with the lighter. No one was around.

Old Jim nodded to him, asked, "You got another cig?"

Man Boy Slim hesitated, then offered him one.

Old Jim lit and took a drag. They smoked in silence for a while, then Old Jim asked, "Do you know who I am?"

Man Boy Slim shrugged. "Owner of the bar . . . I guess."

"You don't sound convinced," Old Jim said, thinking of the scary film Man Boy Slim had talked about seeing with Drunk Boat, twenty years ago.

Man Boy Slim took a drag of his cigarette, smoke spiraling from his nose like a sad-looking dragon. The bags under his eyes, in the sunlight, were practically caves.

"Yeah, well, it's just the tells, you see. That give you away."

"The tells. Do tell, Man Boy."

"You've got all these tells. But the biggest is, you ask questions not like you used to live here but like you're writing a book about the Forgotten Coast. And you act like you know me, Jim.

Why is that, pray tell? *And* you act like you knew poor dead Drunk Boat. What's that about, Old Jim?"

"You found a rabbit with a camera around its neck, didn't you," Old Jim said. "Way back when, I mean."

Man Boy Slim's jaw opened and shut, opened again, like he was a mullet out of water, gasping for breath. While a vibration built in Old Jim he couldn't deny. An itch for the old ways, for the directness of that. Did Man Boy Slim sense the danger yet?

"Who the fuck *are* you? Who sent you?" A hint of menace in his voice, to go with the flicker of fear, as if he still didn't quite understand the danger.

"What did you do with the camera? Other than view the footage? You shared it with your girlfriend, didn't you? With Samantha?" The Mudder.

"Who?"

The way of all questioning. The bad acting. The faux innocence betrayed by the widening of the eyes and the fatal inability to look directly at the questioner.

"Don't fuck with me," Old Jim said. "You don't want to fuck with me." He just wanted to punish someone for still being in the dark. He wanted to remember what being in control felt like.

Man Boy Slim dropped his cigarette, rubbed out the burning end with his shoe. "I'm going back inside. I don't have to answer squat."

Old Jim pushed him into the wall. Hard. Then closed the distance, punched Man Boy Slim in the gut, so he slid down the wall onto his ass, clutching his stomach.

"Don't get up and don't make me do that again," Old Jim said, squatting in front of him. "Answer my questions unless you want more of that."

Still no one around, Man Boy Slim slumped there, arms around his knees, Old Jim rising to loom over him.

"Start talking or I start kicking."

"She wasn't my girlfriend." Man Boy Slim said it quiet, sad, like it was something Drunk Boat had teased him about back in the day. Like Old Jim had knocked loose the memory, so it had decanted fresh.

"Actually, I don't care what she was to you. The point is—you got a camera and both you and Samantha viewed the video on it. Did Drunk Boat see it?"

The look on Man Boy Slim's face was enough.

"Let me guess—what you saw unnerved you, so you had your friend watch it, too."

Man Boy Slim miserable, but Old Jim recognized the usual relief, too, as if he wanted to confess.

"It changed. Each time it changed."

So, there it was, out in the open, Man Boy Slim flushed like a quail. But that wasn't enough. He needed more of a push.

"You asked who I am. I'm the guy who, if you don't tell me what I need to know, you'll be brought to a black site and the experts will take you apart looking for answers. Maybe they'll never let you out of there, or maybe they'll exile you to some godforsaken island and you'll never see the Forgotten Coast again."

Conjuring up a persona more like Jack, because once Old Jim had kind of been Jack.

The terror in Man Boy Slim's eyes—he'd imagined something like this already, and not just as one of the Forgotten Coast's paranoid conspiracy theory wet dreams.

The way he started talking again, but in a different register, subdued, beaten.

"The first time, Samantha watched it. I couldn't get the camera to work, but she could. I was bivouacked out in a tent in the swamp. She used to come visit and sometimes we'd fish in my rowboat. Then I watched it, then I had Drunk Boat watch it. Sam didn't see much, or she wouldn't talk about it. She said . . . she said—"

"She said what?"

"That it made her feel bad. It made her feel bad in the way you feel when you think something terrible is going to happen and you can't do anything about it."

"I don't like that answer. Try again."

The sunken-in aspect of Man Boy Slim's gaze began to turn the fear back onto Old Jim.

"She said it showed everybody disappeared, gone."

"You mean dead? It showed the biologists she was with dead?"

He shook his head, slow, like he still didn't understand it himself. "No, it showed the coast, like overhead, and there . . . there was just *no one here*."

"Were there any other details you can remember?"

"It wasn't like a nuclear disaster or anything like that. It was more like everyone going about their business one day and . . . just *not there* the next. How is that possible? How would that be possible?"

Did the chill live in Old Jim's body or the wind off the sea? Jack's "prophecy," brought to him by illegitimate sources, precogs and bullshit artists that the rest of Central didn't believe in.

"And when you viewed it, what did you see?"

A tic pulsed under Man Boy Slim's left eye, like something small inside the skin was trying to get out.

"I saw an army fighting a strange light between two mountains," Man Boy Slim said.

The shock of that, the shudder bang in Old Jim's ears. What if the biologists had gotten the dream of the green light *from the cameras*.

"And what did you let Drunk Boat see? That killed him?"

A guess, meant, even in denial, to keep Man Boy Slim on his back foot, like another punch to the gut. And it hit the target, and in Man Boy Slim's confused, anguished expression Old Jim could see that what came next, he'd held on to for a long time. The exhalation of breath, the way the words came tumbling out.

"He saw his own death. He saw himself in some sort of ec-static vision, like, Blakean as he put it, being torn apart by the Tyrant. He saw every detail of that, and I could have spared him ever seeing that. I could have never shown him the camera, never caught that first rabbit. Never gone anywhere near Dead Town."

Man Boy Slim had caught the first rabbit. The timeline changed in Old Jim's head.

"Do you think you caused what happened? Because you didn't."

"I killed my best friend," he said, slumped against the wall. Which brought them to the boat.

"Is what happened on the rabbit camera video what hap-pened in real life? Were you there? And the Tyrant killed him and injured you?"

"I was there, and, no, the Tyrant didn't kill Drunk Boat. The camera did. *I* did."

"How did the camera kill Drunk Boat?"

"We tried to destroy it."

"Because you thought destroying the camera would save Drunk Boat?" A weird, animistic logic to that.

"No. The Tyrant was just a myth. The footage was just some really creepy bullshit. I thought. Like, doing a psychological number on us. No, I did it because Drunk Boat got real de-pressed. He was more oracular about it, he had too much imag-ination. And I wanted to stop dreaming of the green light. And I did think the camera might be somehow . . . dangerous. People might come looking for it."

"But it didn't go as planned," Old Jim prompted.

Man Boy Slim let out a sob. "No. It went wrong. I thought we could just dissolve it with this bleach mix I'd used for other things. But there was a reaction. It caused an explosion."

"And instead Drunk Boat died and you were injured."

Just to carry Man Boy Slim through the horror of that, to

leap from boat to land. Old Jim didn't care about the details, like how Man Boy Slim had tried to make out like his injury came later, which also delayed anyone finding the motorboat.

"Yeah. But the camera was still there, the nub of it. Damaged, so no one could see what it had shown us."

"And then you did what?"

"Hid it. Hid it far out in the swamp, because I couldn't just throw it in the water. That felt wrong."

Man Boy Slim had gone chalk white, appeared to have some trouble drawing breath.

Time to take his foot off the gas around the bend, so he could accelerate again.

"What about the piano out at Dead Town? What were they playing? What kind of music?"

"Well, you know it," Man Boy Slim said in a whisper, staring at the ground. "You just played it in the bar. One reason I wondered about you."

"What?" No, that had to be wrong. That was wrong.

"Yeah, that's the music they played. Old piano music. Just like that."

Old Jim laughed. "That's bullshit. Not just like that." Trying to throw the echo back on him, but now he felt like he was in retreat. He didn't want to hear Man Boy Slim talk anymore. He wanted to kick him, punch him.

"I'm just saying—"

"You keep that shit to yourself, okay? You just tell *Samantha* to contact me. On my phone at the house."

"I can't. I won't." But Man Boy Slim sounded like a beaten dog.

If before his face had looked like chalk, now he looked like a truck was about to slam into him.

Old Jim wanted to tell Man Boy Slim that some nights he took the Mudder's journal out of the safe and read it before sleeping. That he knew the Mudder better than anyone.

Instead, he said, "If she doesn't contact me, it will go very badly for her. And for you. Have her call my number at the house." He scribbled it on the back of a Village Bar business card and tossed it into the man's lap. "Keep your mouth shut. Show up at the bar like you usually do, and it'll be like it ever was. Otherwise . . ."

Old Jim left that threat hanging in the air and walked back into the bar.

What a man did next depended solely on the man, and Old Jim didn't quite have the measure of Man Boy Slim, even now.

*"Every stream will meet the sea, / and every sorrow have its day."*

Time would tell.

Later, Old Jim took a book from the shelf above the love seat, *The Monkey's Paw and Other Stories*, and went out back for a breath of fresh air, trying to get clear again. A canal lay beyond the gravel parking lot, with a raised berm flanked by tall reeds, and if you followed the path, you came upon the bridge—sturdy, wooden, with wire crosshatching beneath the railings so no one could duck under to leap into the marsh.

Birdsong and the persistent trickle of water. Minnows stippled the silted brown water beyond the railing, as iridescent in the sunlight as a living oil slick; the pattern of their intrusions on the water's surface felt soothing and the railing was pleasantly smooth and whorled.

What did it mean to see your own death?

He'd read part of "The Monkey's Paw" before Gloria had come in with the fishhook, curious about how it had influenced the band. Was Monkey's Elbow the result of "be careful what you wish for"? Even as he wondered if he'd violated the sacred rule with Man Boy Slim: any action might have an equal and opposite reaction. Energy moved from vessel to vessel. Status quo made sense at times, if you weren't sure yet that you could deal with the consequences.

Before, he'd had the usual frissons of appreciation for the timeless quality of the tale told—the truth in uncomfortable observations like "the way that middle age is wont to regard presumptuous youth" and the son's worry that wishes fulfilled would turn the father "into a mean, avaricious man, and we shall have to disown you."

But now he also read it, almost against his will, with a spy's eye for detail. Hidden motivations and hidden agendas. The opening game of chess struck him as a series of messages, put him in mind of how the resistance communicated under repressive regimes. And did they live so far out in the sticks so their elicit activities would fly under the radar?

The Sergeant Major with the monkey's paw felt both baldly symbolic and beyond the writer's intent. For a member of the military to basically use the family as subjects to test a weapon felt perhaps too on the nose, perhaps because he couldn't forget Jack's spiel about poison gas, and it lived ominous in his head, to think of the uncanny object as a *made creation*, a kind of experimental weapon developed by the military to use on a civilian population. The way the paw got people to self-destruct, like it was also a psyops threat.

Not only couldn't he get the idea of the paw as a weapon out of his head but echoes of the house centipede made him uneasy. "'It moved,' he cried, with a glance of disgust at the object as it lay on the floor." Seeing faces in the fire.

But then, when he came to the son joking that they'd find a big bag of cash on their bed "and something horrible squatting up on top of the wardrobe watching you" it put him in mind of the spy's life and the way Central operated. "He was caught in the machinery." A man was frantically trying to find the monkey's paw in the dark, like it was the opposite of a grenade. Even though it was a grenade.

When the nature of the couple's last wish became apparent, Old Jim stopped reading for a time, then finished and closed the book. Life was more complicated than that, life had to be, and his daughter wasn't dead. And he wasn't trying to bring her back to life, and yet still it struck him that way.

A terrible genius to the idea that people could wish themselves into poverty, injury, death, psychic damage. That, in fact, given the freedom . . . that's what they would tend to do. The way things almost always turned out. All you had to do is give them a window of opportunity. A tiny, shriveled paw. Wish upon a star. Wish upon a paw.

Disembodied voices. House centipedes. Psychics in subs thousands of feet below the surface, seeking a mystery. A name from the past uttered at the right time, to the right person, having such an effect. A terrifying vision told by a fool to another fool, about a camera that was not a camera.

And, in the end, as in the story, all that might be left besides horror and regret was a streetlight shining on a "quiet and deserted road."

# INTEGRATION

## 011: THE PATRIOT

The dreams of the biologists after the Rogue had been potent enough to result in catastrophic damage. But the Medic had been subject to none of that psychic damage in the aftermath of the Rogue, because the Medic had fled, or retreated, or "disengaged," however they put it in the file.

After debriefing (file missing/withheld), the Medic didn't skip a beat, reassigned to another top-secret mission. So as the biologists huddled in the remains of City Hall dreaming dreams gifted to them by rabbit cameras, the Medic had been eating three squares a day somewhere, living in relative luxury at a Central safe house.

One biologist survived longer than the rest, despite her dreams. The last entry in her journal read, "They are coming. We cannot hold them back." When the Central rescue team reached Dead Town, she "put a gun to her head and pulled the trigger, despite our pleading with her to stop." In her jacket pocket, they found a horrifying account of her last days and clutched in her hand like a talisman the bobber from a dead alligator.

By then, the Medic would've been happily preparing for his next assignment, reading through mission directives and protocols. Maybe slowly chewing bites of a ham sandwich while doing so.

A consummate professional.

Despite his need, Old Jim felt a reluctance to speak with the Medic, who through Cass had agreed to meet at the lighthouse. This despite his prep, as if thorough prep were not enough, and he would need some kind of cleansing ritual after. Almost against his will he got out of bed the next morning and at the appointed time drove to the lighthouse. Reluctant, too, because the truth was he didn't much care for the lighthouse.

A toolshed stood precarious next to the lighthouse building. It marked the last moment before a ridge of soil and coquina morphed into a line of rocks stretching out to sea, parallel to the beach. At low tide, the place where soil and coquina met rock felt like a good place to meet—shielded from the lighthouse road by the shed, but good lines of sight otherwise.

The lighthouse, looming in its disorienting swirl of black and white, felt like it would fall on top of him. If Saul the lighthouse keeper was up there, he wouldn't be able to see Old Jim through the little windows in the side of the lighthouse. The point was to watch the sea, not the ground.

Soon enough, then, a heavy-set barrel of a man in a leather jacket, flannel shirt, and jeans, with black boots, walked down the trail toward him. He'd lost most of his hair, this man, but white strands floated out to the sides like wisps of fog. He had the gait and build of someone who lifted weights but also drank a lot of beer, with a potbelly jutting from the bottom of his shirt, a jacket bursting tight across the shoulders.

The man's face as he approached closer had the pugnacious quality of an old-timey boxer, and his hand when he took it from his jacket pocket had a meaty aspect, fingers stubby and rough, although with carefully manicured nails. His handshake managed to be both clammy and dry, making Old Jim withdraw from it even as the Medic tried to clasp more tightly.

The Medic stated his (false) name, his rank in the Brigade, said he was proud to serve his country and would answer "any questions I can for you."

Old Jim was still staring at the stubby fingers, now quiescent by his side, wondered how, as "medic," he'd been at suturing wounds or bedside manner. His voice had all the elegance of a rusty ax slowly being pulled from deep in a thick log. He masticated words like if he didn't they would come out the other end uncomfortably whole.

"I've got respect for you, coming on at your age to run things, you know?" the Medic said, which felt like a way of telling Old Jim he'd done his homework, seen his file, too.

Preamble and greetings he'd lavish on someone who was deserving, so he just got down to it.

"I'm going to ask you some questions about the Dead Town expedition." The chance of mics and other surveillance was practically nil, so the Medic should feel comfortable.

"Sure, sure. I'm up for that. I truly am, you know. Sir."

His face had such a thick cast to it, such broad features, Old Jim wasn't able to read him, didn't know how to take the addition of "sir."

"When the generator died, what happened to the biologist who disappeared?"

The Medic shrugged. "Same as always, sir. He'd discovered the secret of the generator and the conditioning didn't work anymore. I told him to be quiet about it. He wouldn't, and I had to eliminate him."

What did it matter now, the continuing shrugs appeared to convey. It mattered to Old Jim, but he needed to pretend it didn't, even though hearing it uttered so plain felt like an abomination. The casual complicity, as if Old Jim should agree it didn't matter.

"The secret of the generator?"

"Yessir. The subliminal messages. The whole point of the thing, as I saw it. Save lives in the long run, you know. Central cleared me, said it was a solid decision, said the circumstances were not ideal. Being at war and all."

"At war?"

"With infiltration of the coast and all. And needing the hypnosis experiments to proceed. Self-defense if you think about it, sir."

"Self-defense?"

"Yes, sir. He would've killed me and others, if not. Because of where his mind was at."

The Medic was as futile as a file in his matter-of-factness. The Medic could state his truth without shame because Central had validated it. This aging man with the wispy shreds of hair and the sausage fingers who talked of murder with such ease. It made Old Jim deeply sad, sick almost, to think that the Medic existed in the same operational universe with him.

Why had the Medic not been exiled to his own island?


Something about a faint pencil-mark erasure in the Mudder's journal had raised another question for the Medic, made it possible to pivot away from his disgust.

"And how many people were on the expedition?"

"How many, sir?"

"Yes—what number." Was the man stupid or stalling?

"Oh yes—common misconception, sir, the way the files present it, I'd imagine. Twenty-five, not twenty-four. One got eaten during the alligator experiment and bled out."

The thought came to him, in that brief interregnum when

Old Jim couldn't think of what to say, that this was another joke of Jack's. That this person was an actor like Cass was supposed to be, at the start. Except, the Medic was too bad at it; he had to be real. The information he was giving Old Jim had to be real.

"Tell me about the alligator experiment."

The Medic frowned this time, withdrew into himself, his gaze distant, hands in his jacket pockets like he'd suddenly gotten cold in the sea breeze.

"Not my area, sir. Not my story to tell, not that one. Look for key words 'Teacup' and 'China Shop' in the archives. Might be what you need."

He had a frisson of insight, about something Jack had said, back at Central.

"No need," Old Jim said. "I know it was an experiment to see if people would do some 'routine' task while also, without remembering it, perform other, more clandestine tasks. To see if they could be programmed." He drew up short, had almost added "right?"

"Yessir, that's about it," the Medic admitted after a moment of hesitation.

"Teacup, though?" Old Jim said, in a cheery tone. "Really?"

"Yessir. Full tea service on a tray. He was holding it. Almost made it the whole way through the line of gators while they did up the harnesses and prepared for release."

"The Tyrant, huh?"

"Yessir." His face had brightened at the mention of the name. "Always was the difficult one, sir. Still might be. For someone."

Not my problem, that emphasis. Not at all.

A man had died and the man-eater had been allowed to escape into the swamp, there to form a pact with the Rogue. Intolerable.

Staring up at the lighthouse, finding it hard to look at the Medic, feeling ever more disgusted, he thought of another, more current question, one pertaining to Henry, in a way.

"Why did they switch the lenses? The lighthouse lenses, between the one on Failure Island and this one right here?"

He'd seen it in the files, from five years ago, and it had nagged at him, recognizing how much effort it had taken, how much convincing it had taken of the Coast Guard, which had jurisdiction over lighthouses.

"Sir, the Brigade at that time felt they'd learned all they could from the Failure Island lens. Subjected it to all kinds of hocus-pocus fiddley-diddley. And now it was time to turn to the one on the mainland, but it wasn't as easy to access, being more of a tourist spot. Thus the switch, sir."

"Is that all?" He meant the herculean physical effort as well as the bureaucratic one, but also stuck on how stupid "hocus-pocus fiddley-diddley" made the Medic sound.

"Well, sir, the Fresnel lenses—they're a powerful magic," the Medic said, and maybe there was a wink there, too, and maybe there wasn't. It felt like the leprechaun version of something Henry would say.

Maybe he should have been adding another task to the long list, about the types of experiments the S&SB had done to coax "magic" out of lighthouse lenses. Yet he was still stuck in the moment where the Medic had watched as a man had been killed by an alligator.

When Old Jim had said nothing for too long, the Medic said, "We have been looking for signals, sir. And, now, I understand you will be looking for traces?"

"Traces?"

"Because we want it to come out into the open."

"You mean force it?" Old Jim asked, and wondered what worlds lay between his definition of "it" and the Medic's definition.

"Yes."

"Why?"

"So we can control it or destroy it."

"Do you think that's my mission?"

"What other is there, sir?"


The seas were calm, bereft of much interest except seagulls and pelicans. The brief knife of a dolphin's fin could have been a wave. Out on the beach, the girl Gloria walked with her mom, but on the far side, and he only knew her by her red windbreaker and something solid in her walk.

He was undecided about the risk versus the reward of asking the Medic directly about Henry or the rabbit cameras.

"How long have you been with the S&SB?"

"About a decade, sir." Correct. The file told the same story. Before that, overseas, but on another coastal "job," mostly acting like a "foreign entity" inflicted on someone else's shores. After all, he'd already had the experience of being an infliction.

"Have you been to Dead Town since?"

"Since what, sir?"

"The expedition."

"No, no I haven't."

"Why not?" Old Jim asked.

"Haven't been instructed to. The lighthouse is our focus now. Have you been?"

"I'll get around to it," Old Jim said.

The Medic nodded, and there came a shift in the wind, some indiscernible mote removed from the arc and wheel of the heavens, Old Jim overtaken by a feeling he couldn't identify. An urge to dive down into the heart of things.

"Did the Mudder escape with you?"

"Who?"

"The woman studying the fiddler crabs. On the expedition."

"No, sir," the Medic said. "She wasn't with Central. Only I was."

"Did you ask to see the files? About what happened during the storm? With the stranger?"

"No."

"Did you ever investigate further, in any sense? Or receive further information from Central? As regards the stranger."

"No, sir."

"Do you have any thoughts about the identity or current whereabouts of the stranger?"

"No, sir."

"So you have no idea who the stranger might have been?"

"No. Sir."

Was that crumbling of his features . . . that he was about to cry? To bawl, perhaps? Perhaps not. He couldn't read the Medic at all, as if he came from a culture so foreign they only had five or six words in common.

"Was he part of Central's experiment? The stranger."

"No. Not that I was aware."

"Who would have been aware, if not you?"

"I wouldn't know, sir."

The Medic kept shuffling closer to Old Jim, for reasons Old Jim couldn't fathom, and Old Jim kept stepping back, so that now they stood where the rocks formed a rough semicircle with the startling gleam of a sandbank jutting out to form the rest of the circle, in shallow water.

It felt like a spotlight, with the dark, rich blue of deeper water to both sides.

"What do you think happened out there, to the other expedition members?"

"You mean besides 'the Mudder,' sir? Because I think you mean the Mudder got out, too. Which . . . I never knew that before."

The Medic said it with no particular malice or interest.

No, he ate the meat and potatoes put in front of him every

day, and that was enough for him. No strange dreams for him. No Rogue running riot across a field of smoldering rabbits. He slept the quiet sleep of the certain, and Old Jim almost envied him.

"I'll ask you again: What do you think happened during the storm?"

"Manifestation of the foreign entity," he said in a solemn, almost worshipful tone.

"And how do you define 'foreign entity?'"

"An entity that is foreign, sir."

"Can you elaborate?" Old Jim asked, and he could not keep a current of sarcasm from his voice.

"An old, old force in the world."

Old Jim didn't like that answer. It sounded too mysterious. It conjured up an ancient army headed toward a gap in the world filled with green light. As if some religion had infiltrated Central, this way he kept encountering a quasi-mystical element even in how Jack talked about where he got his intel.

"How would you name it?" Old Jim asked, as he noticed how close the Medic had drifted toward him.

"Unnamable, sir. That's what the Séance and Science Brigade is here for, sir."

"To name it?"

"Yes, sir. To name it."

Old Jim gauged the waves, the distance, the risk, and knew he couldn't stop himself. He came close as if to end the meeting, shake the Medic's hand.

Then he shoved the man off the rocks, as hard as he could—toward the sand and shallow water. Watched as that particular barrel managed to put his hands out, break his fall. Get to his feet with surprising agility, arms covered in sand.

Standing there in that semicircle of spotlight staring at Old Jim, devoid of outrage or anger.

Somehow that chilled him more than anything. That the

Medic didn't sputter or wave his arms or shout. But just stood there, in the waves rippling over the sandbank, staring at Old Jim.

Staring and staring as Old Jim walked back to shore over the rocks.

## 012: OLD DECOMP

The darkness of the night beyond his desk beguiled him now at times, the way it could feel like the prow of a boat and the mutters of the open waters beyond almost like words rising from the depths. A key from the kitchen hook sometimes slipped into his hand now as he went out onto the deck to enjoy the sunset. As if he had the muscle memory of some other place, and there having been too many other places to identify which one. But he liked the solid, cold feel of it in his hand, an old key, brass, with complex teeth.

If the key in his hand oddly calmed him, like playing the piano, so too did receiving the news that Jack had gotten him the Dead Town evidence. Although it was Jackie, not Jack, who in curt fashion gave Old Jim a caustic call to let him know it had been delivered and where to go to "wade through it." She gave him the address, then said, "Next time, even if it's Central you need, go through me, not *him*." Chain of command, breached, didn't know his place, but still couldn't say Jack's name over a secure line.

It would feel good to escape them both for a while, along with the files, S&SB management, and Village Bar duties. Escaping, too, the sea debris reports of his predecessor, which still came by fax as if no one had told Central the man was dead.

"Round trip, get in the truck," Old Jim said when Cass came

around for their regular debrief later that morning. "We've got all the Dead Town expedition files waiting for us. Just a bit of a trip."

"Sure thing, boss."

He decided to take that as earnest, not sarcastic, in part because he'd kept the weight of intel on him, so why shouldn't she feel lighter than he did?

Maybe he was just getting used to her, but it felt more comfortable with her there on the passenger side than it did empty. Even if he did have to move some maps and file folders and toss a couple of fast-food bags into the back.

"Did David Sheers tell you anything?" Cass asked as he adjusted the truck's side mirror, which had gotten turned inward somehow in his travels.

Had the Medic told him anything? Not really. It was more that the certainty of the Medic had disturbed him and felt like an implacable force, but he regretted pushing him into the sea. It felt so childish now that he hoped Cass never found out.

"Name, rank, serial number. What I do know is he's dangerous. Watch your back when he's around."

"I always keep a physical distance when we have to meet, have someone else in the room with me."

Even saying that, Cass had a serene aspect about her that Old Jim hadn't seen, like they'd done this a hundred times before. As if, in another reality, they'd been running this op for a decade and been through the wars together. The smile she gave him as she'd hoisted herself up into the seat, one hand on the doorframe, conveyed a trust neither of them had earned yet. Was that just a young-person thing?

"Don't you want to know where we're going?"

She looked over at him with a glint of weary mischief. "I've just come from hearing the early-morning complaints of a bunch of psychics, séance freaks, and submersible techs. Just get me as fucking far away from here as possible. Even if we're driving right up to the gates of hell."

He gave her a raised eyebrow for the hyperbole. "Almost. It's between here and Bleakersville."

"Everything is between here and Bleakersville, Jim."

Well, she had that right.

"Hank's Premium Memories" read the sign at the address, with the legend, "When Yer Hankering for the Best." A storage-locker business converted out of what appeared to be a doppelgänger of the Starlight Lounge. What was it with the long barracks–pillbox style of local architecture?

"Hankering for a better slogan," Cass said as they approached, still rife with manic energy.

Old Jim said nothing, not sure he liked her joking tone.

"But seriously," Cass said, sitting straighter in her seat. "This looks like a great place to get ambushed."

"Agreed. You strapped?"

"Yep. You?"

"Yeah." The guns were old, from the archives, but effective.

With all the add-on structures, the place was not just cruel to the eye but an actual maze, so Old Jim parked out front, next to a trashy green sports car right in front of the office.

The white guy behind the counter in a bright red shirt and dreads gave them a map. He drew an arrow with a ballpoint pen to indicate a circular structure out back. "Just walk through this front building to the right," he advised, "and leave your vehicle here. Back lot's rutted."

"Too rutted for a truck?" Old Jim asked. Maybe he sounded incredulous. Maybe he almost wanted to argue about it, given the state of his nerves.

"Too rutted for a tank, buddy, in my opinion. But do what you want."

"Thanks, buddy," Cass said, and nudged Old Jim away from the counter.

So they took the advice, although Old Jim didn't like leaving the truck, and they walked through the main building to the back. It had dozens of doors and more empty corridors off to both sides. Their footfalls echoed and he could hear the wheeze of old plumbing.

Out the other end, through a glass door propped open with a cinder block green with mold, and into the huge gravel lot beyond, littered with a scattering of shotgun shells. The smell of motor oil and burnt rubber was almost a taste in his mouth.

A welter of potholes full of muddy water dominated that space, and his thoughts slid from the Medic's blithe description of murder to an even more visceral place where the texture of tadpoles and eels brushed against his skin, and maybe that was just how unclean he felt after talking to the Medic, like the potholes were an accurate depiction of the man's soul.

"I don't like those potholes," Cass said. "If this was someplace else I'd sweep those holes for mines first." Where had she been, then? Before?

At the lot's far corner, maybe seventy feet away, a windowless stone silo squatted, framed by sprawling pines and oaks behind. A kind of stone approximation of a yurt, with a vaguely chimney-like protrusion just above the roof.

"That feels like a remnant of someone else's history," Old Jim said.

"Good times," she said sarcastically.

"In theory, they've shoved all the evidence from the Dead Town Disaster inside." But something already felt off, even if he couldn't put his finger on it.

"Did you request they dump it in a brick shithouse with bad vibes, or is that Central giving us the finger?"

"It's not brick."

"You know what I mean. Looks like the place a serial killer takes his victims to."

"I do know what you mean," Old Jim said.

But they came close anyway, across that messed-up parking lot. The potholes had the look of terrestrial tidal pools, with ankle-turning potential and a disturbing aspect of cloudy water, even though it hadn't rained recently. Old Jim didn't like how his face appeared distorted every time he looked down.

The tower-silo's pockmarked stone had dull green discolorations across the curving surface, mapped to splotches of lichen. Some underlying assault that expressed itself as a melting of the shell rock used to build it, so that a swell of breaking lesions appeared out of that rough surface. The door had a small "24" painted in white high up to the left. Coincidence or Central having a grim laugh?

Old Jim caught a whiff of rotten eggs, of dead animal, but that might just be coming from the seepage ditch before the tree line.

"How do we get in?"

"There's supposed to be a hidden latch. A key inside to lock the door on the way out."

Cass gave him a sharp look of disbelief, standing there together with the disquieting door.

"Security by obscurity? So anyone could come along and open this damn door."

"Highly unlikely. And probably Jack's idea, not Central."

"Met him twice, in group meetings. He asked me too many questions."

"Best place to meet him, though," Old Jim said. "Now help me find this latch." Jack didn't ask "too many" questions of any old grunt, that was for sure. Her file had caught his attention—a file Old Jim still hadn't seen.

She just stood there, arms crossed, while he felt absurdly like he was patting down the door for weapons. No, he realized, she wasn't just standing there, but *watchful*, like she expected an ambush—checking lines of sight, so no one could sneak up on them unexpected, because truth was, they were exposed, and not even the side of the truck to shield them. Fact, too, the way Cass carried herself, there was no tell about her weapon. Shoulder holster, maybe . . .

Ah, there was the latch, disguised as a rough jut of stone next to the door, and no doubt now that this place was Central's in the discovery, and had been for a long time.

The odd satisfaction of the click, as if he had solved some larger puzzle.

He shot Cass a proud smile, and the door opened outward—unleashing a rotting-fish stench mixed with a chemical odor so strong it sent them both reeling back across the land of horrible potholes.

"Shit," he said, his boots wet. Waterproof, but the water had a viscous quality.

"Jesus Christ, Jim, what died in there?"

Well, everything, apparently.

Back at the truck he had a thermos of water and a supply of fresh handkerchiefs in the glove box, for which he got mercilessly teased even as Cass accepted a couple to cover her face.

"Hankering for a handkerchief, Jim? You running a black market for handkerchiefs? Anyway, yeah, this'll work." Pulling herself together, looking like a bandit because she'd chosen a black one.

"I have the handkerchiefs," he said in muffled fashion from under his, white with red polka dots, hoping moistening them would deaden the smell, "because you never know when you'll need one." Although really it was one of those habits the reason for which was lost to time and history. Too many ops, too many rituals.

"Right, sure, I can think of tons of uses." Then she sobered, or he thought she had, but said, "Let's hit a convenience store after this, Jim. Make some money on the side."

She was about to walk back out across the parking lot, when Old Jim frowned, held her back with one outstretched arm.

"Let's wait under the awning a moment." He'd heard something or thought he had.

Something clicked behind her eyes and she hugged the wall with him.

A moment later, a pickup pulled up in front of the stone silo, bucking over the potholes like the driver had done it a million times before and didn't give a shit about his truck's suspension. Three men clambered out, in jeans, T-shirts, baseball caps, armed with rifles.

Cass had her sidearm out so fast he still didn't know where she'd drawn from, silencer screwed on in seconds. A brutal-looking Beretta. The look on her face told him she was prepared to have a firefight right there, in the parking lot. He could see now how the open button-down shirt allowed her concealment but also a quick draw.

"Don't," he said. "We're not law enforcement. We're not even supposed to be here. Not officially."

She gave him a hard glance, softened, nodded, lowered the Beretta, but didn't reholster. Fair enough. He had his Walther in a shoulder holster in easy reach, and a tiny Central-made pea-shooter strapped to his ankle. One bullet.

The men had assembled in a row and now were firing furiously at the side of the silo, kicking up stone chips and dust, until they had exhausted their ammo. Then they jumped back in the truck, which popped a wheelie and drifted in a shriek of gravel before finding purchase and roaring out of sight around the corner, leaving behind a smell of burnt rubber and a haze of black smoke from the tailpipe.

"What the fuck," Cass managed to get out.

Old Jim had already emerged and, hands on his hips, stared out at the stone silo.

"What if they come back?"

"They won't," Old Jim said. "Those were really low-caliber rifles. Not enough juice to penetrate that elephant hide. Local talent, but not yahoos or killers."

"Huh. How'd you know?"

That felt good, he couldn't deny it.

"Just a sense you get after a while. I think they thought we were in there, and they were just supposed to scare us. Surprise us." Maybe even sent by whoever had left the belt buckle for Cass. Had the same feel. Peevish.

"The attendant must be deaf," she said.

"I bet he won't be there when we leave."

"But who, Jim? *Why?*"

He shrugged. Did Jack or Jackie hate his request more? He didn't like to think the men had been friends of Man Boy Slim— that would be a whole different matter.

"Let's just get on with the job and get out of here," he said.

Kicking at the gravel, plop, hit a pothole.


The damp handkerchiefs helped enough for them to pull the door open and survive the interior. Although the door slammed shut no matter what you did, so Old Jim found a loose bracket to serve as a door jam and Cass groped around and found a flood-light in the wall about ten feet up, with a cord . . . and, well, then they were looking at a "metric ton" of half-rotting evidence arranged amphitheater style to leave a space in front of the door free.

"Do you have a problem with dead things?" Old Jim asked. Because he did, sometimes.

"Only if they're coming after me," Cass said, deadpan, but he could tell she was unsettled, too.

Barrels with large jars stacked atop them formed the lower level, with boxes and display cabinets next, so high the piles against the wall disappeared up where the light could not reach. He ran his little pocket flashlight over contents that crushed his mind with the sheer density, the intense mania, of vast numbers.

"I expected banker boxes full of files and, uh, photographs of this . . . evidence."

Turtle and tortoise shells stacked in between the cases. Taxidermied fox squirrels, the skins of raccoons and otters and mink. Some cases had fallen open and out cascaded preserved dry feathers of house swallows and purple martins.

Cass poked half-heartedly around the edges. "This is a display case of bat skeletons. This one is full of butterflies."

"Never get through it all."

Because it was spooky. Because of the stench. Because of how the darkness of the whole formed the shape of a creature looming over them. Because some of the jars preserved in ethanol had been deposited roughly and cracked, so the chemicals had leaked out. Because the stacking structure seemed chosen without thought for getting any of the samples out of the silo.

A rickety stool had been set up in the middle of the room and under what looked like a handful of parking-lot gravel a piece of paper awaited them. The circular nature of the evidence assembled around it made the stool look like an act the audience had come to see. The audience in this case: the lower layers of jars of sea and river creatures, stacked five high.

Thankfully, his nose had numbed itself or the handkerchiefs

were holding up. Had there been a deliberate lag between stacking the jars here and letting him know they'd arrived? Just to add to the general ambience?

"There's a message, I think," he said, and stepped forward to pull the piece of paper out from under the gravel, held it up to the flashlight with Cass perched in close, breathing a little shallow in his ear.

But all it said, in large handwritten block letters, on Hank's stationery, was:

## HAPPY JACK

"Happy Jack," he echoed. Happy Jack?

"No, Jim," Cass whispered, like they were in a church, not an amateur abattoir. "Happy, Jack."

"That's what I said."

"No. It's a question, signed by Jack. Are we happy? No."

"Oh."

"Aren't you glad Jack wants to know if we're happy with this shitshow? And that some underling wrote it down wrong?" Ah well, ah hell.

This was what men who had learned nothing did. Men who didn't mind repeating versions of their lesser selves.

"You're a mighty stain on the world," had been Jack's call sign once, and Old Jim's countersign had been, "And you're a horrible mess." Followed, in more dire circumstances, with, "Are you the one dying?" "No, I'm the one knifing you in the back." A life around Jack eroded the wall between do and not do.

The message wasn't funny or clever, even if Jack thought so. Because what Jack was telling them stank worse than the specimens. That they were welcome to whatever they could pick out of the remains—if they could stand the smell. That instead of a respectful fulfillment of Old Jim's request, Jack had dumped on the edge of Bleakersville the complete inventory of samples the biologists had taken over that long summer twenty years ago.

No linguistics report. No analysis of any kind. Just every collection of butterflies and moths and stick insects. Every row of pinned iridescent beetles. Every tadpole euthanized for science but then abandoned to an archive or warehouse . . . probably not even at Central, Old Jim realized, for Jack to give him this so quickly. But somewhere closer.

And Jack telling him that he disagreed, that this wouldn't help Old Jim neutralize the Rogue, that he was barking up the wrong stone silo. This sad, tired detritus. So maybe that meant they *should* catalogue it, that Jack had gotten sloppy and didn't realize what he'd given them.

"Do we try to go through it all?" Cass asked, as if reading his thoughts and with an edge of anxiety in her voice.

"No," Old Jim said. "I mean, *I* do."

"No way. We're in this together." Cass, muffled through the handkerchief, both of them trying not to talk too much and let in the stench.

Such a complex knot of feelings in his stomach, with her saying that. But also a sense of comfort, somehow, like maybe someone actually had his back.

"Right," he mumbled. "Take a stab at it?"

Cass nodded, and not perfunctory, but like she really got it. No files, no analysis from Central. Just . . . the raw stuff. Rawer by the minute.

"Must be something here," he said, even though he was used to doing uncomfortable tasks that led nowhere. Prying anything out from the stacks would take patience.

"It's okay if it's a dead end, though."

Old Jim had never seen an end deader.

"Maybe try as long as we can stand it . . ."

But Cass was already rolling up her sleeves, which Old Jim found reassuring. She was going to roll up her sleeves and get to work.

So they did. For a time.

There came a moment when he'd thought they'd found something. High above, in the murk, the deep-water feel of it, as if they were lost along the bottom of the sea, lost amid shipwreck, lost amid debris and artifact, lost amid ritual and Jack's wrath.

"Get that for me?" he'd asked.

That broke down Cass's mask discipline, and out poured too many words: "Can I climb this mountain of crap to get that for you without falling down and burying us both? Because, what, I'm younger? I'm fitter? I'm more expendable?"

"The middle thing," he admitted, reluctantly.

She considered him a moment, there in the dark, in the stench, protected by his handkerchief, and then said, "Catch me if I fall."

"Break your fall at least."

But he took it serious, watched her keenly, arms outstretched, and if she'd fallen, he would have caught her. Or hurt himself trying.

Cass, anchored by one arm and one foot, leaning out over the abyss. His flashlight turned on her in that upper darkness, and from that angle, the forced perspective, the creatures in the foreground, she looked so very far away, and her face so pale, that his heart gave a little, a kind of twinge, as if she had become too remote and was fading away from him, too far to return safely.

"No," he said, "no," and reached out with one hand toward her, then dropped it as he realized what he was doing.

"Stuck," she called down after considering him a moment.

She was grasping for a small red object, wedged between

kegs and boxes and display cases stacked as if by some madman who had become an expert on balancing objects atop each other. And this one bright red thing catching his flashlight beam in a way obscure to Old Jim, there near the top.

"It's really stuck," and now she was frowning and shining a light on him, as if worried . . . about what? That his paralysis meant he'd lost his mind. He could not control his expression. Had the smell gotten to him, or something else?

"Cut it loose," he said. "Drop it down to me and let's get the hell out. Or just come down." Every word was torture, the handkerchief failing.

Did he know she had a knife in easy reach? She did. Of course she did.

Later, safely out of the silo, Cass would tell him that the object had been stuck amid the Mudder's fiddler crab cases, which were illogical, misfiled, difficult to understand. Because most, the closer she looked, had the wrong labels. Filed not as the fiddlers they were but as butterflies, beetles, frogs, dragonflies, anything but.

How far had the delusion spread?

They lasted exactly twenty-nine minutes before they couldn't stand it any longer and fled, including a terrible moment when it appeared the door wouldn't open and then, pushing together, it did, thankfully.

The door made a clang as it shut behind them and they tumbled out into the sunlight. Like grave robbers. Like bandits. Like escapees from the wreckage of the Dead Town Disaster, released from those unearthly jars of creatures so long dead and yet newly dying a second death. Reborn anew.

Blinking, ridding themselves of the cursed handkerchiefs and laughing even as Old Jim believed they both had expected more gunfire.

But there wasn't. There was just the potholed parking lot, the bright sun on their faces, and they both took big, deep breaths, and staggered around, bent over at times with the hysteria of aftermath.

In the truck, he felt exhausted and unclean, like he needed a full decontamination process, or at least a shower, Cass with a look on her face like she felt the same.

"Well, that was terrible and disgusting and worthless," Old Jim said, as they sat there contemplating the road through a windshield stained white by bugs.

"You think so?" Cass said, weary but impish suddenly, as if the engine that drove her never slept. "Because maybe we learned something valuable. About the habits of the locals. About how fucked up our mission is. About old decomp. Like, avoid it. In fact, I'm going to call this place Old Decomp on the map."

"I need a bar," Old Jim said. His legs felt rubbery. He couldn't shake the weird potholes, the deep-sea drainage, all of it. "Not to drink. Just a quiet place to rest a bit."

"Sure," Cass said, giving him a sideways glance, "but I'm driving."

On the seat between them lay their treasure: The red bobber attached to the tracker, from some long-dead alligator subjected to a pointless experiment during an expedition come to ruin.

## 013: SEPARATING THE INGREDIENTS

Stacky's T-Stop had no pedigree to speak of, but at two in the afternoon no clientele, either, and just the right amount of bleach smell slapping out from between the saloon doors leading to the bathrooms to make Old Jim begin to forget chemical smells and rotting things. At an empty adjoining table, the relic of a blackened chicken finger rose above the wax paper covering a red plastic basket, admonishing him to only order water. For Cass it was a burger and fries, initially a beer, then, with a nod to Old Jim, a bottle of root beer instead "because the taps here will be salty and sour."

"It's okay if you drink," Old Jim said, kind of mumbled it. Didn't know what to do with her thoughtfulness.

Camaraderie still felt unfamiliar to Old Jim, like he'd forgotten the rules. Or the rules with Jack had been so different than the norm. Stuck, too, on the locals shooting the silo, which resonated more deeply with him the more the moment receded from him. While it seemed to have had the opposite effect on Cass.

They'd situated themselves in classic desperado fashion, at the back of the bar, on the same side of a table for four, facing the front door and whoever might burst in, guns blazing. While the bartender, having delivered Cass's burger, downed a couple of side-by-side shots of whiskey from behind the counter.

Old Jim watched, incredulous, as Cass dissected her meal, using her hands to separate the top of the bun from the burger on her paper plate, place it on a napkin, and then carefully airlift to the side of the plate two tired pickle slices, a scrap of lettuce, a bit of onion, the slice of underripe tomato.

Then she removed the bottom of the bun, placed it on the napkin, and cut the hamburger into eight equal pieces. Which she considered as would an artist some new masterpiece. At which point, she took a bite of bun, then speared a piece of burger and ate it with some pickle, lettuce, and tomato, chewing contemplatively.

Only stopping when she saw the look on Old Jim's face.

"What?"

"Are you checking for bugs?"

She finished chewing, wiped her mouth with a napkin, gave him a look, and said, "You mean like a centipede? No, I like to see it all separate and then have the right ratios. And I hate onions."

"I've never seen anyone do that before."

"I always used to eat this way, before the military tried to train it out of me. You should try it."

Try it? It would drive him crazy just to witness the process more than a handful of times.

She speared another hamburger chunk and repeated the process. It bothered Old Jim that she was going to run out of pickle, tomato, and lettuce before she ran out of burger with bun. It bothered him that she might actually worry about being a target.

"I'm going to give the alligator tracker we found to the psychics."

"To do what?"

"Sniff it," she said. "Pick up the trail."

"Oh, like hunting dogs? To find an alligator."

"That's about right."

Even as every night now, in support of actual science, he turned on the alligator tracker, hoping for a hit. "Maybe that'll turn up something. Jack wants to see real progress."

She wiped her mouth again, said in a way that made Old Jim think she was talking about him at first, "Control freak. Maybe too happy about distant messaging and hypnosis." But she meant Jack.

"What did Jack tell you about Dead Town?" Old Jim asked, thinking of the Rogue.

"A high-level summary report. But it felt incomplete. Was there more to it?"

"Yeah, and I can't keep it just in my head, and I think it's important, even though it happened twenty years ago."

Cass said, "I'm listening," and the last piece of hamburger was gone. She ate so fast, and yet savored everything.

So Old Jim gave Cass more details about the rabbits, his theory of the generator, his theory of the Rogue—all of it. Dumping it on her in that back corner almost, he felt, like Jack had dumped the specimens on them. Only keeping to himself the fate of Team Leaders 1 and 2. That felt personal, or irrelevant, or . . . he wasn't sure, but he omitted it.

While Cass just kept swigging her root beer, as if he were catching her up on the latest baseball scores or a ten-year history, month by month, of the high-tide marks during storm surges. Even when he didn't spare her his pieced-together vision of the Rogue shrieking as he ran across the blackened field and, somehow, as Old Jim spoke, he felt as if something evil or evil-adjacent was emptying out of him—and the relief of that he hadn't expected, almost as if he felt physically lighter. And even though he knew the weight would return, that he'd only banished it for a time, the absence meant something.

When he had finished, Cass held up her empty bottle of root beer and shouted at the bartender like a drunk, "Need another!"

"Come get it yourself!" he half shouted back across the empty room.

"Fucking service around here," she muttered as she got up, putting a hand on his shoulder to steady herself.

By the time she had exchanged words with the bartender, put her coin on the counter, and sat down beside Old Jim again, he expected she'd tell him he was a paranoid fool—maybe a delusional one. That there was no "Rogue" as he or even Jack envisioned him. No possible way that the events of twenty years ago meant anything to the present day.

But, in fact, she'd split the difference.

"That was a lot of old decomp you spilled," she said. "I was told that the expedition was a complete success, but I guess not. I guess, you know, *the opposite.*"

"No one made it home. Not really."

"But what if we separate out this idea of 'Rogue,' as you put it, from the rest of the story. Move away from him laying waste to the expedition with, what, experimental weapons or mind control? Because maybe focusing on that obscures the *purpose* baked into him."

"How do we separate that out? He basically killed them." Surprise that she could dismiss that apocalyptic vision from the dead meadow so easily. That felt like she'd had the intel earlier than today, or did she just have leaps of intuition?

"More like reckless endangerment."

"Maybe," he admitted, although he was pretty sure Jack didn't see it that way.

"So I think about what it would take for someone to *do* that," she said in a whisper tinged with awe. "To be part of a twenty-year op? And he might have another twenty ahead of him—we don't know."

A peculiar, almost unknowable look had overtaken her that he couldn't break the code of. He had a sensation of intel that lay far beyond him and had passed overhead in the night, headed for a distant star.

"The mission is . . . personal . . . to the Rogue in some way."

"The mission is *everything* to the Rogue," Cass said. "He'll endure what almost no one else would. Do you do that for God, for country . . . or for something else?"

Old Jim felt close to an answer, but then it was gone again, and an uneasy silence came over them, until he felt a kind of pressure, a need to acquiesce.

"I'll think about that. I'll think about what it means. Or doesn't mean."

"Oh, I don't know what it means, Jim," Cass said wearily, as if she were older than him and more jaded. "I just know the answers lie so far outside the box that there is no box. Speaking of which, the cameras. Did anyone do an autopsy on them?"

Old Jim felt a chill come over him, like crunching on the ice in his water had given him a headache. "Not sure what you mean."

But he did know. Maybe it had been in the back of his mind without realizing it.

"They look like toy cameras or something. Fake. I don't know why. That's what got me thinking about it."

The chill cantilevered into his body like something was curving down into his system to infiltrate it.

"An autopsy? They probably took them apart . . . But you mean . . . a real *autopsy?*"

"Yes. I mean a real autopsy."

"The weird description of the cameras by the Team Leaders was put down to hallucination."

"Consider for a second what it would mean if it wasn't a hallucination . . . what if they did change?" A kind of guarded look to her gaze, as if expressing the idea seemed dangerous to her. "No one at Central saw a 'living' camera."

"A living camera," Old Jim echoed.

"Yes—and we don't know what a living camera means."

Somehow, Old Jim wished he was back in his office watching an alligator tracker that never registered a hit.


Later, exhausted, headed home in the truck, caught in an epic downpour that made Old Jim drive at a crawl through half a foot of water, Cass said to him, "You know, sometimes I feel like I've been shipwrecked here. It's like I don't have the right tools, and I'm supposed to improvise. It feels impossible." Half weary, half frustrated.

"But we do have the right tools."

"The tools are rusty and broken," she said, and sighed.

"If we fail, I'll suffer, not you, trust me," he said, to change the trajectory. Driving through the water made him feel as if he were neither on land nor at sea. Gliding through a limitless expanse.

She sat up a little from her slouch, like he'd caught her out somehow.

"Trust you? Do you really think I can, Jim? Or that you'll be the only one to suffer?"

He shrugged, didn't reply, even when she stared at him, just concentrated on driving. The rain assaulted the roof of the truck and the fresh smell came with a drop in the temperature, so it was almost cool.

Something had burnt out in him, some last flare of resistance, and he felt hollowed out and small and maybe a little foolish.

"No," he said finally. "You'd suffer, too."

## 014: EVERY SORROW

The green light and the cleft between the two mountains, but this time an army of house centipedes poured into the gap in endless legions, against a barren, silent landscape. He woke gasping, as if he'd been deep beneath the sea, the little key cutting into his hand.

The world was filled with forgotten places that had been something else once, had contained something else once, renamed by whatever you did there now. The idea frightened him when it came to him as he woke during the night in the kitchen, sometimes sitting on the chair, with his head full of the rabbit cameras, alligators, and a fading image of a burning candle. An empty vessel.

A meadow of wildflowers was no better or worse a trap than

an abandoned quarry where once he'd sat in winter, in a heavy coat and thick beard, and posed like a barbarian for Jack behind a rusted, broken-down metal desk. Jack had snapped some shots with the frozen waterfall cascading down the levels behind and laughed and the next night they'd come back with the informant and done what they had to do. It was no less beautiful the second time.

The alligator tracker . . . tracked nothing. The further examination of Old Decomp's contents proceeded laborious through third parties, low-level players on Failure Island brought over for a perhaps useless task. He'd asked Jackie for files on agents killed or gone missing the past thirty years, seeking anything Rogue-like, but there had been no reply. Maybe that was Jack telling him they'd worked that angle, found nothing.

The weather had turned colder, merged into fall, and he had so little that he wanted to report to Jack.

Still not enough sleep, so when the phone rang, it woke him up. Had he been nodding off, in the middle of the day? How many days since Old Decomp? For a moment, he couldn't remember.

The surprise: It was the phone for "tourists," as Jack had called it, not the red phone for Central.

"Old Jim here," he said, into the receiver.

A sense of heavy breathing at some remove made him fight the reflex to hang up, and instead he waited out the silence.

The static parted and a voice came through the line.

"You threatened me if I didn't call, but I have called and called and you never answer. Not one time. Why would you do that to me? I've done nothing. Nothing wrong. You should just leave me alone."

The voice had a musical intensity that disconcerted Old Jim. The person was using some sort of distortion device, just not the type that made your voice sound muddy and gruff. No, instead, this person sounded lyrical, almost birdlike, but a big, aggressive bird, not a songbird.

"Does it work both ways?" Old Jim asked. "The voice distortion? What do I sound like to you?"

"You sound like an old man to me. How did you know?"

"An educated guess."

"You threatened me. You wanted to talk." The voice rising in panic.

The Mudder. He'd known, but it still came at him like a flash of heat lightning. The anti-Medic.

"Why disguise your voice? I know what your voice sounds like from the tapes."

"You can't trust voices to just be voices."

"What do you mean by that?"

"A sound leaves a trace. Like a parasite, in order to exist, sound needs a host."

That felt personal. Of course, that's how she felt. How unsettling and terrifying to continue her research in the middle of an expedition she felt was full of zombies. The generator. Her notes.

"What can you tell me about the expedition that wasn't in your journal?"

"I have no value to you. That's what I'm *trying* to tell you. You can just forget about me."

"Did you see who attacked the expedition, at the end?"

"No. I told you, I don't know anything. I was already far out in the marshes by then, leaving. Why won't you believe that?" A hint of hysteria rose through her voice.

"What did Man Boy Slim tell you about the situation?"

"How the fuck do you think I got your number?"

Old Jim cursed. He was blowing this, head too buried in the reports and procedures. Now he did feel an urgency—but also panic that he didn't have the right questions.

"Tell me more about the rabbits, the alligators, then. Even if it was in your journal."

A hesitation, then: "The rabbits made the alligator worse. No one wanted to say it because it sounded crazy, but the more rabbits the alligator ate, the more atypical it behaved. It did all kinds of things you don't expect from an alligator, to write about it, that seemed crazier. In the moment. Because we just wanted to forget the alligator experiment."

A terrible thought occurred to Old Jim.

"Did members of the expedition eat those rabbits, too?"

"I wasn't keeping track. I never did. But that's not why the alligator behaved strangely."

"Then why?"

"Because it ate some rabbits that had cameras around their necks. It ate the *cameras*, and that was the problem. That's what changed her, the Tyrant. I think."

What would it have meant? To eat a camera that was not a camera? He felt light-headed, realized he hadn't had breakfast, couldn't remember having had coffee. Why was that?

"What about the stranger?" He had to come back to the Rogue. "He talked to you in the bar once. A man whispered in your ear. Man Boy Slim might've called him 'the Rogue.'"

A strong sense of violation in the Mudder's reply: "How do you know that? How do you *know* that he talked to me?"

Anything he said might provoke her, so he said nothing. There was a long pause, and he thought he'd lost her.

Then: "Men always whisper in your ear. It's disgusting."

"I think you know what I mean." Surely she remembered what the Rogue had said.

"I'm sorry."

"What?"

"He whispered, 'I'm sorry. I'm really sorry. It should be different already. But it isn't, so I'm doing my best.'"

*I'm sorry. I'm really sorry. It should be different already.*

While he digested that, she rushed into the gap. "That's all he said. That's it. Like a lunatic. I didn't know him. I never saw him again. I thought he was drunk and he'd mistaken me for someone else."

"What was his voice like?"

"Ordinary. So ordinary I can't remember."

"Are you sure he didn't say anything else to you?" Something that had affected her mind, and she couldn't remember because the Rogue didn't want her to remember.

"I'm telling the truth!"

"Was it after he said he was sorry that you had the idea to leave the expedition?"

"No. He said nothing to me about that." That hadn't been Old Jim's question, but no point asking again.

"Why did you leave the expedition that night? That particular night?"

"The hurricane was coming on strong. The expedition was falling apart. It didn't take a genius to see that, and I was scared."

"Not because the stranger had told you to leave?"

"No!"

"I believe you," Old Jim said. But he didn't know what he believed, exactly.

"No you don't."

Maybe he didn't. It would easier if what the Rogue had whispered had been a confession, a reason, something that didn't leave Old Jim in the dark holding a strange key.

"Did you see the stranger that night?"

"No. We were already out on the mud flats, me and Man Boy Slim. Too far away."

"Did you ever see the stranger after that?"

Silence. For too long.

"I just want to understand," Old Jim said. "Help me understand. And then you'll never hear from me again."

"What is there to understand? There's nothing to fucking understand because nobody will ever fucking *understand* it. Don't you get that?"

"Where did you see the stranger?" Old Jim said, patient.

A sigh like the Mudder was expelling every ounce of oxygen from her body.

"He was shucking cameras like oysters. We saw him the next morning with the Tyrant shucking cameras like oysters."

"I'm not sure I heard that correctly," Old Jim said. "Could you repeat that?"

"You heard me right, old man. We'd gotten lost and we saw him through the binoculars across a lagoon. And he was melting down cameras, like in a bucket. Like *shucking oysters,* except keeping the shells? Harvesting them. And he tossed the rest to the Tyrant, who gobbled them up. Right there by his side. Like a fucking pet."

"How did he do this?"

"You won't believe me."

"Try me."

"He stood over them and he breathed on them and he . . ."

"He what?"

"He drooled on them."

"You mean like he spat on them? Saliva?"

"Just what I said. I know it sounds funny, but the more he did it, the more material he'd tossed in the bucket after he'd . . . he'd 'shucked' the cameras . . . well, it was like dry ice or something."

"He spat on the cameras in a bucket and they steamed and smoke rose up."

"It was long-distance. I don't know what I saw. Why do you keep pressing? It doesn't matter. Fuck you. That's all I remember— don't ask me any more about it."

What had the cameras been coated with? Some psychotropic substance? Maybe even contact with a harmless substance would make them bubble or seethe?

"And the rabbit cameras . . . you viewed some of the video footage."

"Yes." She sounded sad now, not defiant.

"How would you describe it? The footage."

"If you saw it, you would have run as far away from that place as you could."

"What does that mean?"

"Will you stop asking questions then? Will you really just leave me alone?"

"I will. I promise."

"But you keep *saying* that. You keep saying you'll stop, but I don't *know you.* Maybe you're not even who Man Boy Slim thinks you are. Maybe you're trying to keep me on the line to triangulate my location right now. I won't be here long. I won't be here at all. It won't work on me and—"

"I didn't mean to—"

There came a formless, primal scream from the phone and Old Jim held it away from his ear as the Mudder began shouting. The Mudder had begun to spiral and Old Jim hadn't recognized it in time.

"You see a place like the coast, you see it, but it's different and impossible things live there and the lighthouse is a glowing green spear and out at sea you can see ships split in half and if you walk too far you reach a point you can't go any farther and you're trapped while all the impossible things are hunting for you, all the monstrous things you thought were only in your dreams."

Said breathless, in a jumble, and he had to work hard to make sense of it. To see how the sentences fit together.

"Take a breath. Just breathe." He was trying to avoid saying "stay calm" even as his own heart rate had spiked. That would just send the Mudder over the edge.

"But *I* can't forget and *you* can't forget I ever existed, which is what I want and you can't fucking do it, can you? No you can't. I want you to forget and either you or someone else will come after me and ask more questions I can't answer and I'll have to give the same answers and I'm sick of having to think about this, you understand. I'm sick of worrying about people finding me and asking, and I don't know if I believe you. I know I don't dare believe you. How am I supposed to believe you? The fact is I can't and someday you'll come for me and so how can anybody have peace of mind in that? You can't. You can never have peace of mind. Something terrible is coming. It's still uncurling from that long-ago moment. I know it, and it's going to kill us all every one of us. It'll kill you and me and—"

"I want to assure you that no one else even knows—"

"Goodbye. Fucking old man. Stupid fucking old man."

But there came no click of the phone. Instead, Old Jim heard a loud crack like a handgun firing, a weight hitting the floor and then the receiver banging a table. Or so it seemed.

He waited. And waited. The line remained open. He didn't know what he was waiting for—someone else to pick up?—but instinct told him not to hang up.

"That was good acting," he said finally, maybe to no one. "But I know you're still on the line." The gunshot had been a recording. He knew it hadn't sounded quite right, like from a television show.

"Fuck you fuck you fuck you fuck you fuck you. Leave me the fuck alone or I'll kill you. I'll come back there and I'll kill you. I'll—"

Old Jim placed the receiver back on the phone. It was the kindest thing to do. For the Mudder.

Maybe no one had really survived the expedition except the Medic.


Old Jim tried to go back to work, but he couldn't. The sense of being caught in a trap or a maze, the suffocation of that.

He escaped to the porch instead. Didn't quite know what to do with himself. Sitting on the porch doing nothing helped, a bit. Yet even doing nothing, he was allowed solitude for only a brief time.

Because soon enough, Gloria arrived on a bike, reckless over the ruts in the yard, clutching a crumpled paper bag against one handlebar. She careened to a stop in front of the porch, let the bike crash to the ground, and hopped up the steps so fast she had to skid to avoid pile-driving through him and his chair.

Her face was flushed from the exertion, and her hair was so thoroughly wind-tangled, she kept having to brush it away from her face. She smelled like a kid who had been exploring mud and swamp all day. Her boots told the same story.

She dropped the bag on the table next to him.

"Mom's cookies. No raisins. Just oatmeal and also chocolate chip. Thanks for taking the hook out of my foot."

"You're welcome," Old Jim said, looking in the bag. He had so little interest in talking to her, wanted her gone so she wouldn't interrupt thinking about the Mudder's words.

"You should read the note. It's from my mom. She likes you."

"Your mom doesn't know me well enough to have an opinion about me. And neither should you."

Except she knew he had taken the fishhook out of her daughter's foot. That would be enough for some people.

"Just read the note."

The note read "Thanks for taking care of my daughter. Maybe I can buy you a drink someday as thanks. Trudi Jenkins." Sure. Right. Maybe they could go on a date while psychics screamed in submarines at the bottom of the sea. That seemed likely, seemed right. The absurdity of his life overwhelmed him. The sheer unnatural quality of that life.

"Do you like the note?"

This insistence on him liking the note irritated him. Caught at the wrong moment or the kid was genuinely cloying.

"Yeah, I like the note fine. Thank-you notes are good to write."

"Mom says that, too. She writes letters sometimes."

His interest perked up.

"You ever write letters?"

"No, mostly I draw things I see. Starfish. Lighthouses. Pretty rocks. Should I write letters?"

"Well, depends on to whom," Old Jim said. "Sending a letter means something." Or, it would, unless you wrote a hundred of them, to someone who never received them.

"What about that man you pushed into the sea? Will he get a letter?"

So she had seen that.

"No, he will not get a letter."

"What about a postcard? Is that okay?" She was looking at him with an earnestness that made him smile.

"When you only care a little bit, yes."

"So he gets a get-well postcard?"

No, he gets a fuck-off-and-die postcard.

"Sure, why not. He can have one. Everybody can have one."

"You sound like you need a postcard," Gloria said.

He laughed at that while she stood there, mouth open like she wanted to laugh, but wasn't quite sure why they were laughing.

"Is there something wrong with you?" she asked.

"Yes," he said. "Now, you should go."

She hesitated, gave him a look he could not interpret, and got back on her bike. Now he could see, half-hidden by trees, that a car waited at the end of the driveway. Her mom. So maybe she didn't roam as far as he thought.

Old Jim watched her go, wondering how he could dissuade

her from coming back. The premonition of the urge to deploy her if she did come back, to turn her into a little spy who reported to him all unknowing.

By then, Old Jim had almost forgotten the wreck and ruin of the Mudder. He almost felt like he was just some washed-up guy who deserved cookies for taking out a fishhook.

Every sorrow might have its day, as the song went, but perhaps joy could, too, sometimes.

If joy meant oblivion.


Later, though, the itch came back and Old Jim went inside and pulled the rug out. The safe (and it wasn't strange, was it, that he'd spent the time on that, or that it seemed to have taken no time at all?) appeared to him like a greedy little mouth, with its twin dials for the combination like eyes, and how could he be sure that somehow the safe didn't open a link to Central, such that whatever he put in was immediately taken out on the other side back in the sterile cathedral?

He pulled the Mudder's journal out, closed the safe, replaced the rug, and sat on the couch. No one had physically examined the Mudder's journal for a decade. When he had first seen her journal in the secure, climate-controlled environment, a kind of weight had lifted from him. Even having to view it via gloves shoved into a sealed chamber usually reserved for plague bacteria or radioactive objects. An unexpected grace and beauty, swathed in darkness, the light all concentrated golden on this artifact from a now-ancient conflict.

What he'd left in that space in the archives approximated what he held in his hands, even if he trusted no one would request a viewing in a month or even a year. Some reliquaries were not in high demand at Central, while others likely were hauled out at Brute meetings like, well, a monkey's paw. Anointed with unholy water, blessed, prayed upon.

As carefully as he could, Old Jim pulled the journal from the plastic protective sheath. He was looking forward to revisiting it, with the idea that parts might mean something different after the phone call.

Except . . . all the pages had been slashed to pieces with something like an X-Acto knife and then patiently pushed between the covers to fit in the plastic container.

He stared at the desecration, mind blank, truly shocked.

Someone had come into his house to do this. Someone had known the combination to the safe.

A kind of message from . . . whom? From Central? Belt buckles. House centipedes. Rifles firing into the side of the silo. Secret minder or Failure Island sicko or the "Bad Slack" of the Rogue? He felt bereaved, shaken.

But it felt like a test, as well as a message. So he replaced it in the safe, adding the strange little key, too.

Then he went into his office for the nightly ritual of turning on the alligator tracker. The usual moment of disappointment, which this time would also be the relief of normalcy. The relief of knowing that there was no Tyrant out there, possibly no Rogue from twenty years ago.

He flipped the dial on the tracker, watched as it came on. The familiar green of nothingness. No signal to receive. No trace. Like he wished his mind would be: empty, at peace.

Then the dot blinked red. It blinked red. He almost fell out of his chair. He peered at the coordinates, compared them to his foldout map, heart beating rapid.

It was . . . it was . . . in the middle of Dead Town? How was that possible. He tapped the side of the machine as if it had malfunctioned.

The dot shifted to a different location.

Shit. A scramble to look up those coordinates. Middle of a marsh, of course. Nowhere. Literally nowhere—nothing nearby, no roads, nothing. As remote as could be.

The dot hovered there for a moment, flashing against the green circles like mosquito coils. Then it began to move. Rapidly.

It took a moment to realize the dot was headed directly toward his location. At speed. As if whatever lay out there knew he was tracking it.

Old Jim shut off the tracker. He pulled the plug out of the wall. Then he took the whole apparatus and he went out onto the back deck and he tossed it into the darkness.

"You can have it!" he shouted. "Take the fucking thing!"

Who kept fucking with him. Why couldn't he shake his dreams.

He had no clue.

## 015: THE MONKEY'S PAW

There came onrushing the Friday night of the Monkey's Elbow gig, like a great beast coming for Old Jim. When a new Commander Thistle would join the band for one night only.

Cass had called several times, but he hadn't picked up. He needed time to think, to connect the dots, and he spent whole days drawing and redrawing diagrams that showed the Mudder, the Medic, Man Boy Slim—3M for short—in relation to the Rogue. In spite of himself he kept trying to see some pattern that fit Cass's operational acronyms.

But it seemed impossible. Cass's intensity about the Rogue, the idea of some higher purpose for him, some reason that ranked above God and country—it infected him at times, got to him in a way that felt like a yearning. Like he, too, needed such a purpose.

He escaped the trapped feeling of that, and what felt like dysfunction, by letting the bar job overtake him as the place began to fill up. A certain amount of good feeling in recognizing Trudi, Gloria's mom, with a wave, and less of that feeling noticing Man Boy Slim walk in. But that was put aside as the pace of mixing drinks, pouring beers, quickened, thankful that the Village Bar had only a rudimentary toaster-oven menu.

Soon enough, the band took the stage, with acoustic and electric guitars, violin, keyboards, drums, and the vocalist, traditionally sans instrument (to broaden a limited pool). Trudi was on tambourine, like usual, the rest less familiar to him. The boisterous applause from a packed, standing-room-only crowd shook the wooden foundations and Old Jim gasped despite himself, no dust settling from the ceiling, no impact of missile or bomb. Just a band that, sometimes, drew people here from all over the county.

Monkey's Elbow had some rules about their twice-a-year "Commander Thistle" as lead singer, a role held otherwise by Brad the lighthouse volunteer. You could not use your real name onstage, and Commanders typically used masks to disguise their true identity, even if you didn't have to be a spy to figure out someone from their body language.

Another reason the crowd had swelled: Every volunteer lead singer had to write a new song that would be recorded only for a limited-edition small-batch pressing. To be purchased, along with T-shirts, from a weary-looking gray-haired woman in a long drab skirt standing behind a rickety foldout merch table.

Commander Thistle came up after the regular members of Monkey's Elbow, a bulky man dressed in a strange hat and long trench coat that, from behind the bar, Old Jim paid only half a mind to as the drink orders came in. But the audience oohed and aahed at the elaborate nature of the disguise. Maybe because if you knew Commander Thistle, say, was the butcher down the street, you might not take his singing seriously.

But, then, somebody at the bar had said it wasn't a popularity contest.

The man's voice fit his image: rusty and slow-roasted, with a hint of barbed wire, rasp but no twang. Nothing of the sea in that voice, oddly enough. At least, as Old Jim thought of the sea, or even the way the sea had served as a backdrop to the squat barrel of the Medic's own raspy voice before Old Jim had pushed him in the sea.

> *Shining out like shining out like shining out*
> *So the dark so the dark is no longer to blame.*
> *Shining out like shining out like shining out*
> *God in his tower and Man in his berth*
> *Shining out, shining out, shining out . . .*

The *"shining out"* became less divided as it repeated, until the commas had been obliterated and it could as easily have been *"out shining out shining."*

He wondered if the song lingered in his ears from Central research, or just déjà vu from other songs. A moment of *recognition* in the words he didn't understand. For the song or the singer?

Looking at that implacable mask, he wondered what he didn't know about the here and the now. Not the past, with which he had become intimate. Not the future no one could see, but maybe what existed here, outside of the Brigade, Central, the Rogue. The man's weighty head tilted forward as if to topple, mask still disguising his features. It was disconcertingly, with the tricorn hat, a premonition of the guillotine ushering in a new age.

As Commander Thistle launched into another song—"Down in the Marshes, Up in the Sky, I See My God"—Cass walked into the bar.

A whole new wave of energy burst in behind her, in the form of five fishermen just off shift, ready to drink, and the festivities became more jubilant. Cass looked askance at the noise of them, walked up to the bar, and asked Old Jim a question.

But he couldn't hear over the music. He motioned to his ear and she looked exasperated, waved her hand, like "talk to you later," and said hello to a man and woman dancing to the music, who led her closer to the stage, so the three of them were swallowed by the crowd. Old Jim kept serving drinks.

Maybe, for one night, they could both just be civilians.

O weary night. O ceaseless journey. For, how long could a band play without pause when their lead singer was made of solid stone?

Candle, flame, or vessel? The question came to him again as a long treatise in his head about the limits of a middle-aged man's endurance, being both owner of a bar and in charge of a secret mission, the limits of which had become murkier and murkier.

As the night wore on. While he washed beer mugs and gave Sally backup support, changing out a tap, then another, the rage of conversations as energy-sapping as the repetition of nautical terrors and misfortunes from days of yore. Were they now secretly a colonial-era pub? Wrung out the dish towel, had to hand dry as the dishwasher decided to malfunction. Couldn't be sure he was hearing the lyrics right, or maybe there was no right way. Because so different.

> *Oh, to be the burning light*
> *sinking beneath the waves.*

*Oh, to escape this nameless plight*
*and dive into a whirling grave.*

The way the black of Commander Thistle's mask felt like stark night, like stark night staring back at him when he woke distressed. Despite the neutral expression on those wide features, the mask captured the beginning or very end of a scream. A sense of violence or disturbance lurked beneath the impassive gaze, the suggestion of thick lips in the pale flash of the mouth hole.

He checked. The key was back in his pocket, but he did not remember opening the safe. When had that happened?

Man Boy Slim had come up to the bar, and Old Jim was instantly on high alert. He tried to find Cass in the crowd, but he'd lost her.

"You know what I learned today?" Man Boy Slim asked. The band had finished their first set, so Old Jim could, unfortunately, hear him.

"No, what did you learn today?"

"Well, Old Jim, what I learned today is that what appear to be the stubby legs on a caterpillar are actually proto legs—they're completely fake. The real legs are on its face, if you can believe that—can you believe that?"

"No, that's pretty interesting," Old Jim said. Man Boy Slim appeared to have lost his fear of black sites, or an ass-kicking.

"So, anyway, these fake legs still help the caterpillar move around. Real fake legs. Imagine that. Can you imagine that, Old Slim?"

"I can imagine I'm not serving you another drink, that's what I can imagine."

Man Boy Slim wiped at his eyes like a fly had settled on him. "Yeah, well, it means something, philosophically. Like, would you recognize a caterpillar as a caterpillar without its fake legs? And what if the caterpillar's disguised as something else to begin with? And if you carefully pull off the fake legs, would it walk on its face?" Man Boy Slim started giggling at his own rhetoric. "Walk on its own face."

"Profound," Old Jim said in a neutral voice. Was he high?

"I have to take a leak. But don't go anywhere. So many tales left to tell you. So many tales to tell on you."

Old Jim watched Man Boy Slim head for the bathroom. The distress in the man. How it probably meant the Mudder was unrecoverable, that Man Boy Slim would never find her, never talk to her again.

He needed a break, felt like he was suffocating.

Outside was cool and dark, the streetlamp in front having gone out and the county in no rush to come around to replace it. Just a tinge of moon and the triangle wedge of blue-green light from the neon sign shouting "Village Bar" that let him see. That lulling sound of tide and sea, the hunkered shapes of the houses and other businesses, few of them lit up, along with all the cars and trucks here for the concert. The band noise buffered by the door, distant enough to hear himself think.

He began to feel at peace when a boy and a girl stepped into the neon blue-green, their faces striated by it, bodies whorled and swelling because of it.

No, not children, not teenagers. Adults. They just had that aspect, dressed all in black, the man in particular—the kind of youth preserved in aspic you saw mostly in centaurs and aging child actors. She had a demeanor of golden-haired innocence he couldn't quite explain, sharpened and estranged by the neon light. Her gaze was feral, her teeth sharpened by shadow.

Two undead freaks, trapped here by the seaside, in the off-season. Or maybe they were about to sell him some form of God. Someone reeked of turpentine.

"Hello, Jim," the man said, with a foreign accent. He had small eyes in an oval face, was stout but no muscle behind it, and had a stilted look to the slant of him. Like his neck wasn't properly connected to his body.

"Do I know you?" Old Jim asked. He had his peashooter at his ankle and a knife at his waist, but not his Walther, because he didn't like having real firepower around the bar.

"I think you do. In fact, I think you know all about us. You're the Night Commander, after all, pulling the secret strings of Valhalla."

*Night Commander* said smarmy, disrespectful, and then Henry waited to gauge Old Jim's reaction, when Old Jim knew he wanted to say more.

"The secret strings of Valhalla, huh? Sounds important," Old Jim said. Or meaningless.

While Suzanne stood there as mute as a wax museum statue of herself.

"And I know all about you, too—your insomnia, your sleep-walking," Henry said when Old Jim said nothing. "All your pacing back and forth in your office? I understand it's a lot of responsibility running our organization. Must wear on you, Night Commander."

Jesus. Compromised. Surveillance? At a distance, from off-property.

"Got a point to this?" The point Old Jim felt he might have to emphasize was a quick kick to Henry's groin and then a retreat back into the bar.

Henry had come closer while Suzanne hung back. A good disguise, Henry's indeterminate age. You might underestimate him based on youth if you didn't know better. The adroit use of makeup and the put-together look of pressed trousers and crisply ironed shirt under a tailored blazer, along with good genes, give a sense of perpetual youth, if also a whiff of school uniform.

But one day, maybe decades hence, this man's head would sink like a shriveled apple into the ruins of a waiting wattled neck.

"We want to know who your boss is, Night Commander. You run tricky Cass and maybe someone runs tricky you. And we want to know where the rest of the resources are—the money we need to do our critical research. Where is it? Why withhold it now?"

Critical for who? For what purpose? A half sister who followed him around like an unpaid intern.

"Are you one of those Ouija Hicks that roam the coast? Is that who you are?" Maybe pointless to pretend he didn't know who Henry was, but narcissists didn't like being treated this way.

But Henry just laughed in a thin-lipped mirthless way. "If so, you're the head hick, Night Commander."

"If a bird flies long enough inside a house is it still a bird?" Remembering the questions the psych had asked him at Central.

Henry looked confused, struggled to respond.

"Do you exhibit glib and superficial charm?"

"Is there something wrong with you, Night Commander? Something breaking down, perhaps?"

"Here's another one," Old Jim said, his own special nod to the the manual for identifying psychopaths: "A belt buckle and a brick are traveling in opposite directions, away from each other, the brick at the speed of a snail on a bad day and the belt buckle at the speed of a waistline expanding at the rate of three inches per month. Which one will reach you first, if you stand at the exact opposite end of the universe? The snail or the waistline?"

Henry smiled, revealing the affectation of sharpened incisors. Old Jim felt like he'd hit his target, and also suggested the "Night Commander" might be deranged enough to do anything.

"So, which is it?" Old Jim prodded, left hand resting on his knife.

"Did you like how you were greeted at the silo?" Henry asked.

Before Old Jim could answer, a group of fishermen came sprawling out from the bar. They looked as rough as bare-knuckle boxers. Henry kept a cocked finger like a gun pointed at Old Jim, even as the two retreated, receding and receding until they were gone, taken by the darkness.

As if they really were vampires. Except, soon after, Old Jim heard the cough of a car engine starting and he figured they'd decided not to fly away.


Old Jim had no stomach for going back to the bar after that. Not right away. So, instead, he braved the wall of sound long enough, Monkey's Elbow raving on again, to duck into his office, and from there through the storeroom and out back, in search of the little bridge. There was just enough moon and glow from a back window of the bar to find his way.

He could see the lighthouse's beam shining out, moving on, shining out, revolving three hundred sixty degrees to take the entire measure of the Forgotten Coast. The smell of salt and brine from the coast came up quick on the seething breezes.

Henry had unnerved him, maybe more in what he already had gleaned about Central's operation than his demeanor. What did he mean about the money? Resources? Was that just a shake-down? Or something else?

The dull vibration of drums and bass guitar weakened, strengthened, as the distant front door opened and closed, opened again, along with the rough wail of Commander Thistle. "*The stars start to glow / and the sun shines its last.*"

He'd unwind for ten minutes and then return to help Sally. Get his shit together, talk to Cass, maybe, about priorities for next week.

But when he stepped onto the bridge, he heard a sound in the water as of an animal moving away into the marsh. Some beast large and ponderous.

A figure arose at the other end of the bridge.

Old Jim stood completely still. The figure was just a silhouette.

"Man Boy Slim? Is that you?" Old Jim asked.

The figure said nothing, remained motionless at the other end of the bridge. A nothing smudged by night.

It wasn't Man Boy Slim.

"Who's there?" Old Jim asked. "Who are you?"

But he knew who it was.

Whispering at Old Jim, whispering and whispering like a floating flame over the mud flats. Whispering and whispering, intent on the whispering, like some psychic, like some phantom, like something ancient and yet new.

The Rogue.

He tried to drop to one knee, pull the peashooter out of his ankle holster. But he couldn't. He couldn't. It was too late.

Because the Rogue's words were slamming into him now, slamming into him and drawing him close, reeling him in and drawing him out, until he was as thin as taut twine and nothing at all was left of him. Nothing at all, like it was always meant to be.

Except, Old Jim's mouth was opening wide and wider still to vomit words, to erupt words toward the Rogue. Words in patterns he had never learned, words meant to harm, and he heard the Rogue shriek as if he'd been dealt a physical blow.

Even as Old Jim was falling. Falling down a deep well, a flight of stairs, into a crevice far beneath the sea, with no oxygen to breathe. No pulse. No heartbeat. Nothing but dark sky above.

Until his body felt like a vast blackened meadow with the rain coming down.

Ah, Cass. Ah, Genevieve. What had he done? What was he still doing?

Then there was nothing but darkness.

# DISSOLUTION

## 016: WATER LIVES HERE

Old Jim stared out from the banks of a sandy, slow river held in deep shadow by ancient trees. Ravens walked on the flat rocks in the middle of the river. The dark of the canopy felt intense, the sun coming through only as a dappling, branches reflected in the water. He was a vessel with a guttering candle, left on the bank, and could not move. He was the water or the air, and neither the air nor the water could be called just that, if you looked close enough. People lived invisible and impossible in the water, or had become the water, or something else lingered there and he could not change his view to be certain. All while there came the pull of a distance he could not discern through the trees, a green light, a cleft between two mountains and he had the sense that if he just traveled farther down the river, he would see—

The sounds of distant gunfire—one, two, three, four gunshots or shouts. The ravens, like splotches and ruptures of blackness, became spooked by the noise, rose, and disappeared into the trees or became the trees.

He woke in an unfamiliar bed, a lounge chair opposite with Brigade files on the seat. From the way the cushions had been pushed flat, someone had been sitting there a lot.

His eyes and mouth felt dry. His head seeming to weigh more than his whole body, so he couldn't think of moving. He thought he'd seen Cass the last time he'd woken up, her hair short and the wrong color, as if in a dream. He struggled to rise, but all that happened was that the sound of water over the rocks came close again, and in no time at all, he was in the water, becoming the deep water, becoming . . .

Woke again to the sensation of a centipede curled around his brain, under his skull, fast-fading.

"Stay still, stop trying to move," Cass said, but gently, from somewhere overhead or to the side, from below or above. He hadn't been able to open his eyes yet.

"You snored like gunshots or shouts, or someone did," he tried to say with his dry mouth, but it came out in a mumble or an exhaled breath, wasn't important anyway. He had a pain in his abdomen, like a muscle strain, but also as if someone had placed a stone egg inside of him, next to the muscle.

He opened his eyes. Cass had pulled up a stool bedside, her hair short and blond, just like he'd thought.

"You're lucid? You know you're in the loft bedroom of my apartment?"

He nodded.

"Water?"

He nodded again.

Cass offered him a glass of water from a table next to the bed, helped him sit up, held it for him as he drank. There was a softness to her that surprised him.

"Let me check your pulse and take your temperature."

Her gaze told him it was important.

"C'mon, at least your pulse, or I'm not telling you what happened."

Now he got it. She was concerned he might be impaired in some way. So he offered up his arm. He felt helpless as she held her thumb on the vein in his wrist, counting.

When she'd finished, she carefully placed his arm back by his side.

"Pulse is a little high, but not by much. Good."

He lay back in bed, ghost to a headache, the skylight in the slanted roof framing the crisscrossing branches of trees. Did she live in the forest? White walls balanced by rustic wood for the ceiling. Someone had undressed him and put his pajamas on him. He felt vulnerable, exposed.

"Your hair . . . ?"

"Call it combat ready. You've been out of it for a while."

An impatience and energy was rising in him.

"So, what happened?"

"A lot." A curious mixture of frown and smile lived on her face, and he could see the tiredness in her eyes.

"How long?" He tried to keep the panic out of his voice.

"Three days," Cass said, giving him an evaluating look. "I brought you here so I could keep an eye on you."

"Three days?" That took him by surprise. "I don't remember that—getting here. Or much else." His mouth opening wide and wider still to erupt words toward the Rogue. There was a deep ache throbbing down his back and left arm.

"Are you ready to hear everything?" she asked, with kindness.

"Yes."

She hesitated, still assessing him, then said, "Someone ambushed you at that little bridge. I shot at them as they tried to get away. Pretty sure they took one in the chest. Someone torched Old Decomp. And the psychics on Failure Island found an alligator harness, using your bobber."

The alligator harness felt like a trap somehow. How he felt about the Rogue was complicated, but it was hard not to mourn the stone silo, all those peculiar and oddly beautiful dead things no longer even a memory of flesh, but just gone, forever.

"That's a lot," he said.

"I told you."

Old Jim rose half up out of the bed, but Cass pushed him back down.

"No. Stay in bed a bit longer. Just to be sure."

Covers thrown back, Old Jim could see his feet. He was wearing socks with a bunny pattern on them.

"All I had, promise," she said.

He decided not to challenge her on that.


A couple of hours later, Cass helped him downstairs and dumped him in a chair at the kitchen table. He had no doubt she'd hauled him upstairs herself and wondered why she'd made the effort. A leather couch, another TV, and a terrarium full of water and plants next to the couch.

"What's in the terrarium?"

"Two clawed frogs that look like plastic and don't move much," Cass said. "I call them Jack and Jackie."

Maybe he should have found "Jack and Jackie" funny, but he didn't.

She brought him some coffee. "Not sure you need this, but . . ."

He took a sip, his mind lighting up.

"What did you tell Jackie?"

"That you have a cold, that's all. I wanted to let you decide what to tell her." While she cracked eggs into a bowl, looked for a whisk.

"How'd you know to look for me? At the bridge?" She'd seemed distracted last he'd seen her in the bar.

"I noticed as soon as you went into the office. I think I've told you not to use that back door for breaks . . . and I've been keeping an eye on you."

Emotion so strong it surprised him.

"Thank you."

Cass poured the eggs into the frying pan, contemplated the sizzle and pop.

"Jim. I wouldn't have been caught dead on that bridge after dark. Fully exposed. A sniper could've ended you. And there would've been nothing I could do. You know that, right?"

"I'm not myself." Had he imagined shouting at the Rogue, and its effect on the man?

"Are you sure?"

She was asking if she could rely on him. Checking his pulse again.

"Any chance I could get another glass of water?"

"It's already there." Miraculously, it was. Right in front of him.

"While you eat breakfast, let me tell you about what happened on the bridge."

Cass had found him by the screams that cut off suddenly, at the entrance to the bridge, on his side, trying to get on all fours, bruised and weeping. He was striking out blind with his knife, such that Cass thought he had impaired vision.

At the far end of the bridge, Cass saw a figure moving forward, and put two rounds into the general direction of his chest, which caused him to dive into the reeds beyond the bridge, soundless, so she didn't know what she had hit. Cass had the definite impression that it was a man. No, definitely not Henry. No, not anyone she'd recognized, like Man Boy Slim.

Moving cautiously, Cass had ventured as far as the end of the bridge, saw no movement, heard nothing, except what might have been a gator in the middle distance, in the water. Blood spatter on the boards led into the grass. Enough blood to believe she did him damage.

There were no fingerprints, no shoe prints, nothing but the blood. She'd sent samples to Central and then wiped the scene clean. After securing the site, she'd tended to Old Jim, making sure he had no critical injuries. He'd put down the knife by then, despite having no recollection of having drawn it. Disoriented, his eyes were bloodshot. Cass recalled that he had kept talking about a candle and a flame, "some other weird shit." A winter journey.

So Cass had gathered him up and gotten him into the bar office, put him on the cot they kept back there for naps, and gotten Trudi to examine him, there being no Brigade medic within easy call.

"You thought Trudi would be happy to return the favor."

"Something like that."

Old Jim found himself more concerned about Trudi seeing him like that than the breach in "protocol." What was protocol when you used psychics like sniffer dogs?

Trudi could find nothing wrong except that Old Jim had "obviously experienced a trauma." Cass had alluded to "a history of seizures" as cover and, after Trudi left, had taken Old Jim to her place.

By midnight, Old Jim was deep in sleep and she'd gotten word that Old Decomp had gone up in flames, someone breaking in, lighting a match, and boom. "The chemicals in the jars acted like accelerant. The stone held but became an oven, baking it all until the roof eventually blew off." The outer structure, burnt out, still stood, but the contents had been obliterated for the most part.

By the next morning she'd received word that the psychics had identified the general coordinates of what they believed to be an alligator harness identical to the one they had been given.

"Oh—and here. One thing from Old Decomp survived. Must've been hidden among the sample trays."

She placed a photograph on the table.

It took Old Jim a moment to recognize what she'd taken a picture of: small, half burnt and inchoate, slurred by flame into less of a compact object than a memory of its function.

The remains of a rabbit camera from twenty years ago.

Funny, how the world could change so quickly. A week ago, he would have rejoiced at finding a camera. Now, he recoiled, had to force himself to relax back into his seat.

"Send it to Central as soon as you can," Old Jim said. He didn't want it anywhere near him, Cass, Failure Island.

"I already did. I didn't handle it. I didn't let anyone touch it directly."

Old Jim nodded, relaxing. He didn't believe Jack was that sloppy, that R&D was that sloppy. They would have found a camera in the biologists' samples long ago.

So how had the camera gotten there?

He thought he knew.


## 017: NOTHING TRACKS


O ld Jim got dressed. He asked for any new reports he'd missed to be brought along when they went out. Didn't he want to rest? No, he didn't want to rest. He felt an attenuated rejuvenation in that moment. Sally could mind the bar, the psychics would self-medicate and self-manage on Failure Island for another day. Jackie could cool her jets.

They would visit the beach not to catch his breath, but to see where Cass had found the harness. And then? Then maybe he'd rest or maybe not. But hadn't he just rested? And now he had to catch up, outthink, outrun the source of that "rest" for him.

He'd survived the Rogue, and now it was time to plunge ahead, even if that meant transport via Cass's crappy hatchback, with its lurching five-speed.

They drove to the coast amid an impossible yearning on Old Jim's part—impossible because he didn't know what he yearned for, an incurable, reckless energy rising in him. An impatience with his dreams, an irritation with piano music. Beating a rhythm against his leg with the fingers of his left hand. He liked that the weather had gotten cold, that maybe they'd see glimpses of winter, soon.

They reached the little strip of beach where the harness had been found, parking in the cul-de-sac of concrete that marked the farthest point of civilization. The coast all around consisted of wildlife refuges and state parks.

Old Jim found the trees here strange—either dead snags like ragged spikes sticking out knee-deep from the salt water or the sand pines that grew gnarled but tall, with few lower branches but a sudden opening up to a verdant green fan shape at the top. Nothing else grew here. Nothing much suggested other than the stark idyllic, other than the vague outline of a freighter at the horizon line, well beyond the chatter and swift glide of gulls.

Sift through thin lines of dead seaweed and barnacles to know your future, or maybe just your past. When what he really needed was to know what the hell was going on in the present.

He sat on a fallen tree trunk become driftwood, at the edge of the cul-de-sac, Cass standing beside him, shielding her eyes from the glare. She surveyed the beach as the wind buffeted him in a way he found comforting. Eternal.

"What is that?" he asked, pointing to the "structure" in front of them. A half circle of stone in the shallows just offshore, cradling the mud flats that had formed in front of it. Three more jagged spines of tree trunks stood in front of the stone, evenly spaced. The harness had been tied to one of them.

"A place that was different once," Cass said. "And will be again."

The water had crept inland, as water will, and the trees had died of it, and what had been a kind of observation point had been buried in sand and reduced to a ruin—a crumbling fortress for fiddler crabs. He hated that he now saw anything unusual as suspect.

"How close were they?"

"Who? To what?" Said softly, like she was considering something shimmering far out at sea. The place had that effect. Was it calming or was it just so much bigger than them?

"The psychics. Tell me about it."

"Beacham's Point, they said. Very specific. Only this one way in and out. They saw it 'in the thoughts,' as they put it."

"*Whose* thoughts?"

"I don't know. The ones who saw it are still in a sub at the bottom of the sea, conducting other research."

"They must have said something."

"Just that, and I quote, 'a mind had revealed itself and we could read it amid the static.'"

"I don't believe it," Old Jim said. "I mean, I think the Rogue lets them see what the Rogue wants them to see. Or did."

Cass was giving him a look and he just stared out to sea.

"Full report soon," she said, "but you have to admit they were right. Do you want to examine the harness?"

"No."

"Brigade forensics will be all over it, but I doubt they'll find anything," she said, sagging down beside him on the log.

"What about all these tracks?"

One reason he hadn't wanted to walk on the beach was to think about the tracks first. He could clearly see Cass's boot prints out to the snag, although not back. But from the suggestion of a double imprint on some, she'd just stepped back the way she'd come, to avoid contaminating the scene further. Smart. He wouldn't have thought to do that.

"Yeah, there's been a lot of traffic on this beach. Popular with animals for sure."

Cass's were the only human prints. But he could see paw prints, cascading lines, bird feet, and a thick dislocation as of something wide pulling itself along parallel with the upper shoreline, positioned between two lines of sea wrack.

"What do you see?

"There's a lot if you know how to interpret it," Cass said. She rose, pondered, pointed: "Raccoons there, lots of them, a whole battalion of raccoons. Herons. Tons of shorebirds. A bobcat. A couple of snakes, though sometimes opossums drag their tails. You've noticed there are no shoe prints except mine, I hope."

"Snakes on a beach?"

"Happens all the time."

"How do you know this, about animal tracks?"

A wistfulness he put down to homesickness in her reply. Like, maybe she thought she could never go back there.

"I learned it growing up in a place like this. Different latitude and longitude, but similar. I had a dad who took me fishing and hiking. You didn't have that?"

"No."

And what he had now, even in this calm place, was still the feeling that he had gotten in over his head. But she hadn't mentioned the most disconcerting mark on the beach, so maybe she felt the same.

"That long, wide track, like something sliding through . . . ?"

A massive creature, with imprints to each side, as if something like starfish hands had been uncontrollably shaking against the sand. With odd traces of coquina and moss to the sides.

"A very, very large alligator, I'd guess."

"It swam out of the sea?"

"Alligators do that here."

They were silent, then, staring at that premonition of the past, Old Jim contemplating Cass's tracks in the sand. The way the harness had been tethered to the snag. This idea that the Rogue had been "hiding out" for twenty years—it still didn't make sense.

"The Rogue didn't burn down Old Decomp," Old Jim said.

"He didn't," Cass said, in a vaguely distracted tone. Was she still intent on his physical condition?

"The Rogue wouldn't have left the camera. The Rogue would have taken the camera. And what would it accomplish, anyway?"

The way the Rogue had adapted to circumstances, to be feeding cameras to an alligator. Whatever that meant. More likely Man Boy Slim left the camera, burnt the place down. In which case, who cared?

"I've been thinking about how we're floundering." Still in that detached tone that worried him, as if she was weary after taking care of him for so long.

"Why do you say that?"

"While you slept, I got the blood sample analysis back, the one from the bridge. Not human. Alligator blood. I'd made up a story about wildlife studies relevant to 'foreign entities.'"

Old Jim considered that—the part where the Rogue was actually the Tyrant.

"Are you sure—"

"I shot him. Twice. In the chest. There was no gator. As far as

I can tell, despite there being no body, the Rogue is in bad shape right now."

The Rogue could have killed him on the bridge—could have used prosaic methods and means. Shot him. Stabbed him. Bludgeoned him with a baseball bat. But instead, the Rogue had tried the same trick as before. The house centipede trick.

So why hadn't it worked? Or worked as intended? Or had it failed? It must have failed.

"Here's your gun, by the way," Cass said, and unclasped a shoulder holster, heavy with metal, and handed it to him. "Ammo's in the car."

He stared at the Walther like he'd never seen it before. Well, he guessed he was behaving normally, if she'd returned it to him.

"We have to go to Dead Town," he said. "Now."

"Why?"

"Because everything started there. Because in my office the alligator tracker had blinked red there."

Because Dead Town was like a suspect he had to rule out.

He felt her gaze on him, realized if she objected, he wouldn't push back.

But all she said was "Dead Town it is then," and walked back to the car.

While he contemplated some version of eternity. That end-less horizon of sea, that peculiar altar to the memory of ruins. All the little fiddler crabs frozen in front of him, next to their holes, wondering what he would do next.

Wondering if he would be merciful or lay waste to their homes, burn everything down.

## 018: THE DEAD

**N**othing like the old days, those old days he'd never known on this Forgotten Coast—now there was a halfway reliable route you could take to Dead Town.

On the way, he found out Cass liked to listen to punk music. Cass also liked to race her hatchback down dirt roads, not much caring about the jostling, her window open a crack, so dust still swirled in, but she grinned wider like that made it better. With the punk music blaring, which just sounded like noise to Old Jim.

"Did I tell you I used to like off-road racing? This 'stupid little hatchback' is actually souped-up, which I didn't expect."

He'd been so impressed by how spotless Cass's car was that it had taken him a little while to realize when it didn't fall apart after ten minutes that Central must've had the shocks reinforced and swapped out the engine block.

She radiated such an unencumbered joy when she had to shift gears suddenly or when they threatened to drift and mire on the sandy parts of the road. Relishing the challenge, leaning forward in her seat to see better what hazard lay ahead, whether whipping branches or even mud in the ruts from the recent rain. But then settled down, tapping her finger against the steering wheel during some song at odds with the music on the radio, which fizzed and spat at times, reduced to static, then cleared up, fizzed, cleared up. Repeat.

"No country stations?" Old Jim asked.

"You like country?"

"No."

She laughed. "Punk isn't for you. Is that what you're saying?"

"I don't even know what this is." It struck him as the opposite of *Winter Journey*, which agitated him.

This feral energy to her today that he recognized, this nervous energy because they were headed into the unknown. She loved movement, he could tell, was happiest in motion. And she'd had to look after him for days.

As they watched the countryside roll by: meadows and forests, run-down shacks in the middle of nowhere, farms gone to ruin, overtaken by pine trees and vines. Every once in a long while a man with a shotgun and a hunting dog who stared at them with a stoic interest.

✦

Old Jim noticed that Cass's mood dipped when she had to slow to a crawl, a creep, at the turnoff onto a road lined by barbed-wire fence and overgrown with long grass, ending at a locked gate flanked by a bog and a thicket of wax myrtles.

As she took the key out of the ignition, her smile became flat affect, her gaze inward-turning, and her body seemed to take up less room.

He checked his firearm, put a new clip in the magazine, while Cass reached for her pack in the back seat.

"You ready?" she asked, opening the car door.

"Yeah, sure," he said. "Born ready."

She winced at the cliché, but it was no worse than her own quips. Just like old times with Jack, is what had him frozen. In a car. On foot. In a helicopter. A prop plane. A boat. Bicycles once. The terrible bad old times. No, it would be nothing like that, would it?

"I'll take point," she said.

"Expecting trouble?"

"Low probability the Rogue is here, if alive, coming back to the scene of the crime," Cass said.

"If the Rogue thinks like other people."

"You watch our six. I'll take care of the rest."

She'd produced a machete from the trunk.

"Bloodthirsty." Besides his gun, all he had was a camera slung over his shoulder. Didn't know what he'd be taking photographs of, but that was kind of the point.

"It's going to be overgrown. Try to keep up, but if you need a break, let me know."

He trusted her at least enough not to protest that he could keep up.


They approached from the north, down the east side of Dead Town. From the files, Old Jim believed no one from Central had been there for more than a decade, and no one else had, either, from the evidence of the curled-over remains of barbed-wire fence and the number of monstrous blackberry patches Cass cut through.

Then it was more tall grass across a dirt path that ran beneath the oaks that guarded Dead Town's northern reaches, leading them to a trail of coquina-like gravel shot through with vivid, low-growing yellow wildflowers.

Cass kept looking back to make sure he was keeping up, but in her silence let him know she was checking behind them as well. That made him oddly calmer.

The meadow, when they reached it, was a riot of purples, yellows, oranges, white . . . so many colors and hues, so it became a kind of impressionist painting, framed by the searing blue sky with stretched shreds of clouds, the sun reflecting like liquid diamonds off the marsh water.

It hurt to look at without squinting, and Old Jim didn't know if that was the light, the beauty of it all, or what he knew about the place, but he could have stared at the meadow forever. Here the biologists had stood and drank beer and joked around and tried to ignore the odd echo of the piano from the marsh, and here, too, they had slaughtered rabbits and then themselves been undone by the Rogue.

"Beautiful, but not what we're here for," Cass said, as if reading his mind, and he realized he'd almost fallen under a spell. She gripped his right arm to guide him, as if she couldn't trust he would pull himself away.

They walked into Dead Town, onto the main street, the eroded asphalt of the road cracked by vines and tree roots, overpowered by grasses that exploited every fissure. The huge, monstrous oaks looked as if they had erupted overnight amid the buildings.

City Hall still anchored the street, but unlike the surrounding buildings, it had all four walls and a roof.

They stood side by side, considering it. As if they still had a choice.


Cass insisted on making him wait at the bottom, machete left propped against the stairs, while she took the steps two at a time and checked out the roof, the third floor, the second, and then back to the first.

"I don't think anyone's here, or has been here for a while," she said, popping out of the doorway. She looked more relaxed having done the sweep.

They skipped the first floor, which had a vile smell and a vista of the moldy shambles of foldout cafeteria-style tables. But the second floor, which had been the tourist center, looked more promising from the doorway.

Ample light spilled into that space from the front-facing row of glassless windows, revealing a long room tormented by neglect, and, again, mold. Oddly sweet-smelling.

The ceiling sagged in low, with tiling and plaster come down everywhere in wide strips along with eruptions of a disorienting pink insulation.

Ceiling lamps with shades shaped like oranges hung via cords, some fallen so far that they dangled just inches off the ground, while others had smashed into the floor, and still others hung with eight feet of space beneath them.

"I hate this place," Cass said.

"There's a path," Old Jim said. "To the chair. See it?" He pointed to the first chair overturned on the first rug. Someone had cut away some of the wires and lamps, while tricks of perspective suggested obstacles where none existed.

"I just see a mess of wires and junk."

"Patience."

The jangle of lights drew the eye toward the far end, with more overturned chairs, ruined green rugs with geometric patterns, and a far counter that must have once featured tourist brochures. A curtain on a broken metal track had become a white-green blur he didn't much care to think about.

Three booth alcoves lay against the left-hand wall, through the cords and lamps. A huge leather chair sat in front of the center alcove.

Some disturbance on the dirty floor drew his attention and now he saw not just the main path but something else.

"Could you hunker down as low as you can get and look parallel to the floor?" he asked Cass.

He expected a joke or some resistance, but instead she got down on her knees and lowered herself into a modified push-up position, looking like she had her ear to the floor, listening for a secret sound.

"I see it," she said.

"What do you see?"

"It's like a tunnel. Fairly wide, higher than your knee, leading to the chair. Like, something swept through from the doorway and . . . crawled . . . toward the chair. Flakes of dried mud, traces of dead moss, and kind of . . . an old smell. Swampy."

"An animal's trail."

The dot blinking red in the middle of Dead Town, and his heartbeat blinking faster now.

"Yeah. Up here on the second floor. Somehow."

"Like the alligator tracks on the beach?"

She got up off the floor in a hurry, wiping her hands on the back of her pants. "No sand here, but I think so."

"Let's use the conventional path," Old Jim said, and led the way, through the forest of messed-up lamps, to the center alcove. Simple once you'd seen it, like someone had layered a series of bead screens to form a trail. Not simple to avoid brushing against a cord or shade, so that a wooden jangle followed them.

The trail ended at the booth alcove and the large leather swivel chair, which was covered in streamers and loops of a material like gauze or shower curtain. The slant of the sunlight left the alcove dark.

An enormous rug lay to the left of the chair, cleared of debris. The thick discoloration across the rug, impressed on that surface over time, did suggest the shape of an alligator.

"A man and his reptile." He was already taking photographs. "The Rogue has somehow trained an alligator, probably the Tyrant, to serve him. To, what, perform a few tricks? Guard him, like a dog?"

Cass backed against the lamps swaying behind her, didn't seem to care that she set off a chain reaction of twisted rope creaks and dull chimes.

"I don't like the thought of that," she said. "The Rogue with a pet alligator holding court in Dead Town. How do you hide with a giant alligator by your side?"

"He moves around a lot," Old Jim said, not convinced of the words he was pushing out into the air. "He must be comfortable using rivers and swamps the way we use roads."

Funny what you noticed and what you didn't, even with training. Something about the swaying lamps made it difficult to pick out details. At the edge of the rug, in a weird shadow cast by the chair, Old Jim spied something the size and shape of a pork chop.

"Is that a . . . bone?"

Cass got out her flashlight. "Dried-up old haunch of something. Snack for a pet?"

Old Jim almost said, half joking, *It's a friend*, but caught himself, because he didn't like what he meant by that.

"A helper? Somehow?"

"Yes, some kind of help, mission critical," Cass said. "Don't touch the chair."

Under the flashlight's glow, Old Jim could see that a peculiar residue like golden pine dust coated the chair back, only missing from the seat, swathed in that rotting white fabric. Without the flashlight, the residue was practically invisible, but it had a hint of moisture to it, like when humidity made Old Jim's deck boards sweat.

"What's on the seat?" Cass asked.

"Curtain remains, like at the back of the room?"

Cass nudged the edge of it with her boot. The edge crumbled like a wafer, made more of the material into dust.

"Reads more like husk than fabric," she noted. "Samples?"

"No, just photos. Let's not disturb anything else. He might not come back, but let's try to make it look like we were never here."

But that wasn't the reason, not really. Something about the suggestion of samples made him nauseous. Something about the failed expedition and all of their samples, stacked to the ceiling. He felt faint, like he needed water. He took more photos of the chair as if it might make him feel better, then had to stop. Some realization was coming to him from a long distance away, slowly dawning, but he couldn't quite articulate it yet.

"Here," he said, holding out the camera, "you take some and give me the flashlight."

She took the camera from his hands eagerly enough, probably happy for the distraction.

"Maybe you really did hurt him," Old Jim said. "Maybe you did, and that's why this place seems abandoned."

"I'm going to map this whole place with photos, even the parts off the 'path,'" she said, and began to walk carefully to the rug side of the chair, documenting every stain, every discoloration.

She was using the flash, so he just shone the light on the wall behind the chair, curious about the hints of wallpaper. Maybe a pink flamingo pattern once, but now only gray pieces of it stood out against the off-white stucco beneath.

Some graffiti written there, just above the chair, so faded and mold-covered he hadn't noticed before, like a ghost of a tag. Scrawled in black: NO CHANGE. BUT TOO EARLY, WRONG SEASON. Then a few anarchy symbols, it looked like, but just written with a ballpoint pen.

Then more words he couldn't read, written small, unobtrusive.

He leaned awkwardly over the chair to read what had been written there, the chair pushed back in the attempt.

A kind of symbol drawn there, too, unfamiliar to him, with a stylized lighthouse in green. Mutterings rising in his head, phrases that he didn't know where they came from, as if waking from a dream.

A series of words, in the casual scrawl of someone thinking aloud. Some of it he couldn't read, but then he found part he could read.

*"Follow every shiny glimmer / down the winding river bend; / The air will hit the trees / like a whistle or a ring of thunder."*

Old Jim felt a lurch, a misstep, an endless abyss. That wasn't the *Winter Journey* he knew.

The metal crumpled from the bomb underneath and he lost control of the wheel and smashed against the mountain shoulder, the heat gushing into the compartment, and he couldn't breathe, no one could breathe, and the carrier twisted, toppled, careened off the road and down the slope, toward the limitless blue above and below.

To the side of the words on the wall, the same person had scrawled a name. A person's name.

His true name.

Trapped into blackness, into nothing, trying to get out as the flames rushed through.

## 019: FAILURE TO DEAL

A sound like a song, like music and yet not. It had a delicate quality, a questing, searching pulse, with a depth in the echoes and a comforting familiarity. It nested in Old Jim's head, a sound that could never have emanated from a human throat, and yet what nonhuman could make music that felt like far-distant home? The beauty of it overwhelmed him as he peered down a tunnel in the reeds toward the water.

The song came louder to him, and a glimmer at the end of the reed tunnel of water stirred by wind. The hint of some wider, deeper movement, and he, drawn to it, began to crawl forward. The song made him courageous, or was it just a fey fascination he could not break. *"I'll singe every falling wave, / green field, swallow tail. / The sun up from the depths, / as I follow a flaming trail."*

The broken reeds under his palms scratched despite the cool mud beneath and in that enrapturing cocoon the brackish smell came to him fresh, and a vast and alien eye at the end of the tunnel. *"You'll find me in the scrub, / across riverbeds and distant shores; / you'll find me in bitter mist / hover fly, bear witness."*

Was he hallucinating? Was this his death?

There came a slap of the mighty tail against the water, a suggestion of a massive body submerging.

The music ended, abrupt, and the Tyrant had vanished with it.

Left standing by the water's edge, alone.

Dread choked him as tears fell wet from his face. He came to himself in the dead meadow, overcome by emotion that made him hide among the cascading stalks of the wildflowers, that made him grasp at the dirt on all fours, as if the feel of it could anchor him. A scream in his throat he couldn't contain or escape, that left him raw, defenseless. The the the this this this this.

The Tyrant dragging her weight through the mud, over and through the biologists, the thrum and hum of her body like a memory of the song.

Something in his brain kept misfiring and he kept crawling on his hands and knees through the heart of the meadow as if he feared a sniper. But would he fear the tracery of bullets overhead now, there among the mosquitoes and the biting flies? And he thought he should get up, get up, but the terror hit him again, that the Tyrant lay somewhere behind him, closing fast, but no, it was not an alligator he feared or should fear and . . . Instead he found a clear muddy patch at the far end of the meadow and lay there on his back in a soft, comforting wallow. As if he were one of the biologists from so long ago, and he stared, mindless, at a harrier hawk as it passed back and forth above him, stitching some obscure message into the sky.

All the reverie of the dead beneath him, around him, in the molecules of the air, the water, all this great fecundity of life—and what was his life in comparison? Nothing but signal, nothing but openness, lying there wounded.

He wondered if his daughter thought of him ever, and how and why. If it was still with any form of kindness or affection. If she had regrets. If she was happy now. If it sometimes tore into her the way it tore into him.

And he might as well have lain there a century as an hour. He didn't know if he could get up again. The smell of the mud mingled with the flowers, strong, earthy, and so full of a fragile, trembling fragrance that he wanted to stop weeping, to take root. To be mindless here and become lost, taken away and dissipated into the sky with the flock of cranes he spied swirling higher and higher still. To forget everything, to remember . . . nothing.

Until Cass found him there, a frantic look on her face as she stared down, and him without the energy or gumption to rise. He thought, perhaps hoped, that she would back away from the fading anguish of his affect, from the place in his mind that he thought he had moved past but kept returning to against his will. For he felt in that moment that she could have slain him with the wrong look.

"You scared me," she said. "You just disappeared."

He said nothing; he was incapable, and her words came to him from a great distance. But it was true: He had vanished and now had come back into himself.

Cass slid down into the mud beside him and she held him and he cried into her arms. She said nothing, did not shudder or pull away, just allowed him to be there, letting it all out, again, until it was gone—truly gone—and he was empty and lost a century or more, down in the mud, in his thoughts.

Then she took his hand, his weathered, worn hand and she told him a story. About herself, about her past. It was sad and funny and tragic and complicated and terrifyingly personal, what she told him, and although it would become, in time, just the fading memory of something beautiful he had heard once, he kept it close and fiercely private and personal.

She released him then and he didn't dare say a word, for fear of feeling ashamed, for fear of it being the wrong word or a damaging word, wondering what, if anything, he had done to deserve this gift.

Nothing, he had done nothing.


When he had recovered himself enough to sit up, she said, "We don't have to go back there."

"I don't want to."

"We can just stay here for a while."

The sun felt so distant and he liked it that way.

After some span of time that escaped him, Cass said, "Someone has damaged you. Badly and with intent. Over time."

He tried to say something about the mission, the Rogue, but couldn't quite get it out.

"After what happened at the bridge, I shouldn't have let you come here."

"No," he said, "you couldn't have stopped me. I don't need rest."

"That feeling might fade. It might not last. And then you might need to go to a hospital."

When he didn't respond, she sighed and lay back against the mud and reeds next to him.

As the bees and the wasps and the butterflies went about their business, oblivious, tending to the bright flowers.

## 020: ENDLESS NIGHT

All the warp and weft of aftermath. How it lived in his bones and his flesh so that he felt inhabited by another and made into an empty vessel. Another's body that had carried out the mission where he'd hit the roadside bomb. Another who had lost a daughter. Holes in his head that corresponded to the holes in the Old Decomp parking lot.

"You have to get over losing her," Cass had said on the drive back. "Just forget you had a daughter."

"I don't know how." Saying words that felt remote from him.

"*They* don't want you to know how. Central."

He had no answer for that, but he could tell Cass didn't like his silence.

"I need you to hear what I'm trying to tell you. Central made me write a letter to you, as your daughter, before I came here. I was supposed to give it to you the day we met. But I couldn't. It was too fucked up."

That other life. The one where he'd dumped all those letters at her feet. Jesus. How much bleak and terrible shit had she shielded him from?

"Thank you," he said.

She reached out and took his arm by the wrist. Held it for a time, released him.

"Heart rate is little high, but acceptable," she said. Sighed.

When they reached his house, Cass waited to drive off until he was at the door. As she left, he couldn't quite put a finger on what was wrong. Because something was still wrong.

Old Jim lurched into the kitchen, found his way by the dim light over the stove, as if his eyes had become sensitive, because he didn't want anything brighter. Water in a rinsed-out glass, and lots of it. He gulped it down and still he felt thirsty, although he didn't feel hungry at all. The place smelled musty, but maybe it always had and he hadn't noticed until now.

The strange version of *Winter Journey*, mutated, had entered his head, clashing with the original. *"The air bleeds through cypress knees / go forth god / body bent / my half prayer spilled / through every wild glimmer."*

If he went into his office, he'd have to sit in the awful chair of a dead man. If he went to bed, it would just be a restless tossing and turning, eyes shut but mind open. Cass had asked if she should come inside and wait until he got settled, but he hadn't liked the idea. He felt a kind of guilt over her concern—that she risked something expressing concern, a kind of instinct he had about her, one spy regarding another. Instead, she'd develop the photos and circle back for a debrief.

Old Jim checked for new faxes, found that Jack had relented about the Exiles, a bit, and graced him with Central's R&D about the cameras. He felt superstitious about the informality of the kitchen, took it into the office and got into the monstrous chair.

What caught his attention right away was R&D's request to reinterview the exiles—to talk to Team Leaders 1 and 2. That "to understand the substances and compounds and pheromones that created this object, we need to better understand the context of the object's capture."

The Rogue, out in the wetlands, "shucking cameras like oysters." What if that was R&D too? Just from a different direction?

Not only did Central's R&D refrain from calling the "object" a "camera," but from the context of the request as it went through various subagencies to the Relocation Program division responsible for the exiles . . . it was clear that R&D did not know about the Dead Town Disaster. That R&D had been led to believe in the "accidental discovery" of "the object," and only a clerical error in filing had allowed them to discover the names of Team Leaders 1 and 2.

Who, exactly, at Central, still knew about the Dead Town Disaster? Was it just Jack and a handful of his underlings? Did Serum Bliss enjoy the same level of secrecy? He had assumed Jack must still report some detail of his operations to higher-ups at Central, but what if that wasn't true?

Such that when he saw the file on a prominent Brute at Central pressing R&D about the rabbit cameras, he realized why R&D had been told nothing. So they couldn't tell anyone else.

Equally, in the other direction, Old Jim's mistake in his requests beyond what Jack had given him was departmental. The further information on the cameras originated with R&D and had not been reported back to the department that had interrogated the team leaders.

Which meant that the entire purpose of studying the camera had metastasized as extracting any advanced or proprietary technology, to then apply to Central's own surveillance equipment. But not just cameras—scopes on sniper rifles, the optics on bomb-sniffer robots, the proprietary elements of new microscopes.

"The alloy appears neo-biological in its compression," the "crude analogy" that of "how lichen adheres to a rock, and is unable to survive without the rock, how moisture accumulates and is held in the rock, but also the lichen." These kinds of "bindings" exemplified "the relationship between materials in the object."

But it was also clear from R&D that although they could replicate by mimicry the properties of the object, they did not understand the object's initial purpose, coming from a purely extractive point of view. Nor had the video component been working in the cameras provided to them.

Information helped, even when it made things more complex. Old Jim felt the tension in his body loosening as he read, leaning back in the chair. Even when he noticed a piece of paper sticking out from the space between the far bottom leg of the desk and the wall, hidden by the whiteboard leaning there that he'd never bothered to put up.

When he moved the whiteboard, Old Jim found a pile of burnt faxes. At first, he thought it might be a quirk of his predecessor, who had smoked. Have a cigarette, burn a fax. But when he pulled them out, the ash smudging his hands, he discovered they were all recent, and they were all lyrics from *Winter Journey.*

He pulled up short, let the damaged faxes fall to the floor beside the chair, as if they had been tinged with a poison. Tried to wipe the ash onto his pants. His hand swept across his pants pocket and there came a kind of pearly click or slight clang of one piece of metal against another. He frowned, didn't remember having put the strange key in his—

Down in the depths, rising, and by the river's bank he looked out on the ravens that were not ravens and the rocks and the green canopy, resting there as vessel, candle, flame, and the branches of the trees were opening and opening up to reveal, far off, the two mountains and the green light in the cleft between them as if it had always been there, waiting, and he'd always known that, too. He could hear a distant hum or music or chanting and it came from both the water and the air, as if both were full of invisible lives that made sound through the branches, through the river reeds and moss.

Hidden lives. Hiding from the green light, even as the army marched toward it. They must march toward it, they must fight or be destroyed. In their antiquated armor, their old weapons, their grim aspect. How they flowed into the landscape the more he looked upon them, became less bodies than waves or torrents pouring into the breach.

It was cold, very cold. He was shivering and his eyes didn't seem to want to open. There came a voice he half recognized, half didn't.

"Get in the barrel and stay dead. Get in the barrel with the others. There you go. No use resisting now. Just get in there nice and snug. Cover yourself in the fluid and don't get any on me. I don't need it, only you. It should be quick. You'll all be in God's eye soon, as it should be. What you did, it must have gone against God in some way. So just get in the barrel. Get in the barrel. Shouldn't be this long. I want to go home."

A new set of sounds, like the man had wrenched someone's arm out its socket, that soft, hollow, distressing crack. Followed by the same sound again, like he'd done the other one. But no scream, no sense of another person.

Somehow that sound made him go dead calm. Some muscle memory, some training that he hadn't fully used in a while.

Was this a nightmare? He would wake up in bed, and he'd just missed a step, been so tired he'd fallen asleep standing up. If he didn't open his eyes he would return to sleep, to some kind of sleep.

But the cold felt more like being in a walk-in freezer and even with his eyes closed, he received a premonition of a blast of blue light, as if it wasn't quite the usual, not quite real in the usual ways. The man stumbled about now, splashing liquid and sound, too corporeal to ignore.

Old Jim realized he was sitting in a chair with his arms around a huge sack, like a mailbag, which sat in his lap like he was clasping a pillow or about to hand out gifts around the holidays.

The splashing like dunking, dunking, and the faint smell of some unfamiliar chemicals—and now he was fully awake and terrified. How had he gotten here? Had he been drugged? If he opened his eyes, the person moving around might notice. So he kept them shut.

He still had his peashooter in an ankle holster. He still had his knife in a sheath at his waist. And a yawning chasm of doubt.

"Get in there. Go down easy. Don't resist."

The blue lights flickered against Old Jim's eyelids. The pattern made him think one or more of a bank of lights had gone out or malfunctioned. The "mailbag" had the unmistakable slight shift and crunch of money in banded stacks. He knew it from a couple of dozen payoffs.

The voice rough, with a cough behind it like a smoker. "Yeah, like that. God loves you. God sees you. This is his path, his way. Go drown now, happy. All's well."

The sound of squishing, of sloshing, made his heart rate spike again. As did how he couldn't quite trace the voice, but knew it anyway. Along with a strong sense of déjà vu that he'd spent many hours listening to this man talk.

The key in his pocket, waking up on the deck after sleep-walking.

"Why always this now, Old Jim," the voice muttered, and his eyes would've shot open if he hadn't controlled himself. If he hadn't realized the man still thought he was . . . asleep? That wasn't quite it. But the man thought they were accomplices. And the man was big, looming, the voice rumbling down to him.

He dared to squint one eye open . . . and, yes, he was holding on to a giant sack of cash. He was sitting in a chair with a key clasped in one hand, hugging a sack of money, listening to a psychopath talk about God while stuffing things into barrels of fluid. A psychopath who might be a mail carrier. Who had stolen a lot of cash.

The man faced away from him, clad in a . . . a tricorn hat? Plus a full-body black coat of some kind . . . bathed in that dark swimming-pool blue glow . . . bending over a large barrel that came up to his waist, and a thick hand gloved to the elbow pushing at some rag doll, some broken approximation of a person, with one naked foot and leg below the knee lolling at an unnatural angle over the side.

On the floor to the left of the man, two more bodies half in, half out of an archway to a much larger room than the one the man toiled in, the one Old Jim sat in a corner of clutching a money bag. That room was more like a small hangar, cavernous with a high ceiling, full of the same quavery light . . . and full of barrels, in some places in the back stacked three high.

He thought he recognized one of the two bodies on the floor, peering around the mailbag, using it as cover. A mid-level Brute from Central who Jack hadn't liked—a "thwart" as Jack sometimes put it. The bloodless face turned sightless and eyeless toward the ceiling.

Did he try to run? Did he try to reason with . . . someone doing terrible things with barrels? Did he just fight like a thousand devils because he had no choice?

Abruptly, the huge man doing the stuffing stood up abruptly, turned, too late for Old Jim to disguise his gaze, to close his eyes again.

Old Jim stared right at him.

The black mask was so thick and wide it appeared at first made of stone, wrapping around to hide even the man's ears. The buttoned pitch-black flaring trench coat hid his clothing below the neck. At some murky point the trench coat left off in favor of huge old-fashioned black boots, with huge silver buckles, tarnished by age or lack of polishing or an eye toward authenticity. He hadn't been wearing those onstage.

Commander Thistle, from the bar. Commander Thistle wedded to his Monkey's Elbow costume for unfathomable reasons. Commander Thistle shoving bodies into barrels like some kind of fucked-up nightmare. Only Jack could be doing this. Only Jack.

He prepared himself to draw his knife, but Commander

Thistle only considered him a moment, grunted, half turned back to his work, then turned to Old Jim again.

"I told you, Old Jim, to keep your eyes shut. Shut your eyes. Peon. Serf. Shut your eyes. You serve them like a marching automaton. You serve them like *there's no risk in the reward.* Like *water lives there.* Like *you are on a long journey and have taken no rest.* So close your eyes now. Close them."

Old Jim felt the pull of those words, like someone was trying to stitch his eyelids shut, like a specter hovered close with the needle and thread and if he'd just relax, his eyes would be shut forever in no time at all and he could just fall back into dream, back into a nothingness that meant no knowledge, no complicity.

Except, there might be a new dream now, to replace the old one.

And Commander Thistle might be satisfied with Old Jim's acting, or, while Old Jim descended back into that prison of nothing, he might stuff him in a barrel anyway.

Old Jim wrapped both hands around the money sack. It was very heavy, and he rose from the chair and stepped back a foot or two to give him a little extra distance from Commander Thistle.

In that ultra-blue light, that lapping, watery blue light, Old Jim could tell from the shoulder slump, the downward look, that Commander Thistle did not appreciate the interruption of his tasks. That he just wanted to get home. Maybe wax philosophical in his fucked-up brain about what it took to fit a man into a barrel properly.

"I'm leaving now, Commander Thistle," Old Jim said, his voice raw and more fearful than he could have hoped for. "And you're going to let me."

A long, mournful sigh from Commander Thistle that Old Jim did not find hopeful.

"I see," he said, with a resigned kind of crooning groan. "I see how it is. You're the resistment type. You're the meat thinks it isn't good enough for God's will. Well, I'll tell you, if I'm good enough for the mote in God's eye someday, you're good enough for it now."

The nausea that came over Old Jim had to be suppressed with anger, with the memory of past discipline. Disgust at this private cosmology, this pathology grown out of control.

It wouldn't help to plead, but it might buy him a moment or two, to reason with a God that enthusiastically wanted people shoved into barrels.

"Listen to me," Old Jim said, money bag still held out in front of him, unsure if he could reach and extricate his peashooter before the Commander could close the distance. "I'm an agent of Central and I'm going to walk out of here *now*. If you don't let me, you are going to die here. Do you hear me? Do you understand?"

God's eye could fuck right off. Could take a flaming arrow to its core and burn and kill God dead.

The black mask betrayed no emotion. Commander Thistle scratched the back of his head, shook himself like he couldn't quite find the flea, sighed in a great outrushing shuddery breath.

Commander began to reach into one vast pocket of his outfit.

"Don't do it!" Old Jim shouted, and pulled out his knife, held it with his left hand while still keeping the mailbag between them like an awkward shield.

But all Commander Thistle took out was a folded piece of paper that he delicately unfolded and then began to recite phrases from, looking up at Old Jim between each.

"'Consolidation of authority.' No? How about 'have your house in order'? 'Risk equal to reward'? 'Check under the seat for change.'"

On he rattled, while Old Jim felt only a fizzle and tingle, knew he intended an effect similar to the generator on the biologists so long ago. But he was free of that, and the Rogue had freed him, even if now he might be bound in some other way.

Commander Thistle put the piece of paper away, as if it had accomplished its purpose. "Now get in the barrel. This barrel." He pointed to the barrel with its lid off next to the barrel already full. "Get in the barrel, Old Jim."

He'd noticed a small door behind Commander Thistle, a way out maybe, or just a dead end to a supply room. The archway felt too dangerous, put himself in Commander Thistle's grasp. Maybe just let the immovable object come to him.

"I am the hand of God," Commander Thistle bellowed. "I've been here before you and I'll be here after. Get in the barrel! Get in the barrel!"

Old Jim sighed. He could die here, now, and yet he felt a kind of tedium, a boredom, with Commander Thistle's demeanor, the way the mask almost seemed to make him as stupid as stone.

"You can get in the fucking barrel," Old Jim said.

Commander Thistle charged like a bull, arms outstretched, and Old Jim twisted to the side, smashed the man in the face with the money sack as he stumbled past. But Commander Thistle managed to reach out a hand and get a grip on one side of the sack, swinging Old Jim farther behind him, the momentum almost tearing the sack free, and they were pulling the sack from both sides and Old Jim couldn't stop pulling because if the tension slackened Commander Thistle could charge him again, so they swung and circled while the fucker still spoke to him about God.

The sack wasn't up to the stress. The bag burst open and the money tumbled and exploded out, single bills and banded bills hitting Old Jim and Commander Thistle in the face, sliding to their feet. Old Jim lost his grip on the bag and went skidding up against the wall, Commander Thistle the other direction, knocking over the barrel full of bodies, which sluiced out the archway and came to rest in the other room.

Old Jim tried to get to his feet, but Commander Thistle was on him then, smashing into him like a truck, so he landed hard, air out of his lungs, and he had to gulp for air, prone next to the steel table.

But his arm knew what it was doing. His hand knew, too. So that even as Commander Thistle tried to bring enough pressure down to choke Old Jim to death, he was stabbing upward at Commander Thistle to the left side. Stabbing and stabbing with his knife through the man's overcoat, which was thinner than it looked, and some thickness beneath. And Commander Thistle roared with pain but kept trying to bring his forearm close enough to crush Old Jim's throat while the bulk of him held Old Jim prone and all Old Jim could do is keep stabbing as his breathing became more constricted and Commander Thistle kept roaring with each new stab. And Old Jim could feel the slickness of blood on his hand, on the knife hilt, but not enough by far. Not enough and he began to see black dots, even as, futile, he tried to arch his back, and Commander Thistle was still raging thick on top of him, a fucking boulder in human form.

Feeble stabbing ever more feeble fuck he was going to be a person in a barrel. Commander Thistle was going to break off all his limbs and fit him into a fucking barrel and he'd never find his daughter and never see Cass again and he knew—somehow knew so strong—that the Rogue didn't want him to die. That this was not the way it was supposed to end. It couldn't end. Even though he could hardly breathe now, and his right arm fending off Commander Thistle was beginning to throttle his own throat with the weight put on it. Fetid breath so close it almost seemed to come from his own mouth.

But then the weight left him. Commander Thistle rose staggering, clutching his side. The slickness there disguised by the black suit, but still some kind of dark faintly luminous purple. The blood that was coming out of him. That was too much for him to continue.

Up he rose, Commander Thistle, and loomed over Old Jim.

"I'm immortal," he rumbled. "I will never die. Pathetic remnant. Lost child."

Old Jim braced for Commander Thistle to leap on him again.

But, instead, quicker and more nimble than any big man should be, Commander Thistle ducked past him toward the little door, and as Old Jim swiveled to watch, shoved himself through that too-small door, and then into some wider space that brought in the smell of the swamp, and Old Jim could hear the echo of his running steps toward an exit, toward the world beyond.

Fucking hell. The fucker. The fucker. He'd fled like a coward. Old Jim stared after him in disbelief, the way they'd been grappling and then not, the weight had fallen away.

Groaning, he reached down, bruised, for his peashooter, felt better with it in one hand, the bloody knife in the other.

Old Jim stumbled through the door, out into the night.

"Jesus." A familiar fence and lights through the forest beyond.

He had emerged from the biowaste facility, just three hundred yards from his own house.

Outside, girding himself for ambush, because Commander Thistle hadn't gotten into the rusting old white van in the facility parking lot and driven off. So where the fuck had he gone?

Old Jim got his legs moving, once out in the night, under the moon, headed for his house, and how could he not, soon enough, see Commander Thistle, repatriated with his thistle wilderness, ponderous—because there was a giant swath smashed through the reeds past the trees. The man was built like a Mack truck, but bleeding a lot.

Was he running in the wrong direction? Disoriented?

But maybe he meant to head toward Old Jim's house. And now he realized the smell of the man, the stench, he'd smelled faintly in the kitchen before. Maybe that's why the office chair was huge. Oh fuck, what if Commander Thistle could lock him out? What if he meant to destroy documents or get Old Jim's Walther or send for help?

The heavy, wet thwack of Old Jim's boots against the mud, the whispering rasp of his clothing against the saw of the reeds. This feeling that, like some windup automaton, he might run out of time as he headed for his house.

The moon a jagged sickle overhead. The smashed reeds made him flinch for the Tyrant, Commander Thistle's back now visible jerking and torquing ahead of him with the effort of running over uneven ground, but Old Jim was closing the distance, closing, because, yes, Commander Thistle, like a tank leaking gasoline, had begun to slow down. Running, then fast walking, then staggering, and with Old Jim just twenty feet away, Commander Thistle swayed more like a reed than a slab.

Old Jim's house was close now, only about a hundred yards.

"Stop," he hissed.

He wasn't sure the bullet in his peashooter was enough to end this giant.

Commander Thistle half turned, to contemplate the black gleam of water to their right.

"Go to your God and beg mercy for your sins," the man said. He'd given up trying to stanch the blood and no longer held his hand to his side.

"Who sent you? Who do you work for?"

"God sent me."

"No, God didn't fucking send you, you great fucking asshole."

Commander Thistle coughed and bent over to vomit great loops of blood, could not get back to his feet again. Knelt there, unsteady.

"You were supposed to be asleep," he said. "You weren't supposed to ever wake up."

The chill that came over Old Jim. Never meant to wake up. Never meant to fully sleep. Trapped in limbo.

"Jack said you might be difficult," Commander Thistle said. "Now you'll be difficult for Jack. He'll put you in a barrel himself."

Jesus Christ.

"Stuffing bodies in barrels is God's work? Is Jack God?"

Commander Thistle's voice came back weak and thready to Old Jim.

"They're all Brutes. They're all bad people. They needed God now. They got God now. Stop chasing me. I just want to sit by a window by the sea." Plaintive, like he was losing touch with whatever reality he'd chosen to live in.

Old Jim relaxed, lowered his peashooter. There wasn't anything he had to do now.

"My God is near but yours may be nearer," Commander Thistle whispered, Old Jim so close now.

The giant behind the mask toppled and sprawled, finally silent, into the ever-present reeds. He expected the body hitting the ground would make a mighty sound, but it was muffled, less reverberation than vibration.

*"But quick! The water slows, / its surface turns to glass."*

Commander Thistle lay awkward on his side, dead, the blood of the ruptures from the knife bubbling up pure, unhindered.

*"The stars start to glow / and the sun shines its last."*

Godspeed, Commander Thistle, down to the fiery pits of hell, where Old Jim hoped he would be stuffed into a barrel for all eternity. Any sympathy he had left Old Jim meant to apply as salve to his bruised ribs.

He limped back to the house to recover, to think about the next steps, before returning to the biowaste facility. Only the porch light was on. As he reached for the living room light switch, he stopped dead. A figure sat on the couch. In the dark. In his house.

His hand wanted the real gun, the one he'd left in his office.

"Hello, Jim," Jackie said. Some aspect of her dark, functional clothes glittered in the shadows like chain mail. No one would ever mistake her ways for those of her father.

He left the lights off so she couldn't see the distress on his clothes, grabbed his jacket from the kitchen table and put it on. Then took a seat in a chair in the farthest corner from her.

"You're sitting in the dark in my living room. For how long?"

"For a while," Jackie admitted, and she didn't want to look him in the eye. "I thought you'd be here. Where were you?"

Had she heard anything? Seen anything out the window? He didn't think she'd be sitting there so calm. She could have waited outside and shot him on the porch, under the bare bulb, if she'd wanted him dead. This was true.

"What was so urgent it couldn't wait until morning? That meant you couldn't come back later?"

"I'm being recalled to Central," she said. "To answer questions about what's been happening here. And not by Jack. By *Central.*"

Oh, sure, he understood her just fine. Serum Bliss was under the radar, except maybe now it wasn't. Someone high up the chain of command had caught a whiff of it, the decomp wafting up from a barrel, or heard the lilting, gentle sound of distant gunfire against a stone wall—or maybe something had come up in a random sweep of ops.

"What *has* been happening here?"

Had Jack kept her in the dark about stealing from his own op? Or funding the Brigade in devious ways? He couldn't quite see it clear.

"I leave soon and I wanted you to know. This might take a week or it could be a month."

He considered that a nonanswer, didn't like it.

"You want to know if I have intel that can help you survive an inquest, is that it?"

Brutes taking verbal baseball bats to the old breed, while Jack stuffed Brutes into barrels. Or maybe both sides were playing almost as rough. While Phantoms, if they existed, laughed secretly on the sidelines. A kind of internal civil war.

A coldness spread across the chill of her sharp features, and she sat up, rigid.

"Earlier today, while you and Cass chased ghosts or whatever it was you thought worth doing . . . we lost two submersibles. The psychics on board set them on fire from inside when they reached the seabed. Because they were in contact through distance messaging with others on Failure Island, three more S&SB personnel are in comas, nonresponsive. The building caught fire and we don't know why yet. For now, files and records are being evacuated and any Central personnel with them."

"That's a shame," he said. He had no surprise or shock left in him.

The shock, instead, registered on her face. "You have *nothing* for me? No analysis? No guesses?"

He shrugged—and as if she took that as provocation, she took something lying in the darkness of the couch next to her and tossed it at him. The entanglement of it as he caught it felt familiar. A red bobber, a tracker.

"Or was this just a waste of our time?"

"Where was Henry?" Thinking of belt buckles in parking lots.

"We're looking into Henry, but it's unlikely," Jackie said. "He relied on that place to analyze what he's found at the lighthouse."

Debatable, the logic of psychopaths, but Old Jim didn't want to debate it.

"Where in the building did the fire start?"

"Forensics lab, we think."

The alligator harness would've been in the forensics lab. Maybe that was a coincidence, or maybe it was the point, the Rogue still one step ahead of them.

Old Jim decided to give her a stale crumb, while he mulled his choices, given the number of dead bodies, the large amount of money lurking just out of view through the forest.

"We found something at Dead Town that might be an old sign of the Rogue," he told her. "We took photos, will file a report."

His ribs ached worse when he breathed; his hands had cuts and dried blood on them, yet in some ways he felt sharper than he had in years.

She was leaning forward now, intent. "You know, the next one they pull in to Central will be you. Jack may have Central still thinking you retired here, but not for long. They might trap-door this entire operation and disappear us all."

The closest Jackie would ever get to pleading, but Old Jim was unmoved. Numb.

"Then I guess you'd better be convincing. Good luck with that."

It didn't even matter that Jackie had turned into knives again, in the way she stared at him.

"Get us something we can use, Jim. A villain. A scapegoat. Anything."

Burn fuel to protect themselves, create sacrifices. He wanted to say, *You can't give me up or Jack goes down.* But soon enough Jack would find out Old Jim had crossed some invisible border and whatever bond Jack saw between them would break. He didn't know what that new world would look like, but it might be grim.

"I'm working on it," Old Jim said. "We haven't had enough time, but we're close." Any old reassuring bullshit he could think of.

"I sent Cass back to Central this evening, as a delaying tactic. That also allows me to tie up a few loose ends before I join her."

The surprise of hearing those words, disorienting, like he was back in the biohazard facility, sitting in a chair with his eyes closed, holding the bag. They were going to debrief at the Village Bar. They were going to find the Rogue.

Cass's hand on his wrist, checking his pulse.

He'd stopped breathing, had to remember to start again. How Cass had stared down at him from the ladder at Old Decomp. How he'd stared up, ready to break her fall.

The empty chair in the apartment as he recovered, her files strewn across it.

"Are you still with me, then, Jim?" Jackie asked.

Grotesque to him, that she said it like she was truly concerned.

"I'm sure you're right. This will all blow over."

He forced the words, clipped, out of his mouth. It wouldn't help Cass to express concern for her. It might doom her.

Old Jim rose, opened the door, stood there, waiting for her to leave, jacket zipped tight.

"I guess you're done, huh?" Jackie said, giving him an appraising look.

"I'll hold down the fort until you get back."

She looked wary as she got up and paused there in front of him. As if she could read his mind, how some part of him wanted to scare the shit out of her. Make her feel what he was feeling.

"Good luck at Central," he said.

Jackie stared at his messed-up hands, which had begun to throb even worse. The blood crusted across his enflamed knuckles.

"What have you been doing tonight?" Jackie asked.

"Just sleepwalking again," he said. He couldn't look at her.

"Is this about Cass or the mission?"

"I'm just tired," he said, because he was tired.

"You're not going to wind up drunk on the street again?"

"No."

"She'll be back. If Jack survives. If I do."

Said quiet as she walked by, into the night, into the distance.

He closed the door behind her gently. Lines from *Winter Journey* a pressure in his head. *"Now, I see a shifting signpost / shimmering beneath my gaze, / but I must travel on, a ghost . . ."*

For a long time after Jackie left, Old Jim just sat there, in the dark, pondering his next move, if he had one.

Cass was gone.

Again.

# IMMERSION

## 021: STACKING THE CHAIRS

A vessel broken, a need to find his way to the green light, a dry feeling in his throat. The way the world around him seemed both brighter and duller than before.

Break down the wells, clean the grates, plug the taps, wipe and polish around the taps. Clean the counter and all other surfaces around the bar area. Sweep the floors. Stack the chairs. Old Jim knew the closing duties at the Village Bar. But he had no checklist for how to clean up the biohazard site, no checklist for how to cope with Cass being gone. Or how to cope with feeling so beat up that he only got two hours of sleep, and then it was already dawn through the bedroom window, and he felt an urgency to get things done.

What things? For whom?

He returned to the biohazard facility and did what he could to clean up enough to maybe confuse whoever came by to investigate. True, the money would be gone, because he meant to transfer it to bags and a better hiding place, but everything else he did was meant to buy him just a little more time.

The unpleasant need, with a handkerchief over his mouth and nose, evoking Old Decomp, to decant some of the bodies in the barrels, to identify the ones he knew. Mostly lower-level operatives, as if that was all Jack dared, or by some other logic that escaped Old Jim.

Five barrels with a piece of red tape on the side. Ten with orange to mark the money and documents and photos, some of which looked like blackmail material. An inexplicable green to indicate that the rest did, indeed, contain biomedical waste.

Some version of intent laid bare by the documents he found in an old-fashioned briefcase that must have looked tiny in Commander Thistle's hand. And yet the documents clarified nothing. Studies on "the sweet spot of psychopathy and far-seeing" mixed in with falsified ledgers for the Brigade, a report on out-of-body experiments to "other dimensions" rife with encounters with "beings vaguely reptilian, like crocodiles or alligators," receipts for meals at a bar in the city of Hedley, which lay beyond Bleakersville. Photographs of Old Jim walking into the Village Bar didn't bother him, just added to the sense of the site like some Central midden, a grab bag of impulses and obsessions. Had that been due to Commander Thistle or some impulse from Jack that manifested as a kind of madness subsumed by paperwork?

Jack using the Forgotten Coast as his garbage dump, his bank, his liquidation center. There was a map by the barrels that indicated a transit system: break the bodies down here, deposit the remains somewhere else. But even those instructions felt arcane, optimistically alchemical, with what must be the dead hand of Commander Thistle having ritualized this new decomp into superstitious "sites of power." The sad, too-human diversion of logic into unmarked graves—places marked as "watchers and talismans before God" under trees, in abandoned old slave graveyards, in the dunes overlooking the sea.

If not for Commander Thistle's pathological quixoticness, it would have made sense, in a way. Remote. Nominally under Jack's control. Already bearing the scars of past ops. But it also meant Jack had become a monster. The Brute of Brutes. There was at least six submersibles' worth of money in the barrels. As he stared at that mute array that screamed so loudly at him, he realized that there was no escape. Not really.

This vision he kept having now: of Jack, creating the seeds of a shadow organization within another, a kind of parasite that would soon enough live in the dead husk of the host—or, paranoid thought, some greater power manipulating Jack . . . and meant to plunge Central into what? Chaos? A cleansing fire? Or just corrupt Central with mind viruses, misdirection, false ideas. So that, eventually, Central would *be* the shadow, eaten up from the inside.

How long until Jack found out about this breach? Probably less than a week, but no way to be sure because he'd neglected to ask Commander Thistle about his reporting protocols.

He could run away, forge a new identity, but he felt too ancient to pull a Mudder.

Distracted by what he had wanted to tell Cass that had kept slipping his mind. Maybe nothing. But maybe that a mission could be a dysfunctional masterpiece that existed almost like a piece of brilliant but unhinged music. All these strangers shoved together into one purpose, choreographed into a rapid, tight precision around some objective. One bond, so that in life-and-death situations you could depend on someone having your back, taking your pulse.

So that in the end, over time, all that mattered was *the moment*, breaching the perimeter, kicking in the door, with people you trusted more than a partner, more than anyone else in the world. So he wasn't going to run away. He was going to stay, and he was going to push even harder. For Cass.

As he finished cleaning up, Old Jim had to sit in the same chair he'd occupied before, opposite Commander Thistle, amid the signs of struggle he had not yet erased, the scuffs and smudges he hoped read like normal wear and tear. He felt less emotion than a lack of emotion, which bothered him.

His whole body was sore and buffeted, his throat raw. He had to finish burying Commander Thistle, make him into an inconspicuous mound amid the marsh grasses, under the sun. No strength and no stomach to stuff the man in a barrel.

The huge, bloodstained leather wallet he'd pried out of the man's back pocket identified him as "Gus Waldron." What a name for a monster.

There hadn't been much in Gus's pockets, but still more than there should have been—the kind of sloppiness you risked when you recruited a nut of a homegrown operative. Like the folded sheet of control words . . .

Jack had been manipulating him from the outset, and the Rogue, dead or alive, had released Old Jim from Jack's spell. From Jack's bad intentions.

Shouldn't he be able to see his life clearly now?

## 022: VETERANS OF THE PSYCHIC WARS

Old Jim woke in the midafternoon, on the living-room couch. He hadn't meant to sleep so long, or at all, but his body had needed it. This was his night to return to the Village Bar after "being sick." But now that felt dangerous, so he called Sally and said he'd be taking one more day off work. No, he was fine. Everything fine there? Yeah, except Man Boy Slim was sullen and drunk, and wouldn't leave. Mudderless, rudderless. Go with God, just not Commander Thistle's God.

"Oh, also, your daughter called and asked you if you'd feed her pet frogs while she's gone."

Cass. He felt a lurch, a dislocation, a surge of . . . pride, triumph? In how she'd managed to get a message to him.

She'd left something for him in the frog tank.

Maybe Old Jim had been too out of it before to notice, but it felt like a kind of dream, how her apartment stood at the end of a tortuous series of dirt roads amid a mature pine forest. How the afternoon sun came down in a healing way, to then spill golden over the soft pine-straw forest floor.

A series of sleepy two-story rustic wood-frame town houses appeared, nestled into the landscape at odd intervals, such that Old Jim thought he'd reached the last one, gotten lost, only for another to appear teasingly out of the canopy. A true maze of looping switchbacks and the whole time he had a sense of gently falling forward into a ravine. Or a cleft between mountains. No, he had to put that from his mind.

At the end of one wandering lane, closest to the wilder woods: Cass's place, with the souped-up red hatchback out front. For a moment, his hopes leapt up to defeat his pain. She was still here. But of course she wasn't.

Around back, he smashed in a window, using a rag from the truck to muffle the noise, and opened the door through the pane, entered with gun drawn. No sound, no sense of anyone inside.

He cleared all the rooms before approaching the frog tank. No one hiding in the closet to surprise him. But as he looked around, he saw the signs of what he took to be Jackie's intrusion — not in the place being trashed but in how clean it was, how the cushions on the couch were so perfectly placed, and not a hint of clutter. He was willing to bet Jackie'd had the place swept after Cass left.

Still, he checked in the usual places, hopeful he might find something Jackie had missed. But, upstairs and downstairs, the place had been picked clean. Or perhaps Cass had done it herself, anticipating Jackie going through her things.

Even the bed had that look of not being slept in.

He decided he might as well feed the frogs, but of course there were no frogs in the tank. No safe under the floorboards, no frogs in the tank. Had she taken them with her?

A little pirate chest at the bottom of the tank belched water, but Old Jim didn't think whatever Cass had left him would be inside. No. The chest drew the eye with the flashes of gold paint, the movement. So, he upended the jar of food flakes onto the side table, found nothing at the bottom.

The tank had a thick layer of pebbles beneath the water and a line of green algae at the water line that appeared unbroken against the glass.

Gently, he reached down and trawled, tried not to disturb the sediment, let his hand search through the roughness of the pebbles. The small pleasure of that pitted texture against his fingers soothed, distracted him from the pain in his shoulder where Commander Thistle had hurt him.

He had almost given up when he felt a smooth touch against one finger, felt an electric excitement.

There it was: a tiny plastic packet, easy to miss.

He extracted it, dripping, out of the tank. Inside the packet was a key and a number on a slip of waterproof paper: 92544.

Sitting on the couch next to the tank, he stared at the number. While the lid of the treasure chest rose and fell. Storage locker? Some unit at the Old Decomp storage place? No. It had to be simpler.

It took a while longer than it should have, maybe, but when he'd solved it, the answer made him exclaim and rock back on the couch.

The order of the numbers had obscured the possibility, because there were only six separate apartment complexes, but if he reversed the numbers to 44529, the key could be to another apartment: unit 4, apartment 4529, farther up the slope. If 4529 existed.

Old Jim's pulse quickened. Maybe Cass had a second apartment. Because she didn't want anyone to know where she lived. Because she knew Jackie had a key to this one.

Sure enough, after some driving around, Old Jim found 4529. No one was around and he wasn't even sure the apartments to either side had tenants. The key fit perfectly.

Inside Cass's real apartment, Old Jim had a moment of blurred déjà vu. The layout was the same, with the same white walls balanced by rustic high wooden beams.

He decided to start upstairs, just the routine security check, one more time. The bedroom was different. She'd dragged a bare mattress up there and had converted the bathroom into a darkroom. He thought she'd sent the film to Failure Island, but instead she had developed it here.

The main difference between apartments was that Cass had used the white space of the bedroom walls to track the Rogue, Henry, her thinking about the Brigade. Most of the S&SB personnel had their headshots taped to that wall, along with their role, rank, important details about their past, their points of view.

There, too, the question: "Did Henry kill the head of ops?" With a checkmark, as if Cass had confirmed the origins of the belt buckle.

The Rogue's wall consisted of oddities and contradictions, with the same image from the trail cam twenty years ago, photocopied, with her scrawled note: "The sleeper awakens." He wondered if she'd found it in his pocket when she'd brought him to her apartment, after the bridge, and copied it then, or earlier.

Not much he didn't know already on the Rogue wall, except

a brief section about a man shouting at schoolchildren at recess through a fence twenty years ago, one hundred miles north of the coast and to the west. Cass had noted that the stranger "clutched the chain link so hard he left blood." The man had then retreated into the swamp. The list of names beside this news item must be teachers and students, and Cass had been crossing them out, one by one, as she'd checked into them.

What did that mean and when had she obtained all of this intel? Long before he'd given her the full files on the Rogue, he gathered, from some of the penciled-in date notations. He remembered her intensity about the Rogue after Old Decomp and should have felt betrayed, but what he felt instead was more complex, because the apartment key felt like trust.

Transcripts from the Mudder's conversation with him lived on that wall. References to his conversation with Man Boy Slim near the front door. Which meant that Cass had supplemented Central's bugs with her own. He remembered her severe Realtor's business suit, bulky enough to hide surveillance equipment, the way she'd looked around the bar.

"Mission critical: What is the Rogue actually reacting to with its actions?"

It? That stood out, handwritten on a piece of ruled notebook paper and attached by a piece of duct tape. Did Cass think the Rogue was a machine?

On the desk in the corner, though, is what he felt she had left specifically for him: three items neatly laid out as if the ultimate debriefing. He took the order seriously—two file folders and a photograph—and considered each in their turn.

When Old Jim had read through the first folder, he sat back in the chair, numb, considering why he didn't feel more.

Because Cass, somehow, had obtained secret documents pertaining to spells meant to bind him. Starting with the lyrics of the *Winter Journey* songs he loved, with enough context to make clear that when Commander Thistle had worried Old Jim might be slipping, a little refresher of the lyrics helped bind Old Jim's soul.

"*My back may tear, / my feet may break, / my heart may storm and rage— / Yet I will stay my course.*" The song seemed quaint, old-fashioned now, and his fascination with the suite from some other life, because it was . . . the way he knew, staring at those lyrics, that every time he'd sat down at the piano, he'd reinforced the vigor of his secret mission, submerged his own true self.

At first, Old Jim didn't know why many of the documents in the file served to reveal the extent of Central's interference on the biologists' expedition, their use of the generator to send out subliminal commands, their use of the alligators as the Medic had indicated, and even detailed analysis of the experiments conducted on the Tyrant prior to her "joining" the expedition. Which included alligator-specific drugs for increased alertness, negative reinforcement, a regimen of control and of freedoms, along with supposed "brain augmentation" that had turned the creature into a kind of battle-scarred veteran of Central's interference.

But then he saw Cass's point, because Central had integrated what they learned about conditioning into the very program that Jack had hijacked, to mess with Old Jim's head. Then Jack had set Old Jim loose in the archives, to, in a sense, explore the genesis of his own condition. Had Jack gotten a kick out of that? Rationalized it, somehow? The idea that Old Jim would research and analyze the origins of the pathology imposed upon him?

The grotesque truth in Cass's handwritten note on the last page: "Reviewing the old files on the biologists' expedition was part of your conditioning, Jim. That's how fucked up Jack is."

The perversity sank in along with a smoldering anger, even if on some level he felt beyond surprise.

To distract, he went on to the second file, which focused on Old Decomp, with a note attached with a paper clip to the front: "I didn't like the potholes." No, she hadn't.

He flipped through it, still trying to adjust to this command center, this access to Cass's mind. The sharpness of it. The way it contrasted with the person who supposedly had failed at her prior mission. The person who separated the ingredients. The person who made goofy, off-center jokes.

Maybe this is what you did when you failed and you wanted to rise again from the ashes. Maybe you tried to do everything you could to solve the mystery on your own, saddled with a partner who kept falling apart on you. Or maybe this is what you did when every last bit of what you'd said about yourself, what Jackie had said about you, was a lie.

The file contained the infrared spy-satellite images of the area Cass had referenced on the way to Dead Town, and zeroed in on the stone silo. The potholes stood out because they formed a pattern, as Cass had said, with a rough X down the middle and a circle around the outer spokes. Rough, yes, but clearly discernible. If it had been defined by red blinking lights he would have thought it resembled a helicopter landing pad. But, in the context, who knew what it meant? Or if it meant anything at all.

The potholes under that scrutiny had "exhibited unusual properties, similar to the residue from neo-biological substances and related molecular disturbances."

A type of "pollution" that should not be there, given the history of the place. Yes, the silo had been a burn site before the storage unit had been built next to it, around it. But only for the usual: paper and wood and other "nonchemical waste."

The site had also been used to incinerate the remains of the biologists twenty years ago. That information Cass had written by hand on the report, so it came from elsewhere. He felt sick to his stomach. Jack must have chosen the silo to dump the expedition samples for that reason.

The intensity of the report bore down on Old Jim, as did the last page, which cited a fire department incident dated to three days before the Rogue showed up at the Village Bar. The parking lot had been on fire. The firefighters had to put it out, cause given as "arson, gasoline," with the speculation that bored teenagers had been responsible. End of story. Nothing further, but Cass had written "entry point?" in the margin.

Entry point? The little hairs on his neck rose. Like the Rogue had . . . *arrived* there?

Cass had flagged two other items in particular: The first indicated that a review of the history of the site going back a decade showed it had "changed significantly" in the past few weeks, a phrasing that, no matter how he rifled through the pages, came with no further explanation. Second, that the parking lot residue matched enough of what had been found on Aguilar and Numi twenty years ago that R&D had wanted to reinterview them, and by that Old Jim knew they wanted blood samples and a full physical as well as a talk.

Except, they could not be found.

What did that mean? The vast outlines of something moving through the deep, of processes that had gotten well beyond contain.

Every next thing left for him felt like distraction from the last.

Old Jim picked up the photograph from Dead Town, which showed the back wall of the second floor of City Hall, behind the chair in the alcove. On the back, she'd written: "There are people at Central, despite the odds, who care about an actual future. Who believe in something *real*. I'm coming back, promise."

Promises could be threats. Promises could be meant sincerely, but never kept.

Who the hell was she?

The silencer. The expert aim. The inconsistencies.

Was she a Phantom? Was this what a Phantom did? The rumored faction that never stepped into the light. The "third way" that found both the Brutes and old hands suspect, crude, and nearsighted.

Old Jim doubted she had ever failed on a mission in her life. Maybe she hadn't been desperate to convince Old Jim to keep her around, so much as make sure that their day-to-day interactions not betray who she worked for.

If everything was up for grabs at Central, then maybe she was suggesting that they could be allies. Offering that to him.

He stared at the photograph for a long time, trying to figure out why she had left it for him. But, as with the address, he finally found it there in the photo—passed this final test.

The faint, indistinct suggestion along two sides, marred by shadow. If he had to bet, Cass was trying to show him the outline of a door. Cass was telling him that a secret room lay behind the chair on the second floor of City Hall, in the heart of Dead Town.

That the Rogue's lair might lie behind that door.


Downstairs, on his way out, Old Jim checked the fridge, because his mouth was dry and he had a sudden surge of thirst.

But the fridge was empty except for one thing.

A pomelo.


## 023: THE NIGHT COMMANDER


**N**othing lived in Old Jim's head driving back to the house except the need to return to Dead Town, to have a secret room solve a mystery in a way Cass's secret apartment had not. To see his mission through to the end, no matter what that end might mean. They all wanted him to do it, every possible master he might answer to, even if he wished to punish some of them. He believed Cass wanted it, too, and, perhaps, that meant he worked for the Phantoms now.

A quick dinner of leftovers and back into his office to retrieve a duffel bag into which he placed duct tape, earplugs, a flare gun, a hunting knife, some of the money from the barrels.

While he'd been gone, a new fax had come in. Like a spasmodic quiver from the dead hand of his predecessor, the sheets of paper consisted of the latest sea debris reports, which had become stranger, wilder over time. Dead birds in droves, deep-sea creatures come to gelatinous ruin on the shore, a "tar-like substance" being tested by the Coast Guard, "a diaphanous soft exoskeleton, unknown origins," and more dead sea creatures. Dolphins. Sharks. No storm to account for it. Mostly in remote places. Mostly just more data to sift through pointlessly. He tossed it on the pile of damaged faxes. Let someone else sort it out.

Old Jim stepped out onto the back deck at sunset, thought he'd retrieve a handsaw he'd left there, too. The sun was almost gone, had the dark-blood aspect of a bad egg yolk running down the side of the sky. He ignored the illusion that the birds wheeled to avoid the streaks. How the black-blue parts of the sky churned with some occult energy.

A shooting pain in his head as something smashed into him and a second sun opened up in front of his eyes. He crumpled back onto the deck, ears ringing, blood pouring into his eyes. He wiped at it feebly, slid down to the deck floor, back to the railing.

Familiar shoes appeared in front of him. Almost as old-fashioned as Commander Thistle's. Henry had laid him low with a heavy blow, maybe brass knuckles. He pawed for his gun in its shoulder holster, but a hand ripped it off him and tossed it out into the darkness. Old Jim tasted aluminum and disinfectant, wondered from a distant place if he had suffered a concussion.

Henry punched him once in the jaw, then stood back. It hadn't been a solid punch, Old Jim had turned his face, and it almost gave him back some equilibrium. He struggled to rise and Henry planted a foot on his chest, kicked him back against the railing. Okay, then, he'd rest there for a while, ribs burning inside like they had caught fire. Wipe this blood out of his face, figure out why his left arm felt numb and creaky.

"Hey, Night Commander," Henry said. "Calling the Night Commander. Still with us?"

Old Jim ignored that, trying to clear his head, because the fireflies had come out and there were so many tiny warm yellow points of light that he couldn't be sure which were the sparks lighting up his brain from the damage.

Henry squatted to look him in the eyes, but stood far enough away that Old Jim didn't think his numb left arm could reach for the knife in his boot before Henry kicked him again.

The deck light had come on, giving the vampire a wax museum look—the exaggerated glower of his hollowed-out expression that hid a twisted pleasure.

A faraway glaze to his expression as he launched into a speech, an underlying quaver to his tone that bothered Old Jim, maybe more than the beating.

"What I want you to know, Old Jim, is that you've been a failure here the whole time. Because of you and your kind we're behind—and because of you we don't even have the right equipment to conduct our research. And because of you, our records to date are almost useless. Without our hands tied behind our backs, it took just a week to get results at the lighthouse here on the mainland. Just a week. And you're not even with the Brigade are you? You're . . . you're a sort of foreign entity."

That Henry might be a talker had not occurred to Old Jim.

"I don't know what you're talking about."

"And now this fire, this catastrophe," Henry said, talking right over him. "Did you set the fire? Was it you? Because you couldn't let me take over?"

Old Jim almost missed Commander Thistle's stripped-down pseudo-religious jargon.

When he didn't respond, Henry kicked him in the ribs. Old Jim felt something shift a bit, like his body might come apart at the seams, and he curled up on his side, the fire raging stronger and trying to breathe shallow to avoid more pain. Now he could reach his knife, and he willed Henry to come still closer. Just a little closer.

But Henry didn't. He kept orating—about money, about lost opportunity. About lofty goals. About the dark sciences and how they weren't Ouija Hicks but the future, and why would the Night Commander want to get in the way of that? Which led back to the question: "Where's the money? Do you know where the money is?"

The money wasn't in the barrels anymore, grasping for what he could say to buy some time. His knife was itching to find Henry's throat.

"It's at that storage unit place—before you get to Bleakers-ville," Old Jim said, wincing as he spoke. "In the stone building out back."

The place that had "changed significantly." The only place he knew and Henry didn't, and maybe he could escape into that dense forest behind the silo.

"The one that burnt down? Do you think I'm stupid?"

"It's in the ground, buried."

Henry thought about that a moment, while Old Jim got himself into a sitting position. The more Old Jim saw of Henry, the more something seemed wrong with the flow of the man, as if he had experienced the onset of some wasting disease.

"I need medical attention. You'll get the money, but you need to get me to a hospital." Worth a try, just to get a reaction.

Henry sneered. "You're talking just fine so you're coming with us. Get up."

Us?

Old Jim gauged the distance again, but Henry, he saw, had a gun on him, too. That and the little signs of mental stress and anxiety made him feel that Henry might decide to just shoot him. That vibration of energy. A kind of constant vibration below the surface of Henry's skin. Possibly on mood-altering drugs. Someone who might slip up along the way.

"Okay, I'll take you," Old Jim said, like it was still his decision.

But when they walked out front and Old Jim saw it wasn't Suzanne waiting there, he stopped short so abruptly that Henry almost bumped into him.

The Medic.

Shit.


The Medic took his knife, peashooter, and truck keys. The Medic bound his hands behind his back. The Medic, dressed the same as at the lighthouse, smelling of boot polish, whispered in Old Jim's ear as he came close, "You pushed me into the sea, sir. Jack said to tell you, 'You should've gotten in the barrel.' Like a good boy. Sir."

So much for having a week before Jack found out. Now Jack was having Old Jim brought to the quarry, the back alley, the hidden place by the river. Now Old Jim was going to find out what that felt like, because while an amateur psycho might've botched the job, he doubted the Medic would.

The Medic got in on the driver's side of Old Jim's truck and Henry shoved him into the middle, so they were squeezed together like awkward livestock. The Medic was going to kill them both, and whether Jack had ordered that or the Medic had taken a special interest didn't matter.

As the Medic pulled out, Old Jim said to Henry, "I heard you found something in the lighthouse. I can help with that. What did you find?"

Henry couldn't help himself, not on his favorite topic. "I found what was hidden. It wasn't hard. It escaped, but I held it, I had it in my hands. It *saw* me."

"Shut up, Henry," the Medic said, and the glint in his eye, the cold-blooded calculus of that look, made Old Jim panic.

"Listen, Henry, listen to me. This guy doesn't care about the lighthouse. He doesn't care about what you found there. He will—"

With surprising agility, the Medic turned in his seat and slapped Old Jim across the face. Old Jim slammed back against the seat, stunned, added to his injuries a dull ache and white dots in front of his eyes. An open hand from the Medic was the same as a fist.

"Shut up. Sir."

The godforsaken dirt roads the Medic favored made tunnels in the darkness, the startling white of sand and dirt in the head-lights ethereal, the trees curving over in a way that made them seem alive and interested in Old Jim's fate.

"*I follow dry riverbeds, / in peace, I make my way.*"

He was going to die at Old Decomp. He hadn't gauged the timing well enough, or the intensity of Henry's hostility. He'd never make it to the secret room.

"*Every stream will meet the sea, / and every sorrow will have its day.*"

Old Decomp, how it had fallen on sad, hard times in the harsh glow of the headlights. The fire scars, black against the gray, in rough tongues and shredded triangles of damage. The suggestion of the top of the turret having blown off like a teapot kept on a stove too long.

The potholes that in memory had been of hideous regard held that aspect now, a kind of flicker around their edges in the peripheral vision of the headlights. Cass's report kept rolling around in the back of Old Jim's brain, as if that could help him now.

The meat barrel that was the Medic squashed out the side of the pickup and soon enough he and Henry were pulling him, protesting, out into the parking lot.

The Medic held him by the arm while Henry got a shovel out of the truck, tossed it on the ground at Old Jim's feet.

"You're going to dig up the money. Wherever it is."

"No," the Medic said. "He's not. We will. He's dangerous. Has no God." Another one, like Commander Thistle.

"He's going to kill you, Henry," Old Jim said. "He's going to kill us both." There, he could say it, could imagine it. Somehow that was a relief.

Another blow to his ear that sent him off-balance—the Medic had that move down pat—and he managed to fall to his knees north of the potholes, in the gravel, restraints cutting into his wrists.

This was the kind of place, like the quarry so long ago, where he'd always expected to die. It wasn't the worst way to meet an end. He liked how the insects chittered on regardless in the trees beyond the light. How he could hear a barred owl's loopy mating call so clearly. How none of what lay beyond the headlights cared about what went down in the back lots of a bunch of shitty storage units.

He felt a pang of intense regret, of sadness, the cause of which lay somewhere in the trees beyond the light.

"What spot, sir," the Medic said. "Where, exactly."

"Right there," Old Jim said, after a moment of pretending to orient himself. "Waterproof wrapped and one bag per pothole. Some of them." Would that buy him any time at all?

"You said it was in the silo!" Henry, almost shrieking as if he were unnerved by the place, or the potholes. In the shadow and spotlight, the potholes appeared of uncertain depth and the fuzziness of the slight glow made the quality of the water dubious.

"No, I didn't." Always make the enemy unsure of itself.

"You did!"

The Medic reached down, picked up the shovel, threw it effortlessly into the middle of the potholes. It came to rest with a scraping sound that seemed to last too long.

"Dig it up, Henry."

So the Medic was going to kill Henry first.

"What?" Henry truly didn't understand.

"We start by believing him, Henry," the Medic said, as if talking to a child. "Then we punish him if he's lying."

Henry hesitated, then nodded. Maybe he was thinking of all the times he'd appeared to be a psychopath to normal people. Maybe he was thinking that he should try doing what someone said for a change. Maybe he was just figuring out when to replace the Medic's beady eyes with pebbles.

Henry walked into the headlights' glare, into the middle of the potholes, holding the shovel. His head lay at an odder relationship to his shoulder than usual. He looked around as if having decided none of the potholes looked promising.

"Henry, when are you going to start digging?" the Medic asked.

Henry appeared flushed around the edges, as if about to break into tears. But he began to dig into the potholes, half-heartedly. First one, then a second, both times his shovel finding no purchase, sliding off the gravel. The third time, the flat sound of the shovel hit something hard, and he forgot his caution, elated, and got on his hands and knees, letting the shovel slide to the ground beside him.

A hand shoved into the hole came back empty.

"There's nothing here. It's just some sort of cement block in this one."

"Try another one," the Medic said patiently. But Old Jim standing beside him could hear the way the Medic's breathing had become more rapid. The slight tensing of the Medic's right hand.

Henry looked eager now, like he going to put some heart into it—like he would get up off his knees and pick up the shovel again. Old Jim even believed from the almost-happiness on Henry's face that maybe he was wrong. Maybe they weren't both about to die.

But Henry couldn't get up off his knees. His knees appeared stuck to the ground, or was it the hand still in the pothole that had gotten stuck?

The way his long sleeve runneled downward like black wax into the hole.

How the sides of him rippled as they liquified and fell splashing and thick in streams and pools of nothing like flesh, to feed the holes, which throbbed and hummed green now, come alive in a way that made them seem like too-regular tidal pools on a sheet of rock next to the sea.

How Henry screamed and screamed, like he was being taken apart at the seams. How he spasmed and tried to pull free, but still he was stuck.

Old Jim's veins turned to ice, the pain in his ribs ossified a century in a moment.

The Medic, mouth open, couldn't stop watching, the sound coming out of his mouth indescribable but like some sort of huffing creature trying to catch its breath.

A wave of odor, swift and thick, roiled over them. Heavy,

electric. That must be what you smelled when the remnants of a person became molecules in the air.

The smell made the Medic bend over in distress, taking two steps back, and, as he tried to straighten up, the man's gaze swept over Old Jim, and even in that uncertain light and shadow, he could see that the Medic, too late, understood what Old Jim was going to do. Because he'd done it before.

He rammed into the Medic, drove him into the writhing, seething form of Henry, used the impact to fall to the side, clear of the potholes. Henry reaching for the Medic, as if the Medic could still pull him free even though it was too late for that, and how the Medic screamed where Henry's liquid arms touched him, as if made of burning lava, and how the Medic kept falling into Henry, that never-ending abyss, until Old Jim couldn't tell which part was the Medic and which part was Henry, and had to look away even as the screams of both began to die.

How Henry and the Medic continued to melt into the parking lot and wash away into the murky water of the holes like something escaping a prison. How the Medic, oddly, became impossible to discern first, and yet Henry still thrashed there for a time.

Like something returning home, all of him, forever, and in the last extremity there came only a gurgle from what was left of Henry's face and then even that was gone, like something crumbling in the tide and swept out to sea.

A final sob, a final questing of the remains of one last waving hand, and then Henry was gone.

Old Jim stumbled to his feet, to the truck. He could not look back.

He would not look back.

## 024: THE TERROR

There was a secret room in Dead Town. That's what the photograph appeared to show, in stark black and white, a spectral outline, a possibility. How the tracker had lit up and shown him Dead Town, Main Street, not some desolate place out in the swamp. How that had to mean something other than a malfunction.

He'd thought about calling Jack when he drove by the Starlight Lounge, but what was the point? The place might be staked out, and Jack would just tell him to come back to Central and debrief, which Old Jim would never do. No bargain to be struck, not with Jack, and, he felt, no time left. The pathetic questions Old Jim would've asked Jack—why he had used something precious like the piano as a tool to harm him. Even as all the intricate details of his work for Central came back to him in that moment, like something he was letting go of. Like something too delicate to have been real.

Every rut and bump—he felt it in his body. His left knee wasn't solid, even in the truck, with no weight on it. His ribs made him wheeze, but he told himself the injury lacked the sharp dagger of pain that meant he should find a hospital. He stank of fatigue and dirt and strange parking lots. Henry kept dissolving in the reflections on the windshield. The Medic kept appearing in the middle of Henry, falling into the oblivion of a terrible death.

By the time Old Jim got to the gate at Dead Town, he was in a mood to smash through with the truck. So he did. He didn't want to walk far in the dark, so close to water.

Then he slowed the car to a crawl and cut the engine close to the dead meadow. He could've used Cass's help, but some part of him liked being there alone, as if that's the way it was supposed to be.

The night felt unoccupied to him as he crept down Main Street, the moon strong through reflecting clouds, so he could see without the flashlight. The oak branches created the shadows of monstrous figures across the ground, the moss shining silver off the limbs.

City Hall lay dead and dark in front of him soon enough, and he paused only to listen to the silence—cut through with the chitter of bats, the chirps of flying squirrels.

Old Jim put in his earplugs, in case of an earwig, a centipede, and then went inside. He climbed the stairs with a slowness that felt like delay but veered more toward caution, then negotiated the maze of lamp wires on the second floor until he once more stood in front of the middle alcove.

All was as before. He gently moved the chair to the side, as quietly as he could, and then to a position behind him—a barricade against the unexpected creeping up on him. The moonlight slanted through the windows but did not reach the alcove, so he turned on his flashlight to examine the wall.

It held such a history of abuse over the decades, seen that way, in that stripped-down light. The ravages, the indignities of time, of people passing through long ago. The way the wallpaper, and part of the wall, had rotted, dissolved, been idly pulled down in strips, probably by bored teens smoking cigarettes and telling tales about the Cavalry.

And in the middle of all that, the words and his true name.

The power of seeing that name felt distant now. Inert. Dead. It had done the job of finally unlocking him, and how he wondered if the Rogue had written that name other places—anywhere Old Jim might eventually encounter it. Or if it only existed here, and if so, how had the Rogue been sure he would see it?

Just a name he'd gone by once, no more or less real than "Old Jim," and what name he would have at the end of all this he did not know.

With trembling hands, flashlight awkwardly positioned between chin and shoulder, he traced the line he thought he saw, remembering the latch at Old Decomp and thinking again about the idea that the Rogue knew Central's tricks. Such a thin line between knowing and not knowing. Such a secret hiding in plain view. Central had mentioned no secret room in their report twenty years ago. Was it possible they'd missed it?

Somewhere low, as he bent to his knees and squatted, the line broke for an inch or two, down there in the shadows near where once, perhaps, an alligator had slept on the rug like a faithful dog. It broke just enough for his finger to find a depression, an indentation, and to know to both push and pull.

With a pop, a door appeared, pushed just an inch inward. No light shone out from within.

He stood up. He pushed the door open, just enough to enter, and he stepped inside like a thief, like the Jim of old.


The inside was a mirror of the outside room, just smaller, as if the walls here had been insulated with more foam, built with thicker wood and drywall. It had the same high ceilings, here made obvious by the lack of dangling lamps, and spread out before him lay a simplicity he had not expected, as if the Rogue had less complexity to him than in Old Jim's imagination.

Across the center of the floor, rendered black and white by the flashlight's gleam, he saw a series of what appeared to be glass jars over rough indentations in the floor, in the pattern Cass had shown him on the Old Decomp parking lot infrared scan. The exact same pattern. The X, the circle around it. The two spokes of the X held little coagulated piles in each declivity. The one closest to him revealed itself as twisted, burnt pieces of what could only be rabbit cameras.

The glass jars had an uncomfortably organic feel to them, and a cloudiness he did not like.

This debris meant nothing except that the Rogue had been a

madman, that he had been the kind to believe in monkey's paws and psychics, in perverse pentagrams and the occult. What practicality was there here? What purpose and use?

But Henry's fate had taught him to be careful not just of who whispered in your ear but where you placed your feet.

He wrenched his gaze away from the crumpled rabbit cameras to examine the rest of the room. A ragged sleeping bag lay in the far left corner behind the devil's floor display, dusty and ripped in places. The well of darkness in the right-hand corner came into focus as a vast watermark or fire scar. The indentations in the foreground had the look of suffering fire damage, so perhaps it was the same.

Almost as if tightrope walking, as if the pattern hid some secret depth, Old Jim made his way to the left-hand wall and what had been written there. Checking the far-right corner again before he turned his back on it. He did not like the curious discoloration of it, the vague circle of it, the sense he had that it might be as recent as yesterday or as old as the time of the last biologists huddling in the stairwell, awaiting rescue.

The sensation of lingering on words was peculiar now. He did not like to do it, to scrutinize, preferred to glance, to skim and move on, as if in the cursory slant of his regard he might be spared the power of whatever stared back at him from the letters.

Diagrams, too, featuring the pattern on the floor, with markings and words he could not decipher, as if the Rogue had written out complex formulas for use—but for what kind of use, Old Jim could not tell. Diagrams of energy and dispersal.

There was a pattern to some of the diagrams, a sort of improvisational quality he could sense, and much of it involved the Tyrant, the way the diagrams suggested jury-rigging, suggested that the Rogue had in some biological way used the cameras to create a symbiosis with the beast, and he didn't know if he had used the right words in his head, but there came a kind of chill that was realization—that at some point the Tyrant might have become not the Rogue's servant, but some kind of coconspirator. Either the Rogue or the Tyrant modified to accommodate that.

He felt like a caveman encountering the schematic for a spaceship.

In the end, the diagrams spilled off the wall and onto the floor, because there were three pages of further diagrams and notes and names and phrases, including notations to "protect" or to "kill." He glanced at them, folded them, put them in his pocket for later. Someone wiser than him might have to interpret them.

He halted next in front of a sentence that felt like a confession: "I did not mean to do that to them." No teenager had scrawled that on the wall. He could see where it repeated, faintly, ever lower on the wall, as if written in a frenzy.

Then, roving higher on the wall, where it might have required a ladder, Old Jim spied a list of names in three neat rows. About twenty names, maybe more, but not on a cursory glance the names of the Dead Town biologists. Craning his neck to try to read the names, he realized they'd been written where a person sitting against the far wall could read them with ease. Maybe start a morning there, contemplating just those names.

But he stopped trying to catalogue names when his flashlight flickered, realized with a curse it would give out soon, and he still had the opposite wall to examine as well. So he stepped past the bulky sleeping bag that looked like a bundle of clothing had been shoved inside and then the watermark to come close enough to the other wall to read it.

"It was winter then, late summer now?"

"The piano is different. Does it matter?"

"Why is there a Commander Thistle?"

Saul Evans's name, in a delicate hand, and written next to it "the carrier must remain the same."

Henry's name.

Gloria's name.

His name again, but expressed just as "Old Jim."

Cass's name, but not her last name. Just "Cass." Her name had been circled and a greater circle created so that he stood back a step to almost the edge of the bizarre pentagram on the floor to take it in.

Gloria's name at the center and Cass's name on the periphery, with lines from "Old Jim" to Cass and Gloria, and from Saul Evans to Gloria only. With a question mark.

He was so puzzled that he didn't feel alarm or dread. He just didn't know what to make of it. Some secret op so vast and obscure and with so many moving parts perhaps the Rogue himself had lost the thread. Was that why there were question marks beside the diagram?

Gloria's name surprised him to the point that he had to wrench himself out of reliving her visit to his house with the cookies, as if what she'd said to him could bring some essential secret out into the light.

Did this mean the Rogue had them all under surveillance? That the Rogue, in his own way, had been watching all of them. The strange behavior of the alligator tracker. The feeling of someone or something in the marsh.

Even through the earplugs, he thought he heard a sound like a drop of water falling into a deep well, felt a wetness on his face. The hairs on the back of his neck stood up, like he did know but couldn't think of it yet and a chill overtook him.

His pulse quickened and he had to stand still for a moment, to catch his breath, to let the resumed ache in his ribs subside. It would hurt much more if he started to hyperventilate.

The weight of the darkness from above felt oppressive in that moment and he realized with something like panic that he hadn't swept his flashlight up that far. Now it felt like someone might drop on him from above. It felt urgently like someone was about to ambush him.

He didn't want to see what might be there.

He had to see what might be there.

When he swung the light up, no one clung improbably to the ceiling, waiting to drop onto him, and all his breath, which he had been holding in without realizing it, came out at once.

Something registered at the edge of his peripheral vision. He swung the flashlight onto the sleeping bag. Had there been a movement?

It lay harmless, motionless. Empty?

Into the silence came again the odd drip of water, more urgent now, more as of a body rising from a swimming pool. Of a body pulling itself from a pool of water partway onto land.

He did not want to turn farther to his right. He did not want to be in the room anymore. His mind had gone blank with terror at the sound that should not be there, the sound so thick and weighted as of a very heavy person in the room with him. So that he was back at the bridge behind the Village Bar. In the dark. Feeling like he was alone. And this time he was, with no one to save him but himself.

But he turned anyway.

As there came such a rush of fast, immeasurable speed, as the blackness there raged into abundant and ferocious matter.

The Tyrant.


There was a way in which it was so real and immediate and yet also felt impossible and drawn out. Maybe he could not contain the feverish intensity of it and also the overwhelming beauty of it, how he could be reduced down to his bones by fear and yet also feel so alive.

For there, impossible, in the back of the room, a pool of water of limitless depth had appeared where the watermark had been, the edges stippled with the faint bioluminescence of specks of uncanny algae and duckweed.

While, in the center of that space, filling it, the great head of the beast known as the Tyrant had risen, the last living member of the Cavalry, to regard him with a carious yellow eye—erupting from those supernal waters toward him, the mighty head so armored in scales reflecting its own strange light, as of tarnished silver with the gleam shining through the whorls of that.

The way the bioluminescence at the edges of the pool leapt up as the Tyrant leapt up and intensified, so that it formed a collar around the great beast's neck, and then fell away, exhausted by the velocity.

Old Jim screamed, dropped the flashlight, and it skittered across the pentagram, went out forever.

He could not escape. He was in the Tyrant's jaws even as he turned to run. Wider and wider until the pressure held him entire, and he surrendered, lay limp as prey. He thought he was about to die, anticipated the rending of his flesh, the crack of his bones. But that moment did not come.

For the Tyrant had him gently in her jaws, just the slight febrile pricking of those teeth, held tight but not too tight, against his clothes, his skin, and that maw wide and deep enough to hold him secure as he crumpled into agreement with his fate, and he knew somehow, instinctually, to hold his breath as the Tyrant receded back into the pool, into that impossible body of water, that impossible impossible water, and together they disappeared down, down into the depths.

## 025: NO GOD HERE ON EARTH

T hen there was just the field of golden sunflowers across the wetlands, so rich and full of light as the Tyrant crushed her way through them, carrying him limp in her jaws, that his vision blurred before the intensity of them and he became un-moored from the moment and he was just a relic, an object mov-ing through a field of gold, toward an unknown destination. No one had ever held him so intimately, so without judgment.

Time passed and he felt lulled by the sound of the reeds, the calls of birds, the blazing sun to match the blaze of sunflowers, until, finally, they came to the edge of an open space, amid the trees. A lake, a lagoon. A place so remote that perhaps no one had ever seen this vista as he saw it now.

The Rogue like a dead commander laid to rest, arms folded over his chest, floated in the clear water, a pale, wavery visage from the surface, wearing clothing that flickered and lingered with the light, the shadow, so that all but his face became the sand, the aquatic grasses, the dark blue of the deep water, the light blue of the water in the shallows.

The Tyrant deposited Old Jim on a divot of land that erupted from the edge of the lagoon, then she slipped into the water be-side the Rogue. A green rowboat lay up against the divot, at Old Jim's feet.

Shining from all sides, the surrounding halo of the swamp sunflowers at the lagoon's edge, thousands of them, so was it the sun that made Old Jim squint or the flowers? While from below, the Tyrant came up out of the depths of the deep blue and embraced the Rogue, who subsided into her and was enraptured by her, and there was nothing of him that was not encircled by her and nothing of her that was not a part of him.

As the Tyrant brought the Rogue close, Old Jim saw that he

had lost his camouflage, breathing and yet not breathing, the red brittle starfish of two bullet wounds in the chest. The Rogue's eyes were closed. The Rogue was dead-alive. The Rogue was staring at him from the belly of the beast, and he wondered now whether, in that connection, he had an audience with the Rogue or with the Tyrant, and whether it mattered.

The Rogue's left eye opened. That cryptic eye, that alien regard. Staring at an organism become other than a man, but sheltering in a man's body. What was this new thing that looked so old?

There was the sensation of liquid glass passing through Old Jim and the shards sliding through his mind and then gone. And with the touch he knew Cass's aim had been true. The Rogue had been mortally wounded and lay now in a kind of never-ending sleep or coma, surrounded by the flowers, yes, but beneath the surface, the dim glimmer, the glint of a darker gold and the same pattern across that shallow bottom, mapped to the secret room, to the parking lot of Old Decomp. And that the Rogue had known Old Jim would come, but not when.

He vomited up all the old words once more, reflexively, as he had at the bridge, but the Rogue just smiled wearily and waited for the assault to end, and by this Old Jim took the Rogue to mean that the force of those words held no sway now. That there had already been countermeasures, that the Tyrant, singing to him every night from the marsh even as Commander Thistle sang different words, had torn him from his dreaming state . . . into another.

Because the deep truth of it was that, somehow, impossibly, the Rogue was from Central or had originated with Central, long ago and far away.

"Will you tell me what this means?" Old Jim asked. "Please."

But the Rogue without the Tyrant was nothing, he could see that now. This peculiar pale man who rested in such a repose that in the dead bliss on his face, Old Jim envied him the obliviousness of that.

Because Old Jim wanted, needed the same, and so that's what he said to the Tyrant: "Let me go. Let me rest."

The great beast roared, a thunderous, guttural sound steeped in swamp water, in the black reflecting water beyond the lagoon, the land beyond the sunflowers. This water that had protected her these twenty years and there was the unraveling or unspooling of some hidden mechanism and the Rogue fell away, down, down into the depths and from the Tyrant's open, roaring mouth she breathed out upon Old Jim not words but a cloud of golden particles, so that for a time Old Jim believed he had been dusted with sunflower pollen.

He could see again the armies in the green light, and how some among their ranks bent over as they walked and appeared to be concentrating vast amounts of mental energy toward the strange light. That, on occasion, they cried out in pain, reared back, their eyes rolling into their heads—and quavered in their form, became light, became wave, re-formed as human. As wagons crunched along over an endless plain of bones.

And he gasped, because now he could see that they marched not toward two mountains, but toward ridges across a seabed where the water had receded as some force had expanded, and here, now, from the Rogue's vantage he could see the remains of vast ships and how, at their back in the far distance, the remains of the lighthouse shone out.

The distant future, not the past, and the future was where the Rogue came from, a future unbearably uncertain, a place where everything was fluid because of what was coming, and if he had no place here, if he had no way to come to rest, the Tyrant told him, he might once he crossed that divide.

But first he had to do the thing he always had, would always do, and what did that mean, when you were a spy, and yet what was one more role to play. Because he hadn't been supposed to find the secret room, the way the history went, because there shouldn't have been a need for a secret room, for a Rogue, for an intercession at Dead Town. He could see that now as the dust that wasn't dust overtook him. The dust was just another kind of language, and perhaps the biggest mistake he'd made was not believing the biologists' accounts in a literal way.

Because earplugs hadn't helped him at all, and that meant they couldn't have helped the psychics on Failure Island any more than the past could ever defeat the future.

And he was falling away, as the Tyrant too now fell away, for the moment was coming and he could see the word for it, the words the Tyrant had given him: Area X. Nothing in the end could placate Area X. The land overwhelmed with a spark from the lighthouse, and what came out manifested under the ground and spread and even when it did not seem to spread it was spreading, and though the coast was still and silent, the people who had been there would still exist in some form, in some place. How this would always happen and yet it could happen in ways much worse. It could happen so that no one ever survived.

Yet Old Jim wasn't going to get to the end of the mystery, though he'd almost run the gauntlet, been given the outlines. An agent of the future acting on the past, but lost in the variables, unexpected collateral damage, mortally wounded in the process of trying to change . . . what? Forced to go dormant, underground, to evade the enemy, to avoid the very fate he wished to change—the future colonizing the past, as if every moment had a permeability that could neither be denied nor controlled, like an outstretched hand with the water draining off the sides back into the river. A man walking beside a huge reptile in the reeds. With all of history on the horizon.

The Rogue faded fully into the gold, deep into the gold and the water, enfolded in the Tyrant, who laid him to rest with a gentle affection.

**ABSOLUTION**

To sleep, to dream, to rise again, someday.
And what day would that be, and did it matter?
Old Jim wondered if he would be there to see it.

## 026: THE SOUND AND THE SIGNAL

The green rowboat with scars of past encounters, with Old Jim in it, and the Tyrant leading him by pulling a rope at the prow. This mundane act, the tactile nature of the landscape around him, made the visions fall away before the crush of swamp sunflowers and the marsh reeds turned russet in the afternoon light. Light, every particle of it a miracle.

How the way the Tyrant moved through the water made the flat, wide nose of the boat nudge wavelets ahead with little gasps, how even through the grasping pockets of water that escaped around the sides of the hull there rose from the bottom the long green fingers of aquatic grasses.

There was nothing in his heart other than relief, of coming to some kind of end, to some kind of answer, even if it required a belief that he still had to muster.

The sun burning down, burning away, held him rapt in the aftermath—and then the sprawl of night sky, torn at by the pale tower of the lighthouse, releasing shapes like the retreat of birds and bats from Dead Town so long ago.

As the night dulled the marsh, the Tyrant sang out to him and soothed, the *Winter Journey* transformed, and what message did the alligator share with him? Saturated with the sight of the great beast, the sky, the water.

The pilot light of his fear had gone out, and he was neither candle nor flame, but only vessel, and the Tyrant sang words to him he half understood and must obey. What he scribbled on a piece of paper. How he was commanded. But he felt no terror or shame in that obedience, only a kind of sureness of vision. That this was necessary, that this was right.

For, in time, he would shed his self, drift down deep, the bridge a shadow above him, become nestled in the water and the reeds, staring up at a well of distant golden light, soon infiltrated by a green tint.

He was just water, moving through a long tunnel formed by the curving reeds, and at the end of that tunnel, which was time, lay the Tyrant once again, and the Rogue, and perhaps Cass, too, and perhaps she would be the one who extended a hand, told him, "You made it," and pulled him out of the water into a new world.

When the boat reached the edge of firm land and a trail back toward the Village, he didn't look back, heard only the sounds of a massive alligator dragging herself into the heart of the swamp.

As he found the road to the bar, a peculiar light made the beacon of the lighthouse beam seem to be tearing through a veil, a conspiracy of atoms that would not obey the normal rules. The black sky, when the beam moved on, a vast wall and a field of stars, and the sky-stars blurred out as of something moving through and past them.

Soon enough, a little car moved slowly past him: Henry and Suzanne headed to the lighthouse, pale faces in the dark. They did not see him or he was no longer something that could be seen, and there came from somewhere a fading urge to catch up and end Henry a second time, along with so little surprise at seeing him alive.

In the bar, he did the things he knew they expected, with precision, and he said the things he usually said, and then he sat down at the piano. There was nothing left in his head now, except what burgeoned beneath the surface, what the Rogue had put there to save him, to change him.

The real Cass, at ten, at the piano, protesting her incarceration on the bench at first, but then banging the keys with him. "Don't stop," he was saying or she was saying. Or it'll be over. Just don't stop. Just keep going.

There was the signal and there was the sound. The signal he had committed to memory, both the rage of it and the distress beacon to the future buried in it by the Tyrant, and that was not his concern as the shadows began to overtake the bar. As the bar darkened and there came a great thrashing and screaming.

The sound would be love as long as he was able. Love for them both—the false daughter and the real one. For what did it matter which had abandoned him and which had chosen to stay by his side for a time, or why? He could not hold on to the grief of that, wanted only the joy.

All the ways he was being released into the world and the world released into him. The simple relief of that even as his fingers came apart at the piano, the wound in the world that kept attracting the candle, the flame, the vessel. The way he could be in all three places at once now—the present that had annihilated him, the past that had never left him, the future that held him still and trembling like a bird caught in a biologist's net.

He could see Cass, his daughter, so clearly. He could see the accident, the aftermath, what they had done to him, and the way he could not go back and fix anything, but at least he saw it now, understood it now. The cruelty of Jackie telling him that his failure on a mission had been his false daughter's. That place by the searing blue sky, the searing sea where he'd betrayed them all and never been right again.

Following the green light, joining the army that labored there, the Exiles there now, too, staring back at him, waiting for him to catch up . . . or that's how it seemed to him, as if he had risen above the bar, the marsh, and was leaving that behind because there was no world now. And there had never really been, and Old Jim was just someone Central had pulled apart and remade.

And yet, in some way, some human way, he had still been himself, a self, underneath it all. Underneath it all, he had survived, somehow.

Here are the keys.

This is the music.

Let the music mean something.

Just do as I do.

It doesn't need to be perfect.

Nothing is perfect, ever. Nothing.

I forgive you.

Can you forgive me?

*There shall be a flame that knows your name.*

But, perhaps, he knew its name, too.

# THE FIRST AND THE LAST

## ONE YEAR AFTER THE BORDER CAME DOWN

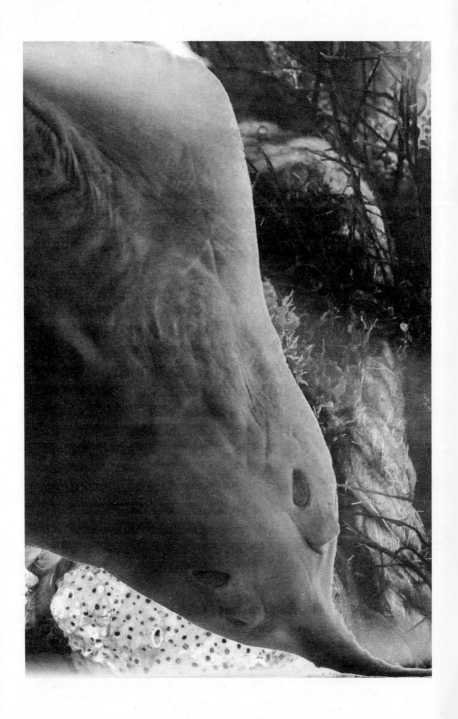

# 1=FUCK THAT CHICKEN

## LOVE AND GLORY HOLES

J ust twenty-four fucking hours until they crossed the fucking Border and nothing Lowry didn't know, for fuck's sake, that Jack hadn't told him, and he didn't know anything, fuck. Not for fucking real. The world felt like it was in shackles and the only fucking way to deal with that shit was to become so abso-fucking-lutely free he could claim his existence as an act of fucking defiance.

Nothing on the news, oblivious to the SR's first expedition, nothing in his sordid past, nothing about the other exped mems skewed him different. Sail-la-fucking-vee. They were going to sail off into the distance like a boss. Even though the actual coastline they'd fuck up had not been much discussed, so they'd never think of the fucking horrible things that occurred waterside when the Border came down.

Lowry's on-again, off-again mission-loathing manifested, and festered, as hate for the fuckling suit he would have to wear to cross the Border into what they now called Active Area X. The inner layer covered his skin so fucking perfectly, like an extra-large condom over his huge cock, that Lowry felt entombed: an organism had wrapped itself around him to suffocate him, to slowly dissolve and cheese-grate him into nothing but feeble as fuck motes of dust and light.

The slight rasp of air circulating only, fuck, gave him the claustro sensation of being digested, in a way beyond grokking. He was only an expert on digesting dead flesh—which felt shitting great most of the time—and for his own safety he should let, fuck, the, fuck, suit happen. He should just let it, fuck, happen. He should.

Fuck? Fuckfuckfuck.

Similar feelings about Sky, the expedition leader, a blonde Lowry currently banged on the side, clandestine. Another mish, near completion. Stress relief, fuck, for them both, he figured, but he couldn't stand the clammy feel of her body for long, almost attached to him as after a fuckathon she shoved herself up against his back in sleep and, fuck, *put her arm around him.* The texture held wrongness, body heat oppressive, fuck, and he had to pull away, and let her fall, fuck, into sleep again, while he put on his clothes and left.

Which made sense, right, fuck, since no one should be banging anyone else on the expedition, those were the rules, even though so many members were fucking other members, fuck, that it was like, fuck, an orgy erupting en masse while crossing the Border, with other borders and boundaries disrupted, no longer valid. If, fuck, they ever had fucking been.

A huge stretch of intestines, fuck, formed the corridor from the Border to Active Area X. That, too, a kind of suit, fuck, and intestines made sense to him not "corridor," because no one could convince him, fuck, it was straight, but the Director, fuck, kept talking "a straight shot" instead of "a coiled mass."

If he thought long enough, fuck, then fuck would stop appearing in his thoughts, fuck. It came out of his mouth too much, fuck, so fucking fucking fuck stop it. Stop saying it. Not a condition, just a nervous tic, more fucking clear the closer the day approached, but maybe all the drugs, too, fuck. Some experimental as fuck. Fuck. Fuck on a clear-sky day, hopping into the truck to be fucking carried away to fuck all fucktown. Area Fuck. Southern Fuck Reach.

There. No fuck.

Fuck.

Lowry liked Sky, just couldn't stand her sometimes, fuck, and Lowry knew she must feel similar. A relief, fuck, so it could never become serious. She had a girlfriend, fuck, or a girlfriend and a boyfriend, something ambidextrous, back in some non-fucked-up mid-Atlantic state, which is where Central pulled her from, and must've been a find, beau coup creds, given what it would take to tempt her, fuck, because she'd been high up in the *unnerved brass*. What Lowry monikered anyone above, while below was just a mass of *basement twhuts*.

Snagged a bouquet of flowers, fuck, and snatched a ring ground-zero'd with a diamond splinter, fuck, before this last time, fuck, and who knew what kind of sleeping arrangements they'd have beyond the Border or if anyone would even be in the mood. Fighting off the unknown with their glorious automatic rifles, fuck, forging ahead for the glory and the power.

Flowers and the ring made an ironic statement on the conditions of their fucking, fuck, but somehow, when Lowry had handed Sky the white lilies and proffered the ring, fuck, it had become something more serious or mysterious—fuck, and why not? He was going to be shoved like a Vienna sausage into a truck and hauled to the Border like a Vienna sausage and then all the fucking anonymous sausages, standing upright, would fuck off into the unknown. So was she, fuck.

The look on Sky's face became clouded, vague, as she said, "Ah, well, Lowry, you're surprising me here. I didn't know you were one for a grand gesture."

Fuck fuck fuck fuck.

But he was—he was!—and he couldn't control the pulse of impulse, and didn't, as then, fuck, know when he was succumbing to the impulse, the disease, the sentimentality that he'd tried to crush and crunch inside him like a field of broken glass, a diamond fragment . . . still, that quality was, fuck, a part of James Danforth Lowry, son of a bunch of deceased shitheads and fuckfaces reaching back to old fuck farm money in the Midwest.

Forget about chickens sent across on leashes. Forget they would be thrust through the Border like a cock thrust through a glory hole in the back of that bar in Bleakersville that Delmas, no fucking psychic, had mentioned one too many times.

## FUCKLING PICKLE JARS

Stupid security breach in the damn middle of the Southern Reach, fuck, the unholy reliquaries, centered around a goddamn tombstone, fuck, what a pain, that, fuck, they couldn't remove for twenty more years, out of fucking respect for a dry bag of bones underneath that had owned the doll factory the gov had bought to find the space for the command center, fuck. All the enviro regs in the world quashed, fuck, but this ancient fucker leered up at them from almost dead center of the main building, and would for two decades more. Fuck.

And the only disrespect or concession or whatever the fuck it was that meant they'd piled all these jars of finned fuck specimens around them—all the deep-sea critters, so it was a glass room of dead marine spectators fucking graveside, fuck, and the old dead guy, fuck, could not have thought in his shitting will to put in the clause "shall not be overshadowed by dead sea proteins." So, fuck, now hemmed in and frayed by these glorious fuckers in their surveillance chambers of clear glass. Backlit by a spectacular set of tech rave lights on "perpetual memorial mode" as even the most drama-crazed Eurotrash bro could wish or fish for in a lifetime of snorting the white stuff, fuck.

This clarity of neon blue, yellow, green, red, and then some ill-advised return of a too-light blue on the bottom shelf, fuck, all of it on the shelves looking like the liquor wall at your fav swank bar. So, fuck, less rave than smash a hole in a jar, pick it up with both hands, decant it into your face and learn by taste the briny secrets of the Southern Reach. Seaside moonshine, aged in the dark depths. All of the creatures, fuck, samples from the seaward side of the Border come down, none of it useful, fuck, none of it, fuck, helping know what, fuck, happened, but still they kept it there, all cute creepy maybe a fuck-you to the oldster in the ground who made them keep his gravestone.

Including, fuck, the cheery-looking dapper little shark, tail fins down, squat face peering out with a wicked smile, like a fucking stand-up comedian in some backwater failing seaside town with a bad beach, about to launch, fuck, into a, fuck, old-fashioned shipwreck of a performance. Listen, folks, have you tried the halibut? I halibut you haven't. Costs too many clams.

Fuckfuckfuckfuckfuckfuck.

Others lagged not far behind. Cuttlefish Lad, with the tricorn-hat-looking tail at the top, jammed into a jar too small, so, fuck, the eyes bugged out at the bottom, perpetually shocked by his fate, like anybody at the Southern Reach, fuck. Or maybe Downward Diving Shark was his fav, because he liked all the sharks, being one, for the fucking gravitas on the face. The texture that, fuck, seemed plush like a stuffed toy from childhood, and that expression almost priestlike, so you, fuck, could tell DDS anything you felt, even about priests.

In this chapel, this cathedral. Ah, fucking god, it was all death, wasn't it? And yet with those glass shelves, fuck, the jars all lit up like Christmas in that square room, a little cramped, but the ceiling, fuck, so high up it got lost in darkness, perfect as a storeroom once they cleared, fuck, the riffraff out.

While down below, in the center, surrounded by low gray metal benches set into the wall . . . the gravestone with the, fuck, improbable patch of dirt and grass, so, fuck, that a goddamn mole breached security once or twice, well, you could sit there, fuck, and meditate, while all the weight of hundreds, fuck, of dead souls stared hard at you. That was worth the price of admission, fuck, because where the hell could you see anything like this? Nowhere, fuck, except, maybe, depending, what did he know, Area X itself.

Chaste Dickdrcd, the fucking name on the tombstone. Couldn't make that shit up, unless Central had, for psyops reasons, though, fuck, what would those reasons be? Saint Dick Dread the Chaste. Chase that Dread Dick around the room, breaking glass with baseball bats. The ghost that remained steadfast, reliable. And, fuck, maybe that also drew Lowry to the room, that and how his security clearance, fuck, just barely cleared that limbo bar. Chin, above, or maybe limbo bars worked the other way, but still it felt like being in limbo, sitting in that, fuck, space. Also, Whitby, who had become his fucking default-o confidant on mish-sensitive topics favored the room, so it felt comfortable.

So those were all the whys he'd given Sky the ring and flowers there, fuck, in the one fucking place in the whole goddamn brutarian Southern Reach complex with, fuck, the most character and, fuck, the most history. Except she'd recoiled or coiled, couldn't tell which in that light, over the monstrosities he, fuck, saw as old friends. And him in-fucking-articulate arggle-bargling it in trying to explain he, fuck, had more in common with them things in jars, fuck, than the things in bars he shared space and time with, fuck, his fellow exped members. Estranged, fuck, strange, 'cause none of them had problems with extra skins. While these fine fellows, fuck, secure in their jars must sympth with him. Must simp for him. Must, oh fuck these drugs were so good and so invisible to their piss tests and he knew from experience fuck fuck fuck that his expression and his words came out not all chewy and elongated and melty how it felt but pure and resounding and, fuck, like he had the resolve of backbone, even when he did not.

But yeah, so, fuck, Sky had unnerved him with the blasé blast of a response, the coldness, fuck, of that place a refrigeration of both sea friends and his regard for her, and now, fuck, he spiraled more, fuck, thinking there was no anchor, no anchor, except the anchor of being encased in a second skin, fuck fuck fuck. Somehow, sentimental, fuck, he'd begun to think of a future post-mish, maybe back in the land of Midwest farmhouses, maybe somewhere, fuck, more esoteric.

Yet, too, he had to admit, fuck, he'd ruined it by expounding fucking fuck on the fact that the tombstone of Boonies Landowner Doll Factory Founder lay atop a colonial fort, the last foundational remains of such, fuck, and Lowry had strong feelings about that, especially on the drugs.

The fucking invaders had fucked it up to begin with, with their pograms and their shitty forts dumped on the landscape like they fell from the sky as alien spaceships, each polygon or hexagram or whatever shape they chose, drawn up like thrusters on a central space capsule. So maybe the forts were the ass-end of the spaceships, and the rest had detached and fucked off back into the sky to their home planet, because they sure as fuck had seemed like aliens. Spreading disease and death and a stupid fucking language that Lowry still hadn't completely learned.

Like, what if they'd had spaceships made of some dense wood or stone and they did fall out of the sky on entering the atmosphere because they were incompetent and made it wrong. But, anyway, as he'd said to Scott Landry, who got him the drugs, when Landry had put forth this theory, the thing was that those forts didn't belong in the fucking area and the whole Active

Area X didn't belong, either. It might be invisible, the Border, but the imprint was the same. Like a bunch of fucking stone forts had smashed down into the firmament . . . and just stayed there.

Just fucking stayed and spread and how the hell had anyone lived in those things in this climate anyway? What a disaster. So they would be inside an invisible fucked-up fortress that was enclosing many earlier fucked-up fortresses, as surely as if the invisibleness were visible and made of coquina or whatever other stupid-ass materials the invaders had used, and just sproinged up out of the ground. Just sproinged up out the ground, as Landry put it, and Lowry who called it "widescale anthropology," rude-corrected by Landry to "That's just history, man," couldn't erase from his mind this idea of all these spaceship forts landing and all these invisible walls sproinging out of the earth like, well, not like suddenly erect penises, because they were the wrong shape, but the word sproinging was like that, this suddenness was sudden fucking yeah it was and then their fucking moats and cannons and so on and so forth.

To which rant Sky appeared immune in, fuck, a romantic sense.


## HAUNTED BRASS


The great final briefing. An anti-briefing, by the haunted brass, the unnerved brass, the brass not fucking going into Active Area X, swerved up by the Director the day before the mission, Central like an elephant that ate its own giant turds as they came out.

Lowry had cooled it on, fuck, the fucking drugs so maybe he wouldn't spew mid-spew. The standard words, in the standard ranks and rows of high-salutin' sentences. How there was the possibility the expedition would be met by soldiers still alive in there, from the army base, navy seamen from the destroyer cut in half by the Border, who might've swum to shore, to lead a fucking resistance against . . . what? No one knew, still. At least, no one would tell *them*. But morale was high, and some of them just high.

Jackie there for a time, Jack's daughter, looking imperious and crew-ella-effing-deville. Rumor had it, around the locker rooms and in the playpens they called the exercise rooms, that Jackie had just gotten out of Area X—not by the skin of her teeth but the skin of her ass. Felt the breeze of that Border on her butt hairs. Doing one last thing for dear old dad, fuck, some skuldug-gery alluded to like smarmy subtext in the files.

The way it got told, fuck, which wasn't the way it happened, no doubt, fuck, it was like stalling out on the train tracks. The Border came down and chopped her car in half like a butcher with a cleaver. And her there in the front seat, fuck, the metal sheared as fine as if with a precision laser so it was like one of those slices of the human body at those fucked-up museums that gave Lowry the chills.

As fellow misher Karen Hargraves would have it, like some sadomasochistic storyteller, the cut had been so close it had sliced away the layer of her pants waistband jutting in a soft *v* past her underwear, left her untouched. Stupid fucking story, fuck, the anatomy of it made no sense, but that breathless moment of be-lief, that idea of brushing up close to something so absolute and alien, and in that moment . . . what? Did you shit yourself? Piss yourself? Cum all over the place until you had no internal organs left? Or just sit there like a dumb statue, traumatized forever?

Maybe it had happened to someone even if not to Jackie. Maybe that's how it sounded so real and un-fucking-real at the same time. Like an encounter with God, if God wasn't just a fucking terra-cotta joke shoved on a stick and sold to unsuspect-ing shitheads.

All twenty-four of them, fuck, had been made to gather in the Southern Reach cafeteria, which still had a plastic-rubber chemical new-place smell, so Landry at Lowry's bidding called it the "catheteria," which still felt like fucking largesse.

The rest of this fucking ridiculous section had been the part wrenched and recruited out of retirement as a factory making children's dolls. Way out in the middle of nowhere, it had died along with the tourist attraction Doll Land, fuck, just a bunch of smashed foundations among weeds on a back road that led to the town of Hedley. The Southern Reach so loathed these origins, none of the documentation mentioned it.

Fuckfuckfuckfuckfuckfuck.

Now Doll Land bespoke multitudes of high-end thrill seekers, people in the know who had clamored to join. No sense of the "existential threat," as Whitby—world champ exped alt, a twee too-cheery enviro scientist—put it. "What existential threat?" Lowry had asked. "Oh, you know." "No, I do not know," Lowry had fuck fuck fuck snarled. "Well, the unknown. The fallacy of thinking we know what's going on in there, just because of a chicken." A chicken. Fuck Whitby. Fuck Whitby's chicken. Just . . . fuck all that.

But Lowry thought about the chicken, without a contamination suit on, navigating that dank corridor from the Border to AAX, fuck, and some small part of him wept over that fucking chicken's terror. While the Director droned on about all the insignificant things, which was anything that happened now, before getting on with it . . . and Lowry thought also about how the arrows of the sprightly, colorful cafeteria carpet pointed out toward the just landscaped exterior, which included a scooped-out artificial holding pond and some gaudy stupid benches painted in shit stripes of primary colors, which no one fucking used because of the heat and no tree cover.

How they'd covered up the doll factory real good. You could barely tell, although Lowry had this fucktastic disaster scenario in his head where after the Director's droning, fuck, he'd tug on a string and a thousand doll heads would come tumbling the fuck down from some hidden panels in the ceiling, fuck, rather than the customary party balloons.

The old chain gang getting the lecture, plus (poor double-fucked exped alt, X-alts, fuck, the exped membs calls them) Whitby Allen, at his usual seat at the back of the room, facing out. Like he expected bounty hunters to burst in, fuck, chain him to a wall, sizzle-brand his ass, and dry hump him all the way to jail—and was fucking ecstatic about it. No one had dropped the basket or kicked out, or whatever the hell the expressions were that tumbled through Lowry's head along with all the other stuff, fuck, so Whitby would remain a Behind, which was another way the exped membs ref'd the X-alts.

"I'll be there in spirit," Whitby ventured, fuck, probable belief that all twenty-four wolves staring at him from time to time thought dippy-shitty sheep thoughts. "I hope not," Lowry stage-whispered back, "'cause you're needed here." "Look for the tag TOT," Whitby said mysteriously, fuck, with a thin smile. "Remember that. And then you must run, because you won't know what it is." "Like, jog?" Whitby shook his head, whispered "trash or treasure, trash or treasure," like a sinister parrot, but then said no more, in part because the fucking Director had begun to look at them as if they were misbehaving schoolboys at some fucked-up boarding school where everyone took turns whipping the shit out of each other's bums of a fortnight, to leg-trembling excess.

Extra drone: "The natural state of men living side by side is war. The natural process of peace is to side with war. This expedition goes in peace, but with the capacity to wage war." Did it? All twenty-four of them?

The deep-sea fish stared out of their jars at Lowry and it seemed to him they were fucking judging him. Even dead in their jars, dredged up from the bottom of the goddamn ocean, trawled to be truths about AAX and they'd failed that—so fuck these fucking fish for judging him. He was about to be a hero, along with twenty-three other heroes, well, fuck, maybe more like nineteen other heroes because some didn't seem like they had the gumption for it, would wind up in jars themselves, floating for-fucking-ever until Central carted them away to be jar things in some invisible warehousing space that no one would ever see and the dust would collect on the jars and even though some would be human-size, fuck, you wouldn't know until you fucking wiped the dust away whether it was some goddamn sunfish with an accusing eye or Private Shithead Crapseed, giant octopus squish-jellied or Colonel Kickedbucket.

And which one had the worse fate, the scientific experiment or the guy or gal who didn't turn this huge opportunity into a win? Lowry knew the fucking answer to that. Oh my fucking god, this fucking fuck briefing would never be over, not in his lifetime. The expedition would start five years from now, fuck, and they'd all be dead from standing in this spot, pissing themselves, dehydrated, all that training down the drain, where the fuck was Landry with more drugs he was running out of fuck fuck fucks, which now felt very wrong, so he knew he hadn't maintained a level but was coming down, and that couldn't happen until he was out of the suit skin suit skin suit skin shit now he had to stop saying suit skin and get more drugs for the fucks to replace suit skin suit skin suit skin. And, finally, the briefing was over and all the brain powers sucked out of all of them jumped right back in and amid the muttering and little chuckles they decamped to the catheterrarium to see what new lunacy Whitby Allen might have in store for them, theory-wise.

What might greet them inside Area X? Nothing had come out. Not a thing. But the great final briefing? That came out, fuck, kept coming out, and might never stop.

## SCROLL CALL

**M**orale-boosting booster of a briefing received, roll call came next, which meant the stink eye for Lowry from some, because the Southern Reach had let him keep his mane of golden hair. Because he'd snarled deadly enough, or barked enough, or expelled his organs like a sea cucumber when they'd tried to insist. But they knew why they'd brought him on. Charismatic and direct, a little nutty, the craggy good looks, the athlete's build, the fittest member by far. Resolute jaw. A comedian as a bonus, could tell a great joke. Unpredictable moves. Bright blue eyes, "piercing" some women called them. Yeah, baby. Keep the mane. Be a downer during roll call all you all, all you fucking want, all you shaved scalps and close-call twhut cuts.

Still, who the fuck didn't feel quasi-invincible on this mission? They all did, even the psycho psychics. They had trained like banshees, like windmills, like robots, like pixie fairies made of some unbreakable metal. Pumped up on adrenaline and, some, drugs. All the best equipment, why not use it, Lowry was itching to use it all.

Director Captain Chef the kind of paunchy, white-dress-shirt-wearing, tan-blazer-wearing, navy-trousers-wearing motherfucker Lowry preferred to think of as overseeing a physics lab or a high school as principal, but not well, did the old hem-and-haw at start of roll call, like they weren't highly trained, highly motivated mofo pros. Jumping up and down on blocks while screaming insults at their parents. Enduring temp extremes while "girding" their minds against "contamination." Shouting "yes please may I have another" while lashing each other with whips while they wore heavy clothing and helmets with masks. Practicing hiking the fucking football in a wind tunnel. The usual.

If Lowry fidgeted, fuck, in that interregnum before the

names, it was twofold: Some tiny abnormal piece of him, deep inside, worried that this time the Director would leave his name off the list.

But, also, there were too fucking many of them, which got on Lowry's nerves, because there were also, as he'd explain later to anyone who would listen, too few of them. But, for the roll call, just trying to remember the names, let alone the personality behind a name . . . just awful. A chore, a horrible task. That was Tommy Ugh, that was Gretchen SuperGroper, that was Prick the Super Psychic. Redundancy, yes, but twenty-four felt like Central expected attrition not insurgency followed by conquest, or even just a plain old walk in the park.

Dan Henkel looked like a walking talking unlit matchstick with legs. Christopher Formsby was too tall. John Fu told stupid bad jokes. Frank Delmas folded his arms as a preamble to pedantic lectures about nothing any twhut would want to hear. Marie Bukvic believed too strongly in the supernatural, so he always saw a black cloud over her head. Joanna Easterling was all right, but in small doses, due to her fucking way of repeating what you said as a question to give her time to think. And so it went and so it goes. Lowry bonded with himself first and foremost, and he believed that was right and true.

Jamal Winters grated and got on his last nerve for the simple fucking reason that Winters was second-in-command and Lowry believed he should be second-in-command. Animal, visceral reaction, and Lowry believed in allowing those, encouraging those, as the true fucking reaction. None of this bullshit of pretending. That led to repression, heart attacks, soft cocks. Fuck that shit. Also, Jamal had a wonderful personality and good leadership skills, and that pissed Lowry off because in AAX none of that might matter. They might get there and figure out "good leadership skills" got them all killed. Been there, done that. Checkered history, but also he'd played chess and played fucking well for a long time. He was ready to jump in when Jamal failed.

Lowry only took an interest in a few of them because the rest might be cannon fodder despite their bona fides. But he'd been wrong before, fuck, so tried not to alienate any of them but Winters. Although he knew most of them hated him on principle. Yet, would any of them fucking die for him on the mission, the way he would for them? Like, he would fucking dive in front of a burning bus full of killer whales with a monster on the roof directing traffic while shooting RPGs out of its ass—for them. *All* of them. Any of them. But he fucking *liked* very few of them, except Landry, Hargraves, and well . . . maybe just those two. Sky didn't count because she fucking counted too much.

At first, fuck, he'd liked Hargraves because she fucking accorded him respect, understood who she was talking to and how poised on the cusp he was—and not just because, like fucking usual, she wanted a special gold-plated invite into his pants. Cusp of greatness. Cusp of valorous deeds. Cusp of solving AAX (he had theories he had never fucking shared, because only AAX deserved to hear them, like he was facing the Sphinx and figuring out its riddles).

But, then, Lowry'd fucking figured out she was taking the piss out of him, as his Britcrumpet friends on prior mish's had put it. Trying to piss-take him, a bit. With a smile that never changed a degree, so it was hard to tell. Plus, Hargraves, along with three others, were top brass, haunted brass, protected species, fuck, the rumor papermill belching out the smoke signal that they came from long histories of military service at the highest levels.

So, over time, he'd figured out Hargraves was the Great Pumpkin, if someone else jumped out of a fetal position from a huge pumpkin in a ghoul costume. Hargraves was like if a bunch of intelligent knives with an education had first become a huge colander of talent and then morphed into a human being right before you used the huge colander to get the world record for boiling broccoli or some such fucking record.

Who the fuck knew *what* she was thinking. He just knew she

was thinking, all the time, and it made him fucking nervous. Something always got in the way of liking her—and it was Hargraves who got in the fucking way. She was always tripping up the like so he wanted to keep distant and not treat her like a drinking buddy. Except she was like a drinking buddy to every fucking buddy else.

So why couldn't he commit to even just that fucking kind of buddy relationship, let the water slide off his back, not some other duck's back? Maybe because Hargraves reeked of competence and commitment. Besides him, she finished first in almost every fucking thing. Open a goddamn can of tomato paste, she'd make her own fucking can opener and have it open before you'd have half a chance to gnaw a hole in the metal with your own fucking teeth. Ordered to bash gophers with a mallet at the county fair and she'd bring her own multiheaded mallet and bash all the gophers in three goes and take the fucking huge teddy bear the goddamn disgrace of a fair-fake thought no one would ever attain and she'd stuff it full of sticks of dynamite and carry it on her back like twenty fucking miles with no complaint, jogging the whole way if Sky told her to—and probably Lowry if Lowry told her to. Then explode it all over whatever colonial colonic fort she'd been told to blow up. And that was just irritating as holy fucking fuck fuck, wasn't it?

Landry disagreed like a fucking asshole, about Hargraves and about Winters. He also didn't think Formsby was tall or too formal, but then Landry was tall as fuck, a flagpole in a storm, a lighthouse to guide you home. Just put a blazing light in both his eyes and turn him on. Of course, he'd lead you astray because he'd be giggly high the whole fucking time anyway.


Roll call, which was such basic fuckstoic stuff. Like, if some of them didn't answer, weren't there, where the hell could they be? Also, not a damn thing in roll call about sleeping arrangements.

Everybody was celibate and stored their fucking genitals on a shelf in their lockers next to their fucking deodorant, according to the Director.

Even if, perk of alpha order? Scaramutti diddled Singer as if it were a sacred duty and the church would go bankrupt if he stopped, while Winters reached back across the rows of names to subject Bukvic to his no doubt unimaginative thrustings. Did artist colonies operate this way? He'd heard tell but never been close enough, except once tiptoeing through one after midnight, on the way to a firefight in a forest. But the mish felt like a too-close commune already, minus the skunk pot smell, exped somewhat secondary. And what of it? They had the best of everything, why not fuck out any fear. Fuck. Out. That. Fear. Let it go. He should be a goddamn motivational speaker, and maybe, with the right publicist, he would be, after this mish. This mishmash.

Then they were all still kind of there, milling, malingering, and Lowry watched Whitby's grin hit a glitch before it flared forth once fucking more. Poor Whitby. Always the fuckee and never the fucker, succor not suckee. Hypnotists and jugglers, acrobats and psychics, fire-eaters and crypto-ecologists had gotten their claws into the exped, and Whitby's rather déclassé, anti-bohemian creds . . . did not cut it.

So. The first expedition, it numbered twenty-four.

18 Skyla Overbeck (expedition leader, naval intelligence)
13 Kalliope Benner (biologist)
14 Sherri Binder (archaeologist, psychic)
15 Samuel Bronen (surveyor)
04 Marie Bukvic (psychic)
05 Frank Delmas (military)
22 Joanna Easterling (hypnotist, military)
06 Jon Erlickson (physicist, some anthro)
10 Dambeku Ferreira (military)
21 Christopher Formsby (psychologist)

11 John Fu (physicist, no anthro)
07 Norayan Fussell (psychologist)
12 Karen Hargraves (military)
19 Dan Henkel (medic, military)
20 Angela Hernandez (biologist)
03 Rebecca Hinojosa (biologist)
09 Peng Jiamu (biologist)
01 Scott Landry (medic)
24 James Effing Lowry (hero)
23 Danika Miles (military, anthro)
02 Marianne Rodgers (biologist)
08 Sophia Scaramutti (psychic)
16 Tamesha Singer (material sciences)
17 Jamal Winters (medic, military)

ALTERNATES
Whitby Allen (cosmic star child)
David Read (cosmic dipshit)
Jenny Spirling (not dipshit, not cosmic, not going)

The numbers Lowry drew on the sheet with a blue ballpoint pen each roll call had a secret but simple significance. No god-damn soul but Lowry, no twhut or bastard would ever be privy, although maybe once he'd fucking told Landry because they'd both been so fucking high.

Some positions had changed due to new intel, but most had held steady and with the slight singe of burning metal as of a fucking Gatling gun exhausted from continuous fire. First through last to die, drop the bucket, smash the flask, end up ashes. No point rating the fucking riffraff of the alternates, as he had no idea which of them was more likely to succumb to a slip-and-fall on the Southern Reach's over-waxed concrete floors.

The numbers had analysis behind them, with no bows to fucking bastard esoterica like friendship. Which was why the number-one candidate to drop dead sooner than later had always been and always fucking would be . . . Scott Landry. Nothing personal, Scott. Nothing personal in this chart I keep making where you fucking kick the fuckets right off the fucking bat.

Landry was cool, though. Lowry thought Landry was way fucking cool, but also that Landry would be the first to go. Nothing wrong with that. One thing was a friendship based on Landry giving Lowry the fucking drugs that made him think or say fuck too much, but also kept him on this plateau somewhere high up close to Mount Olympus. Landry and Lowry, buds, sitting in a tree D-O-I-N-G D-R-U-G-S. Landry and Lowry meeting out back after Lowry had visited Sky so they could do more drugs. Landry made things pop and frizzle. He always had the right amphetamine mix and he fucking gave it up a lot. Everybody knew. Nobody cared. Came with the territory as a perpy exped memb who owed allegiance to both the army and Central, got to raid both their fucking pantries. But they were all supermen and superwomen. In the prime of their fucking fitness. Who gave a fuck what they did, so long as they showed up and kicked ass?

"Storm the torpedoes! Damn the Speedos! All hail!" had been his and Landry's battle cry for a while, forced through obstacle courses and the like. One of those things you couldn't explain to anyone else, but made Landry and Lowry laugh so hard their sides hurt.

But kicking ass was hard work, fuck, even ahead of time, in abstract, and the drugs kept him even-keeled rather than keel-hauled. He took one almost any time he thought about putting on the suit. He was taking one right now, and then another, over at the watercooler, sneaky as roll call progressed with all the speed of a blocked colon. He fucking fuck fuck had taken two two earlier while in his apartment in the complex on the army base outside of Bleakersville, behind the barbed wire and giant tiddlywinks, propped up by guards' automatic weapons or bazookas or land mines or something, and guard dogs. The usual kit.

So now he was fucking ready for the sausage-skin suits, ready to face his fucking fears in the fucking right way. With all his fucks in order and on the rise. The rise of the fucks, yeah.

"You have to bring all the drugs into Active Area X, Landry," Lowry had told him and nodded now at Landry across the table and cocked his finger at him and winked, to emphasize the point he was mind-pushing in Landry's direction.

*Alllllllllllll the druuuuuuuuuuuugs.* Yesssss baauss. Yeah, it's gonna happen. *They're going to sausage wrap us those chancy motherfuckers. Need to smuggle the drugs.*

Oh man, that had given him a great idea he wanted to shout at the others, but now had no time to execute. Even just getting the design done would take too long, an epically sad thought.

Because "Fuck Out the Fear" should really be on a T-shirt.


## NO REASON TITTY


L ast fucking lunch in the cafetorium after the last words from the Director, all these fucking *lasts* lashing at them, at him, while someone had put on a morale-inducing film as a fucking backdrop. A Great Nation thanks you for your service, fucks its thanks right into the fuckservice of propping up a rickety fuckscreen while not a fucking soul watched this ripe ol' tripe.

Lowry felt his left foot tap-tap-tapping no matter how he tried to stop it. The usual Last Words, bleached of meaning, prattling over images of military helicopters blat-blatting over some jungle. About honor, duty, honor, duty again. Had they not already had this at the briefing? Risk-reward ratios mentioned prominently and other weird sayings. Shit-tastic.

Round table, none of them fucking Lancelot or Lancelottia, Lowry staring at his pallid lunch as if it should be lobster and a

bottle of champagne, because it should. Even if they were promised immortality in the afterlife that was Active Area X. Fuck
that.

Stale bun of disappointment. Fillet of flat fucking flounder
that looked like it came decanted from the jar room, with some
dirt and tombstone on the side. Mixed vegetables someone had
thrown from a great height, stepped on, smashed, and then used
a buzz saw to render into a fucking mash before boiling them in
a pot with too much water. A pint of milk like they were wee
bonny bairns in some school lunch program not fucking earthbound astronauts about to put a beatdown with nunchucks and
automatic weapons on a fucked-up "foreign entity."

"Why'd you agree to sign up?" Winters, to the room in general. Sky had checked out of the conversation, and Lowry ad-
mired that commitment to not letting her fucking nerves go for
a scrum. She'd be wound as tight as a Swiss watch anyway. She'd
be sweating orders through her pores as practice.

Loud agreement to a word Lowry didn't like. Twhut twhut
twhut.

"Cock." Also loud agreement.

Whitby blushed in his corner, squirmed, very high-schoolish.
But Lowry squirmed too. Blinch, twhut were approved terms.
Cock was fine except when it wasn't. Twhut we owe the honor,
Your Honor. Twhut is on the agenda today, Winters?

"Love."

"Death."

Now. That was real.

"Is this just a banal Rorschach test? Using words?"

"For the witty re-partying."

"Tour of France, tour of underpants, that old beret's dirty
rants."

"Still time for some Bleakersville glory-hole action, assholes.
I'll be there with my cock gently shoved through a hole almost
too small for it until seven. Stall three, my lovelies."

Except Lowry's quip made them all go quiet for a time. Fuck f f. Time counting down and counting out more twhutty repartee.

"We're like the colonists in days of yore," someone said, and even Lowry winced. Fucking shitheads on wooden ships finding the wrong fucking place and spearing wild pigs on their arrival and eating them off spears el dente like fucking snacks. And, also, they had no honor, not really.

"Who said that? Who fucking said that?" Winters, again asserting himself, like he'd been made second-in-command or something. And he was, with Lowry third. He thought third, couldn't remember if his request had been affirmed or if they'd made it more complicated than that.

"Spreading death and disease? I think not." This from Erlickson, somewhat fucktatingly tedious to Lowry in his anthro role. The basic 101 lectures should be subtext, fucking subtext. Explain not the furies of the past at a catheteria table.

"Finding honor and glory in courage," Easterling said, down two spots and wrong. Sometimes you had to run like a little brat from danger.

"Foraging for scraps from an unknown entity."

"Titty," Lowry offered, to break the mood.

"More likely we will injure it than it us." Erlickson, who was moving from six to four on Lowry's fucking list, rapidly.

"Find the off switch, we just need to find the off switch."

"Who the fuck just said titty for no fucking reason?" Lowry asked.

❧

All the most important haunted fuckers, from the Director on down, fucking vomited from their mouths all the time about the fucking "off switch." As if the mish exped would saunter into Area X and find a huge red fucking button like a giant toadstool, sans caterpillar, and all jump up and down on it until the fucking thing depressed and Area X would just go away and they'd come back to endless thankful reach-arounds and ticker-tape parades.

Lowry preferred to fucking assume Area X had eaten the off switch and that meant if it still existed they'd have to dive down Area X's throat to find it, experience a thousand fucking stings of hell to get at it, battle their way down to the bottom of the sea, climb a sudden mountain. But still the Director was "off switch this," "off switch that" like a fucking broken record that someone had smashed over Lowry's head.

What if Area X wasn't even truly "on" yet and thus no off switch, but somewhere there was an on switch. What if they fucking turned Area X on instead? Hideous thought, hideous truth that gave Lowry vertigo.

There in the catheteria, Whitby's grin had glazed over and Lowry didn't know what to read into that. He couldn't fucking tell. Was their banter boring? Was their banter passé? Was their banter an off switch for Whitby? What did he know that made him so fucking glazed?

Exasper-fucking-rated with himself. Because: Why Whitby? Why fucking Whitby? Whitby who was like an old duck, or whatever the fucking phrase was. Freak, piece of work, crackpot, coot, fruitcake, black sleep, no, black sheep. Not his type. But still Lowry sought his guidance. Were his instincts better than his conscious brain? Maybe. Still, oddly—fuck it, incomprehensible—that Whitby'd been the siren Lowry had listened to most over the past months, lost in the mist.

"How'd you get this gig?" he'd asked Whitby once and Whitby had said, "Teachers. Love of nature. Someone yelling at me from a school fence."

Okaaaayyy.

Whitby Twitchby Snitchby.

Fuck.

Almost time.

# THE OFF SWITCH

The Director shortened "Active Area X" to "Area X" at exactly 17:00, their on-base curfew. Like a fucking coward, although he couldn't finger why it felt fucking cowardly, only that the Director felt fucking cowardly, so must be fucking cowardly and maybe "coward" could become his fucking drug word not fuck but fuck there it was again, fucking creeping in.

By then, Lowry had snuck into Sky's quarters, because she had her own private suite, even if it still just boasted a damn bunk bed.

"Sawed off that shotgun like everything else," Lowry said.

"Exactly," Sky said. "Like everything else." She had expressed more than once concern for what she called "the paucity of our supplies." Lowry thought living off the land sounded fucking fun so had always kept quiet when she brought it up.

Except for all the regs imposed on fucking foraging, lousy with regs like fucking head lice. More like mind lice, like the sea lice in their jars, chewing away on the gray matter until all that was fucking left were roll call cells, briefing cells, and, yes, regs cells.

"Except the number of expedition members," Lowry said, another perpetual fucking sore point, hand on her left breast. Where he preferred it, his hand fucking loyal in that way—and she, too, preferred it. He thought. Except she also didn't fucking care for anything too complicated in that arena, nothing that might seem more like he was trying to tune in a fucking radio station.

"Two less psychics than I'd prefer," Sky said. That would leave two and a half. Which was two and a half too many for Lowry, except one of them had weapons training or knew how to play fucking bass guitar at least.

"The psychics go first," Lowry said, left it cryptic whether he meant get culled, be pushed on ahead as bait, or what. He ran his finger in the approved counterclockwise motion, not pausing because that tickled her. This could fucking go on for a while, but that was a-okay. And he just agreed with her sometimes for the fuck of it because personally he did believe there were too many other fucking fail-safes. Yes, burn the psychics as witches, but also torch the fail-safe anthropo. To the funeral bier with you, metaphorically speaking. Ex-fuckling-filtration had been his specialty, the anthropo shit secondary, if useful, especially if you tossed in some psychology and stirred the pot with some sniper experience.

Fuckable fucking fucked fuck future terminology for college degrees that fucking fell fuck apart in the fuck field like fucking paper bags filled with fuck water. Landry's cocktail mix this time blew Lowry's mind, pills ground up into one bolus for his throat to receive . . . the fucks were incredible, the number of f-bombs going off in his head, trembling off the charts on the tip of his lips.

What thrilled his fucking blood, what Sky didn't know as he continued as if she were a safe and the fucking combo would unlock a blow job but also a bomb would go off if he didn't find the right numbers soon, was that the civilian degree had just enough community-college vitality for show-and-tell and that was about fucking it.

Central, or Central's emissary rather, had popped up to fucking embed him, as Lowry saw it, as Central's right hand on the mission, to be the lion at the heart of it, the king beast, the secret leader if it all went to shit, despite cocky predictions and cokey ones from Landry.

The thrill of how Jack Severance, Central's bright and shining spymaster—from way back a legend, legion, and lesion in the field (boil of vengeance wreaked upon the enemy)—talked him up in private to people he met but didn't know but must be fucking fucking fucking important if Jack intro'd them. Wanted him as an extra set of hypervigilant eyes "from my perspective," in addition to his actual secret fucking mission.

Although, if Lowry was fucking honest, Jack was a lot to take in, especially the first couple of times. Jack had the fucking effect or affect of a human can opener fused to a walking talking oldie. His beard—fake for the occasion?—peppered with salt already, the red burnished glow to his face either perpetual fuck sunburn, fuck, or some skin ailment that could not be simple-slapped off his features, but it lent fucking urgency or at least a scorched authenticity to all Jack fucking said or did. He wore surf-brand button-down flowered shirts with a silver cross on a chain around his neck, with dress slacks and shiny dress shoes it looked like his granddad's granddad had bequeathed to mother-fucking him.

Lowry would meet at Bleakersville's bleak as fuck Snucker's Balls Pool Hall, him forsaking the true fucking name as fuck-false for sure. And there, in a back room that smelled of chalk, pesticide, and jizz, Lowry gave him reports on progress, including what he thought about the Director and Whitby.

Why Whitby, he didn't know, but Jack had his eye on Whitby like a fly on a juicy piece of dog shit. He had an eye on Whitby, Lowry wanted to tell Sky, like the Dark Lord with a hard-on looking through a peephole while jerking off to some local fuck folk singer's version of "Hey Nonny Nonny." Could get your eye poked out that way, but breach or not, Lowry'd "breathed not a word" (Jack's pumped-up spy talk) to Sky or anyone else.

She could lead and he would follow and back her play, making happy humping loyal gestures and roasting the dumbfuck part of his personality—currently fuck fuck fuck wrestling with the sentimental part of him as he fought off a burst of tears at the thought that he might never cup Sky's breast again if things went wrong. A whopper of a bad thought, right up there with playing fucking tiddlywinks and weeping at a shit-tastic sappy movie. Or was this some other emotion welling up that he dare not put a fucking name to? No way.

Sky thought corners had been cut prepping the exped for the mish. Lowry thought that might be the point—haste. You had a fucking foreign entity that had taken over part of the coast of a country "and it's a goddamn miracle," Jack muttered once, over his stale pale ale, baptized in the salt of the Forgotten Coast's marsh flats, "that we covered it up and sold a bullshit story. Put an expedition in there too? This country's damn heroic, puts her mind to it, not that any slob out there will ever know."

She'd never know Lowry had fucking pushed Jack on that, asking Jack to "slip us the super weapons, you know, the stuff that's experimental but it's particle waves or shit like that. Can blow the fuck out of shit. I'm good at that, Jack. Blowing holes in things. Fuck this anthropology shit. Anyone can do that." And Jack had been all like, "Yeah, yeah, barrel boy, you got the best stuff we have, even your video cameras—we R&D'd those out of evidence recovery on other ops, including captured cams of foreign entities."

Well, Lowry liked the sound of most of that, but not "barrel boy" and not the way Jack said "foreign entities," which didn't ring up right at the fucking register. He said it like a strand of hair snatched from fuck knew where had been perpetually caught between two of his teeth and he was using it to floss while he said "foreign en-tities." And later Lowry figured it out: Jack-in-the-Box hadn't meant to say it. He fucking hadn't meant to say "foreign en-tities" or tell him about the damn cameras at all. So what the fuck did that mean?

But Jack-in-the-Box must've thought it didn't matter, because the next day, from the Southern Reach chaplain herself, Lowry got the full instructions for the "seek-mish" as he liked to call it in his head—most of which involved some ancient fucking dude named "Old Jim" who Jack O'Lantern thought might still be alive in Area X. A guy Jack said had been "compromised by a foreign entity and affected by pre–Area X infiltration." Along with a phrase that caught Lowry's eye about a "secret room in Dead Town."

Delivered unto him via a cavity scooped out of a fucking Bible like it was a book melon, which Lowry found priceless. This new intel that Jack didn't give a fuck about Bibles or, thus, religion, and thus was also a bit more like Lowry despite the cross at Jack's neck. Hell, he would've taken that paper, devoured it, and shit it out patriotically, except it said "Burn When Done" right at the fucking top. So ashes to ashes it—

"Stop dialing long-distance phone numbers and put yourself to better use," Sky said, slipping from his grasp and pushing him into a lower position. "Twenty minutes and then you should go." Next round of checks on quarters by fucking security, she meant. No nookie or cookie until crossing Bordersville into the unknown.

"Aye, aye, captain," Lowry said, and shifted his fucking priorities to where the fucking expedition leader fucking wanted them, right there in that fucking place he love-hated and it was going to be all right, this mission, this fucking mission was going to be fine and they would all come out of it alive, they surely would. Even if he didn't believe in the off switch as he tried to find the on switch.

He noticed out of the corner of his eye that the lilies had not survived the trip to her suite, just the vase, which sat next to the little ring on the nightstand. Would she put the ring on for fuck's sake? Or had she and it didn't quite fit? He didn't mean this fucking second, but had almost blurted it aloud, which also almost meant he'd been talking sentences into her like some kind of erotic mesmerist.

Fuck fuck fuck. His jaw felt detached and numb and he was drowning and all the jars of dead things had gathered to watch what was not a fucking spectator sport. Breathe through the nose. Breathe. Goal had been five minutes to save his jaw from clenching in stress over crossing the Border because even with the fucking drugs, it was already clenched from the fucking stress of being about to cross the fucking Border.

Jack had slapped him on the back as he walked out, "That's my boy," kind of the same way Sky did now, to indicate the twenty minutes was up. He was pretty sure it had gone spiffy, but mostly he was happy to disengage and fall away down onto the floor for a bit, on his back, his arms outstretched and his cock tingling along with his mouth. Peach-stung fruit of more distant youth. Fields of wheat in summers where he'd sneak a fruity beer and sit in the shade of an oak along a dirt road, getting gently drunk.

Shit. He was going to have to cross the Border, in a stupid skin.

## REVERSE PUFFER FISH

So, then, in the end—the fucking end of the beginning of it all—they faced the suits in the special wing of the Southern Reach reserved for the equipment, with the disconcerting look of a fucking high-school football locker room. It shouldn't look this fucking way, Lowry's senses screamed at him. It shouldn't fucking ever look this way. It fucking shouldn't.

"Are we going to the moon?" Hargraves asked, but she had always asked something like that, during the run-throughs.

Tremor of an almost laugh, and then fucking death silence, except the exhalation of Dan Henkel, medic and heavy mouth breather both. Lowry sharing a glance with fucking Sky, who broke it off like it had been a too-long piece of fucking peanut brittle. Date night over. So Lowry had to resume negotiations with the fucking suit he hated so much.

Worse, some problem with the fuck fuck fucking forward post position, pre-Border, where they were supposed to "get dressed" as Sky put it. "For the formal dinner party in hell." Like, one day they'd be husband and wife attending an awards ceremony for Best Fucking Secret Exped.

It felt to Lowry—and apparently only him—like wearing the skin of another human being and then putting over that a fucking constricting fucking tight turtleneck sweater made of rubber . . . that covered his entire body. And then, over that, a fucking deep-sea diver's suit—of the kind popular in old silent films, where the air line to the surface or air fuck pipe or air fuck tube air something gets tangled or cut and years later at the bottom of the fucking sea "they" find your jellified, algaed, nutrient-rich corpse, still constrained, still being destroyed by the goddamn suit. The gleam of bone peering out through all the human excesses of liquids and goop and just plain old shit-your-pants human grossness.

God, he stank already, something he fucking hated to do, to stink, just putting on the suit, sour from nervous sweat. Only so much cologne he could ladle on to cover it before somebody like sensitive Easterling the hyper hypnotist went all westerly on him and complained she was allergic. Well, fuck her and the toad she rode in on down shithead road. Her face could puff up to the size of a . . . a puff adder . . . a puffer fish . . . and her throat tighten to a hot wet rope, twisted taut for all he fucking cared. He wasn't going to smell himself the whole shitty trip. But, in fact, she said nothing, except "Good luck," and he felt totally fucking ashamed for about two seconds, which was two whole seconds he wasn't thinking about the fucking corridor into Area X.

Then they were all in fuck fuck fuck their suits, so ballooned up in that garish, tightish space that there came the vague scratching sound of the outer surface of the suits rubbing up against other suits and the more they squirmed, waiting, the more it sounded like a basement full of gimps. Bring the ball gags, the rubber helmets, the whips, and the giant dildos. They were in for a fucking hell of a ride. Area X, yeehaw.

But all they could do was shuffle-shuffle like sumo geishas until the guys with the special clearance came in with the wide dollies to scoop them up, two or three at a time, and wheel them through a cellophaned door to their pathetic doom on a fucking truck ramp, to be loaded up like human-size souvenirs commemorating some shitty catastrophe, "some human-size trophies," Fu the physicist said.

With their helmets on and locked in, "to avoid contamination before the Border," except "contamination" was there, here, everywhere. How Lowry wanted to just fucking divest, divest, divest, and scamper on all fours across the Border, howling at the moon or sun or whatever celestial body happened to be on fucking offer.

Shoved so tight together in the truck bed that Lowry couldn't have fucking moved if he'd wanted to, human sarcophagus being offered up as sacrifice to an uncaring god of no particular nature, since they had no fucking clue what kind of god animated Area X, or if a god had anything to do with it at all. Maybe a demon, a devil, a sphinx, a gryphon, a talking head on a spike.

Staring at each other from the humidity-tinged helmets—air valve open for now, but filtered fucking pure. Lowry hoped they wouldn't have to use their oxygen tanks on the other side, or stay in their suits. It felt so wrong, got under his skin, to be sitting so close, surrounded on all sides by such beautiful, fit people and unable to touch, to feel . . . much of fucking anything.

Let the dicks commence to reveal themselves through the hole, like "guess the cast member." Who would go first into the breach they called the door in the Border? Not I said the fly, not

I said Lowry. Put a psychic first—they should know what was about to happen to them. Old joke, would never be tired, though.

A rush of sadness, out of nowhere, just as suddenly obliterated by the lurch of the truck hitting a pothole, forward, to the Border.

Just like the chicken before them.

## NEKCIHC EHT

**C**hicken fucking noodle soup. Chicken fuck stuffed with another bird, like duck? Chicken broiled. Chicken fucking fried, with fries. Chicken shoved in a microwave, irradiated on high. Chicken boiled in a goddamn pot for hours and hours to make it less tough, just enough so you could sell that shit at a fancy French restaurant.

Fucking fuck fuck Whitby had told Lowry about the chicken. *Why* had he told Lowry about the chicken? *Why* had Lowry let him? But it was Lowry's damn fault, too, because he could've put that on someone else. He could've told Sky. He could've been K-I-S-S-I-N-G Landry, scratch that D-O-I-N-G D-R-U-G-S. Scratch that. DOING DRUGS. Sitting on a goddamn motherfucking branch and doing drugs . . . he could've told Landry the chicken story, gotten it out of his head. Because he didn't fucking even know why it was in his head.

This had been when Lowry thought of Whitby as "that strange little prick," or "that straight albino pretzel," or "that starving marshmallow showin' his ribs." So cheery "out of season," as the saying went.

That fucking fuck last had been chumming it with Landry, snorting something while shooting something fucking else. It had been white stuff and brown stuff and red stuff, maybe. So anyway, Whitby, new to the job and so damn fucking cheery no matter what, still convinced he'd make the expedition. Maybe stow away in the suit of someone more voluminous, fuck, get lost in a fold like a sail, only discovered taking off the fucking suits on the other side.

Back when Whitby clearly had hope and esprit des corps rather than the fucking corpse variety that metastasized later as black humor, sleeping too much, drinking too much, and talking about shit in evil ways. No one else saw Whitby as the fucking prince of fucking Denmark or whatever, but Lowry could tell the shift.

Of course, fucking Whitby had cornered Lowry in the hauntable dining digs to tell him the fucked-up chicken story. Although mainly because Lowry had been pissed off with his comrades for reasons he forgot and sat next to or near Whitby to have distance from the rest of the twhuts. Use the Head Twhut to keep the other twhuts off him. Lowry had taken someone's meat portion, gibbering on a thick pile of napkins, and pilfered an apple just to make a point. Also now fucking forgotten. The meat likely wasn't quivering or gibbering, but even back when Whitby told him the fucking chicken story he was pretty high. Pretty damn high. Aspic—his pilfered meat was glubby aspic with murdered fruits.

"Do you know the story of how they tested the corridor?" Whitby asked him. "How they field-tested it, I mean to say?"

"The corridor from the science department to the catheteria? Do tell."

"No, from the Border into Area X."

Lowry sighed—a huge, heaving, melodramatic sigh meant to exhale all the air in the room that he'd been saving up in his lungs. This guy. This fucking guy, at lunch. This Southern Gothic happy happy small-penis guy, fuck, who probably had to pay for a reach-around when freebies existed everywhere in the universe, for miles.

Whitby had, at best, made the prancing pony team armed with mallets back in college. Or not even that, but clotheshorses or hobbyhorses, and they'd been swatting each other's bums with mallets and the balls had all been just clicking and dancing around on shiny lawns, forgotten. Then, continuing this line of thought, Whitby had probably been kicked off the team for freezing up from the stress of accidently riding his hobbyhorse to death—a first—at the Extended Rallies, or Balls in One, or Horsey DeComp, or whatever they called the stupid fucking horse stuff at fancy prancy universities.

Lowry had been so invested in his vision of . . . what? Incompetence? Coming in last-ness? . . . that he totally fucking forgot it was his turn to talk.

"Robots, right? Funny, fancy prancing robots with weird hats and weathervanes for heads?"

Whitby shook his head with such enthusiastic negation Lowry feared the fucking thing might fall right off and spin across the floor.

Lowry looked at his aspic jiggle, juggling interior fruit slices via some dubious molecular equations, and debated leaving the table for the table with the popular kids he currently hated. All laughing about some dirty joke, he fucking hoped.

But . . . the chicken beckoned. The chicken coerced. The chicken chided.

"Okay, Corporal Fresh Fuck III, tell me about the chicken."

"I'm not—"

"Just tell me. Tell me now before my jiggle settles, man."

"So, I learned this information from the robotics department."

"The whole fucking department?"

"From a woman who—"

"Never mind. The chicken?"

"Yes, so," Whitby continued, undaunted, which Lowry grudgingly began to fucking admire, "they did send in a robot on a track, but it became stuck halfway through or ran out of energy, but, anyway, they brought it back and sent in the backup chicken instead. A chicken in a harness with a lightweight rope attached to the harness."

"So?"

"They put the chicken in the robot carriage and unspooled the rope—a very thin, very long rope, because they didn't yet know the length of the corridor—but at some point the robotic carriage encountered some obstacle, but the chicken went toward the light in front of it."

"The light?"

"The opening at the other end. And because they'd put a small, primitive camera on the chicken and the chicken went through the hole—they knew it was possible for a person to go through."

Lowry, hooked: "Wait—what do you mean? And how many times did they do this? Just once? And what happened to the chicken?"

He didn't know why, but he felt very invested in the stupid fucking chicken all of a sudden. He could imagine the chicken drawn by the light, hoping for something to peck. Was there a juicy worm in the fucking light? Surely light was better than the damn darkness. Fuck the darkness, head for the light, chicken. You can do it. You can make it. I know you can.

"More of a rooster," Whitby said. "A fighting rooster of some kind."

"The chicken was a motherfucking rooster."

"Yes, I believe so. I believe I misspoke about the chicken."

"Choke the fucking chicken, Whitby."

Whitby laughed, high-pitched, startling, never wanted a repeat performance of *that*. "So what happened to the chicken-rooster is they had to pull it back to get the camera from around its neck. And that's what they did."

Relief mixed with the existing aspic nausea. The chicken

had been all right. But then realized he was fucking making assumptions.

"But . . . the chicken? The rooster, I mean?"

"Oh, unrecognizable. That's the really great, interesting part—it didn't resemble a chicken at all any more, but at least the camera was intact. Anyway, that's what I heard."

That's when Lowry did leave the table. Left his aspic fruit behind for Whitby or whomever. Because of the sloshing stack of bullshit. The expedition might be compromised by fucking and the army might pull shit like sending a chicken over.

But no way the Jack-in-the-Box he had come to know would allow Lowry to risk his life based on that kind of fucked-up shit.

But no way had the chicken been the first expedition. Because all the people trapped in Area X—they had been the real first expedition.

What had the chicken-rooster looked like in the end?

Whitby never fucking said.


## KCUFFUCK


**Y**ou fucking sugar count. You fire dick twhut flying cocksucker. You cock cocksucker sucking cock with another cock you goddamn piece of shit. Fuckbuddy long-dick penis shitter. Drown in an outhouse you fuckland fucklord reach-around meat-beating county old hallucination. Get your claws off me fucking dark lord, dark fucking whisp get you gone and off of me. You fucking low-carb crisp of a fucking fuck. You mind's eye sphincter. You asshole-licking lying treasonous sons of blinches lying in the long grass with your fucking dicks in your hands. Fuckside fuckling fuck-a-mole fuckshot fucksicle fuck fuck. You witch you witch you witch. Goddamn nothing mother-humping bastard of a twhut-whipped fuckup. You pathetic blinch ghost fool-fellating your own dead body's cock with some other mouth. Shove it where the sun don't shine with all the rest of your fucking hoarder's booty. See how I care you filthy flapping dick dying in the sunshine, shit gatherer. You talking talking walking shitstorm of a shit stain. You wallowing swallowing fuck go get fucked skullfucked fucking fucked fucking fuck fuck ah make it stop get me out of here."

Lowry only realized his voice was saying these things from the look on the faces of those around him, the echo on the comms. The silence on the comms after all the shouting.

Who had he been talking to? Who had he thought was in the tunnel behind them? Who had scared him that much? No idea. Not a clue. But he shook it off, could pretend it had never happened, would never happen again. Besides, some of that had been decorum, Lowry trained not to say the bad words. So it was twhut and blinch forever. His sisters had beat the real words out of him.

Ah, hey, he was stone-cold sober now, staring out at a hazy horizon full of trees—how could there be so many trees—and couldn't say the f-word. Even thinking it made him nauseous. What the f-f-f-f had happened. Where were his swears?

He threw up in his helmet, staggered to the side, sitting down heavy on a rock, throat raw. Oh holy h---s oh holy f---s. Oh solid ground. Even with the filter, and through the vomit, Lowry could already smell Area X and the sun felt heavy on his face, even dulled by the helmet. Heady mix of humidity, a vegetal thickness, expressed all around in undergrowth and trees familiar from the Southern Reach. A jarring rhythm or distant sound or hum in the air. Like a dessert made to look like a hamburger, a sound that shouldn't have been a sound so he couldn't describe it, except as a creature, a subtle monster grating against his teeth, popping from his jaw.

By the time he'd recovered, the Border had pooped out almost everyone. Sky had ignored his outburst and barked out the roll call head count, moving among the writhing bodies of sausages not yet oriented, struggle-fighting to regain motor control, to stand. A writhing mound of giant tardigrades or he didn't know what, but it was natural/unnatural the way they couldn't come to their senses, kept falling and getting up and falling. As if they'd suffered some natural disaster, been half electrocuted in a freak storm, some enduring yet fading trauma.

Sky's movements in her suit became more frantic.

"Marianne? Rodgers? Marianne?"

But Dr. Marianne Rodgers, the junior wetlands biologist with the startling blue eyes and perky nose, never answered, never made it through, would never be found, had to have vanished "in transit" as Winters put it later. Couldn't take it. Couldn't take whatever Area X whispered in her ear, whatever it showed her that it hadn't shown the others.

"One sausage down, twenty-three to go," Lowry said, amazed at how old his voice sounded. Like a cracked statue in a public park. Like a man in a coffin a thousand years. Like whatever the vultures couldn't bear to eat.

He couldn't imagine being lost in the corridor. Although maybe she had made it back to the Border? "What a story that'd be for the grandkids: I got stuck in a magic culvert and did nothing except get lost and come back and yet here's a medal pinned to my chest for no reason. At all. Could be. Could be." Unaware he'd muttered most of that aloud over his comms.

But they all knew it couldn't be. She was gone.

F-f-f-f-f-f-f-f-f-f-f-f-f-f-f-f-f . . .

Cascading alarm about Rodgers, which turned most of them into suit-clad synchronized dancers, who drifted out of the crude circle, regaining motor function, but then drew close again, precarious, to form a ragged flower-petal design. Except the edges were as sharp as trauma, as sharp as something that could rip you apart. If anyone had seen it from above, and Lowry kind of hoped not because they had no air support.

Hoped yes, though, *Let's get this party started. Let's see what greets us here.*

Ten, fifteen minutes, in the chaos, that's how long it took. Sky barking orders no one at first thought to follow—all that training circling the drain, not able to escape for the clog and heavy fog in the brain pipes—before anyone realized Jon Erlickson lay in a fetal position on the ground. Known by the prominent duct tape across his chest with his name in all caps with Magic Marker. Like his parents had been afraid he'd get lost his first day of school, but because everyone knew he'd been terrified no one would know who he was in the suit and even though against regs, what was the harm?

Had it been a bull's-eye for Area X? Lowry would ask Sky later, just to make sure she was still talking to him. But also because doubt had pierced him.

Henkel and Winters tended to Erlickson awkwardly on bended knees in their suits—their quivering forever tombs, their embryonic inverted doughnut holes—while all the other earthbound astronauts gathered in a circle, no doubt blotting out the sun for Erlickson during his last moments. If he wasn't already dead. Lowry abstained, noted, destined for his memoir, that the butt patches on the suits exaggerated glutes so much there was a crinkly shelf or human flesh ledge around Erlickson, Henkel, and Winters on which he could have rested some of the medical equipment.

Although not communicated directly, more through psychic osmosis and group feeling, and some seeing . . . Erlickson's suit had fused with his body so hard that his helmet had form-fitted to his face like a scene in a gangster movie where they suffocated a snitch with a plastic bag. What had Erlickson done to Area X to deserve that? What had the rest of them, to have to see that shit.

Somehow, when they straightened Erlickson out, it became clear the whole suit had shrink-wrapped him, and the glass helmet, now a profile of his face, had begun to turn from tinted copper to a milky white . . . white pores like the maggots in tapioca pudding (or that was how Lowry perceived the evil that was pudding) and Lowry wanted to vomit again, peering in on all that as the tapioca moved slightly—a kind of rasp, and he realized they were witness to Erlickson's last breath, juddering through the goop of not-milk.

"Take off your suits!" he screamed into their helmet comms so hard some held the sides of their helmet heads with their hands. "Take off your suits. Contam! Contamination!"

As he scrabbled at his helmet latch. As he gibbered pointlessly, swears still snuffed out. But instinctually, he knew this was true. Knew he was right. Or so close to right as to be no difference. Their suits, as he had always known, would betray them. Their skin might betray them too, but at least it was part of them, more a civil war than a foreign invader.

F-f-f-f-f-f-f-f-f-f-f-f-f-f-f . . .

The straps and traps and clasps and lapses on their lumpy chastity suits, their elaborate costume for clowning chumps up for adventure—frantic, because he'd realized Erlickson had only been *two in line ahead of him* in this cosmically fucked-up grocery store checkout, check-in. And what happened had happened *in Area X*, not in the corridor.

Was he still shouting? Did it matter? No one else had the balls or ovaries or moral equivalents to say what needed to be said. Yet, slowly, then swiftly, the others followed his lead, even as Sky ordered them to wait, to wait, to wait and become squishy tapioca pudding in a fancy multi-million-dollar flesh bag.

"No more flesh bags, flesh bags no more," just saying whatever rant came to mind, but still avoiding the f-word for fear he might burst into flames now that the drugs didn't work and he couldn't quite remember if the f's had been effin with him before the drugs in quite such a profusion, as if f's were a million minks in one of those terrible farm places, with not enough room between each f and like forest fires some places the whole world would burn if he started saying the word the f word in such close proximity and profusion oh my god was he losing his mind when would this shitting suit come off come off, get the sausage off the sausage.

Ah, then, divested of his own death, gushing forward into the exhale and inhale of the unrecycled, and the feeling of the humid air, redoubled, beautiful rot, thick and thrusting and ready, the squawk-tweet-chirp of the birds, the sudden onrush of such a more intense blue to the sky, all of this better than sex, at least better than sex in that moment because who knew how he'd feel in another moment, but released into a kind of paradoxical paradise. It gave him a hard-on because, hell yes, he was alive, not like Erlickson. He breathed deep, even as he kept, melodramatically now, having fun, feeling like an actor taking off a period costume after the play, removing his exoskeleton, but keeping his bones and his skull. Although his skull was a bone, technically.

Soon enough, Lowry felt weightless, gorgeous, and lusciously naked, along with the rest, most reaching for their trail clothes in their packs. But not Lowry. He beat his chest with one fist like half of an old movie, then left off seeming celebration in consideration of the death of dear departed Erlickson, who, to be honest, he had hardly known. Happy enough to let his dick dawdle and dangle there in front of all of them. If he could've swung it like a vaudeville entertainer with a cane, he would've, then taken a bow. For hadn't he saved them all?

"No compelling reason for clothes," he could see putting in his report to Jack after they got back. "Especially clothes that betrayed us so hard and so badly." Terrible thought—what if Dr. Rodgers had transmogri-died and was also sploosh in the suit with Erlickson and they just couldn't see her amid all the viscosity, the slime, the squirm.

No, f f f f f f no. No.

What if, here, they could be free to burrow into each other's skin to protect themselves? Burrow in deep for freedom's sake. Maybe the people he hated most on the expedition would allow the loan from time to time. Even as he recognized this as more spiral, more panic, disguised as experimental ideation.

Another terrible thought: If suits could collapse into hard jelly, what use the hiking clothes? It would always be hot here, unless it wasn't, and that, too, the biologists, there being no meteorologists among them, would put a finger to the pulse of temperatures, take samples of pieces of sky, to see if this cracked, brittle shard they'd knocked loose with a hammer tasted better than that piece, trying to forecast the next week, while they all cowered in their skins and . . . and even Lowry realized he was beginning to spiral, not twenty minutes out of the cave mouth or symbolic vagina or whatever the psych-witches back home would no doubt assign it without the imagination to just think of it as a conduit between states of being.

While in front of them, the high pile of discarded suits grew and grew—some of them entire and some in pulled apart pieces. A grand, frenetic molting into their original forms to mark the start of this glorious asshole of an expedition. Should they burn it now or leave it? What if they had to mix and match to make it back at expedition's end, or were they going to do it naked, like the chicken? Mound. Mountain. Here lie the remains of some peeled astronauts we cooked, cracked, and ate.

Somewhere under there lay Erlickson.

Lowry, staring at that f f f f f site and sight, wanted someone to hug him and reassure that Erlickson and Rodgers had failed to follow some vital protocol, although what it could be other than don't die and have no damn bad luck, he could not imagine. They'd been no less fastidious or "with it" re: the program. But, still, that they had been their own worst enemy. That must be the fundamental truth. Better you than me. Better the rest of the yous than me.

While the rest of the you yous stared at him like he'd forgotten to bark out another order, all in various stages of dress or undress, with some like him, perhaps dazed by death and disappearance so early, unable to put on pants quickly or competently, and falling over on their sides and having to do it with butt firmly on the grass. Some butt to butt, a sensation he loathed like it made him unsure of whose butt was which, especially if your butt had fallen asleep. This made him giggly, an impulse he suppressed as he could not tell if that impulse came from his face or some aftershock influencing his face.

Soon only Sky, the one who had tried to stop them, still wore her suit. But something in looking around at everyone in their trail clothes and Lowry still naked exerted too much peer pressure. Even as expedition leader, and the practical matter of all the rest's divestment of trust in the personal architecture provided to them by the Southern Reach.

Zippers unzipped and then the arms she pulled out from the suit, then stepped out of the legs, and soon enough she was naked in front of them, these people she was supposed to lead. Standing there with her arms by her side, with a look both defiant and vulnerable.

F-f-f-f-f-f-f-f-f-f-f-f-f-f-f!

"Come on in, the water's fine," Lowry quipped, and he meant it gentle, maybe even affectionate. But it did not hit that way. Fell flatter than a topographical map of flatness. Even though in every way looking like a goddess, Sky had ascended and showed herself to be above the fray, above even Lowry's useful/useless panic. And he a Neanderthal or first man of some sort, there in that bird-shrieking, anxiety-inducing Eden-not.

"Get dressed, Lowry," Sky said, even as he couldn't stop staring at her, at all of her, as naked as the day she had been born. For a pang of a forlorn moment, Lowry wished he'd never volunteered, that she had never volunteered, that it wasn't probably now that most of them would die here, given twenty-two was less than twenty-four in only twenty minutes. At that rate, they'd all be dead well before next sunrise.

"We're free now, though," he said. "We're free."

"That's an order," Sky snapped.

"I'll get dressed," Lowry said, even though he didn't want to get dressed, because he felt naked without his f f f f's, without his drugs, and knew Landry was nearby but could not visually locate him for the nod that meant the drugs had come through unscathed.

The chill he felt was due to that, and also because some part of his mind knew that how he had behaved might not be considered normal or un-histrionic, and also that he might have been wrong about taking off their suits, because now they might be subject to every pathogen in the air, in the soil, in the water.

Together, Lowry and Sky dressed in their trail clothes, facing each other, to an audience of twenty, not twenty-two, and a pile of dead suits.

"I fucking hate you," Sky hissed in his ear as they headed toward base camp. "Get it the fuck together."

That was where his f's had gone, Lowry thought, sadly. Into her brain.

Would he ever get them back?

# 2=JACK-OFF LIGHTHOUSE

## SOME OF US WILL BE QUEENS

The prolonged, desiccated horizon like the roof of his mouth without the drugs. The glare of the blazing sun, as noisy as a car alarm, sizzling in his face. And them, swaddled by base camp like fucking babies. This false comfort that if they pissed their pants everything would be okay. That they would "establish" this fucking place that had been miraculously built before their "first" expedition arrived, and not a soul among them questioned that bullshit?

Whitby had said, "Don't be surprised if it's brighter," and Lowry at the time had said, "Brighter than what? Your mother's—" But Winters had given him the stink eye and he'd aborted that thought, replaced it with another. That Whitby kept saying things like some kind of demonic travel agent. That on the one hand sounded okay or good, but on the other hand, when you thought about it . . . this was bad. This was something you'd like more of Landry's drugs to process. Or sunglasses, except they already wore sunglasses everywhere, so maybe that's what Whitby meant. But, mostly, Lowry wanted to ask, "How do you *know*?"

He could've used some advice from Whitby, too, on exped morale, because he might never forget how some of the team had looked at him just because he'd unleashed more than the usual number of "fucks" and then gotten nude. All those fucks in human form leering and glaring and indifferent encircling him, who, back at the old SR, Lowry had mapped upon his living-room wall, where the abstract art went if you liked to be spoon-fed pretentious crap.

The expedition names, yes, the death predictions, but also who fucked whom or whom all. But to that he'd added other data until the crisscrossed lines in different colors of ballpoint pen he took a fucking step back to look at seemed like one of the psychics' cursed diagrams. If he was honest. In the corner, he'd scrawled, "evil advances with good," but could not fucking remember why.

So many connections. So much fucking life. And what did it all mean? In the end, all these welters of lines, these fucking names, these fucking faces. Reduced down to shapes fated to fucking go somewhere fucking unknown fucking scary fucking it they were invisible weren't they that's what it all meant. A flaming mandala of nightmares or daydreams. A map for the ages. They'd all be fucking coming back. They'd all be fucking each other for all time, because at base, no matter how they looked at Lowry now, they all loved each other, and the mish.

The base camp lay at the edge of pines and black swamp, looking out through a clear space toward the coast, with reeds and marshes in the foreground. When they had, exhausted from the shocks of the day, set up tents and then lifted their heads to the horizon, when they had that luxury, the coordinates of the lighthouse in the distance left most, including Lowry, without words. Best to ignore, although Landry had specific experimental drugs to "destroy visions." What if, though, what Lowry wanted was some other vision? No mere negation? If only he could make some of these decisions, just some. All he would have needed was for Jack's secret mission to not be so secret— that was where his sole authority lay.

Holy fuck, his fucks had come back, even without Landry's

miracles, but he held them close, doled them out sparingly, for fear he still had only a finite supply for now.

While Sky love-bombed them with the language of bases, the value of headquarters even if you strayed from them, supply chains, remembering training protocols, proper camp workflow, maybe even, fuck that, good karma. Juxtaposed with an inserted word from the gaggle of psychics about "prebiotic particles, ghost energy, and establishing mirror rooms." Strange bedfellow, like you'd wake up to a divining rod up your ass with that lot. Lowry fucking hated it. Yet still a sense of strutting and invincibility and how strong they all were, despite that downer.

Where was the fucking off switch when you needed it?

Sky asking if anyone needed "preventative drugs to suppress visions" struck him as a good fucking joke. Suppress visions? They needed every motherfucking vision they could lay their hands on, to counteract whatever Area X might throw at them. Visions to combat visions. Psychics to combat psychedelics. Early days. They might all wind up thinking they were the cast-off suits and never make it out, just liquifying in a pile for eternity, drool rolling down their fucking faces.

There came out of Sky's mouth also the ghost of the Director, noting that the old fuck had asked for "preventative diplomacy if possible," but reminding all twenty-one of them that "peacekeeping allows for self-defense."

"I plan to shoot to kill," Lowry said, and he fucking did. He'd been hired to do a job—several jobs, actually—and one of them was to shoot the fuck out of things when the things needed the fuck shot out of them.

Sky's reply, besides a burning stare meant to reduce his meat facade to a skull face, was to urge them to "Remember the four points of our star," which meant it was a starfish with the limb of shoot-anything-that-moves missing. But the four points were: "evaluate, do not engage, sample, withdraw."

Really? Withdraw to fucking where? What if Area X erupted

somehow in the middle of base camp? Retire in good order to their suits? Run screaming into the bleak corridor that from this side looked like a collapsing oval of fizzy water with a filigree of trembling mitochondria across it. The stained-glass window of some fucked-up nature church.

"In view of the unnatural state of the lighthouse," Sky said, "our rendezvous point in the case of unforeseen circumstances should be the village halfway between base camp and the lighthouse."

Oh, yes, the lighthouse they all kept ignoring while "establishing base camp." The fucking burning symbol on the horizon that should have half of them fuckled and fucked up if not for Landry's fantastic drugs.

Yet the lighthouse did not bother Lowry overmuch, even if like many he avoided a head-on collision with the optics of it in relationship to his eyes, as if it were an abscess or an obscene eclipse. He had expected the fucking lighthouse, or something, to be unusual, not just this banal underbrush and squeakings of marsh rats like a fucking convocation and the birds like normal, inhabiting the sky like bosses.

So maybe they should all compare their fucking versions of reality, using the metrics of the lighthouse, because to Lowry the lighthouse looked like a séance-searing gush-fountain of aquamarine cum spurting from some giant, protean dick.

Which he said to Danika Miles and Peng Jiamu, who happened to be standing beside him and then were held back by Winters, always the reasonable one, like they had meant him some kind of laughable fist violence. Even though Lowry had no problem being coldcocked by Peng and Danika, if he deserved it. Another black eye to write home about. *Dear Diary which I do not keep, got coldcocked again for pointing out a cosmic hard-on.*

"We all kill what we love and love what we kill," he said.

"We all kill what we despise and want to shut up," Peng said.

"That's not the quote."

"Just stop," Danika said.

"Well, what the . . . what the fuck? What the fuck," it was coming back to him, thank god. "What the fuck do you see that's so special you'd take drugs from a fucking psychic not to see it?"

No reply. They didn't want to tell him. They were scared, while Lowry wanted to scream at them that it was a goddamn walk in the park. A haunted, messed-up park, but what had they expected? To be greeted with garlands of flowers and hand jobs?

"Psychics? Not seeing a Gothic tower with your cathedral mother's great big head shoved on top?"

By then Sky had come over, and Winter had cordoned off the other two and led them away.

"Lowry. You're becoming unhinged or dissociative . . . strange."

"No no nope nada. Just me. The usual Lowry." But Lowry felt the lie in how the words came out of his mouth, like they were made of tapioca. Panic, but nothing was oozing out of him.

"I don't believe so, Lowry," Sky said, and he was touched to hear concern in her voice, although not touched to hear pity, preferred just to be touched.

"What do you see?" he asked, to distract himself.

"The lighthouse? I see a beautiful blue-green sea anemone. Most of the others see the same, and some see the lighthouse. A few are using meditation aids because what they see is much worse than an erection."

"Can you hear the sound it makes?" Lowry asked. "The sound like it's seething? The vibration of that? Like it's a real factory, churning out little baby Area Xs or something." The on-switch assembly line.

"No, I do not," Sky said flatly, followed by another "Get your shit together" as she left him there to contemplate whatever glowed green on the horizon that they could not fucking agree on.

"It's a flume, plume, a tragic backstory, a fairy godmoth, I mean mother, who changed into a pillar of neon. Who cares. We are here and we have a mission," he said to no one in particular, as they were all fucking ignoring him, despite how oracular he had been, would continue to be.

A fucking prophet lost in the wilderness, whom no one believed.


That morning, they had discovered that the mound of suits had gone missing. Disappeared. Plum dumbstruck all at the absence, almost easier to believe they'd imagined wearing suits in the first place. No one had an explanation for it. No breach of the perimeter. No eyewitnesses. It was as if they'd melted into the earth, and if that were so, Lowry felt vindicated, although he said nothing. Mum's the word. He feared but hoped he might somehow be blamed, although the task lay beyond the ability of one remarkably capable and ultra-strong man, even given all of the night.

"I have to ask," Sky had said, after roll call and a perversely reassuring twenty-two total, "did anyone do this? As a prank? As a precaution?"

Which concerned him, because it meant Sky was rattled and wanted a lesser, a trivial explanation. Oh, how Lowry wished he could give her that—an answer as insignificant as the eyelash of a diamond he had given her via the ring. Oh how he wished, those quicksilver fishes, that they could stand once more in the echo chamber of jars and he could have a do-over on the saying of stuff.

But, no, she hadn't really needed to ask, shouldn't have asked, because Lowry could see how it demoralized the others and he saw Winters shoot a look to Easterling, Hargraves, and Fu when he should've shot that glance at Lowry.

So when she had walked away to clear her head or to think or to plan the day's hike on the map, he had addressed the others.

He addressed them as he would have wished to have been addressed.

"Don't you see, those of us who survive will be kings when we get out? None of this will matter. None of it."

But he had forgotten to mention what they all thought: Would they survive the corridor without the suits? He also didn't mention that maybe clothes in general were the problem, not the suits. It felt weird to bring up. But, then, nothing had felt quite real to him in that moment and maybe that was the advanced training kicking in.

To not worry. To float careless as a cloud, as the poem went. Continuous as the stars that twinkled, stretched on a motherfucking endless line. The fucking flash of an inward eye, ripe with the bliss of solitude. Because they hadn't found a single fucking survivor, and the oddest fucking part was no one wanted to talk about it.

"And queens," Hargraves said. "Some of us will be queens."

"There you go," Lowry said.

## CALORIE COUNTS

As they continued to just kind of jack off at base camp, spinning their wheels, Lowry wondered, too, if in the course of fucking coarsened human events there had been a blessed moment when the concept of provocation had entered the planning stages. How a fucking base camp felt like one—not just to Area X but a fucking affront to Lowry. Because not only was a base camp too trad an idea for combating something unknown, but who had set it up? An advance team of chickens?

The answer to some shitty questions was to beg experimental drugs off Landry and not worry about it, Landry being in a happy

happy place, always, and not a downer like all the rest. Tossing out uppers like the fucking celebration of an armistice when, in fucking fact, they were just at the start of the war.

So he could not fucking keep still and base camp felt like ultimate stillness so he distrusted it worse, and all who fucking believed in it. He fucking preferred they keep in constant motion across that fucked-up landscape, had the instinct deep in his bones and spleen that his need for motion was the fucking world's need for motion and that the sloth of inactivity, of sitting still, of "establishing" base camp, after the weird fucking deaths, had infected the expedition as a way of defaulting to what they knew and had expected to do, as anchor, but, in fact, it was deadly Area X telling every single last fucker among them to do so. He knew Whitby would understand him, that if along for this wicked ride, Whitby would've raised the fucking issue, somehow someway. Even though it was too late, since they fucking lived here now, apparently.

And if the fuckers in charge *insisted* on establishing a fucking base camp only to leave it—another fucking folly. How in the name of all the unholys and the holy craps was that a great plan, after seeing a man's face fused to his helmet? Which in the meantime rendered them all still, although seemingly in motion getting busy "establishing" the base of the camp so it could be a goddamn safe haven, sanctuary, a place to retreat to, and he already had the sense there'd be no retreat worth the fucking name. More like screaming all their limbs running and fingering their way separately and the head bouncing along fucking behind shrieking "Wait for me!" In which case, more folly still.

Why he expressed this to Winters rather than Sky he put down to the fucking fact that Sky might say she'd had enough of his fucking "bullshit" whereas he saw it as bullet-shit: The truth delivered with velocity. And, also, if Winters did have to take over, until Lowry decided to do so himself, he needed to be in the loop.

"Move, Winters. Let's fucking move."

"Chill, Lowry. Be still." Was Winters telling him to just fucking die? Because that's how he read "be still" now. Winters liked this rhyming too, considered himself a fucking poet who had perhaps joined the wrong calling. Well, he might've joined the wrong calling but if poetry was it instead, he had no fucking calling at fucking all.

"Besides, history favors us."

"Why?"

"This site was a fort once. Someone saw it as having strategic value."

"Oh, this site was a fort once? Where is it now? How'd that go for the folks in the fort? Are they still around? Is it still standing? Anyone other than you remember its name?"

Winters ignored that, said, "You got naked for no reason in the middle of an emergency situation, Lowry."

Just jealous he hadn't dropped trou first. Just envious of Lowry's massive cock, shining in the sunlight as it lolled all the way to the ground in that first fucking glorious moment in Area X before the rules descended again and they were closed in, contained, made to fear what might be dealt with by medicine, remedy, in kind. The base camp was a bad fucking idea. But Winters didn't even know what he was talking about. Even Whitby had known Lowry had something special, some special insight, or why would the loon have spent so much time talking to Lowry. Because he was a fucking clown? No. Not that.

Ah, fucking hell, Winters could just fuck off. What was an expedition but a pain in the ass expressed twenty-four ways.

Twenty-two ways.

"Base" camps also meant other places that were not base camps— meant roving like nomads out from the perimeter of a "base camp," and that fucking process had already started, probably under mish orders from the Director ("imperative to find the fucking off switch, to unhaunt us brass"). That invisible hand from so far off that Lowry felt compelled to tell Sky, *"You don't have to do anything now except what you want. How would they stop you? How would they stop me?"* But he held his tongue. His tongue might need the silence to be credible if some other more imperative blurt overcame him.

So Sky ordered Lowry to assist Easterling with the "side expedition" Lowry knew had been fucking inevitable—she was to take four with her and go forward to secure the village, or if unsecure, to return with intel. The holding of territory when all the territory was potentially hostile struck him as stupid. He didn't know how fucking else to put it. As if the mole from under his tombstone was conducting mish ops.

"You want me to throw confetti?"

"Whatever Easterling wants."

Turned out Easterling wanted him to assemble supplies for their packs, test compasses and walkie-talkies, and make sure they had adequate rations. Five against a village. Central must have some information or some urgent need, and the pang came that maybe he should've gotten himself involved in the side mission. That maybe Jack-in-the-Box (the box being Central) would've told him to do that.

But he didn't trust Easterling, and it wasn't because she said "dude" like "dew-duh," which got old fast. So let Easterling wipe the fucking village clean of demons, witches, and aliens—do the hard, the dirty work and then he'd sweep in behind as the cavalry without a horse.

Easterling, Frank Delmas, Karen Hargraves, Angela Hernandez, Danika Miles—cross them off his list. Figured Area X might have plans for them that they might not like, headed off by themselves. That it was no business of his, despite a twinge for the potential of Hargraves, who, typically, smirked at him in a way he couldn't decipher, said, "Maybe it was my idea. Maybe I wanted to stretch my legs."

No fucking reply for that, so he packed them up and off—and reported back to Sky, who seemed to find him underfoot, so he spent the rest of the day dozing under a shaggy salt oak or whatever, listening to either birds hunt for insects above him or the clanking, trudging, grunting sounds of a perimeter being set up and a fire pit dug and all the fucking rest.

Until the grunts dolloped up changed to shouts of alarm and he raised the brim of his messed-up hat to the news that the first casualty of base camp was by the hand or paw, or whatever the fuck you called it, of an alligator: Sherri Binder, the half-assed psychic whose CV had been so soft the file had gone limp in Lowry's hand, and gooped into the ground.

She hadn't taken chances but the gator had gotten her anyway. It was unnerving. Mating season, according to Kalliope Benner, and the gators were hyperaggressive. The bellows and depth charges of the males in pursuit of females had gotten their attention.

"Whatever else Area X is doing," Benner said, "it hasn't affected the gators."

"Right," Winters said. "That's really what's important here."

"Threat assessment of the real and unreal," Ferreira muttered, first thing Lowry had heard him fucking say.

Stunning. An alligator was just a fucking scaly basset hound that lay sun-dazed, a lot like a log. A lot like a fucking log. How the fuck did you get killed by something that lived in the fucking drink and all you had to do was be moderately careful to avoid? Like, how the fuck did you not see a huge alligator moving toward you across a stretch of wildflowers? How, as a supposed psychic, did you live down dying from being devoured by the most obvious clichéd source of death in the whole damn swamp?

Here, bite my fucking leg. Have a chop. Just take this fucking hand. I want to pet you, are you a doggo, I don't have my glasses or my psychic abilities turned on, so I'm just going to stand here while you eat the shit out of me. Fuck. He could take the first deaths, or thought he could, but this one. It was like she'd given up before they'd even started.

What had she thought the alligator would do? Had she never seen a fucking gator in the swamp beyond the Southern Reach during training? He was forced into fucking incoherence in his own mind from trying to contemplate this situation until he realized that what agitated him was simply the shittiness that maybe she hadn't given up, but this was the way it would be here. That it wouldn't be with a blam but a whisper. A whisper that said, *Why resist?*

Tracks all around the body and actual sightings of animals they *could* have eaten. They could be eating fucking bears! They could be eating otters and dolphins and, yes, alligators. They could be eating herons and kingfishers, raccoons and possums. Deer, lots of deer. Wild pigs! Lots of pigs. They could be feasting on grilled manatee, for fuck's sake. They could be pulling apart the thigh meat of roasted sandhill cranes. They could be eating tons of fish, with no batter. Songbirds were delicious to some— why not crank a bunch of them on the barbecue and eat 'em whole, crunchy and succulent?

Never given a calorie-count chart—a better info chart on a laminated card dangling from a lanyard would've been useful. More than the shit they had—like, charts of the offshore shallows, these topographical maps when the whole place was as flat as fuck.

Because the goddamn energy bars and New Age hardtack in their packs that barreled through their stomachs like a tank smashing through a Shriners' parade barricade—they tasted to Lowry, at least, like fucking freeze-dried sandpaper duck pâté shoved inside a chocolate candy bar and the whole thing dropped in the fryer at a county fair, put on a stick, shoved up someone's ass, and then let to sit for hours before being liquified by burning and then re-formed into a fucking bar and meanwhile there were *animals* to eat all around!

Except Central and the cautious Director forbade it, so Sky did too. Why the fuck not eat them? They should've been able to eat their own suits like body-shaped placentas, born into this new world and needing the fucking nourishment. The suits should've been made that way, so the sausages housed within could feast on the bounty.

Earthworms, grubs, other insects—Area X held a wealth of protein, and as far as Lowry could tell, every other goddamn organism was partaking of every other organism in a great cluster-fuck of devourification. Everything that creeped and crawled and swam—tasty or disgusting on the hoof—totally off-limits, though. Meanwhile, the expedition walked around with swagger and strong intent, breathing the ever-loving air that could be contaminated, too. Why not pluck a fucking woodpecker from the air and chow down?

All over the fucking place. Waiting to be plucked, cooked, and served.

Down to twenty-one, the legal age to drink.

## JACK-IN-THE-BOX

Samuel Bronen, a sick fuck in Lowry's opinion in how he trended toward invisible in every situation, so what a surprise when Bronen popped up like a puppet fucker when Lowry was still in his tent trying to read the Old Jim file he'd prayed out of the Bible.

Fuck that fuck. Lowry didn't really know what Bronen had even done that day, but he had served one useful purpose—he had snuck alcohol in, vodka as water rations, careful to weigh it proper so his pack wouldn't weigh more or less. "Water weighs more by a bit," Bronen had told them, proud of himself. "So the bottles look like I drank some."

"Get the hell out, Bronen!"

But soon enough he'd had enough anyway, and Bronen out there pouring the booze and calling to him as if trying to apologize. So then he had to drink with them and sat there by the campfire, Sky abstaining like a fucking leader should, when all he wanted was to read what he'd pulled out of the mutilated Bible. Yeah, a third fucking time, but maybe some fucking secret meaning would appear like fucking magic.

"You're like my grouchy younger sister," Kalliope said to him. "That's how I'll think of you." The others laughed, except Winters and Lowry. If Hargraves had been there, maybe a third.

Lowry had two sisters growing up and they were older and he felt like he had to work the angles not to be left out or left behind. Mauve and Becka. Tomboys who didn't give a shit what they broke because they were big and loud and strong, and, yes, loved by all. Unbreakable themselves.

"Don't care what we think of you?" Mauve asked him once, after he'd done something selfish and stupid. "Don't care what I think of *you*?" he retorted. "Hell no," Becka said. "Too much fucking work." And they dissolved into laughter and roughhouse wrestled on the living-room couch. While he'd searched for a comeback, and couldn't think of one.

Nor could he now.

Because there was a point, right? Or had he made that up on the fly the sky the why?

The psychics were there. Like hitched twins afraid of the dark. The shuffle, shuffling forward like the shuffling forward of a chain gang or into a Victorian past. They had spent the day issuing "soothing suggestions." Like "Think of the largest, juiciest grapefruit you've ever seen." Like, "Think of a cute little pig at a petting zoo." Fuck cute pigs. Fuck grapefruit. Fuck the Victorians.

As they sat around the campfire, Lowry felt a kind of warmth . . . a kind of loosening . . . that frightened but also excited him. An exhausting exhilaration. As if for all his life he had been trapped in spools and spools of cloth and now someone was unwrapping him until soon there would just be the real him, unmuffled, and the world beyond.

Sad for the other fuckers around him that in addition to the mish-specific files Jack had given him access to, he'd had a quick look at the expedition personnel files. Nothing too drill-down and suspicious, but with the names filed off some personal histories and important moments, and it all mixed anyway with S&SB members, too. Telling those stories around a campfire would be like playing Battleship.

What might happen then? Because now, in the moment, Lowry began to feel the urge to say any damn-fool thing, to do whatever. But he couldn't pin down the origin of the impulse. His mind or some external agent, and how would he know? And maybe for this reason, Lowry resolved while watching the flames to stick to Jack-in-the-Box's orders. A structure, the skeleton, of a plan. Something to hold on to as befit a man. As Winters's face jutted out across the fire laughing at a bad joke by Benner.

Go as far as the lighthouse and then strike out on his own north, up the estuary, to Dead Town. Okay, but while Jack called it "Dead Town," the map, which Lowry kind of fucking believed in, called it "Fort Jones." What the fuck kind of name was Fort fucking Jones? No wonder it'd failed and everybody fucked off to Hedley.

Jack had said, "I don't think the Director would approve of you going to Dead Town. He's a Brute. If things go badly, for the main mission, they might blame me." Lowry didn't give two belches in a firestorm about Central factions like Brutes, or "fractions" as he disparagingly had called them talking to Sky pre-Border. Being blamed he didn't give a shit about, what he cared about was finding *leverage*.

But what did Jack really want, Lowry wondered? Since the fucking campfire kids didn't care if he lived or died now, happy to see him retreat to his fucking tent to resume rereading instructions.

What the fuck was Lowry supposed to put his back into, and what would be his reward if fucking successful?

"The mission first and last," Jack confirmed. "But second, in the Village, these other two locations, and the place I call Dead Town on this map—don't take it, commit this to memory—any files, videotapes, or other documents relating to an operation called Serum Bliss or to Séance and Science Brigade. Bring back everything you possibly can. In the rooms marked on the detail map, you may find money, other types of funds. Note the location of what you can't carry. I have a list of key words, too, that will appear in the lining of your backpack, along with some of the detail-room map intel. Near the inseam for the label."

Not for Lowry the fucking lion to growl about it, but that all fucking stank of some secret op before the Border came down. Didn't take a brain scientist, who mostly just mindlessly removed brain tumors anyway, so maybe it was like a being a brain scientist to suspect Jack feared the secret ops had something to do with Active Area X, which was now fucking Area X. Okay, that was a lot to process, if he really thought about it, like so much beyond his control . . . so he just didn't.

"Can do, boss," Lowry had said to Jack, getting a nightburn from the fluorescent lights in that blank, bleak, black corner of nothing. But maybe he could use this as leverage with Jack later, beyond the promised monetary reward (half now, half to his corpse, or his corpse's widow, whomever that might be), or maybe after he came back he got his ass hauled off to help staff a peace mission to a tiny country in the Fucklord Landlocked

Twhut region. There were so many places he hadn't been yet that looked like fucking fun. Or Central would just swallow him up, a leviathan breathing in a damn minnow through its merciless gills.

"Another thing," Jack had said. "If this guy, Henry Kage, turns up—assume he'll gouge your eyes out and replace them with pebbles. Treat with extreme prejudice." The photo Lowry had seen before, but not with the advice attached. Henry did look fucking dire—like some Nordic gloom flick where a buzzing fly trapped in a room was the only other fucking character.

Jack smiled like some fucking shark showing him Henry, but later Lowry realized Jack was wincing, almost like he was fucking embarrassed, so when Jack told him there would be "consequences" if Lowry fucked up, it felt like Jack really meant *he'd* fucked up and was just kicking that ball forward to Lowry.

Jack-in-the-Box called him "barrel boy" twice during that fucking convo, but also "thistleblower" like it was a compliment, but Lowry fucking despised it and would've gotten in a bareknuckle fight with a brown bear in a bar if anyone had called him a thistleblower. But Jack knew he'd get things done because otherwise why would he have recruited him? Jack wanted the one true thing, he'd known that since Jack had first met him in a really swank strip club, getting a lap dance. He didn't panic. It made him such a good lacrosse player in college, in the Ivy League–adjacent Virginia Creeper league, as someone put it.


Jack-in-the-Box also had given him the False Daughter Project files like it was a fucking sign of trust rather than just another dumbass thing Central had been into. Up to. Stepped in. Tripped over.

The files felt like they'd been written by a bad campfire storyteller, so Lowry had to piece it together, around the fucking redactions.

So, maybe, Old Jim had a dissociative break over the death of this almost-wife and Central rewired him because they'd already spent time on conditioning him, he had all these mad skills, mad kills, and was an asset. Although sometimes Lowry thought Jack-in-the-Box just fucking kept Old Jim around as some kind of a pet.

Old Jim had had a daughter too, sad, messed-up "Cass," but at some point said sad daughter must've seen through him and done a runner, scurried off to some other life, had known everything was very, very fucking off and given Old Jim the fuck off.

Can't have a life without being gone. Can't have a life without being strong. Something something so the lyrics went in Lowry's head. Fly away little bird, far away from jerk dad and his problems Central made worse, made into a different kind of hearse, made him learn some verse, too, it looked like, to keep that conditioning in place.

Old Jim had control words and Ol' Jack-in-the-Box had given them to Lowry, thinking twhut-like that Old Jim lived on instead of being changed into a moonbeam or kibble or something hideous but flappy, the kind of thing Lowry hated worst. Bats fucking sucked. Fuck bats. Smash them out of the sky with their namesake and then eat them whole, on spits. As they chittered outside Lowry's tent like errant punctuation set free from Jack's orders.

Jack put stock in Old Jim, but the file on Old Jim he gave Lowry was nothing to write home about. The guy seemed like a basket case, starting with the ops on which his wife had died, them both in the Humvee, navigating back streets as best they could in the middle of a desert by a glittering blue sea in the middle of a civil war. And rammed by a truck, shot at. She'd died instantly and he'd lost a lot of his memory, including everything about that op, including about his own fucking wife.

So Central used that to construct the idea of a "car accident" and memory loss resulting as a "lesser trauma, removing complicating context," which included that possibly Old Jim had been responsible, gotten them lost, not been paying attention, had been impaired in some way. And then they'd shitcanned him, kind of—admin and desk jobs, until, Jack said, they had need of him on a special special op, off the books.

So it looked like this fucking basket case got fucked up again, from something to do with his daughter disappearing. Like, this guy Old Jim had fan-fuck-tastic luck. Like, the worst, most terrifying luck. Except, also, from the files, Lowry couldn't fucking tell if the "daughter" ever existed. And, like, there was a real "false daughter," another Cass, and what the fuck did that mean?

Why did Jack have to be so scheme-y, all foreplay and no fuck? Or did everybody devoured by Central become that way? So, "false daughter," what the fuck. Something to distract Lowry from no animal eating and base camp. Had they implanted a daughter in Old Jim's head like an angel on the head of a pin embedded in his fucking brain—a brain already full of Central's rusty nails? All those nasty psychewitches down in Central's holding ponds, their basements, their rough-hewn caves. Cackling subterranean while secretly beating off beneath their jet-black robes.

Or, at least, that's how Lowry imagined the jack-off mental tools at Central. How convoluted they were, like the folds of a fucking complicated brain, but the brain preserved in a fuckling jar, hermetically sealed, so what difference did it make?

False daughter, "real daughter," real daughter—maybe in the end who gave a fuck, though it bothered Lowry. It nagged at him hard, despite all the other shit that could've had his fucking attention. That they'd done that to Old Jim. Do that to a man, he's going to fuck with you, if ever he finds out. Lowry would've come after Jack with a nail gun, a dull knife, and baseball bat. Maybe still have to, fuck.

And so it was supposed to look like retirement, Old Jim going to the Forgotten Coast. A gift to a loyal old-timer. While the mission in question was secretly feeding the beast that was Jack with some good old stateside grift in the manifests. Let's turn those manifests into manifestos.

But Old Jim had been smarter than he'd looked and managed to fuck Jack on the money somehow, and Jack needed it back, which is where Lowry came in. Jack acting like Lowry was getting a ticket to a theme park and going to go on some rides. Not, heavily armed and drugged up, to take on the unknown on its home territory.

Because Old Jim had also fucked up Central, "some perfectly good minds, for nothing, after we took such good care of him," Jack said. Something about surveillance tape of Old Jim playing the piano and Central too relaxed and too many people viewed it and "got infected," which didn't make Lowry that happy about finding Old Jim, if the guy could fucking rip off a song and put knives in Lowry's head.

And what the fuck was Lowry supposed to say to this "Old Jim" when he pulled him out of some fucking hidey-hole in the middle of some shit-tastic black swamp nowhere? "Come back into the fold, fucklehead! All is forgiven!" Because no bones about it, Jack-in-the-Box wanted Old-Jim-in-the-Hole brought back fucking alive, not goddamn dead. Unless dead he already fucking be, lying lifeless somewhere by the sea. And they had "every reason to believe based on last comms" that Old Jim still breathed, if in some shaky way. Whatever that meant. Last communion? Last communism? Last commission? Last commensuration? Last commode?

Yeah, "last communications," but the nature of those remained fucking raw, unattainable, not beamed from Jack's mind to Lowry's via mind ray or humble file. Just that look on Jack's face in the dive bar, the smug fucking look of a champion fucking secrets keeper. Maybe, though, Jack cared about the money as much as the other shit.

Oh yeah, the files also mentioned someone involved named

"Schubert," but no fucking context. Who the hell had Schubert been? Someone who reported to Old Jim, is all he could tell, maybe. Plus there was some shithead thug named Commander Thistle who also knew Schubert but Old Jim reported to him?

And Old Jim might've fucking killed Commander Thistle or maybe Commander Thistle was still alive if Area X hadn't snuffed him out like a bad suit. Look for a black mask. "Unpredictable and off mission," read the note.

What was this, fucking Zorro? Fucking sorrow. Fucking fuck fuck fuck all of that.

Down to sixteen at base camp. He fell asleep to the echo of the psychic twins' titanic snores. But when he woke up, they were down to fifteen. Not enough of Landry's fucking drugs in the fucking world fuck fuck fuck fuck fuck.

Hinojosa had disappeared, presumed missing, presumed dead, presumed more fucked than those who remained behind.

Last words, anecdotal: "Pass the scotch, asshole."

## HAUNTED WALKIE-TALKIE TWHUT FEST

The walkie-talkies turned against them the next morning, when Sky tried to contact the Village advance team. Screams. Pleading. A manipulative child's voice, incomprehensible. She had ordered radio silence, all comms off, for morale and because it felt like an attack and Lowry in her tent felt like attack, too, to him. He'd had no chance to re-up with Landry for drugs and felt scraped raw of fucks. Nerve lacking. Nerve fucked.

For a second, he thought she was going to ask him if it was one of his jokes. A long way to go for a joke. But her look was haunted and he didn't like to look at her directly because he didn't fucking want that in his head—that look, from her, from the expedition leader.

Because the strangled quality to the child's voice, how the speech seemed to be trying to approximate something it had heard from afar, distant, garbled, or was being said through a bloody mouthful of broken teeth. Or, and this was why Lowry defaulted to "it" . . . what if the speaker crackling through their comms wasn't a child at all but something else? Would that be better or worse, or just the same?

"Listen," Sky said, and Lowry felt unintended rebuke. He'd thought she'd sought comfort from him, but no: She wanted him to listen to more of this shit, to become more and more embroiled, implicated, in the nightmare that had affected her face such that the left corner of her mouth drooped slightly, like she'd suffered a tiny stroke.

What came out through the walkie-talkies was clear, but not reassuring. Also, her tent was a fucking mess, like she'd torn it apart looking for something or thrashing around in her sleep, and he didn't know what to say to her about that.

"Perimeter wire in place. No intrusion intrusion."

"Yeah, like, any greener and and it'd be blue."

"Say again, red leader. Missed missed that."

"I wish the rations didn't come in this gray color. Paint that damn bar some color, I don't care if the food coloring is bad for you. I I just can't eat gray."

"There's no juice left in that. It's just going to sit there like a toy toy."

That last one from the walkie-squawkies he recognized. "That's a recording of something said at the camp yesterday. They're surveilling us and using psyops on us!"

"No, Lowry. No. They're not surveilling us in the usual way."

They. Who the fuck was "they"?

"That's a recording."

"No, it's not. That's real time."

"How do you know?" He wanted to say, *"That's fucking impossible. Get your shit together."* But the quaver in her voice warned him against it.

"Just turn it off," he said. "Just turn it off and it'll go away." Because if they couldn't even find the off switch on the walkie-talkies, then Area X was a fucking lost cause.

Lowry wishing he hadn't seen the batshit conclusions of Jack's psychics before the Border had come down. That there was a "temporal storm" of obscene proportions, that they were "receiving visions out of the typical order." With directions from Jack not to share with others, who only showed Lowry the batshit barf shit in an empty dive bar while they sat at the upright piano in the corner and pretended to play sea shanties like fucking assholes.

All of which seemed to tell him that Central didn't know an off switch from a hole in their butts and the walkie-talkies might outlive them all. Wishing they could perpetually live in the weeks before going across the Border, in that nervous but exalted energy, that fine and private space.

Sky's face, the way he willed by telepathy that she acknowledge the commitment his gifts had meant. That maybe it might now soothe. But: Fuck. No.

"It's not on, Lowry." Using his name like it was his fault. "It's not on. It's not on. It's not on. It's not on. It's not on. It's not on. It's not on."

He took a step back. Her combat knife was in her hand. His combat knife was in his hand. How had they gotten there? What the fuck had they been about to do with the fucking knives?

He dropped his, but he could pull his sidearm quick if needed. Why did he think he needed to?

"Give me the fucking walkie-talkies," he said. "We're going to take all the fucking walkie-talkies and lock them away."

She looked at her knife, dropped it too, nodded.

"Do you think this means the five who went to the Village are dead?"

"Who the fuck knows."

Had he taken his knife out first and she'd reacted to that? He didn't remember taking out his knife.

He took her hand, which lay limp in his, not so much that she despised him now but that her attention lay so far inward she could not relate to her own body.

So, in the end, they put all the walkie-talkies in the box, and the box started talking to them in *one* voice, in words incomprehensible, but like buzz saws cutting into their skulls, so they stuffed their ears full of cotton, and fuck that, so for once he agreed with Winters: "Let's throw the whole lot in the river." Estuary, really, but fine, Lowry let Winters have "river."

Let that box gargle bargle gasp wheeze with water in the goddamn walkie-talkie lungs. Let that damned choir chorus itself into the fucking muck and filth and silt at the very bottom and haunt some fucking salamander's nightmares.

If the comms were from the past, maybe eventually everything would be from the fucking past, the thought occurred. He didn't want to think about what that meant. Yet, in the end, he had hidden his walkie-talkie from the general confiscation. Just made sure to bury it deep with some of his clothes around it, in his pack, so the dribble of mumbling it resorted to couldn't be heard. Everything might be crazed, but one day he might need to talk to Area X, direct line.

But the very next morning the box was back in the camp, by the dead fireplace. Lowry had a fucking twinge of guilt that faded fast. Maybe his walkie-talkie was the leader and the box of submissive walkie-talkies had come back to the boss of them. Hated that fucking thinking, which was no thought at all but some impulse of the reptile part of the brain to be scared, to be small, to be repulsive. No, his walkie-talkie stuffed inside of four pairs of socks was not the cause of this shit.

Sky just looked at the box like it was poison and retreated to her tent. That left Winters to give orders.

He stood there tall and straight and said, "Let's shoot up the box and take it farther away." He had no tremble to his voice, but no feeling either, at all, and Lowry felt that was a tell that something had slipped away from him the way it had slipped away from Sky. Which meant Lowry third-in-command might have to step in sooner rather than later.

So they shot the box up with their automatic weapons and tossed it, full of holes, back in the river, but far distant.

Cold chill. How had the box gotten back into camp? How was there such a passage of time that Lowry felt starved between lunch and dinner, but couldn't be sure it was the same dinner it was supposed to be. Their compasses had fried themselves. All the equipment for measurements, Winters reported, had become toast, toast, toast. Not fried but spinning wildly, no use to it except to commit all of the electronics to the funny farm for rehab and therapy. Maybe go themselves and slam the door shut behind them.

They would not let the walkie-talkies rule their lives. Where was he again, in the scheme of things? He had a mission within the mission, and this mission seemed to be collapsing around them.

And, in the end, he took his walkie-talkie out into a sudden, black-water shithole of a watering hole beyond the camp and shot it dead. Shot it full of holes, and then tossed it in the water while it screamed at him: "I'm hit I'm shit I'm shit I'm shit."

Goodbye dear walkie-talkie. Sweet dreams. Do not return home. Do not fucking come home.

But he kept his small satellite phone. It had behaved. It had not talked to him.


Where did the fucking time go? They lost more of it all the time like they should fucking chase it down. Lowry couldn't tell. No one knew. Like, were they always around the campfire now.

Always going to be around the campfire now. Always around the fucking merry-go-round they'd go.

But Lowry couldn't get free of the calorie counts, the fucking wildlife. But not just the fucking wildlife.

"Why no moo-moos and cluck-clucks all over the damn place?" he posed to the group in general, to no applause and no response. "Farms here before the Border came down, for sure, folks. Where've all the domesticated moo-baas gone? All the bleaters just fucking vanished, raptured into nothing? We could've had a pig on a spit right now, roasting by this very campfire."

No plump succulent geese? No fucking nothing other than the undergrowth, the untouchable wildlife, the buildings that looked like they'd been mugged and aged fifty years, not one year. And the giant, spewing lighthouse like an oil-derrick gusher in the distance.

Oh, the flaming lighthouse game they still wanted to play, while Landry handed out happy pills. Of them all, Lowry now realized, Landry was the least expendable. Landry could not die, because only Landry now knew the identity of the pills he had in his pack, because they'd gotten all sloshed together.

"It's just a lighthouse."

"I see a snake rearing up on its hind legs."

"Snakes don't have legs. It's a pillar of smoke."

"A tower of ice."

"It's made of insects. Tiny swirling green insects."

"Fucking cocktail with all this good and weird shit in it, like protoplasm and gin and Chartreuse and riboflavin, gentian, electric daisy, maybe a splash of lime with a cherry. I could go for that right now."

Who the fuck could *find* that right now? A cocktail out here was one fucker with a twig swirling mud water in another's cupped hands.

"We don't know what it wants. We don't know where its command and control is. We don't know why it's mimicking us. We should go back—abort the mission." But it was too fucking early to abort the fucking mission. They'd just gotten there and maybe it was the embarrassment of that that felt like too much, like they should keep going.

Sky did not put it to a vote, though. They would continue on, soon enough. To the lighthouse.

They may have become drunk and sullen and started watching each other for some sign of becoming feral.

The mood, man, the fucking mood.


So they sat around the campfire not talking and into his awareness there came a shadow moving through behind them, in the trees, coming down out of the trees like a vast blanket, invisible but thick, filling in the spaces around them until Lowry couldn't breathe, but he couldn't move, either, and he wanted to scream, he wanted to run away, and he could see that the others did too, and yet they could do nothing as if encased in cement, and only their eyes shone out, terrified, and Lowry tried to remember his contempt, his contempt for the others—because they had been trained to ignore or deal with such phenomena, they knew it might happen, and yet so many had lost their shit so quickly. And yet still he couldn't breathe, was suffocating, and the night marched on, darker than dark.

He concentrated on calories, on his rants.

"Calorie count on a gator not including the gristle had to top a few thousand Hamiltons. Muskrat—did they have muskrats or just regular old marsh rats—maybe eight gees."

One of those fucking protected wood stork thingies a thou or coupla, and you could cook the head, stringy-looking motherfuckers.

He stared trapped at Sky opposite him and the thickness was the worst, the contact of skin on skin, but the other skin of such a consistency, a feeling of revulsion and shock from the gliding through, as if it wasn't flowing through and between them, but in some other way touching them. Inside.

Swamp rats like snacks, just pop 'em like hairy marshmallows on a stick around a fire. Pretend you're back at summer camp with some dirty hippie playing the banjo at you. Some marsh rabbit—though they'd been told to especially never put a hit on them.

The living wall had curled around the whole campfire and opposite him he saw Singer disappear into it, just completely come apart at the fucking seams in that moment, screaming and screaming until that cut off as the molecules of body became nothing more than molecules of Area X.

Calories, though, didn't mean edibility. He'd had "alligator wings" once that were tire-rubber quality, but in a pinch . . .'cause what if the protein bars were spiked or had some subliminal taste or message on the wrapper, making them do things or hear things or, fucking hell, feel things. No, he wanted those wild calories. Wild calories were free and everywhere. He could feel the thing cloying closer, the dull hum and rumble and the sensation of flesh moving across the back of his head, his neck.

But fuck if he would be frozen. Fuck if he would succumb to the terror, the paralysis. Fuck that fuck that. Fuck fuck fuck.

He turned and lunged into the backdrop, jumped right into that hell of skin and flesh screaming his own name over and over. He pulled it to him with his arms, bit down hard on that rubbery fucking manta ray, that fucking monster that had been a thing in a jar in his head grown as wide and large as the world.

The wall of Area X felt tremulous, vulnerable, surprisingly delicate. It made him want to protect it, not destroy it. But he'd not have a thing in a jar best him, not now. So he bit down hard and Area X tasted like sour juice, like fresh hail sucked on before it became water, with some acid rain in there and grace notes of fucking merlot for all he could guess. Just gnawing and he was going to fucking eat Area X before it ate him. Even though he should have punctured it with a sharpened metal straw and drunk it like a milk shake or that bubble tea with the little "tadpoles" at the bottom. That he could've just drunk the wall down to nothing, that it would have deflated like a kid's beachball.

He grappled with it to hold firm, like it was a climbing wall without purchase and he was a sweaty-ass climber still jumping up farther and farther, feet in tune to some invisible grips, but really he was just poking holes into the wall, into the fucking whatever the fuck it was, still screaming his own name like a mantra against dissolution.

And maybe in that moment he thought he saw the face of a fucking deity in the wall of flesh, or maybe just a wall of jars exploded to fucking free their essence. But in all other ways, Lowry thrilled to the experience, he leapt toward it, not cringed away. Because he was motherfucking Lowry, nobody's barrel boy. Nobody's fool or tool, nobody's anything anymore except what he fucking wanted to be.

Then it was gone, just fell away, so he was chomping down on night air and he was spitting out what he'd begun to chew because now it felt like carrion in his mouth and also like a vast conspiracy to colonize his throat, and Lowry felt ancient, muscles aching, and he toppled over as did the others. Around the snuffed-out fire.

"Fucking calories," he shouted, still spitting, too. "Just calories, all around us."

While they looked on like nothing had really happened, dulled by drugs or dulled by the reality or all in shock and really he should be in shock too, but he was too excited by his own triumph, and pushing people over to wake them up, dragging out more rations, even sanctioning the banjo that John Fu liked to play, he made them party.

"Some music to get the night the fuck out of here."

Winters staring weary at him, like he was Area X, somehow, instead of the only one to bite Area X in the ass and get away with it. And why the fuck was that, anyway?

But soon even Winters joined in the frenzy of the party, the frenetic quality of it, and they were dancing dancing dancing to the flame and trying to ignore that the flame kept staring back at them with its own eye, but as long as the fucking eye stayed in the fire and didn't lunge out at them, Lowry could deal with that.

"Did one of you sick fuckos cut the eyes out of a hamster and replace them with pebbles? Well, that's what I heard. Back at Central. Looking through your files."

He only said part of that aloud and then defaulted to his own history. Maybe out of guilt. Maybe because he liked sharing it without really sharing it. Maybe because he wanted it out of his soul.

What was it Whitby had said? Sad Whitby. Wise Whitby. Just all the Whitbys in his head. They had said, "You can't escape the past." Or had he seen that on a bumper sticker. Maybe someday he would be an entrepreneur, after he got the gold, and he'd have a bumper sticker commemorating him. His industry. His hard work. The fact he'd jacked up all the gold and used that to become successful. But, anyway, his own history . . .

"Someone's granddad took me to a department-store lingerie show when you were ten," Lowry shouted.

"Your mom made one of you follow an old boyfriend around in a car to see if he was cheating on her but they hadn't dated for years, then had you and your sisters beat him up when he went out to a bar."

Winters had brought the alcohol this time, lapse of protocol unbecoming a second-in-fucking-command and Sky had come out of her shell/tent and just sat there on a log, like a spectator, still in shock. A spectator at her own expedition. Lost. Already lost. And Lowry channeled all of his own lost into her, willed it there, because why should they both be lost, and then relented and stopped, even as a mental exercise, but still she was not fit company to talk to and they all got roaring drunk on Winters's liquor because why not why not?

Shouting and talking loudly disguised the silence of the woods. The silence of the air. The silence in their hearts at the thought of the fucking wall returning. Let there be light! Let there be noise. Let there be more dancing!

Into the middle of all that, Ferreira confessed he had brought a bomb to blow up the lighthouse. Shrugs. I just like bombs. "I have a bomb." "You are a bomb." "Do you think it'll work?" "I don't know. I just thought I'd give it a try, you know." "BYOB. Radical." "So you thought a bomb would work against a gigantic green cum geyser?" For it was still there after dark, spewing, sparkling, roaring incandescent emerald, the most beautiful thing Lowry had ever seen that was also terrifying as fuck.

He couldn't go straight to bed when the others finally did, when they all fucking thought they might be safe, just a little bit fucking safe for a while. He snuck over to Sky's tent, ripped open the flap by mistake instead of using the zipper.

"Want company?"

From the dark corner, Sky and a video recorder, kind of both slumped there, her half curled up.

"Go to sleep, Lowry."

"Are you sure?"

"I'm sure."

"Everything okay?"

"No, Lowry. Everything is not all okay."

"Last chance."

"Get the fuck out of here!"

In the morning, Ferreira was dead of a gunshot to the head,

but no one had heard a gunshot. No trace of any bomb. He'd lied.

Down to thirteen. He thought.

Last words: "Abalone tastes disgusting, by the way. Gonna turn in."

## SLINKY-DINKY PINKY-WINKY

No one slept except Lowry fucking slept like a baby that had been drugged, his mouth enflamed but the outrage of what it had received receding, so by morning with Sky kicking them in the ass to get moving he felt refreshed. He'd made the right fucking decision while they all cowered or froze. Except no one appreciated it, thanked him for biting Area X away. No one gave him a nod or a clap on the shoulder. Like, somehow he'd been fucking complicit and just been acting.

That, some fucking how, he and Area X had colluded ahead of time, choreographed the whole thing, and that wall of midnight flesh would never have hit their encampment except for him.

How did that work? What kind of fucking allies did he and Area X make? Except maybe both of them were fearless, unlike the fearful fucks that were Scaramutti, Landry, Winters, Bukvic, and all the rest. All the cowering masses that didn't know how to face down Area X. Who somehow thought that the best way to win against this place was to just wait and let it permeate them, overtake them, mash them into the soil until they were nothing but the dirt.

But on the playback of what Sky had recorded, Lowry was jumping into that alien flesh, was kissing it, was dry humping it, while the others looked on in horror, but Lowry knew that was fucking false. That the vid was wrong. That this was all wrong, and he'd been biting it, stabbing it. That he'd not been enveloped by it, stuck in, hadn't rubbed his head up against that soft, velvety expanse and nuzzled it and cooed like a fucking lamb or something. He'd been aggro incarnate. He'd been telling Area X to fuck off.

"Winters, you saw," Lowry said. "You saw what happened?"

"We've got to get going," Winters replied, and that's all he said, and by the time Lowry could gather his own shit and pack it up, the whole expedition had headed out and he had to fucking catch up.

By the time he'd reached them again, they'd come to a halt at the trucks. But fuck the trucks. Fuck the fucking trucks. Who cared about the trucks. He'd saved them all from dying the night before and none of them, not even Landry, gave him the gratitude of that. He was the fucking third in line to the crown, to the throne. In a week, if things went bad, he could be leading this expedition. But they all stood there looking at the fucking trucks like he was invisible and he'd done nothing to help.

The trail of trucks looked from afar like kids had been playing with toys. But overgrown with vines, so that ruined the childhood-memory effect, fond times moving armies around the backyard while the parents yelled at each other inside. All of it so subsumed into the substrate that had one year or fifty damn years transpired in the interim. Gear shifts rusted and rotting. No fuel.

What a useless bunch of fucking junk, and he watched with contempt as Winters tried to turn the key and reanimate the dead, living in vain hope of engine rumble like he was a circus freak, an illusionist who had once reassembled a cut-apart rabbit as a fluke and now put on airs, didn't realize there'd been divine or infernal intervention. Not a single fucking tire was sound or could even make a sound if you shoved a pressure gauge into it.

"Push on!" Lowry shouted at them. "Shove off. Ignore this

shit and push on!" "Push on" just a term he'd heard in a war movie once, but it fit.

Bridge over the River Who Gives a Shit. If they were going to ignore him, he'd be the fucking loudest ghost in the world. He'd be the ghost with the most, the one with the fucking megaphone shouting out the truth of the spirit world, which was that it was just the real world when no one listened to it. That was the spirit world. Just people other people fucking ignored. Fucking ignored at their peril. Like a bunch of cowards and shitheads.

Why'd he even have to put up with this crap. Well, for now, he didn't want to be on his own. Because this place was creepy-scary-shitty. But soon, motherfucking soon, he'd strike out on his own and hit gold. He'd be the one who brought back the good tidings, the real thanksgiving, and the rest of them would be still in Area X, shivering in a ditch while some wall of flesh took a dump all over them.

"Where are all the soldiers? No one. No one to fucking rescue. Just ourselves. Just our-fucking-selves."

Sky didn't even tell him to shut up anymore.

But she sure was shouting soon enough.


About two clicks past the stupid trucks, a line of slurping goo people sprang up—a surprise because the expedition had gotten sloppy. Because they'd been fucking sloppy the whole fucking time, like a bunch of amateurs, they were strung out in a line on the trail such that the swoop and tackle of the enemy frags sliced right through them, and Lowry along with Sky, Winters, Fu, Benner, Formsby, and Jiamu on the far side and, dammit, Landry, Henkel, Scaramutti, Fussell, Bukvic, Bronen trapped behind.

How to describe this fucking line of non-people in his incendiary memoirs after this was long past and he had white hair and a beard, or maybe no beard at all and had become an Ichabod Crane haunted fucker who snarled at the neighbors?

Undulating waves of wolves, but made of black liquid and slurping their way across like liquid lava fire, and no that wasn't it but the sight defeated the eye like an eye defeated an ear and a tongue because he needed to see the enemy, not taste or smell them.

By then, Lowry had snorted and swallowed a lot more drugs from Landry, thank the gods. So maybe he was shouting at the liquid things that seemed so joyous in how they could dissipate and re-form and why couldn't all in life be like that? Why did anyone have to commit to just one fucking shape. It was a fucking tyranny of fast-held shapes and what if he just wanted to be a circle or an oval with no end and no beginning?

But he had his automatic weapon out and the depth of his fucking spiraling mattered not because his body understood what he was supposed to do. And what he was supposed to do was kill the shitheads. Kill all the shitheads to protect the expedition.

For now the lopers of the interlopers had re-formed into beings much more familiar and more fey and Sky let out a fearful yip of a shrieking shout because she was gibbering terrified and so was Winters, who Lowry was fairly sure had just shat himself, and that was the smell not the marsh that overtook them.

The enemy had stopped their schtick on all fours and now doubled dead exped mems good, doubled them like they fucking would for psyops and max confusion. They were naked and crying and shrieking and calling out Sky's name, which did her morale no further good.

While Landry, trapped behind that line out of his mind on drugs, was giggling and pointing at them and ranting "Into the armpit of the universe, we're in the armpit of the universe" and "Far far worse shit I've done now than I've ever done before fuck fuck they are ugly." For they were ugly. They were uggos from way back, because they'd mimicked most of the expedition in their gallivanting bipedal numbers. But not just like naked people.

No, it was slinky-dinky pinky-winky shit, loopy and looping, and the flexibility of them at the joints and how they swung around and stared upside down felt like something out a tube of toothpaste. But then they became frozen in form like it had *set* and there came a kind of roughness to their texture more like the papier-mâché of a hornet's nest.

One eye in the heads that watched him, that watched Sky, jutted out oracular, bulged, while the other receded into the orbit, so that if you focused in on that, if you tracked them with binocs, it made you want to throw up, to see both the black hole of the receding eyeball and the quaking jelly of the one half ejected but still hanging on.

While the rest of them were ribbons that had mass, that you could pump water into the lining of to fill out. Yet still they fucking looked like the dead expedition members somehow. The faces. The faces so rubber and coalescing and also poignant, as if they held the memory of something true.

Eels and flatworms came into his thoughts un-fucking-bidden as the doppelgängers began to seethe toward them, to seethe and then retreat, and once again seethe, each time in this sidewinder method coming closer across the marshes, and no fucking evidence at all of feet or stumbling or anything other than this gliding freak-circus act, atrocity.

"Wait until they're closer!" Sky ordered. "Wait and save ammo."

Save fucking ammo? For what? For twenty-one-gun salutes at all their secret fucking funerals? No, he would spray fucking ammo like it was going out of style, like he was some inaugural water sprinkler of bullets at some new municipal park and he was going to annihilate every cardboard cutout of every smiling public official who hadn't sanctioned a fenced area for dogs so everything was dookie dookie dookie that people stepped in.

So he sprayed it, with a mighty hell, with a hallelujah to the

Landrys and alike who might be in the line of fire to get down, so they hit the ground and he just let 'er rip in a fucking cataclysm of bullets, making the weapon hot in his grasp, but he liked the heat and those motherfuckers all fell like wheat before the scythe as someone had said in an old action movie back in the day trying to take yet another motherfucking bridge, except here the "bridge" was the whole bunch of party-crashing freaky-deaky shitheads who had decided to Hey Nonny Nonny their way right through the middle of them.

But he also didn't care for the way the doubles loped across the landscape with half their faces shot off, smiling, mutilated arms outstretched in greeting, like they really were their dead pals.

Didn't like that and also didn't like how the others had frozen but then added their own weapon fire *after* these overenthusiastic door-to-door salesmen had been so torn apart by his own automatic rifle that they couldn't stand anymore and fell back into the reeds like they normally should've long before that.

All this to the cascading smell of he didn't know what. Awful offal but also something so foreign it made him disgusted by the fact that he couldn't identify it, like his nose became intelligent on its own just to revolt from having to smell that and relay it to his brain.

Calm, he danced close while the others hung back and put the parting gift of shots to each of the deadlings' heads, even dared touch the side of one to see if it felt like the wall of fucking flesh—before leaping back, benefit of the enemy's undulating line.

Well, yes, and maybe no, on the texture. More like a manta ray, firm and smooth and a serrated roughness, but with more give and behind it the sense, yes, of something vast, breathing in and out.

Like the line of dark blood leading to a corpse in the snow.

Like some vast quest to a tower they never reached but kept turning in the widening gyre and holy shit holy shit holy shit.

The doubles of the dead had begun to re-form despite Lowry having shot their brains out, and the exped mems trapped on the other side remained trapped, and a mighty horrifying scream came from the doubles as they became their dead comrades again, and a shriek and a bellow like he'd never heard or wanted to hear again, and it was rude and not awesome that he'd killed them, he'd stormed the ramparts like a fucking hero and yet they still *lived*, they wouldn't stay down dead but wanted to be all expantual again when he'd shut them down already, and what kind of fucking party was this, that didn't eventually wind down?

"How do we kill them? How do we kill them? How do we kill them?" Fussell screamed, on a loop that had been helpful only the first two times.

The worst thing was that the feel of Lowry's weapon changed then. It changed so it was a different kind of smooth-rough and when he looked down at it, his automatic rifle had become flesh, elastic, and narrow fishlike, like a fucking gar or something, and it had eyes. And it wasn't just the fucking eyes but the whole situation that made him toss the rifle into the marsh.

Tossed the rifle into the marsh toward the rein-fucking-carnates and shouted at the rest, "Toss your fucking rifles! Toss them!"

Sky and Winters obeyed that command, but not the others and as their weapons turned into some kind of prehistoric narrow long fucking gar with strange eyes, their hands fused to those creatures, the texture like a flaring slime-covered pine-cone, and they could not get free even as those fucking whatever the fuck they were thrashed about and, with a musculature more in keeping with a bulldog or bowling ball, pulled the recipient of their new motor function down into the reeds with them, fins thrashing, where Lowry could hear them being devoured both externally and internally—as he ran really fucking fast to the west, wherever there might be a skimp of trail, with Sky and Winters behind him.

Like, their hearts were exploding into fish but also the fish that was their weapon had started feasting on their external parts. And it was a sound he never wanted to fucking hear again. Yes, they ranted and shrieked like little blinches in the long grass, but he thought it warranted because how do you fight an enemy like that?

Over his shoulder, Lowry shouted at Landry, "Stay safe! Keep the drugs safe!" Oh, shit, he was going to lose his fucks again. He would have to fucking ration his fucking fucks and oh shit did it even matter, if this was the state of the world.

Sky and Winters now, somehow, surging past him in the sprint even though he was fitter than both of them, so maybe shooting so much evil goopy twinky dinky shitty pitty had made him weak.

When they had petered out and stopped, breathing hard, to look back through the safety of a lens, Lowry could see the doubles had risen again to peer at them curious, so fully recovered from their deaths that they had risen twice as tall as before, no longer like humans but like carnival performers on stilts, walking across the landscape of their sideshow.

Before they had well and truly fucked off and left the fugglies behind, there came a moment, too, that Lowry took pause. Even so fey and alien and tall, the winky-dinkys began to look like better copies of the original. They looked more like they *belonged* in that late-afternoon light golden upon the reeds.

It was the imperfections of the reals that stood out, that was fucking inhuman, wrong.

The enemy, Lowry knew, had fucking put that thought there, for sure.

# BEACH OF BONERS, DEATH DESTROYER

F our left, that Lowry knew of: himself, Sky, Winters, and the psychic Scaramutti. Who limped their fucking way down to the seashore by the seaside. In the dark, exhausted, to the calming sound of the tide rippling in and out over the shells. Lowry was still in mow-down mode, vibrating with it, like keep that lawn an inch, maybe half an inch, but no higher. Everything above that, blotto with bullet holes. Rounds ripping through would be fine with him, didn't care what it was, it was going down long before he fucking was. But nothing to shoot at, nothing at fucking all, though he had a fuckling backup rifle would do the job.

The tinkling, pleasant sounds of the water against that rough sand and shells, the lighthouse thankfully gone boring, or maybe they'd gone boring, but either fucking way, it gloomed over them, but did not loom, so that they camped that night as if free of anything but the idea of the beach and memories from child-hood of wet sand and sandcastles, and all the ways in which this grit that got into your underwear, and up your crack as far as cracks went . . . how a fucking stupid experience was rendered nostalgic by the grandeur of a fucking view.

Yet, in the morning, Lowry realized their mistake, for it was not shells that the water lapped against and surged across in the shallow water just offshore but bones. Thousands and thousands of bones.

While on the horizon the fabled dead destroyer from the elongated briefings listed like a blade or wedge. But mostly looked exactly like a destroyer cut in half. And, for a moment, like a vast, half-submerged potato wedge. The magnetic pull of that, Lowry could feel, epitomized by the word "survivors." Of which there could be none, and yet because of "survivors," they all ignored the abso-fucking-lutely terrifying beach of bones to gaze out at that mystical sight, which registered as hope though none of them could fucking reside there.

"Beach of bones, death destroyer," Lowry said, and then couldn't stop saying it. "Beach of bones, death destroyer. Beach of bones, fucking death destroyer."

How was it even possible that the destroyer had mirage-like entered their frame of reference? The charts had it farther out to sea, and farther west.

"This place is undergoing temporal enticements," Scaramutti said.

"Dislocations you mean," Lowry replied. Because Scaramutti only fucking said that to stop him from saying "beach of boners." But it had to be fucking said. Temporal enticements fucking fuck fuck.

Scaramutti just looked at him as if he were the disturbing one.

"The bones. They're not real here."

"They're real somewhere. Say I." Hard to say if one fucking day would make a difference and the prior day would have been different.

"No, they're real here, Lowry," Sky said. "They're real here, we are *seeing them right now,* and so is the destroyer. And we'll take samples—of everything."

As if he were a fucking child making fucked-up beach-of-boner death-destroyer sandcastles out of words and like they were still a fucking expedition. Instead of just four clueless fucking people who'd washed up by a lighthouse and couldn't go on, must go on, who the fuck cared if they went on. But, perversely, Lowry did.

Four people, three of whom had no qualms or cares about security, the way he did. As if the pallid beach dunes they stood upon in a brisk wind wouldn't crumble away under their tents or slinky-dinkys stream out of the sea at them in the night, or crawl toward them undulant from the land.

And, yes, there was a fucked-up death destroyer on the horizon and the bones of what might be thousands of people beneath the shallow water but, surely, they were owed *the sea*—that the sea, reaching it, should fucking soothe, getting there, after all they'd been through in such a short time.

Winnowed down to the mighty Fuck-All Four and who knew who on the other side of the dancing daisy-chain wall of shithead goopy Smurf-flesh might still be this side of fucking mortal, but Lowry bet that by the time they all met up again, if they did, the others would be unrecognizable. Maybe he would be too, although Lowry didn't fucking care if he was profaned or changed after death, on the principle that he would not be alive.

But the sea did not soothe—the seagulls were screaming shit not making it and he could not quite make out what they were saying. But all four of them knew it should not have been words, and Lowry did not like to recall how in the shitty horrifying gap of the killing and resurrection of the winky-dinkys, how their own words had come out funny, disjointed, as if the murder of their shit-gobby doubles had scarred their minds, as if they, not their doubles, had created a crack in the logic of the world.

Oh how miraculous and how deranged, the way the seagulls melted and re-formed, dropped out of the sky and into the sea like eggs cracked open into yolks, splooshing into the water.

The lighthouse up close did not soothe, either, how it still crackled with a hard sheen of electric green if you looked close, but why the fuck would you look close—look away, onto the boner beach and destroyer all dead.

Anyone could make a lighthouse anyway. You could just fucking shove a big ol' fatty dead goose on a stick and hoist it up and set it aflame and have a lighthouse. Hey, fucking presto. So, yeah, anyone could make a fucking lighthouse. Anyone could be a light or a bulb, for that matter. Except not anyone could be a flaming fountain of green ooze ejaculating enthusiastically high into the horizon, against a yellow ochre sky. Nor be ever more fucking boring the closer they got to it.

The great wand of the wizard, the huge dick some amateur psych would say one day, the subtext spurting out of the top. What manner of insult given, to make, to keep making all the inanimate objects of the landscape into portions of one's anatomy, and yet Lowry could not help the impulse, even now, on the beach of bones. Because it did not fucking help to think of that thing as a lighthouse now. So boner it be. It helped not at all to remember the original function, the safe harbor by the sea, the way ships could navigate by its light. There was zippo point to retaining some fucking sentimental view of anything in that fucked-up landscape. It was an anthropological nightmare, this festering need to hold on to the foundations of your vision, your prior frame of reference.

Everyone knew it was not a lighthouse anymore. Why not call it Fuckhead or Bastard or Crate of Monkeys or Shitface or the fucking Pillar of Salt or the Damned Yankee or the refrigerator of souls. Mock it. Scream at it. Anything to try to see it clearly. No matter how ridiculous. And maybe to see it clearly meant to stop worrying about the beach of boners death destroyer.

But, mostly, Lowry mourned what they'd lost to the slinky-dinkys. Landry had been such a special, perfect find, complete with more drugs than an emperor who ruled over a thousand pharmacies and now the fucking Village was off-limits and the first thing he was going to cross off his Jack-in-the-Box list . . . he fucking couldn't. Five things, five fucking places, and now he felt thrown off, adrift.

Maybe he wouldn't have to go to all of them. Maybe Old Jim and the money were still holed up at his place and all he'd need to do is go there after this and have a good old-fashioned heart-to-heart and bring Old Jim home and maybe just shove some fucking bill wads down his own pants as insulation before crossing the Border again. Nobody would notice and he'd still be the hero.

Yet maybe in the end, the very fucking end, he was just distracting himself from the destroyer.

The dark shape seemed to breathe in the distant roll of waters. In Lowry's binoculars, the line of the ship's hull was fuzzy, like the edge of a wall coated in moss. But so, too, was the edge of the circle of each binoculars lens, so after a time he put them down on a rock and did not pick them up again.

Sky swore she had seen people out there and Lowry swore she had not. No instrumentality to peer through could resolve that opposition.

The bones, they crunched under Lowry's feet, snapped under the weight, fucking snapped and ground down while the surf rushed up to greet him like a sycophant and made the ivories tinkle and groan like some dainty sick monk ringing the bells to some tiny fucked-up fairy kingdom. But it was fucking bones. Could've been the bones of centuries of shipwrecked sailors, recruited by Area X. That'd had the fucking gall to goddamn accumulate, the sounds all as unexpected as the reliquary itself.

An unruly ossuary, and the skulls, they all cursed and clacked in their way, their unnerving way, the sand washing through their jawbones to make some stupid point. They were piddling small, too, it seemed to him, like he lost some height entering Area X, or like the water shrank them like dicks or the flesh around people's skulls was swaddled in many more inches of fat and epidermis than known and over time human skulls had gotten smaller, but he didn't even know what that meant except he didn't like crushing the bridge of a nose or the side of an orbital or to make the lower jaw of some grinning fool fucking hang loose, except he couldn't help it, there were too many, his boots too heavy, and he was just smashing skulls like gourds now as he followed Sky to a better view of the damned destroyer.

Lowry could not shut off the irrational fucking fear that one of them was actually his skull, that he'd seen the future and the future was bones and his skull lay there too and he'd smashed it in all unknowing. He'd stove in his own future skull. And now it could never be rewound time-wise into a fat head with a brain in it because he'd crushed it almost to powder. Fuck the luck of that sucked.

All while the doomed destroyer lolled and languished like some dead angular beast that had beached itself.


Sky had shown him the video at some point after the winky-dinkys, the slinky-shitties, whatever the scientific term was for creatures so fucked up he couldn't get them out of his fucking mind. The video showed Sky doing things she'd never done, including screaming at her double on top of a dilapidated picnic bench they'd never fucking passed by, because he would have noticed that, because he loved picnic benches, if only because you could really heap a whole smorgasbord on a picnic bench and you could laze out on the plank full length after gluttony.

But he understood why it unnerved Sky, why she'd been unnerved since she'd seen it back at base camp, and why she hadn't shown it to anyone. Because maybe they wouldn't fucking follow her fucking lead if they thought that was going to happen. Because it felt like a documentary from the future showing that Sky went fucking insane or at the very least bifurcated into two separate but equal Skys, and who the fuck would know whom to follow. And that's what it was showing on the vid—that civil war, and maybe the most unnerving thing about it was how their numbers had swelled, so there were more than twenty-four, somewhere south of one hundred, and each couple of frames of video, more fucking people showed up, like Sky had called a block party on an Area X street and let the booze flow and they'd all get higher than high and say the word "fuck" blissful forever and ever.

"I can't stay here and wait for that," Sky said to him, Winters a bit squeamish about the bones and still on the beach. And who could be squeamish by this point. Squeamish was an imaginary, made-up word that needed to be tossed out of the fucking dictionary.

"Are you listening to me, Lowry?" she asked, urgently, and he nodded.

"Yes, I understand. You don't want to be someone else."

"I think that's a premonition. A warning. Maybe this way something different will happen."

Lowry didn't think the footage had been the future, just a fucked-up horror show, a cavalcade of ghosts trying to frighten them with tricks.

And the more he thought about it, two Lowrys could be fucking tremendous, even three Lowrys or four, if the other Lowrys would just listen to him and do what he told them to do. Maybe that was the fucking point Sky was trying to make—that the double wouldn't do what she wanted, might even do the goddamn opposite of what she wanted.

"How do you know I'm not already someone else?" she asked, maybe because he'd been silent, doing the math on how many Lowrys were needed to give them all back scratches and not leave anyone out, while churning grapes to wine so they could make money while scratching each other's backs and how many Lowrys to climb a mountain and have there be a trail of Lowrys the whole way, how many Lowrys to hold hands and form a ring around Area X, even floating Lowrys out at sea . . . and the fear came out of her so fast and somehow loud he forgot about the bones all around and the other Lowrys.

"I started out this exped talking to the original, and you're still the original," he said forcefully. "I know I'm talking to you, only to you. You are you. You *are* you. You are you are you? I mean, you are you."

The look on her face, so doubtful, had confused him, messed him the fuck up.

"I can't stay here and wait for this," she said again, as if she needed the resolve of saying it twice, though it just made Lowry wonder if she might be her own double already.

Her stare toward the destroyer made his guts churn. Her stare toward the fucking dead destroyer like it was the answer, like she'd done some complex fucking equation in her head and come up with an answer he didn't like . . . that was the fucking look she gave the wedge of half-ship.

"You're going to just fade into the gray lands like a fucking wraith? What the fuck, Sky? I gave you a ring. We committed to each other with witnesses." Witnesses that were dead things in jars, dredged up from the bottom of the sea, but that made it somehow more serious to Lowry, like all of natural history, made unnatural by the Southern Reach, had attended, had consecrated whatever giving someone a tiny ring meant. But also flowers.

Shit. Shit shit shit. Shit.

Shit.


There was a boat. A green rowboat. Why did there have to be a fucking boat? Where had a fucking boat even come from? But Sky didn't seem to care about that question and Lowry's boots crunched and crushed bones as he paced the waterline.

The fucking mirage of it, the way it didn't fucking mean anything, couldn't, not now. Sub-fucking-jective. In a fucking word, a fucking trap.

"It's not real, Sky," he said to her as they kept loading provisions into the goddamn boat. "It's an illusion. A magician's been practicing his act on this beach, and I'd give him an F for fuck no."

"Never known what's real and not, Lowry."

"I know what that giant metal potato half-sunken wedge is. It's not real. It's enticement. It plays on your need for control, the need for salvage. But it's just sea wrack. It's just skulls on a beach.

A false fucking horizon as sheets of metal and matted lashed-together lifeboats. Nobody is alive out there. Not a fucking soul. Can't the bones convince you? All these fucking bones—they're real. They mean something. They're telling you not to go. Don't go, Sky. Don't go. You, Winters, you can go, and Godspeed. Why don't you go, check it out, tell us what's over there behind the curtain, over the rainbow, however the fuck you want to view it, down the fucking sunken yellow brick road. Tell us if you see a magic lamppost while you're at it, complete with a fucking centaur or giraffe or whatever the fuck it was."

It felt like more than he'd ever said before in his whole fucking life, and like a lot less.

"He's a complete Section Eight discharge," Winters said to Sky. "But I think you already knew that."

"No, I don't think I knew that."

"I'm right here in front of you both, you assholes."

"There's nothing for us here," Winters said, and by that Lowry took Winters to mean that they were not Winters, nor Sky, but sneaky fucking copies, and maybe when the dead had come back to life as slinky-dinkys, he'd taken his eye off the ball and everyone on this side other than him was also now a slinky-dinky working for the other side. And had eating the fucking living wall saved him? Was that why he'd not been fucked with yet, or just general strength of heroic character?

Or maybe they were the real Sky and Winters, but the fact he'd eaten the wall had made them fucking paranoid about his true self, and whether he was going to go all slinky-dinky on them in the middle of the night.

"And, again, I must raise the issue of the fucking boat. Isn't the fucking boat convenient? Is this not the most convenient fucking boat in the fucking history of boats. Surely you will not trust this stupid fucking boat. Made of stardust and the applesauce apparently pouring out of your skulls where your brains used to be."

"I can vouch for it myself," Winters said.

"What?"

"I found it. This perfectly innocent boat."

"I don't think you did, Winters. I think you're just saying that so you can go visit the destroyer."

Winters shrugged, trying to not laugh, Lowry could tell, and Lowry had no defense against that laugh, that shrug. No fucking way was he going to disarm and safely detonate that shrug or Winters would've been protesting more, trying harder to sell the idea that he'd blown up the dinghy with his own lungs rather than the fucking thing had been burped out from some eldritch coordinates onto this goddamn beach.

"It's seaworthy," Sky said. "It has oars. We have to try. We have to see for ourselves. There's no one here—anywhere. But there might still be someone out there."

"And it's evidence," Winters said. "Even if everybody's dead. It's a clue."

Evidence? Lowry felt a harrowing incredulity.

"It's a clue like my ass hairs are a clue," Lowry said. "It's not a clue. It's not a clue. It's nothing. There's your clue. What's a fucking clue to you if that's a clue? Because it's not a fucking clue!"

"Help me push the boat out, Jamal," Sky said, and Winters went to the left side while she got on the right side.

"Do not do this," Lowry said. "Friends. Lovers. Comrades. What the fuck am I supposed to do?"

Soon enough while Lowry watched, the two fucking fools, one of whom he once more loudly reminded he'd given flowers to and a fucking ring quite recently were shoving off into the water, headed for a fucking deathtrap.

He watched as they receded into that vast indifference, the arc of sky. He almost wished he had followed them. Even when they did not come back.

"I'll just fucking wait here for your return," Lowry said. "Just fucking loiter around for you." Near sobbing, but he thought that was the lack of fucking drugs, not the loneliness, not the fear of being alone. Even though Jack had said he might have to go it alone. What did alone mean, anyway, here? Soon enough, he'd have a ton of fucking friends, and not like a single one of them.

They just kept rowing and Sky didn't look back and the destroyer seemed to dwarf them much more than just moments before. While still the water made the dead bones and skulls sing.

"Oh god, Sky! Don't go! Don't leave me here! Not here! Come back! I'll do better! I'll be better! Please! Please?"

But she didn't. She didn't even turn around despite his pleading, and he knew she wouldn't come back.

He sank to his knees on the bones, the crunch and crack, the glittering mass of them, and he watched Sky and Winters grow distant.

They had become all the same silhouette, as if their bodies were just part of the boat, wreathed in gray and black, with some glint off the waves of the sun around the movement of their oars.

Lowry watched them for a long time, until he could watch no more, as they appeared to perpetually approach, but never reach, the ship. The lighthouse beam that night was like something refracted through the fucking glass that, diluted, still harvested the world. Not a light that would ever reveal Sky to him lost at sea.

The next morning, he couldn't see the fucking boat at all.

By dusk, the green boat had drifted back, empty, run aground on the bones, and he had his answer.

Winters he could give two fucking shits about, but he could not stand the empty sound of the waves against that hull, the hollowness, the way it meant Sky had left whatever places he might now tread. Fuck.

He flicked a tear from his eye, and liked to think that the jars of deep-sea creatures shed a tear with him, bonded by the bond of being in the same place when he had given her the ring. The delicate, little ring that might now be at the bottom of the sea. If she had taken it with her.

Idly, Lowry realized he hadn't seen Scaramutti for two fucking days. Two days and he hadn't fucking noticed the lack of the jabbering psychic. How, if he had to be honest, it was the one good thing about coming to the lighthouse. The silence of the goddamn psychic.

How fucked up was that?

# 3=THE DEAD TOWNS

## NOT ENOUGH FUCKED-UP STUFF IN BARRELS

Lowry cut the stupid fucking control words out of his sleeve—no Bible for him. The stupid-fuck sounds Jack-in-the-Box wanted him to say in front of Old Jim for this turd of a mish within a mish, mood sour. If just Winters had headed destroyer-bound, Lowry would've been fucking fine, and he and Sky could have fucked off into the next place like first-place champions. If not for whatever brain worm decanted into her skull.

There existed in his head a vision of Winters inhaling wrong on his dinghy-breath and being sucked into the valve, as if boneless, though perhaps that's not the way pumps worked, either, and filling out the inside like he'd made a new suit for crossing the Border, only it was a dinghy. And then, in his own damn boat of himself, Winters could have sailed for the destroyer like a fool for ballast.

But now, instead, Lowry felt like dealing with Old Jim in the old-fashioned way the man's name suggested. More satisfying to his fucking point, but also less blowback that way, of taking friendly fire, because he didn't trust Jack one thousand percent, more like seventy-three, so leery of saying weird shit like no reflection in your coffee or bats be birds, ye olde sailor like thee prophecy.

No, it felt not at all modern, what Lowry wanted to do to Old Jim, even if back at Central, the Warlocks and the Phantoms probably played strip poker based on hunches and faint séance breezes against the drapes of open balcony windows, hoping for a fuck-ugly flying wraith to crash-land like a blue-footed booby right into them.

The point was, Lowry would continue the mission on his own terms.

Yet, there was no purchase, and he kept slipping in his mind, and maybe Sky's choice felt like a personal curse or that he jumped too much at his own shadow, but none of the places Jack had told him to check panned out.

In false-daughter Cass's apartment, Lowry found fuck all, not even the goddamn frog terrarium Jack had told him to check. Water damage, some tables and chairs overturned. Some ruin of a moldy fruit in the fridge, now a green fungal geode. Nor Old Jim's place, except the world's biggest, ugliest desk full of nothing and papers strewn everywhere—and then at what Lowry dubbed the Institute for Fucking Barrel Researchers he found fucking goddamn shitty naught as well. Except the surprise of jellied dead bodies stuffed in some of the barrels and bad stuff in others and it was like a fucking prize from hell he searched for, in being diligent, in doing the job. Like some large-scale jelly and jam preserves operation had gone all cannibal cult.

"There's such a bunch of dead guys and poison in here," he said. "I said, there's a bunch of really fucking dead people in fucking cannisters in this place." Shouting now. "Is anyone going to take responsibility? Anyone? Anyone at fucking all?" The reverberation revealing the tinny aftertaste in his own voice.

It made the reality around him more permanent if he talked to himself now, so long as he never fucking replied to himself, fuck, like some fucktoid doubling, some winky-dinky's voice sneaking up on him, maybe even wearing a shitty polo shirt and cargo shorts.

"Just a bunch of dead guys I do not know." Nor what they had done to get shoved into barrels.

He could swear as he stood there longer than he should have in front of the Hall of Barrels that a giggling came from all assembled—the barrels in their smug fucking rows, in that space like a swimming pool had been turned into a shit performing arts center for barrels and their culture. Yet he had to check each one for the money that apparently did not goddamn exist.

Nothing nothing nothing. He was nowhere. He was fucking lost. What could he do now? Continue to Dead Town or go back to the extraction point?

He decided on Dead Town, tried to cultivate a good mood by talking to himself. But also talking to his sisters now, which wasn't a good sign. He finally had a comeback for them, but they were past caring. Mauve and Becka, the giant twins. Who'd never had to deal with their fucking mom. Who always made him do the stupid-ass things. Was it just because he always caved or did she ask him first? He had thought she asked him first, who knew now? As he trudged.

Maybe a shithead followed him from behind, not good at the craft of being quiet and still. Lowry could track the figure over his shoulder all day long. So he knew, he knew, and yet there was some weird comfort in the companionship.

Sometimes, he cried out Landry's name, hoping for drugs, but really, Lowry wanted to cry out Sky's name, except she'd made her decision, chosen half a destroyer over him. Chosen a beach of bones over him.

Lowry didn't know how long it would take to get to Dead Town. A day. A year. If he were a motherfucking compass, he'd never know north again.

**D**ead Town lived up to its name, and Lowry so sick of scenery he tried to fucking ignore the place until he made his objective: City Hall. Yeah, trees. Lots of fucking trees. A meadow. Marsh. The fucking usual. Move on.

The first floor of City Hall felt stripped and the walls had water damage and the stupid fucking wallpaper they'd used, a blue with shells on it, had curdled to beige and faded as fuck vermillion stippled with black mold, and except for two desks that had been bolted to the floor, nothing else. Someone had cleared it as an infernal fucking dance hall, but anyway some other helpful person had left in black paint arrows leading to the stairs, as if anyone in their right mind couldn't find the goddamn stairs in that place, there to the left, hugging the wall like even the stairs distrusted that empty massive space, that hole opened up in the air by taking all the chairs and couches away.

So fuck it and la dee dah, up the stairs it was, and he took them two at a time like a one-man storming unit, loping like a fucking wolf, scurrying like whatever scurrying thing pumped out death from a sharklike firearm that wasn't going to fucking turn into a creature and bury itself in the ground.

Unusual shit didn't bother Lowry now, if it ever had fucking bothered him. On the second floor of City Hall in Dead Town, he found what had to be Jack's "secret room"—behind a disemboweled overturned chair, against the far wall of what he guessed must have been the world's worst fucking tourist center. Area X didn't want him to tarry here, Lowry felt, yet fucking tarry he would, tarry as proper avenging mish wraith. Damn orange-slice lamps hitting him in the face and he bull-china-shopped the place to get to the crack in the wall. The crack that was a door into the "secret" room. Well, it had become less fucking secret over the years since Jack-in-the-Box intel'd it.

Inside, the junk you found in secret fucking rooms. Stuff scrawled on the walls, a devil's pentagram of a bunch of diagrams on the floor and burnt-out pieces of gunk in the middle of each circle. Some fire-glazed glass jars cracked and in pieces. He wasn't about to fucking parse any of that—leave it to the second expedition. There was no off switch in that dreck, which also held signs of recent ransack.

In the far right corner he spied a wide dirty stain like someone had vomited there or the Devil had pissed for an hour and disappeared in a puff of smoke, big fucking surprise, and the far left corner held somebody's clump of dirty laundry. Well, maybe he'd check out the words on the wall first, then. Held his light up to it, everything fucking stuffy, full of damn pieces of lint almost looking like they were tiny filament worms writhing in his headlamp.

No gold. No papers. So the words on the wall better fucking make up for it. Except, it felt like nonsense, the parts he got, the parts he didn't. Like, who the hell was Gloria? Who the hell was this James guy? Commander fucking Thistle? Spawn of the devil scrawled into that circle. Some circle jerk of conspiracy? Long-ago primitive bingo?

Not so the fucked-up names on the wall, in three precise columns. Because it was all the fucking names of the expedition, and was that meant to be some kind of joke?

That some other expedition survivor had gotten here first and written that shit on the wall? That his name was circled along with Hargraves and other now-dead people? Prankster sick of hiding from all the twinky-dinkys and dunky-wunkys? Smacked of whom, of twhut? He couldn't tell, dull thud in his brain of the inevitable knowledge: He knew next to nothing about his fellow expedition members. Had no idea of most of their predilections other than whom they were screwing, maybe what they liked to eat, and some scrumptious details from the secret files.

So who would do that? He didn't know. He didn't even know who still fucking lived, except that he did. The more he looked at the list, and how it lived there among the mold and the lichen (and didn't lichen need sunlight to grow?), the less he liked the list. The fucking less he wanted to look at that list, or see his own name there. Like it was not a roster but an accusation. Like someone had been assigned to track down everybody on the goddamn list.

The occult pan-dimensional pentagram bullshit on the floor still didn't interest him, but for various reasons Lowry turned to the dirty laundry in the left corner. From this middle distance it looked like some kind of slumpity-dumpity body lay within the clothes, all of which kind of fucking resembled a sleeping bag, except it was instead the sleeper.

The uniform bugged him, the remnants of it, covering what he guessed had def been a person wrapped in a blanket, but now all folded over on him or her, or maybe the him-her had gotten folded. Like, somebody shot them in the back and they fell awkward and over time . . .

Could that be a faded "SR" coagulated on what might have been a sleeve? Fleeting shit-take thought: Had there been an expedition prior to the chicken? But no, it might not even be letters but a kind of stylized snake with a registered-nurse symbol.

Fuck that. He hadn't come to Area X to solve ancient crimes, had he? Let some godforsaken commission of the future weigh in on cause of death. So he ransacked the strange pile for whatever he might find and that was basically nothing. The corpse hadn't fallen dead on top of a bunch of money or papers. No, nothing easy on this mish.

But on top of the remains of maybe a jacket, maybe just a fucking bunch of raincoat tatters or who the hell knew, he found a scrap of paper, with words writ fucking large upon it.

# DO NOT EAT.

Do. Not. Eat? Who fucking put "do not eat" on whatever the fuck these remains were? Like a fucking enticement. Do not eat? Yeah, eat. Eat everything. Eat every goddamn morsel of everything. Do not eat. What weak tea fucker from the expedition had gotten here first and written that?

He totally could eat it, especially now that he saw it might be more like sloughed-off skin, deep epidermis, not a jacket at all. In the right light, of which there was little in this gloom dungeon, it might even appeal. Peel. Peel the skin, Lowry. Peel it.

"You mean like eat the fucking body? The fucking dead body of a dead fucking person?"

Then he wished he'd not said it aloud. Because now he knew what lay in front of him. That it was more than "skin." And also it sounded even more batshit than in his head. But also he sounded fucking scared in his voice, but in his mind his voice was powerful and roared out in a non-frightened way, so what was this damn twhut voice that leapt out of him so quick and easy? It was goddamn traitor, this fucking voice. He should reach down into his fucking throat and find this traitor and . . .

A folded-up dead person that had been here for fucking years. Yeah, who the fuck did that. Eat this guy who'd been lying here like some pensioner waiting for a bus that would never come because there was no fucking bus and because the person was already dead.

DO NOT EAT.

But that must mean . . . eat?

Jesus fuck—eat a dead person. He recoiled from that, sat against the wall, wondering what he should do. He hadn't found a shitting thing Jack-in-the-Box had ordered him to bring back. Like he was some fucking barrel boy. And Jack had told him to "do anything—whatever it takes."

A smell came to him then. Or more that he became aware of

a smell that had always been there. It was an amazing smell, like vanilla and lavender but not fru-fucking-fru cloyfucking. No, wait, it was a savory smell, like chicken in a pot of spices, the simmering scent of that, rising from the stove, curling into the living room on a cold fall day. A taste-bud-tingling smell . . . coming from the dead-skin husk fucking cast-off wax-dribbling figure fucker hidden inside that improbable possible jacket. Secret, self-contained, solitary as an oyster.

Shit. It smelled so good and nary a fucking small woodland creature he'd manage to bag, even since free of the Southern Reach's fucked-up policy on the matter. A good broth on a winter's day. The way the broth would bubble with those golden bubbles, each one on the surface breaking open to add to a salivating scent.

If the pile smelled that good . . . maybe it would *taste* fucking great, too, and any texture infirmities just the price to be fucking paid for, finally, getting a good meal in this hovel, this shithole, this bed-and-breakfast from hell he would not be fucking recommending to anyone.

His mouth watered and he teared up. Oh, it was such a fucking succulent smell, it would have to be a taste of manna. It would taste like moist chicken breast or slow-marinated pork, where the meat just fell off the bone. It could be the chicken from the first-first expedition, Whitby's chicken, and he would still eat the fuck out of it. Yes, just think of it as a fowl. A fattened fowl could be a lighthouse *and* a delicious gorge. Don't be disgruntled or discouraged by what it looked like—if a thing camouflaged itself, that was nothing to do with him.

He reached his hand out and touched the remembered accordion flubber-sweat of the foot part, the tangled shank-of-leg part . . . and found that now it had the perfect crispy texture of the skin on a perfectly cooked turkey. That golden glazed magnificence that made it crinkle and crackle, releasing more of that deliciously fucking warm aroma.

It brought back memories from the farmhouse as a kid, the

truce and peace, sometimes, of holiday dinner, with a chicken, goose, or, yes, turkey, and his sisters so ravenous they put down the verbal boxing gloves and abandoned his prone insult-punched body out in the field to run back into the house to bask in the steam rising off the sacred bird.

Oh, how could Lowry fucking resist? Slowly, still sitting against the wall, he pulled the husk toward him, foot first, until the delicate wafer-thin heel lay clenched in his hand like a fucking unique communion. The heel smelled like the best spices on the best meat in the world, and he didn't bother fucking much about what kind of meat.

The texture, though, felt to his touch almost as bad as when in the shower he'd backed into an ex-girlfriend, butt to butt, and he'd recoiled like her butt was an alien or his was and it was just wrong, that was so fucking wrong, that two butts should touch.

So maybe this would be wrong, too.

Yet, it was with only a little hesitation that he tore a piece of foot husk off with his teeth, contemplated a taste that lit up his buds so fucking hard he almost got an erection. How could he taste a whole feast in one bite? One fucking bite and he was raptured and in heaven, for the texture changed in his mouth and under the crispy crumbling of the skin there came a cooked-through sensation as of pork fat nibbled off the bone and under that some sort of thin layer that brought him back to the chicken—a brined and butter-slathered chicken.

But also gathered around like friends at a holy last dinner with no fucking Judas to betray Lowry, all the other dishes as aftertaste, a Christmas miracle: a great joint of meat, suckling pigs, long wreaths of sausages, plum puddings, barrels of oysters, cherry-cheeked apples, juicy oranges, corn bread stuffing, the fucking cranberry sauce, the fucking green bean casserole, the fucking mashed potatoes, the seething bowls of punch, and, after, the pies for dessert and the eggnog.

Despite this vision, he did not feel full despite all of this satisfying heaviness invading his fine, flat belly. With each bite, Lowry felt hungrier still, so that he could not get enough. Bay leaves and wine for a stew with the remains later, if only he could find fucking bay leaves and wine. And was that wrong, the more he tasted, and the meal more like fondue? Dipper or dippie?

He devoured the first leg then thought better of his gluttony but then fucking hungry again, still with one eye on the cursed watermark, Lowry pulled the other fucking leg to him and that too soon gone until he had no fucking choice but to kneel over the rest of the remains and shove handfuls of collapsed pelvis and torso husk into his mouth—to unpile that fucking delicious feast such that he could eat the goddamn thing down to the last bite, the torso soon just some chest, and with some difficulty Lowry pulled the neck and head out from underneath.

He had known on some level that this fucking moment of truth awaited him. Could he who hated the head of a fucking fish included with his dinner stomach eating . . . a fucking face.

But Lowry had not expected that he would recognize the fucking face.

Whitby Allen's face.

Fuck fuck fuck fuck fuck fuck fuck.

He shoved the head and neck away from him, jammed himself into a sitting position up against the wall again. But as he watched, Whitby's face ballooned to the top of the neck and torso because Lowry hadn't fucking put it all back properly. Whitby's face sat there staring at him, accusing him when he'd done nothing fucking wrong. He hadn't killed Whitby and eaten him. He'd just come across some human remains and eaten them because they smelled so fucking good, and who could blame a man for that given how much of a remnant the expedition was and oh shit oh shit was he going insane? Was this what it felt like? No, it was entirely rational, his decision.

Oh shit oh shit, it was not. Yes, it was. No, it was not. Yes it was no it was not yes it was no it was not yes it fucking was.

"I'm sorry, Whitby," Lowry said to the husk. "I'm so fucking sorry, friend." But was he Lowry's friend? "I didn't mean it. I mean, I meant it at the time but I wouldn't have done it if I'd known it was you. I mean, I probably would have done it if I knew it was you, but maybe not. Hard to tell. But it's done now. It's done now, Whitby."

Fuck fuck fuck fuck. Fuck?

Whitby Fucking Allen.

Except. Well, except . . . Whitby Fucking Allen was an also-ran back at the good old SR building, probably having a confab with a bunch of deep-sea fish in jars right about fucking now.

Not out here. Not on the expedition . . . So reason told Lowry that this couldn't be Whitby. Which meant it must be some kind of motherfucking illusion cast by some twhut offstage, some-body who deserved a goddamn smack for whatever the point of this was. To test or trick them even after deployment? To trap them into passive fucking cannibalism?

With no punch line other than that he'd already eaten so much of Whitby that what did a fucking face matter? In some cultures Lowry imagined eating a local animal's face was a fuck-ing delicacy, and once again, anyway, he felt empty, empty, empty, and all that could fill him was not-Whitby's stupid not-face. All that could satisfy.

It wasn't Whitby. It couldn't be Whitby. So it was fucking fine.

"What would Whitby do?" he asked aloud, and hated the echo of "woodity woodity doo doo."

"Well," he replied because no one else could, "Whitby would eat Whitby's face." Itchby wheat hitchbie ace.

As he said it, he knew it was fucking true. The weird white pretzel would eat his own face. In the name of science. Yes, he would. In memory of the chicken.

"Wouldn't you, you sick fuck, Whitby." Not Whitby. Some-one else. Something else. And hadn't he already taken a bite out of a wall?

So Lowry took Whitby's face with both hands and he crunched down on the fallen-in nose part, which tasted in a satisfying way like marrow and gristle, and he used that inverted promontory to get enough of a grip with his teeth to tear the rest and eat it strip by delicious strip, the neck perhaps the most fucking fragile and delicate, and with its own form of gustatory bliss.

Then, when not a scrap was left, Lowry sighed, burped, and returned, sleepy, to the wall. It had been the best meal he had ever had, even though he didn't think he "knew" anymore after the devouring than fucking before. If anything, Lowry felt he understood less and less.

But at least he felt full. Finally fucking full.

## TYRANT TO KING'S DREAD

Up on the messed-up roof, Lowry paused to think about his next move, to digest, to take in the view back toward the sea. Felt like he stood astride an old fort, a fucking alien installation. What was with these fake crenellations and the ghastly fucking barren stucco, the years of seepage and intrusion, how for a very long goddamn time there had been no fucking body to see the view, to know what had happened just below. Not that he'd been expecting an infernal tour guide, because who knew if that was original or double or triple in this stupid place.

Lowry could see far into the estuary, into the golden light and the scattering of palm trees, gnarled swamp oaks, and, beyond, the coast.

Tiny, but the fucking lighthouse still blared out, flared green in waves, and the marshes seemed light-fucked by the green tendril molecules reaching out like the fake fucking animation of a bad fantasy flick. As if Area X tonight chose not to let him believe it was real but only some acetate overlay, about to burn from the heat seek of his regard. Some fucking onion skin, almost not there, and yet so powerfully there he felt some fear for a second.

This was bullshit. He'd never find gold bars or money or whatever the fuck Jack thought Old Jim had been sitting on, incubating, whatever. Nor even find Old Jim. And Area X would do what it wanted to do and it might take a hundred years, Lowry saw now, to learn all its stupid fucking complex behaviors, cultures, its needs and wants, no matter how slowly expressed or fucking perverse.

He had just eaten a fake Whitby Allen's body molt and was not in the mood for more motherfucking magic tricks.

There were two tired folding chairs drenched in old spattered blood—like, blood that had been poured in unending quantities and spilled all over the floor. Did he even care? No, he fucking did not. Whatever he might've cared about had fucked off in a boat.

What he'd thought might just be loose planks had revealed itself as the splatted remains of a piano come apart in a pile on the roof. Next to a corner so perpetually flooded and yet not fallen in (but one glorious damn day) that tiny fish lived there, amid the algae, and spinning insects. That world had a border too and he could stamp through those waters like a fucking demon or god if he wanted to. But he felt merciful because so shaken, and he held the fuck back, did not do the bad thing. Time and gravity would do it for him and the little fish would pour down to the third-story floor and have to fucking hope it also had become a porous reservoir.

Then it was true dusk, sudden, brutal, and the lighthouse burnt unbearably bright, so that the green light bled in wisps of coronary, in fingers beckoning, until he thought it might all be a disinformation of his eyes, like the black spots, and the landscape lay fucking inert and black and barren, but only his eyes blazed, his vision turned inward, his eyeballs just a miniature planetary playground for the fucking animating impulse behind Area X.

Winters had the bad fortune to intervene then, to appear then, like a fucking jack-in-the-box, but not Jack-in-the-Box, out of the stairwell, as if an apparition conjured by a fatal lack of fucking caring. Because Lowry had thought him dinghy-banished, explicitly wished not to fucking see him, he had popped up. A warning to Lowry to take better damn care to banish by fixation on, in this case, Winters from his life.

"I got free of that destroyer stuff," Winters said.

"Uh-huh."

"Yeah, really. Dead end, just like you said."

"To you?"

He wanted to say, "And Sky?" But knew that was just a trap, that Area X wanted to punish him for eating the molt, or wanted whatever the molt had been, but how did he know what Area X wanted or didn't want?

"Yeah, you said that to me, Lowry," Winters said, even though Lowry knew his "To you?" had been am-fucking-biguous.

"You followed me here?"

Winters smiled long and hard and sharp. "Oh, I've been here a long time, I didn't have to follow you."

Lowry nodded at the truth of that. Who really had to follow anyone in Area X. You just poked a hole in the map and there you were.

"You've got scales turning into eyes all over your body, Lowry."

"So I do, Winters. So I fucking do. Thanks for pointing that out, even though I don't think you were supposed to tell me that. Very kind of you."

Maybe that's why he felt heavy yet light, like he was both opening up and closing down. Yet it seemed unimportant, impotent, fucking stupid, as if the king below and his alligator had no import and their inane convo had some kind of weight it should never have fucking had. Did not have. Because he was seeing Whitby astride a giant greenish-white alligator down below, just walking by as casually as a fucking tourist procession, and he knew that wasn't fucking true. That was not fucking true.

"Did you see what's down below?" Lowry asked, pointing over the edge through a gap in the faux fortifications.

"What is it?" Winters asked, looking down and having located something weird, or pretended to, Lowry guessed.

Lowry shoved him over the edge—feather weight, anvil fall—and he landed with all too much fucking sound. Be fucking still. Be fucking still. Be silent. Rest.

Winters had not been real. Any more than Whitby. Than Lowry felt.

Funny, how Winters looked more like Formsby, or was it Fussell, lying there all broken. But even that—how he'd broken so easily and lay there not moving—felt like provocation. Felt like if he hadn't been Winters, then he hadn't been Formsby or Fussell, either. That Lowry had been right to push him, and maybe the mercy that he hadn't winky-dinkyed him instead. Rest in pieces. Return unto Area X from whence you fucking came. Yeah, that was it. RIP. Rip rip rip.

His hands shook as he watched the fucking pyrotechnics out in the marsh for a while, which might just be in his eyes. The stars came into focus, went out of focus. They oppressed Lowry, dug into his head; he was watching them too hard or they were communicating too much, seeking something. He felt something rising up he could not identify or control, but that clutched at the heart of him. A sadness or an underlying terror that could only be satiated by additional excess, until even that thrill faded and something more extreme beckoned.

Maybe he would still do as Jack had asked. Maybe he should

fuck off to the Village Bar now. Maybe this was where all this had been heading.

Man, did he miss Landry. There had been a pen pal for life. A conversation partner. A good fix. A bad fix.

It was all the same.

## HOARSE TONGUES

It fucking was and fucking wasn't Whitby who now like a horse's tongue slapped atop a butcher's block—a meaty, fleshy tongue, was slapping atop his head, carcass caress descending into that place now porous between gray matter and skull, as if a rough and continual licking had occurred like when he woke after a night of debauchery on someone's lawn with a cat licking his face, but one lick only, and the weight of it just fucking lay there, made him stumble, catch himself, adjust. Slopped and stopped, then disintegrated into his brain like the surface of his brain was full of holes and the thing that was Whitby yet not turned from fat tongue to thin soup stock, had drained right into his mind. Colander, liquid, and maybe it would pass through and he would be undamaged.

Except, it changed again so it was a hundred fingers in a bowling ball that had a hundred holes and he was with his giant sisters in the local alley with a skating rink and the smell of loaner bowling shoes and rancid figure skates and the one telling him to hurry up and the other just shrugging with her huge soft drink and making sounds with the straw, the ice, the dregs as he tried to line up the pins, except he'd never line them up. Gutter balls for a solid century.

A tongue like a pile of meat, like a carcass, a flesh carcass tossed atop a butcher's block and the weight made him repetitious, a weight his mind could not shake off, dislodge, that began, slowly, to dissolve into his brain, so he began to understand what he felt as a tongue was another brain lying atop his own as if both had been decanted from their skulls and tossed on a pile, and still able to feel the odd sensation of that, numb, but not the pain. Not the glistening blood agony of that, the snail track of red pleading out.

Imperfect, the meal to the appetite, or why would he feel anything at all? Why wouldn't it be seamless? Though where this thought came from he did not know. As if he were the meal now and someone gorging on him. As if Whitby's face had disagreed with him, and as he breathed now, a sparkle of golden dust pressed out of him and forayed out from the pores, so that he was expressing the molt, releasing it as it released him, so that he became a kind of vessel, but also a candle and a flame.

While the idea of mind dissipated until there was only the lagoon of clear blue water that was his mind, haloed with reeds, and Whitby's presence a school of golden fish at the core that multiplied and spread out in ever vaster circles, to every corner of him and each particle, each fish, strove to join itself by filament to every other fish floating inside the vessel that was Lowry, and within each new connection he could see the world more like Whitby, or this hybrid thing that had taken on the appearance of Whitby, that had been Whitby for a time, but also had a reptilian eye, a carious eye staring at him from the bottom of the lagoon, through the golden fish and fuck and fuck but resisting meant not seeing it not feeling it for what it really was but his mind pulling up these constructs so he wouldn't go mad. He'd come this fucking far and had far still to fucking go, but he wanted to make it out in a raw, animalistic way, no matter what had overtaken him and was still overtaking him.

The way it had patience. The way it had depth, and how it hid when it had to, came out when it must, the measure of what it had to do, the way it had to do it, and the future it came from. How it came from so far away in time and suddenly Lowry was

there
    air
        was air
            was water.

For water lived there and everything was water and nothing was water. How as it weighed upon Lowry, a presence had weighed upon it, gauged it, and thus it must be disguised, must be water, must be death, be dead, inert. He'd come chasing down something, had gone wrong but right and now existed out there again, waiting for a time to wake, was asleep except now forever in a corner of Lowry's mind.

Across that haunted landscape Lowry strode and he did fucking appreciate how it changed and kept changing, but not how the fucking rabbits kept appearing and winking out, so he knew they were just in his brain, but he could not stop them from being like malfunctioning toasters or strings of Christmas lights, except they were nothing like that at all, but lunging and snapping at him, only to fade the fuck away into golden dust.

While he grasped at the dust as it left him, as if he were a fucking stuffed teddy bear and the dust his stuffing and when the fucking stuffing left him, he was done. That was it, Lowry was over as a reality and a fucking concept.

Whitby Not, the Changeling, this rogue becoming restless within him and wanting out. Wanting to leave Lowry, although Lowry wasn't ready for that somehow, to be without the Changeling, despite the terror, despite the way he sweat dust as he sweat sweat, so he was disgustingly wet and dry at the same fucking time, and the dust spiraled out of him like he was a human fucking crop duster, earthbound scarecrow, still walking out among the fields to contaminate them.

The fucking enormity, the puzzle of it, as if a Changeling molt told him things sideways, even as the dust still left him and the ghost rabbits bit and clawed and fell away, and fucking all of his remaining eye senses and sound senses keeping to the fucking trail through reeds and through limestone terrain, keeping his compass only by the radiating blade of the lighthouse beam, so ever and always the only destination he could have was the lighthouse or he'd never make it. No instinct within him that could compensate for all his senses overlaid and overloaded this way.

How Whitby came from the future but inhabited the past, and the one he'd met at the Southern Reach innocent of either, still peering out at him from the catheteria corner talking to him of blatherTOT and chickenauts, but the molt-owner lay out in the swamps, the marshes, whatever the fuck you called that blue lagoon and he'd stay that way for centuries. That was the thing that almost broke Lowry's brain in the overlay—that this Whitby Not was going to resurrect himself into a future that did not include him, fully repaired from some catastrophic systems failure, and hoped the future he came back into was the one he'd saved . . . from the rabbits? Lowry couldn't grok it to save his life, the way the Changeling's brain and his brain meshed like two different kinds of nets cast out on water that interfered with each other.

So he had to just grit it out, thought fuck of the drug experiences, of Landry, and of what, fuck, Landry's advice would be, and that would be: Riiiiiide it out. Landry would also probably tell him to just lie down for a while, but Lowry felt a powerful fucking urge to put Dead Town behind him and so he kept stumble-walking through the visions in his brain.

A halo of gold surrounding the clearest blue. Out there in what could be a thousand places and not wake for centuries. No winky-dinky could compete with that. An astronaut who had never left Earth, fighting an enemy toward entropy. The glimpses of an army and a cleft between two mountains under what had been the ocean, the way all of the earth and the sky and the water had become a refuge for those who were left. How they had, willingly, willing to change, slopped their way into a different way of being, like seagulls yolking into the waves.

And it became fucking clear to Lowry, or maybe not clear but distinct, like some goal on the horizon that he might or might not be able to describe to Sky if he ever saw her again, like a goal in physical form, an objective, a fucking freak objective, that what they called Area X wanted the past, too, and that was what freaked Lowry out so much he almost pissed himself: The casual way the Changeling's molt told him that the world was gone already. That it might last a few more decades, but it was fucking toast, or most of it. That the fucking thing they fought in here, the way it had no central nervous system, no fucking sorcerer who came out from behind the curtain so Lowry could shoot him in the fucking eyeball . . . that this . . . thing wanted the past, too, in an automatic, thoughtless way. So that there could be no future but its future, no ability to adapt.

He could see even as it faded out of him with the dust, like he was a broken hourglass, so no point in turning him over, how Central had meddled in the business of the Forgotten Coast and how Area X had homed in on that first occurrence, that first appearance of its enemy, and attempted a beachhead there by redirecting what the Southern Reach itself sent through the Border at some point in the nearish future that Lowry had not yet experienced, but maybe he could stop it, except that the Changeling wasn't trying to stop Area X but to just make sure everything happened as it had already happened.

That the Area X Lowry had fucking experienced was the best possible outcome. That Area X would never not happen. There was no off switch, there was no other time in which it faded away or was not activated. But if it colonized the past, then everything would get worse, worse, worse.

With the rabbits now came glimpses of the earth the Changeling came from, the colossus of ghosts of the alien that manifested, in time, after Area X had expanded. The relics of civilizations from wherever Area X had come from, manifesting, glimmering like a mirage, like poems never completed, but it wasn't fucking real. It couldn't be real. This future overlaid upon the marshes.

Neither circular nor square, but in some pattern or geometry that hurt his brain or made his gaze fucking slide away—he could not look at them directly, like he was a wood plank going through a buzz saw when he tried, and through an open door as the saw split him in half came the unbearable light of the sun and as he tried to see past the sun he was being torn apart even if there was no pain but just the crackle and wince of the bleeding light.

These fantastical visions he could not quite credit, that he distrusted, as if they were the residue of drugs he had taken, was still taking, how there came across the face of the Earth such change, such decay and stillness and absorption that how could the violence of that, well beyond Lowry's own fucking capacity for violence, the sheer negation of human life, not be understood as an extinction event. No matter who lived now in the water, no matter how Whitby Not had risen from that time and come back into Area X, that all might remain the same . . . so that Area X might be as it was now, that he might be as he was now . . . how that felt like the most cracked, fucked-up thing. That if granted the wish of any other fucking reality . . . it would be worse . . . than there.

There would be no space for any human soul as the world spun farther off its rotation in the sense of the seasons, the terrain changing as Area X transformed it, and there was so much more spinning out of him with the golden dust and dissipating into the night that made him sad. How the details could not live with him long enough, that he could not see his place in this, that in a way he'd never felt from the real Whitby, some ghost of an influence in his head, some wraith of a cosmonaut stared out hostile at him and did not wish him to survive this, to know these things, and perhaps he would know none of them again when all the dust was gone, but also now he panicked that he would never be the same and began to run toward the lighthouse as if the lighthouse could save him, but really what he hoped is that he would find Sky there, and, yes, even Winters, and that he could explain this all to them before it left him. Because it was leaving him at an ever more fucking rapid rate.

Then, maybe, he would be a real hero. Maybe then he would be a fucking god.

Lowry became himself again in front of the lighthouse in darkness lit by the sliver of a moon that should not shine so bright, the destroyer still there on the horizon, but no tinkling, pleasant sound of waves over bones.

Above, the stars no longer shone but scattered across the sky— like creatures scuttling along the convex surface of a massive planetarium. He'd run out of drugs. He'd run out of molt. He'd run out of f f f f again. The golden dust had left him entirely and he felt flat, unapproachable. The things that energized him disgusted him. Whitby had done that to him, or Whitby's clone, and it was beyond his understanding. He kept close vague memories, said nothing he'd learned aloud, for fear it would escape like the dust into the air and be lost to him.

The lighthouse lay dull and dark, like the night after a rave. No green light—just the lighthouse from mission briefings, but with fortifications now, facing the sea. He did not know how much time had passed. He never knew, now, how much time had passed. The idea of time seemed too ponderous an idea, that it should exist at all, or he had become a ghost and existed on the other side of some invisible barrier.

Spilling out from the mouth of the lighthouse, he could see bodies, the lighthouse clogged with them. Hundreds of bodies, an ever-flowing river of bodies, and as he drew near he could see that they were, every last one of them, the reoccurring body of Henry from the S&SB, dressed in black, that oval, pale face unmistakable, even in a final sleep.

Such a torrent of dead Henrys that they led out to the beach and somehow he knew that if he waited until morning, these bodies would once more turn into a beach of bones and there would not be a trace of them on the lighthouse steps.

But Lowry was headed elsewhere, would not pine for Sky on that beach, give neither lighthouse nor destroyer the satisfaction.

His fucks would return, his self would return, he knew, if he just kept going, to the end.

## VILLAGE DUMP

The Village was a dump. Pure fucking dump, and Lowry had come down from both the spirit-world highlights of eating Whitby creature's molt and the dregs of Landry's drugs. So, low on fucks but also drained like the golden dust had also been, in part, his blood. Pure and utter dump. Not a vacay or top-ops spot. The wind-wracked landscape shoved low to the ground in places between the relics of huts and stone, the sun a howling red halo pierced by the spikes of reeds—and, best of all, redeeming, even, no sign of the freaky-deakys, the permeable people, the winky-dinkys.

And everywhere, on every wall, as if to test Lowry's patience in another way, the graffiti tag of TOT. Here, there, any god-damn where. TOT. Everywhere a TOT TOT TOT TOT TOT TOT Tot tot tot? TOT fucking TOT and Whitby, the real Whitby, back at Central, had warned him about TOT, but what in the flying fuck did TOT mean? TOT TOT TOT fucking TOT. It was going to drive him fucking nuts fucking TOT. Fuckling TOT, and the only satisfaction was that his pilot light had come back and the molting, the urge to eat the molt, the utter ravenous desire to shove all of it into his mouth, had become an ancient-mariner memory from fucking centuries back.

Nor did he feel sediment or sentiment passing by the messages for loved ones on the wall outside the Village Bar. This community bulletin board for all who had disappeared, including those who had left the messages. It had no import, no power, felt obscene—obscenity—so late now, so fucking behind where the times had left them. So he tore them down before he went inside. This sentimentality. This misunderstanding of the truth of their situation. It enraged him or felt like an affront—but to whom? So he tore them all off the wall, he lit into those messages like they were the enemy, and down they came until the path leading to the Village Bar was strewn with the trash of that, and the balled-up negation of that, and he might be weeping but fuck those tears. It wasn't what his brain was receiving but what his body had endured to that point. *"Lost son, Burke, call if seen." "Saul, if you see this, I'm in Bleakersville. I'm safe." "Taking in who I can down the street at 620."* No no no.

Then Lowry had crept inside, shut the door behind him as if it were the door to an airlock and outside lay the unforgiving vacuum of space, as he breathed heavy and deep of the safe air inside. Even if the roof hung low across the far right corner, over a shitty little stage, and the counter itself had been ripped and defiled, flanked by fallen-over stools and on the wall behind the bar the off-kilter dozens of frames of mostly motley fucked-up-looking men, like a tribute to drowned sailors who had been bad at their jobs.

And what was he looking for, in this place where the fatal fucking fool known as Old Jim had lived part of his life, explained his face to strangers, been acting a role? And now here was Lowry, just trying to get by plundering his files, his stolen gold that appeared to live nowhere in the whole fucking universe that was Area X. There, lost in the middle of an alien catastrophe, and yet still Lowry cared, still Lowry hoped to return to the normal, ordinary world, a rich man. That, he had decided.

No dead here, just overturned tables and chairs, a half-crushed piano in the middle left corner, facing the door, and no one on the bench. It was a place to start, a place to look, Old Jim's piano, and something spilling out of the crushed and broken left side, in envelopes. So that he crept through the debris to that breach, to fucking investigate, hopeful he might find what he needed, what Jack wanted.

He knelt in front of the vast flow of letters, more than he could have guessed from the door, and they did not have the look of wealth, the look of money. He opened first one and then another, noting the music sheets from *Winter Journey* on the stand and the blood on the keys.

But they were all letters to Cass, and which "Cass" was that, but from the dates Lowry knew it must be the fucking prehistoric one—before Old Jim had come to the Forgotten Coast for his brief sojourn, and no help to Lowry, though he opened more and more, in hopes that this had been the way Old Jim hid Jack's money, amid the terrible fucking pathetic wreckage of his non-life, his pathetic antilife, this spook of a spy who had caused so much trouble in the end for Jack that here he was, mighty fucking Lowry, on his hands and knees, tearing through pages that pleaded, that raged, that seemed to contain every emotion and every variation of syntax and speech from formal and fluid to informal and rigid, and yet all of it no more intelligible to Lowry than TOT TOT TOT TOT TOT. Taught. Taut.

Fuck it. He tossed letters away from himself, chucked them away from himself, threw them across the room, still felt awash in them, drowning in them, and what the fuck did he care what happened to them now.

Except, unexpectedly, Karen Hargraves stood there, in the doorway, staring at him, and his startlement gave way to relief gave way to something like wariness and even a little spike of fear.

"Hargraves," he called out, too loud, like she stood on the other side of a canyon. "You're alive."

She moved not at all, but stood rigid, alert, watching him, while he suppressed the instinct to step closer. Something told him not to.

But, finally, she gave him a smile, if grim, and she came a few steps farther into the bar, closing the door behind her. Lowry missed the light that disappeared, that she seemed to eclipse.

"So you made it, Lowry," she said, but something in her tone did not reassure, and he kept one hand on his rifle. In case she winky-dinkyed or walkie-talkied, or slick-tongued over his brain.

"The others make it?" Lowry meant the side expedition that Sky had sent to the Village.

"No, Lowry. They did not." Said like she was closing another door.

"That's a shame," he said. "That's a damn shame." Although, did he care? At all? He couldn't be sure.

"How'd you survive?" she asked, although Lowry frowned, thinking he should be asking her that fucking question. Like, she was doubting that he *had* survived, though he stood in front of her.

"The usual way," Lowry said. Unusual ways.

"I survived because it turns out I don't work *out there*. I'm part tragedy out there. But this place, here I do well . . ."

"I'll take your word for it," Lowry said, diplomatically. "You like this place?" He had a genuine fucking curiosity, which surprised him.

"I do."

"You'd rather be here and dead than out there and alive?"

Lowry didn't know if he meant her or, in that moment, himself, but Hargraves said, "I don't think that's the choice. Not anymore."

"It's been hard for you," Lowry said, trying to sound sympathetic.

Hargraves laughed. "Hard. Well, yeah, no one knew it would be like this, did they? Walk in the park, you said. Although you also said 'titty' and 'glory hole' a lot, Lowry, so maybe we shouldn't have listened to you so much. What do you think?"

Lowry thought he didn't like that, the memory on that, the memory it took to fixate on such trivia, but she was already busy wrong-footing him again.

"Going through Jim's letters to his daughter, I see," Hargraves said. "Rooting through them. Like a rat."

He ignored the insult. "Did he really have a daughter?" he asked, only because he didn't know what the fuck else to say.

Hargraves ignored him. "There's nothing in the letters that will help you. No 'off switch,' no intel, so you might decide to put them down and leave them be. You might even decide to clean up your mess and put them all back in the piano."

Lowry realized that his hand that did not hold the rifle still held letters, and he didn't know how long Hargraves had stood there, watching him ball them up and rip them up and otherwise try to destroy them. He dropped the ones he held as quickly as if they'd burst into flames.

"So, you know about Old Jim," Lowry said. "Do you happen to know where he is now?"

He noticed that Hargraves had a wicked-looking handgun in addition to a first-rate sniper's rifle, and that the handgun had appeared in her right hand at some point while they talked, and she'd somehow affixed a silencer to it, very fast. And that this fact confused him in a fundamental way.

"I do happen to know where he is now," Hargraves said, but did not elaborate.

"Well, where is he?" Lowry asked.

"I've been here long enough to figure out Jim, Lowry. To figure out lots of things." And there was a flame burning in her eyes now that he also didn't understand.

"So brief me," Lowry said, trying to sound casual and yet they both stood there rigid at twenty feet, like they were about to draw down on each other, whether Old West or old-fashioned duel he had no fucking idea, except it seemed like a sad waste in either direction, should it come down to it. He didn't want to kill her, but he'd proven recently he could.

"Pretty clear what happened," Hargraves said. "He was sitting at the piano and Area X was changing him and at some point I think he went outside to that little bridge—you know it? Of course you don't, but I do—and he was in agony by that point, Lowry. He was injured and his nerves were shot and he was probably hallucinating because the Border was about to come down, and he was afraid. He was so afraid and so alone and I wasn't there for him and neither were you, you stupid fuck."

"Hey, Hargraves, maybe you could—"

He'd wanted her to turn down the aggro, but she was already barreling through him, interrupting.

"He'd lost a hand, and, from the evidence, the other was eating him, slowly. And he sat down on the bridge, waiting for the dawn. And then he died. He died alone on the bridge, waiting for help. And, eventually, I came along and I found him—or, I found the husk that Area X had left of him."

"Is that right, Hargraves," he said, wondering if he could reach for his gun before she got a shot off. Wondering how the fuck she was scaring the shit out of him.

"Yes, that's right, Lowry." And now he could tell she was mocking him and the moment felt even more wrong.

"Maybe he's still kind of alive, then, if he left a husk," Lowry said. "Maybe you could just show me the—"

"Shut up."

When he'd imagined a reunion with another exped member, other than a false one thrown off the roof for good reason, it hadn't felt like this, hadn't been like this. He'd instead confided all he'd learned—all the wisdom, all the knowledge he'd retained from Whitby Not's molt, and what it meant, and, yes, the urgency of that warned him off speaking somehow, because he felt he'd stepped into some other scenario, one he had less control of, and so he blurted out an instinctual question he'd hoarded since he couldn't access her files back at the Southern Reach.

"Who the fuck are you, Hargraves? Who are you, really?"

Was she Jack's third? And, if so, what was her mission and did it affect Lowry, and he thought it did, it must, the stance she took, the way she regarded him.

The way she took her time replying, like she was lining up a target.

"Who am I, Lowry? Great question. I'm Old Jim's daughter. Not his real daughter, although his real daughter was nothing to write home about. He was better off with me."

The False Daughter Project. She must be lying. He didn't know how to take it, like she'd introduced some element far more alien than anything he had experienced in Area X, so she must be lying.

"Look," Lowry said, hoping to take back some kind of control, "why don't you come to the extraction point with me. And we can sort this all out back at the Southern Reach."

She laughed at that, a disrespectful sound. "Extraction point? You mean crawl back through the tunnel? Even though there's no expedition anymore? And no suits?"

"It's time to go home," Lowry said, thinking he sounded ultra-fucking-reasonable. Though he didn't really think it was time to go home, just wanted Hargraves's hand a little farther away from her gun.

"In time, maybe I will come home, except not through the front door," she said. "But you'll never know when or how. Maybe I'll disappear, poof, like Jim's real daughter for a while. He might appreciate the poetry of that, you know. He might. From wherever or whenever he's watching now." And he could hear the weight of that—the tremor of emotion in her voice, like she'd just come from a wake, and he guessed she had. She actually had.

"Come on," Lowry said, and taking a chance, "I'm Jack's failsafe. I'm the one embedded with the expedition to take over if anything went wrong. And I say we head for the extraction point."

She hesitated, but Lowry understood somehow that he couldn't know what the fuck she was hesitating about—that it might have nothing to do with his question.

"I knew Jim well. I know Jack," she said, finally, there, as they stood in the wreckage of the Village Bar, and a new anger burgeoned in her that alarmed him. "You're not the fail-safe. You're the jackass who takes the attention off the fail-safe. Threes, Lowry. Jack always works in threes. But I'm done being that. I never really was that, because some of us at Central actually believe in the future. And you know what I'm going to do if I make it back? I'm going to wipe the whole slate clean, one way or the other. I'm going to be the one who cleans house. I'll be the one, starting with you."

Maybe the way she said things mesmerized him or he was tired or got careless or just still underestimated her, but Hargraves had her gun trained on him, shot to the chest, and no way could he now raise his rifle in time.

"You're making a mistake," he said, like he was in a movie of his life, not his actual fucking life. "Put the gun down. I have so much to tell you. I have seen so much."

"No, I don't think so. Because you know what I found in Jim's pockets, along with a few diagrams of an alligator in a secret room? The impossible thing?"

"Fuck, I don't know, Hargraves. Put the gun down."

"A piece of paper."

"A piece of paper?"

"And do you know what he had written on it?"

"Drink more milk? Eat more fucking vegetables?"

"Kill Lowry. It read 'Kill Lowry.' And I've been asking myself how he could even have known your name. What happened after I left that he could have known your name. Who gave it to him, why it was important. But, on some level, I've decided it doesn't matter. I don't think it matters why. What do you think, Lowry?"

"I think you should take a breath, Hargraves. Cass. I think you should give this a lot of thought. What it means to—"

"Kill Lowry, it says," Hargraves said, distant, "and you know what? I think I will."

And then she shot him.


## TWO MEN IN A FUCKING BOAT THING

**N**othing was better than getting shot. Nothing. To be shot and still be walking around. He couldn't feel his right arm, or part of his face, but who the fuck needed part of his face. He could still see, and there was warmth on his left side. And he could move his left arm and he could sling his knapsack across his back and still hold his machete. Still had that. Wasn't sure where the gun had gone. Was it still shoved into his pants?

Who had done that? Hargraves? No, Hargraves had shot him. He must've done it. But she'd been quick on the draw. Too quick. Just muscle memory that got him out the doorway. And she didn't follow? Was he too far dead for it to matter? The lighthouse was shining in his face, on the back of his neck, from all positions, no matter how he moved, and only with difficulty and time did the marshes become clear to him, or even the path he shuffled forward on, back to the extraction point. What if there was no suit? Would he attempt the corridor without one? He'd have to.

And then there on the horizon, parallel to his horizon, on another raised berm trail far out, there was a figure gamboling about, swinging its arms and shouting or was it screaming? Was it him? His own true doppelgänger? This was his first thought.

With difficulty he put binoculars up to the side of his face that wasn't numb. Landry. Landry coked up. Landry on meth. Landry clearly on whatever he had left and Lowry crowed in triumph. Landry had made it. At least, made it for now. A salute and a shout out to him, going out with a bang not a whimper, but the shout came out as a croak and Landry couldn't hear him and suddenly Lowry felt nauseous and like a hammer had come down on top of his head, and he staggered and his binoculars swung back against his chest like someone was giving him CPR and he concentrated, one blade of grass at a time, on the trail in front of him, with the lighthouse still stabbing into him from every direction and Landry would just have to fend for himself and come down from the drugs on his own and holy fuck that would be the greatest withdrawal of all time. In the most inhospitable place.

But a short time later, he came across Landry again, this time next to that damned green boat that undulated and ebbed and flowed in its boatness in a disturbing fucking way. A way he didn't care for, that made him think Landry had gone space-age in the excess of his personal drug use, and even Lowry felt fucking unsettled by it—the gleam in Landry's eyes, the way that Landry seemed to have transcended speech but for odd burblings and burstings forth of phrase that said *Get in the boat* so convincingly that Lowry got in the boat, because he was tired and fading and it was better being in the boat with this Landry than being not in the boat and not with Landry.

And Landry had the bag of drugs with him, though Lowry felt fucking good for now. Maybe just because he had someone to talk to who was not the murderer Karen Hargraves, the anti-Sky and not a Winters who had fallen from a great height and lied about the boat before.

Even the lighthouse in the distance, reimagined, felt—or maybe Lowry just fucking hoped—like a newborn thing, a creature that did not yet know the full desire or strength of its own engines. Did it intuit its damn purpose? Flow to flow, the Geiger clicking somewhere. That they at times seemed to be motoring toward rather than away as they hugged the coast with no hint of an engine to propel them but not using the oars either, well, as he said to Landry, that was the fucking shitting pissing yourself bastard part of special ops, of expeditions, of the things you just had to do.

Landry smiled so very, very wide, he was clearly high, and said, "That's rad, man. That's profound," but the words felt fuzzy meeting Lowry's eyeballs, to his mouth-ear hearing them.

"Do you know how you're sounding to others, my glorious Landry. You hurt your own drugs now, not the other way around, you're so fucking high. Enumerate. Reconstitute. Something something I forgot."

There was the wind, yes, and the crashing birds that seemed to have forgotten how to fly sometimes and dashed themselves like glass against rock on the surface of the ocean, and the ones who seemed to have learned to fly too well and were so far-distant and high up that he wondered if they might fly away to the moon. He tried not to notice the loops of sea creatures in the water, and the feeling that the shore wanted to eat them like a mouth. Had the drugs made the fucking birds high? Sprinkling them over the goddamn water.

"We could just fly out to the sea and never come back," Landry said. "Just keeping flying around. Just do that. Do that thing. What did I say?"

"Sail. Motor. Not fly."

"There's sauce out there and I want all of it. I want to walk into the sauce and eat it all."

"Not walking swimming. Not sauce. Water."

"Glide like kings and get the sauce, just for us."

"Fucking swim, motherfucker. Sail, asshole. I mean, Landry, what the fuck are you on because I'm taking the same stuff."

"You tell me, Lowry! Tell me!"

The flushed, peaked look to Landry's face. The carnivorous shadows around his face. Surely cavernous, but, no, carnivorous fit the moment. The tremor to his hands, which seemed to be growing mangroves out of them like a boss.

"Do you like boats, Landry?" Just to change the subject. Just to look away from ol' mangrove hands.

"No not boats. Not boats at all. Yes. But we are not in a boat."

And Landry was right, it wasn't really a boat, was it, he'd just wanted to think it was a boat, to escape Hargraves. It was some creature, low and long against the water, and they motored in the shallows within the shadow of its mouth and the safety railing he thought was the edge of the boat was actually a row of teeth oh shit oh shit oh shit oh shit.

"Landry, this isn't fucking right. This is all wrong."

"This is all wrong, Lowry."

"What the fuck even."

"What the fuck even."

"Shut up."

"Shut up."

"Holy fuck."

"Holy fuck."

"Stop it you fuck."

"Okay."

"Okay?"

"Blort." Or something like "blort," as if to blurt was to lunge.

Because that was when Landry lunged at him and Lowry had to shoot him in the face and then plunge over the side as the mouth tried to close over them both.

Then it was a hard long slog from the shore to the Border extraction point, more and more of him paralyzed, that damn half-face Landry shadowing him from afar and saying shit that was pointless now, like they were not going to have a productive conversation after what had gone down, but as long as Landry obeyed the restraining order in Lowry's head and stayed more than five hundred feet away from the kick-to-curb of Lowry's boots, it was still cool. Or cool enough.

Lord, he was feeling weak and perturbed and hot and the wheel and wreck of the heavens was full of knives that gleamed and kept together like flocks of glittery sharp clouds or flocks of birds and he just wanted to make it to the Border was all. That was all he wanted.

Even with fake Landry out there, holding up the bag of drugs like he was a candy master on some dark ritualistic night, wrangling that candy for the kids. Wrangling that candy while Rome burnt like a candle, like a flame, in the vessel of his brain.

## THIRD SKIN

For a time, then, Lowry felt like he was unconscious but walking still, and for a time, too, as if he had fallen in, footstep for footstep, with the marching soldiers of scientists and psychics approaching the distant green light of the future, as if he were in their ranks, but when he came to, instead, the hole in the ground, the corridor entrance lay in front of him even though he had a nagging thought in the back of his head that he was not himself and even more of his body had gone numb, and was it the bullet or was it something else? The second skin that had always made him queasy. Had made him shocked and shockened and fuck that wasn't a word but it was in his head.

The suit right there and all he had to do is put it on. But it was illuminated somehow by the lighthouse rays and he could see refracted back how the suit was moving. Every inch of the suit moved in a subtle way, as if it were less a second skin than millions of tiny organisms trying to provide the illusion of being a suit. But what if that was just his wound talking? What if he was so fucked up that the suit was normal and his fucking paranoia had commandeered his senses and his common sense. Because he had to put on the suit. Because he had to make it down the corridor if he wanted to live. If he wanted to bring back the critical, the vital info he only half recalled.

He believed he could feel the bullet inside him, like a cold, dead weight, like something you'd put on a tiny scale before you paid out for nuggets of gold found by some dumb-fuck miner up in the mountains of a state you never visited but kept telling friends you would go camping in. Ah but the numbness hurt. It hurt so much, and he wished maybe he could go back to being scales that became eyes from which issued the golden dust.

There was the suit. There was the corridor. He could make it out. He had to make it out. He'd be a hero. He'd be able to set his own terms. He might even run the joint one day. If he could only make it out, he might be the one to defeat Area X. He might be the one. If only. If only. If only he were himself. And of that he could not be sure.

Slowly, with great difficulty, he dropped his knapsack. He dropped his binoculars. He undressed and, naked, stood before his suit and his suit spoke to him and said, "Are you ready?"

And he said, "Fuck, yeah, I'm ready."

But he stood like that, half toppled, for a long time. For a very long time, wondering what to do next. Because he was, as far as anyone knew, the last survivor of the first expedition. Because something felt important about that he could not put a finger on because he could not feel his fingers.

If he could just get into the suit. If he could just get into the suit.

And the suit said, "Don't worry, Lowry. I'll help you get into the suit." And he said, "I'm scared," because he was scared and couldn't stop crying. And the suit said, jauntily, "Don't be scared. Just get into me. Just let me cover you up. Let me just cover this all up." But still he was afraid.

"You see that Hargraves, suit?" He'd been wandering aimless a bit, lost sight of the horizon, even, or the point.

"She passed through here a while back."

"Ah, ah good." And yeah, he was happy for her. Just like he was happy for Sky if she had managed to make it to that destroyer and maybe it had even turned into a spaceship and lifted her into the sky and into a better life than this shit. For this truly had turned to shit, hadn't it, and he wasn't going to be a hero, was he?

But maybe, just maybe, Hargraves was another Landry, splintered into a thousand parts, and no fucking shard of diamond left in the middle to put into a ring and offer in a room full of dead things in jars. Maybe *she* was the dream and he would still make it back and she wouldn't, never couldn't, never ever would. Just him.

"Maybe I *am* the last and I'm going home."

"If you're talking to me," the suit said, "you're long gone, my friend."

"Landry?"

"No, Landry's been dead for a while."

Lowry was in a bad way it seemed, given how ripped up the

suit was, or how it was ripping itself in new ways to bind him into it more securely.

"Anyone else pass through?"

"I told you—Hargraves. She made it through."

"Got any of the good drugs left?"

"Yeah, in my suit."

"But you're all suit."

"Ain't that right."

If he craned his neck, Lowry could see a version of himself that was better than this, somewhere on the horizon but not here. Not here. And maybe he didn't need to be. Maybe he didn't need to be. Maybe for now this was what he needed to be.

"I just need to sit for a bit, suit," Lowry said, "and then we'll cross over." There was comfort in the thought, how if only he could make it across, nothing would change.

And the suit nodded at him, and they watched the sun set over that beautiful fucking place together, propped up against a log, and it was all right and fucking good, even.

For a time.

## ACKNOWLEDGMENTS

Thanks to everyone at MCD/FSG, including my editor, Sean McDonald, for patience and thoughtfulness. Special thanks to Debra Helfand, Rebecca Caine, Hannah Goodwin, Ben Brooks, Nina Frieman, Abby Kagan, Claire Tobin, Alex Merto, Karla Eoff, Vivian Kirklin, and Justine Gardner. Fond thanks and appreciation to my agent, Joseph Veltre, and my entertainment attorney, Alex Kohner.

Thanks to Ann for making the writing of this novel possible and for valuable feedback during various phases of its writing. Thanks to my other first readers for their kindness and comments: Matthew Cheney, Barbara J. King, Ali Sperling, Andy Marlowe, and Eric Schaller. (Thanks to reader Scott Landry for being enthusiastic about allowing me to use his name in the novel, although the character in the novel bears zero resemblance to him.)

I am indebted to Laila Abdanan for a deep first read and multiple other read-throughs while I was writing and editing the novel. She helped immeasurably with several aspects, including the camaraderie between Cass and Old Jim, the character of Jackie, and key aspects of the plot. (In addition to relating to me the house centipede story and caterpillar information, here somewhat . . . altered.)

Thanks to Amelia Faust for bringing to my attention the persistence of an "Area X" in bird brains. Thanks to Dr. Solomon David for detailed information on how a gar would feel held in the hands like a rifle, for the last part of this novel—as well as details about how gizzard shad shed scales.

Similarly, thank you to the following for ideas that helped in the infamous scene of Lowry [redacting] [Redacted]: Jesse Black, a fish ecologist, for describing the texture of abyssal snailfish as like "touching a firm Jell-O salad"; Gina Lloyd, a biologist, for the leaking underbelly slime of hagfish and lizard fish; Claudia Dombrowski for the slimy warty quality of toadfish skin.

Thanks to Amanda Smith, a research fisheries biologist, for a wonderful idea about how a certain kind of alligator tracker might still be working after twenty years. Thanks to Dr. Andrew Merwin, who studies insect ecology, for his thoughts on house centipedes and molts, among other topics. (House centipedes, somewhat misunderstood, are beneficial and complex organisms.)

Thanks to the biologist Emma E. Damm for various consultations, including how it would feel to have an alligator gush through the mud around you if you happened to be lying mud-bound in a blackened meadow. Also, for allowing me to use her frogs and the details of her apartment complex for the novel.

Thanks to everyone at Ology beer bar here in Tallahassee for a list of their opening and closing duties, for use with Old Jim's proprietorship of the Village Bar. Thanks to Livvy the Mousegirl for the charming idea of "hi hi kiss," although it did not make it into the final draft.

The idea for Lowry's attitude toward suits came from reading Dr. Ali Sperling's paper "Second Skins: A Body-Ecology of Jeff Vander-Meer's Southern Reach Trilogy."

The brief quote in the Mudder / Old Jim scene about how sound is a parasite needing a host is (partially condensed/adapted) from *The Order of Sounds: A Sonorous Archipelago* by François J. Bonnet.

Finally, thanks and appreciation to Kristen Roupenian, who, as a student in a workshop I led, had the wonderful gumption to mark up a very early fragment of *Absolution* I left in the break room and tell me everything that was wrong with it. Without that moment, I might never have written this novel.

## SPECIAL THANKS

Special thanks and gratitude to *Absolution* research assistant Andy Marlowe, a multidisciplinary artist and writer (Instagram: @bedroom__culture; website: andymarlowe.com). In addition to providing the divider images between the parts of this novel, Marlowe wrote new translations of the Franz Schubert song cycle *Winter Journey*, psyops variations on the songs, and alligator versions of the songs. Research included compiling monthly reports on sea wrack along the Forgotten Coast, as well as information on biohazard facilities, CIA mind-control experiments, psychopaths, darkrooms, and cultural and historical sites in North Florida. As ever, any errors in using this research are my own.